A COWBOY'S KISS

She got the impression they were no longer talking about painting. "You must be a renegade, Cash Dalton."

He held her gaze, his eyes so blue, they reminded her of Mill Lake in summertime. "Maybe, how 'bout you?" And then his eyes slid over her in a way that wasn't altogether respectable.

"Me? Uh…I'm pretty conventional."

"There's nothing about you a man would call conventional." He stepped in front of her and flicked a piece of tape off her shirt.

She lifted her face to his, hoping she wasn't misreading what was going on here. "Should I take that as a compliment?" *Are you making a move on me?*

"Damn straight it's a compliment." His lips twitched and he tilted his head down close enough that she felt his warm breath on her cheeks. "You know, I nearly kissed you the other day? How weird would it be if I kissed you now?"

She chewed her bottom lip. "Probably pretty weird." But she didn't move away.

His lips hovered barely an inch from her mouth. "Should we try it? What's the worst that can happen?"

It was just a kiss, she argued with herself, trying to dismiss all the reasons it was insane, starting with the fact that she'd just broken her engagement to another man. Her head told her to back away, but her mouth said, "I don't see how it could hurt."

And then, just like that, he covered her mouth with his, tasting her lips until the kiss grew deeper…

Books by Stacy Finz

The Nugget Series
GOING HOME
FINDING HOPE
SECOND CHANCES
STARTING OVER
GETTING LUCKY
BORROWING TROUBLE
HEATING UP
RIDING HIGH
FALLING HARD
HOPE FOR CHRISTMAS
TEMPTING FATE

The Garner Brothers
NEED YOU
WANT YOU
LOVE YOU

Dry Creek Ranch
COWBOY UP

Published by Kensington Publishing Corporation

Cowboy Up

Stacy Finz

LYRICAL SHINE
Kensington Publishing Corp.
www.kensingtonbooks.com

LYRICAL SHINE BOOKS are published by

Kensington Publishing Corp.
119 West 40th Street
New York, NY 10018

All Kensington titles, imprints, and distributed lines are available at special quantity discounts for bulk purchases for sales promotion, premiums, fundraising, educational, or institutional use.

Special book excerpts or customized printings can also be created to fit specific needs. For details, write or phone the office of the Kensington Sales Manager: Kensington Publishing Corp., 119 West 40th Street, New York, NY 10018. Attn. Sales Department. Phone: 1-800-221-2647.

Lyrical Shine and Lyrical Shine logo Reg. U.S. Pat. & TM Off.

First Electronic Edition: July 2019
ISBN-13: 978-1-5161-0924-1 (ebook)
ISBN-10: 1-5161-0924-4

First Print Edition: July 2019
ISBN-13: 978-1-5161-0925-8
ISBN-10: 1-5161-0925-2

Printed in the United States of America

Chapter 1

Cash Dalton put the target in his sights, braced his arm to steady his aim, and pulled the trigger. "Bull's-eye!"

He walked the seven yards to the fence post, built up a second pyramid, and squeezed off a few more rounds, killing a succession of Jim Beam bottles. Or at least maiming them. When he emptied his clip, he loaded a new one and racked up what was left of the bottles for another go at it.

The sun was still hiding behind the clouds, as it was wont to do during a Northern California summer. But Cash could still feel the promise of another hot day. Somewhere, a rooster crowed, and when the wind blew from the north, he got a strong musky whiff of wet hay, horse shit, and cattle. He liked the smell; it reminded him of home, even though he'd grown up in San Francisco. The mountains stood in silhouette against the smoky sky, reminding him what morning looked like in the Sierra foothills. The truth was, it had been a while since he'd seen a morning anywhere.

There would be plenty of time to see them now.

He went back to the line he'd drawn in the dirt with his boot, spread his feet as wide as his hips, leaned forward, and fired.

Bam!

"Excuse me…excuse me!"

Cash jumped, nearly dropping his Glock. How long had his neighbor been standing there? Damn, he was losing his sixth sense.

"Never sneak up on a man with a gun."

Aubrey McAllister glowered at him. She still had her pajamas on. Sleep shorts, a T-shirt, and a bad case of bed head. He guessed the cowboy boots were a last-minute addition.

"It's six o'clock in the morning," she huffed.

"Ah, hell, I didn't realize the time," he lied, scrubbing his hand down his chin through three days of stubble. What he hadn't remembered was her living next door. "Sorry."

She eyed his piece with distaste. "I thought you were supposed to use a rifle for that."

He shrugged. Honestly, he didn't own a .22, just his backup weapon, and because he was permanently off duty, he used the firearm for plinking. "I'll quit now."

"I'd appreciate it." She leaned in and sniffed him. "You don't smell drunk."

Cash reared back. He wouldn't be handling a firearm if he were drunk. "Where'd you get the idea I was?"

She made a point of staring at the shattered Jim Beam bottles. "Look, it's none of my business but you seem to spend a lot of time either shooting things or sitting on your front porch...drinking."

Damn right it was none of her business. "If it's a problem for you, I suppose you could always move."

She shifted her weight from one foot to the other. "I'm just trying to be helpful."

"Last time I looked, accusing your landlord of being a drunk wasn't helpful." He squinted at her, a reminder that he had the upper hand here.

She squinted right back. "Jace is my landlord, not you."

"Jace is your boyfriend, which by default makes my cousin Sawyer and me your landlords."

"Oh, for God's sake." She crossed her arms over her chest. "If one more person...Jace is not my boyfriend!"

That's not what he'd heard in town. Dry Creek was small, but its residents had big mouths. And word was, Aubrey McAllister had ditched her fiancé for his cousin, Jace. Cash had a strict don't-ask, don't-tell policy when it came to his two cousins' love lives, so he hadn't delved. But he sincerely hoped Aubrey was a better choice than Jace's ex. Jace's sons didn't need any more upheaval in their lives.

"Whatever you say, Aubrey." In his experience, rumors always held a grain of truth. He went to collect the broken bottles off the ground, letting her know he was finished with this conversation. She could go home and go back to bed. But she followed him to the fence anyway.

"It's not whatever I say, it's the way it is. Read my lips: Jace and I aren't an item. Never were and never will be. But that has nothing to do with your drinking problem. Your best bet is to accept that it's an issue and get the help you need."

He scooped up the glass and chucked it in a paper bag, perturbed. "Good advice. I'll call someone today and get myself into rehab ASAP. You have a good morning, now."

Cash stuck his Glock in the back of his jeans and started for his cabin, getting only as far as his front porch before she said, "There's nothing to be embarrassed about. There's even a residential rehab center just up the road."

That was news to Cash but not altogether shocking. A few years ago, someone had bought up a chunk of land off Dry Creek Road and turned it into a goat yoga camp. Goats and yoga; who knew? Up Highway 49, closer to Nevada City, the old Jagger farm was now a mindfulness center. So a halfway house wasn't out of the realm of possibilities.

"Read my lips," he said, mimicking her earlier words. "I don't need rehab."

It was on the tip of his tongue to say what he needed was a good roll in the hay before his entire world changed forever. But Jace's truck came barreling up the driveway.

Fantastic, Aubrey had called the po-po.

Jace got out and slammed the door. "I see you're putting your time to good use." He waved his hand at Cash's target setup.

"Anything's better than drinking, right, Aubrey?" He winked, fully aware that it would piss her off, and he wasn't disappointed. Sparks flew in those pretty green eyes of hers.

She threw her hands up in the air. "I'm going now."

"Hey," he tipped the brim of his hat, "sorry for the disturbance." He hadn't meant to wake her; he really hadn't. "It won't happen again."

He watched her cross over the creek on the small footbridge that connected their two yards, letting his eyes wander to her backside and down those long, shapely legs of hers. She was nervy and presumptuous, but her boots were exceptional. Outstanding actually. One of the best pairs he'd seen in a long time.

Jace came up onto the porch, pulled up one of the faded lawn chairs, and straddled it, his eyes filled with concern. "When are you leaving?"

"Day after tomorrow." Cash sat on the top stair, hoping the rotted tread would hold him.

Jace let out a long sigh. For several minutes they sat, watching the sun move over the horizon. Neither spoke but both were cognizant of all the things that were going unsaid.

Jace finally broke the silence. "You ready for this?"

"Nope." Two weeks since the call, and he still hadn't wrapped his head around the situation. By Wednesday, though, he better be prepared. For the sake of Ellie and twelve years of lost time. But he didn't want to think about it right now.

Jace cleared his throat, and Cash eyed his cousin's uniform. Jace didn't usually wear one. It was freshly pressed, with a neat crease down the center of his pants. It reminded Cash of the suits he used to wear in the Bureau.

"You got a press conference or something?"

"Nah, just a meeting with the council." Jace gazed at the pile of plastic bags Cash had heaped on the side of the cabin. "What's in those?"

"A body."

"Not funny." Jace got up, came around Cash, walked to the bags, and untied one. "Whoa, you've been busy."

Yes, he had. The inside of the cabin was a wreck. Cash had spent the better part of a week cleaning it, though you still couldn't tell. "See, I've been spending my time on more than target practice."

"You woke Aubrey up." Jace shielded his eyes and peered across the creek at Cash's new neighbor's place, then came back onto the porch and took his place on the lawn chair. "She was worried about you."

Cash let out a mirthless laugh. "She thinks I'm an alcoholic." To be fair, he'd been drinking nonstop since he'd lost his job. But it had never gotten to the point where he couldn't quit. "What's the deal with her anyway?"

"Aubrey? She needed a place to stay and the cabin was empty. I didn't think you or Sawyer would mind."

He minded; he missed his privacy. Until she moved in two weeks ago, he'd had this corner of Dry Creek Ranch to himself. "Was she living with the ex-fiancé?" It was logical to assume that's why she suddenly needed a place, because one day the cabin was empty and the next she appeared with a U-Haul.

"Yeah, which left her homeless after the breakup."

"A little heads-up would've been nice," Cash said.

"Sorry about that."

Cash hitched his shoulders because it was too late now. Besides, he had bigger fish to fry than being stuck with a neighbor who thought he was a lush and complained about his early morning target shooting.

"Are you two seeing each other?" Despite the rumors, Aubrey had been convincing in her denial. Still, old habits die hard. The former FBI agent in Cash couldn't help seeking corroboration.

"She's like a sister," Jace said. "And Mitch is…was…my best friend. You should know better than to believe what you hear in town. Folks around here are less reliable than a supermarket tabloid."

Cash suspected that was true and wondered why he was acting like a meddling old woman. Jace's romantic entanglements were his and his alone.

A couple of birds squawked overhead, and Sawyer came hiking down the trail that cut across the ranch from his home to Cash's cabin. He had on his dude ranch attire today. Boots that were blindingly shiny and a straw cowboy hat that reminded Cash of something you'd buy from a concession stand at the county fair. The only thing missing was a bandanna tied around his neck.

"No one told me we were having a meeting." Sawyer came up the cabin stairs, squeezed past Cash, turned over a barrel that had been serving as a garbage can, and sat on it, taking a thorough inventory of the porch. "I love what you've done with the place." He turned his eye on Cash, giving him the same raw assessment. "Are you going to the funeral? Because if you are, you should clean up, shave. I've got a black suit you can borrow."

"I'm planning to wear the one I wore to Grandpa's. That work for you?"

"It's better than what you've got on." Torn jeans and a holey T-shirt.

"No one to see me but the deer." And Cash's intrusive neighbor.

Sawyer went back to examining the cabin, lingering on the BarcaLounger no one had chosen to sit on. For good reason; the recliner was infested with vermin and smelled like skunk. It had been on the porch since before Cash moved in.

"All that's missing is the soundtrack to *Deliverance*." Sawyer hummed the opening bars of "Dueling Banjos" in case Cash missed the reference. "For fuck's sake, Cash, you'll scare the shit out of the kid."

"I'm working on it." In its current state, the cabin wasn't fit for him, let alone a young girl. Its best feature was the view of Dry Creek. He could practically drop a line in the water off his front porch.

"Yeah, I can tell," Sawyer said with his usual flippancy, gazing at the old tractor and truck parts strewn across the property, the unstable lean-to Cash used as a carport, and the oil stains on the driveway. The prior occupants, Grandpa Dalton's ranch hands, had used the yard to fix farm equipment.

Cash knew he should've done more to pull his weight. Dry Creek Ranch was beyond rundown. In the last years of his life, Grandpa Dalton had gone through his funds for upkeep and Jace had had his hands full being sheriff and raising two boys on his own. Sawyer had been busy traveling the world for *National Geographic* and all the other publications he wrote for. And Cash, too consumed with his job and life in San Francisco, hadn't noticed that he and his cousins' birthright was slowly deteriorating…until four months ago. That's when their grandfather died and left them the land, the houses, and an outstanding property tax bill as large as the national debt.

"I'll send over a couple of guys to haul this stuff to the dump." Jace zeroed in on the heap of rotting fence rails and broken furniture Cash had piled near an old structure that had once served as a small barn. Slowly but surely, he'd been trying to clear away the debris.

Sawyer chipped at the cabin's peeling trim with his finger. "Some paint would be good too."

Cash wouldn't have time for that before he went to Boston, but when he got back he'd fix the leaky roof, the running toilet, and replace some of the failed windows. In the meantime, he'd scrub the cabin clean and make it as livable as possible, because for now it was all he had, and he needed to make it feel like a home.

"Did you explain about Ellie to the boys?" he asked Jace.

"They know they're getting a new cousin, but I left some of the circumstances fuzzy."

"You okay with all this?" Sawyer asked.

Hell no he wasn't okay. He was nearly forty and still hadn't fully figured out women, let alone a grief-stricken twelve-year-old girl. "She hates my guts."

"She hasn't met you yet, but when she does...yeah, she'll probably hate your guts." Jace grinned. "Look, none of this is your fault. If you'd known, you would've cowboyed up. That's how we Daltons roll."

Maybe, but Cash was ashamed to admit he wasn't so sure of that.

"Go easy on yourself and get to know her," Jace continued. "For now, all you've got to do is make her feel safe and cared for. The rest will come naturally with time."

"And a shower would be good," Sawyer said. "And, dude, deodorant."

Jace laughed—apparently, Cash's hygiene was comical—and got to his feet. "I've got to get going." He bobbed his head at Aubrey's cabin. "Try not to disturb your neighbor again. She's the only one around here paying rent."

Sawyer waited until Jace's truck pulled away and said, "What happened?"

"I was making too much noise shooting bottles." It was a good way of working off steam and getting his head right. These days he had so much swimming around in there that sometimes he wanted to tune it all out.

"You give any more thought to hiring that lawyer I told you about and getting your job back?"

"I don't want my job back." There was a time when Cash had been a true believer in the Bureau, and a stellar agent. Not anymore.

Sawyer got off the barrel and took Jace's chair. "You did all you could do, Cash. They're the ones who screwed it up."

Cash held his hands up. "This isn't up for discussion."

"Fine." Sawyer let out a long breath and motioned his head in the direction of Aubrey's cabin. "What's up with her?"

Cash followed Sawyer's gaze. "According to Jace, she needed a place to live after dumping the fiancé. Two weeks ago, she showed up here with a trailer and a houseful of furniture."

There was now a swing on her porch and flowers in the window boxes. Unlike his cabin, hers didn't have a porch fan dangling from a loose wire or a shredded screen door hanging lopsided from its hinges, or weeds that came up to Cash's knees. He'd heard somewhere that she was an interior decorator or some kind of designer.

"Her and Jace, huh?" Sawyer had obviously heard the rumors too.

"Nope, not according to Jace or Aubrey." Cash chastised himself for not having more faith in Jace. He should've known from the get-go that his cousin wasn't the type to poach another man's woman—not even one as hot as Aubrey McAllister—especially his best friend's fiancée. "I don't know Mitchell well, but he seems like a good guy."

Sawyer lifted his shoulders. "Just know him from when we were kids."

"You remember Aubrey?" Like Jace, she'd grown up here, while Cash and Sawyer had only visited in the summers and holidays.

"Nope, can't say I do. And if she looked anything then like she does now, I would've remembered."

Cash had a vague recollection of a skinny girl with dark hair and sparkly pink cowboy boots following Jace around but couldn't remember if her name was Aubrey. Only that she was a pain in the ass, and Grandpa said they had to let her tag along. The woman across the creek didn't hold any resemblance to that girl. Then again, Cash didn't look anything like his pre-pubescent self, gangly and awkward. Sometime around his junior year in high school, the rest of his body caught up with his six-two frame, and he lost the self-consciousness that had marked him as a nerd during his freshman and sophomore years.

"Looks like she's fixing the cabin up," Cash said, and stole another glance at her window boxes, then at his own porch. He had less than two days to make this place presentable to a twelve-year-old. He had no idea what kind of place she lived in in Boston or what kind of creature comforts she was used to. Hell, he didn't know anything about her, except they shared the same DNA. "You want to help me get the BarcaLounger down?"

"Let's do it." Sawyer waited for Cash to lock up his gun, then they threw the tattered chair onto the dump pile. "Where you planning to sleep Ellie?"

"I'll give her my room and sleep on the couch until I can get the spare room ready." Currently, it held boxes of his case files. Lord knew why he'd bothered to copy all that stuff. Law enforcement was behind him.

"You want me to go with you to Boston? I'm between assignments and have some time on my hands."

It was a generous offer, especially because Sawyer had spent the last year embedded with troops in Afghanistan for a book he was writing and was probably enjoying his downtime. "Thanks," Cash said. "But I've got it." He didn't want to overwhelm the kid with a lot of new faces.

"Let me know if you change your mind. You don't have to take this on all by yourself, you know?"

Cash had never been good at leaning, but when he did, it was on Sawyer and Jace, who were more like brothers than cousins. "Appreciate it."

Sawyer gave him a hard look. "Stop being a fucking island. And, dude, bathe." He got to his feet. "I've gotta go, but if you need help cleaning this place…or with anything…text me and I'll come over later."

Cash nodded, though these days he preferred to keep his own company.

After Sawyer left, Cash collected his spent casings and tossed the rest of the bottles he'd used for target practice on the garbage pile. At some point he needed to stock the refrigerator and cupboards with food, stuff a kid would eat that was more nutritious than his current diet, which consisted mostly of packaged meals he could heat in the microwave. His mother, a health nut, would have a heart attack if she knew.

Furniture was on the list too. He'd been making do with a few pieces he'd brought from San Francisco. Nothing fancy, just things he'd acquired over the years, or hand-me-downs from his parents, much of which was still in storage. But Ellie would probably need a desk, a chest of drawers… ah, hell, he didn't know.

For the next hour he cleaned up around the cabin, then hiked the quarter mile up to the main house to borrow Jace's riding mower. The sprawling rancher was the only building on the property that had been maintained. When Jace's wife left him, he and the boys moved in with Grandpa Dalton and he took over the upkeep of the five-bedroom home. Cash and Sawyer had agreed that Jace and his sons should remain in the house for as long as they kept the ranch. Set on top of a knoll, it had sweeping views of the land, the creek, and the Sierra foothills.

Cash got the mower from the shed and drove it home, cutting wide swaths of weeds and grass in neat rows. The sun beat down on him. Only eleven o'clock and it was already a scorcher. He thought about going inside and changing into something cooler but feared he'd wind up taking a siesta and wouldn't finish the job. So, instead, he stripped off his shirt and used it to wipe away his sweat.

Despite the heat, it was good to be outside, good to be doing something other than staring at the bottom of a bottle. He rode the mower until it ran out of gas and pushed it under a big shade tree. Whew, if Sawyer thought he was ripe before, he would've keeled over now.

He kicked off his boots, shucked his jeans, and cut across the newly mowed lawn to the creek. Then he waded into the middle, where his feet barely touched bottom, and let the water sluice over him, shivering from the cold. Despite its name, the creek had run hard and heavy for as long as Cash could remember. Even in the drought, there'd been enough runoff from the mountains to syphon the water for Grandpa Dalton's garden. This year, with the record snow they'd gotten in the Sierra, the creek was full to bursting. Cash sucked in a breath and dunked his head, then surfaced with a shudder. Damn, the water was cold. He gave his head a quick shake to wring out the water in his hair.

That's when he felt eyes on him.

"It looks chilly."

Cash turned slowly, following the voice to the footbridge that connected both sides of the creek shore. Aubrey leaned over the rail, holding the corner of her skirt to keep it from dragging in the water. The brim of a straw cowboy hat hid most of her face, but Cash thought he spied a crooked smile. She'd caught him naked.

"Yep." He shielded his eyes from the sun. "Nothing like an ice bath to sober you up."

She didn't take the bait, just continued to watch him, then lifted her chin to stare out over the land. The land of his ancestors.

He wanted to get out of the water but was afraid strutting bare ass in front of his female neighbor was disrespectful. He pointed to the sandy bank. "I'm getting out now." But she made no move to leave.

Screw it. If he stayed in much longer, he'd freeze his balls off. He waded to the shore and didn't bother to see if she was looking. Cash had given her fair warning. He headed for the tree, gathered up his clothes, and started for the cabin.

"I only told Jace because I was worried that you…uh…might hurt yourself."

Hurt himself? He'd been an FBI agent for almost thirteen years. Cash knew his way around firearms. "I'm grateful for your concern." He didn't bother keeping the sarcasm from his voice.

She shrugged. "It's really not my business."

No, it really wasn't. "Like I said, I'm sorry I disturbed you this morning. I've got to get inside now."

"Okay. Um…uh…nice seeing you again."

He wasn't sure if she meant seeing him again since their confrontation this morning or from when they were kids. Regardless, it seemed like an odd thing to say when he was standing there, stark naked.

"Likewise." Cash bobbed his head and went inside.

In the shower, he wondered about her. She was beautiful. He'd noticed that the first day she'd moved in. Light brown hair, green eyes, great body. She was also a nuisance, which in Cash's mind erased any of her physical attributes. Still, they were neighbors; best if they got along. He vowed to be more considerate in the future and shut off the water.

While reaching for the towel, he examined the bathroom. It needed a good scrubbing and a few shelves where Ellie could put her toiletries. He rubbed his hand down his face and for the hundredth time pondered what he was going to do with a twelve-year-old.

His cell phone rang, and in five long strides he made it to the bedroom before the call went to voicemail. "Dalton," he answered.

"This is Linda Wilson." She waited for Cash to acknowledge that he recognized her name, but he didn't. At least not at first. "I'm…was… Marie's best friend."

"Oh yeah, of course. How's Ellie?"

"Not good, I'm afraid. She's refusing to come home with you." He was a complete stranger to her. It stood to reason she was leery. "She's threatening to go on a hunger strike if we make her. Ellie can be dramatic, but I'm thinking with Marie's funeral on Wednesday, maybe we should wait and give her time to grieve her mother."

"How much time?"

There was a long pause. "However much time she needs," Linda finally said. "She's comfortable here. We've known Ellie since she was a baby… we love her like she was our own."

Yet after all this time, Marie had chosen him.

"I'll be there Wednesday for the funeral. Why don't we see how it goes?"

"All right. But Ellie's headstrong; she'll dig her heels in."

At least Cash had something in common with the daughter he'd never known.

Chapter 2

Despite the little voice that told her it was a terrible idea, Aubrey went to town. A person could only lay low for so long. Now she knew why they called it cabin fever. For the last two weeks, she'd stayed inside, cleaning and decorating the small log house on Dry Creek Ranch, making it home.

Strangely enough, she liked it better than the three-story mini mansion Mitch had built for her, though the huge house was certainly beautiful. Just big and ostentatious, like a pretty Sunday dress that showed too much cleavage. The cabin didn't have all the modern conveniences the house did. It needed a lot of work, but she loved the hand-hewn logs and the open rafters and the fact that it had been there for a hundred years. But there was her irritating neighbor, though she'd be lying if she didn't admit she was intrigued by him from an anthropological perspective. Since moving in she'd rarely seen him leave the cabin. Most of the time he napped on his front porch with a cowboy hat covering his face or shot beer cans or Jim Beam bottles off the fence post. She supposed that was part of the reason she'd assumed he was a drunk.

Today, though, he'd appeared quite sober.

First, in the morning, with the target practice incident. She hadn't smelled a lick of alcohol on his breath. Then later, Aubrey had watched through the window as he'd ridden the tractor mower in perfect straight lines, making yet another racket. At least the job was too methodical for him to have been drunk. And he had finally cleaned up that mess of a yard.

Later, when he'd stripped down to his birthday suit and jumped in the creek…well, Aubrey had had to stand under the ceiling fan. For a man who spent his days sulking on the front porch, he was in extraordinary shape. Tall, dark, and brooding wasn't her jam—and the guy was a major pain in the butt—but Cash Dalton was quite a specimen of a man. Broad shoulders that wouldn't quit and a six-pack that made her want to join a gym.

She pulled into a parking space in front of the coffee shop and cut the engine. After lunch she planned to go to Reynolds Construction and collect the rest of her stuff. She knew Mitch wouldn't be there, which would make it easier on both of them, though they had plenty to talk about. Plenty.

Aubrey was just about to get out of the car when Brett Tucker rolled his wheelchair down the sidewalk ramp and opened her door. "Hey, good-looking. Haven't seen you in town for a while."

She bit down on her bottom lip and let out a sigh. "I'm sure you've heard the news about Mitch and me." She prayed Brett didn't ask too many questions. She'd never been a good liar.

He nodded. "Like my dad used to say, 'Don't believe everything you hear and only half of what you see.'"

"Part of it's true. Mitchell and I are through." She grabbed her purse and slung the strap over her arm.

He backed up his chair so she could get out of the car. "I'm sorry, Ree. I'm sorry for both of you."

She nodded. "Thanks." Brett was and had always been a wonderful friend. Not just to her but to everyone in Dry Creek. That's why she couldn't bear to tell him the truth.

"I'm not gonna ask about the rest of it because Jace and Mitch are my best friends," he said. "Don't want it to tarnish the brotherhood."

Good, they could change the topic.

"Enough about me." She leaned against the hood of her car, which desperately needed a wash. Dry Creek Ranch was dusty in summer. "How are you?"

"Fair to middling." He grinned that megawatt smile that had made him the most popular boy in Dry Creek. And the sweetest.

Aubrey knew Brett was only putting on a good face. He'd gone from captain of the high school football team and a war hero to sitting in that chair, a paraplegic. A mere month ago, Jace had to talk him off a ledge. Brett had gone from depressed to…Aubrey didn't want to say suicidal, but somewhere really dark.

She suspected he hadn't rebounded, despite his pretense that he had, and supposed they were both keeping secrets.

"Glad you're doing well, Brett." She pushed herself off the car. "Where are you off to?"

"VFW Hall to meet the boys." He did a quick spin in his wheelchair and popped a wheelie. Show-off.

"Be sure to enjoy this fine day." She tipped her chin up to the sunshine.

"Roger that. You take care of yourself, you hear?"

"Roger that." She winked at him and went inside the coffee shop, where she was greeted by a refreshing rush of air-conditioning.

Perhaps it was her own insecurity, but it seemed as if a hush fell over the restaurant as soon as she entered. She knew she hadn't imagined it when Laney James, Jimmy Ray's wife, threw her shade.

Small towns.

She'd lived here her entire life, except for the years she'd left to go to college, and nothing had changed. Everyone was still up in everyone else's business, including her. Only a few hours earlier she'd gotten in Cash Dalton's face about his drinking when she didn't even know the man.

Jace sat at the counter, nursing a cup of coffee, and gave her a smile of encouragement.

She turned to Laney, who hadn't made a move to seat her. "I guess I'll just take my usual table."

"It's Mitch's table," Laney shot back and scowled.

"Then I'll take this one." Aubrey scooted into the small booth at the front of the shop, noting that it hadn't taken long for people to take sides. Then again, Mitch was prettier than her, and whenever the coffee shop needed a repair Jimmy Ray couldn't manage on his own, it was Mitch to the rescue. He never charged, taking his pay in Jimmy Ray's legendary chicken and waffles.

It took ten minutes for one of the waitresses to get around to taking her order, even though the coffee shop wasn't that busy. Jace slid off his stool and snagged the bench across from her.

"Bad idea, don't you think?" she said with a slight scowl.

"Let's give 'em something to talk about." He flashed that signature cocky grin of his, and Aubrey could see why half the women in Mill County wanted in the sheriff's pants.

She shook her head. "It's your election next year, not mine. How was your meeting?"

"Same old crap, different day." He signaled the waitress for a refill on his coffee. Funny how she rushed to do his bidding when she'd made Aubrey wait. "I talked to Cash about cooling it with the target practice."

"I know; he apologized. Again. And now he thinks I'm high-maintenance. And crazy for accusing him of being a drunk."

Jace laughed. "He's not a drunk. He's actually one of the most responsible people I know, but he's got a lot to deal with right now, including a daughter who's coming to live with him in a few days."

"He has a kid?" She didn't know why she was surprised. Cash was about the same age as Jace, and he had two beautiful boys. Jace nodded. "What happened to the wife?"

"Never married. The girl's mother died last week. Stage four breast cancer."

"That's awful." It made Aubrey realize her problems were minimal in the grand scheme of things. "No wonder Cash seems so depressed."

Jace shook his head. "It isn't like that. He barely knew her and only found out he had a twelve-year-old a couple of weeks ago. But that's his story to tell, not mine."

Aubrey was dying of curiosity, but she knew better than to probe. When Jace was keeping someone's confidence, he was locked up tighter than a vault. Unlike the rest of this town, he didn't gossip or give away secrets, not even to her, and she was one of his best friends. Aubrey supposed he'd only told her about Cash because it was common knowledge and she was out of the loop these days.

"You see Brett?" he asked, and they exchanged a glance.

"On my way in. He looked chipper." Her lips pressed together in a slight grimace.

Jace rubbed the back of his neck and let out a long breath. "Ironic, but he's trying for Jill's sake." He stared out the window, disappearing for a while. Jace, Brett, and Mitch had been best friends since elementary school. She'd only seen Jace cry twice in her life: the day his ex-wife failed to show up for their six-year-old's birthday party and the day Brett Tucker came home from Afghanistan a different man than when he'd left.

She waved her hand in front of his face. "Earth to Jace."

"Sorry." He took a sip of his coffee. "What are you planning for the day?"

"I've got to finish emptying out my desk, then maybe I'll brush up my résumé. I don't know if I can scrounge up enough work going solo around here." Working for a developer was the way to go in her line of business and Reynolds Construction was the only game in town. "It certainly doesn't help that Mitch is bad-mouthing me to everyone." She slid a glance at Laney.

"The best defense is a good offense."

She let out a mirthless laugh. "I guess so. You know what's weird?" Her sandwich and drink came, and she waited for the waitress to leave before she continued. "I feel like a thousand pounds have been lifted from my shoulders. The wedding, the house, Mitch…I'm not even a little sad, and just a few weeks ago I was about to marry the guy. What does that say about me?"

"It says it wasn't the real deal." Jace snatched a fry from her plate.

Then why had she stayed? She'd always thought of herself as a romantic, someone who reached for the stars. Yet with Mitch, she'd grown complacent, or perhaps she'd simply gone along with what everyone else had expected of her. Even her mother was disappointed that Aubrey wouldn't be Mitch's bride, despite what he'd done.

"I guess not," she said absently. "Thanks for letting me stay at the ranch. You don't have to if you think it'll affect the election or the boys. I'd hate for any of the rumors to reach Grady and Travis."

"Don't worry about it." He waved her off. "It'll blow over."

"What about Mitch and your friendship?" It hurt to know this had caused a rift between them.

"I'll deal with him in my own time and in my own way."

"Will you tell him you know what's going on, that I told you I caught them together?" She took a bite of her sandwich, even though she'd lost her appetite.

"He knows I know. Why else do you think he dragged me into this with a bullshit story of how I stole you from him?" Jace rolled his eyes. "Back to the best defense is a good offense."

"I wouldn't have told you if I hadn't needed a place to live. You know I'd never want to come between the two of you."

"I'm glad you told me. Like I said, the gossip will eventually blow over. As soon as Cash's daughter shows up, everyone will have something new to talk and speculate about."

Indeed they would. Cash wasn't a Dry Creek native, but his grandfather had been a beloved fixture here. By association that made Cash a local, even if he'd only started living here full-time after Jasper Dalton died.

"What's the girl's name?" Aubrey asked and sipped her iced tea.

"Ellie. I think it's short for Eleanor. She lives in Boston."

"Didn't you say Cash is a San Francisco FBI agent?" She wondered if he was taking time off because of Ellie.

"Former FBI agent." Jace said it in a way that implied there was a bigger story there. Aubrey waited for more, but he clammed up like he always did. Sometimes she wondered if he did it on purpose. Dangle something juicy, then pull it away.

Jace checked his watch and frowned. "Shit," he muttered. "I've got to be somewhere." He pushed away his coffee mug, pulled a few bills out of his pocket, and laid them on the table. "See you later."

After lunch she paid her bill at the ancient cash register. Laney didn't even bother to look up. Jimmy Ray waved from the kitchen, but he didn't come out to say hello like he usually did. Yep, they were definitely on Team Mitch.

She opened the door and immediately missed the coffee shop's cool air. July in Dry Creek. Aubrey walked up the hill to Main Street. Despite being the central artery through town, most of Dry Creek's businesses were on Mother Lode Road, like the coffee shop. The City Hall complex, a gas station, the post office, the high school, the Greyhound bus terminal, a storage company, and Reynolds Construction made up the bulk of Main Street, just a two-lane road that bisected miles of pasture and rolling hills.

She crossed at the light and cut through her former employer's small parking lot and let herself in through the double front doors. Mercedes was on the phone at the reception desk, and Aubrey tried to sneak by. Mitch's executive assistant—Mercedes didn't like being called a secretary—ruled Reynolds Construction like a dictator, chopping off heads for infractions as minor as forgetting to wash out the coffeepot.

"Mitch changed the lock on your office," Mercedes called as soon as Aubrey snuck around the corner. There was a smile in her voice, Aubrey could hear it.

Shit.

She stopped, backed up, and put her hands on her hips. "Come on, Mercedes, let me in. I know you have the key."

"No can do," Mercedes said in a singsong voice that told Aubrey just how delighted she was to be Mitch's gatekeeper.

"Oh for God's sake. It's my personal property." Paint, wood, and wallpaper samples she'd purchased with her own money. Magazines and books she'd collected since college. Furniture catalogs from all the major distributors. And her family pictures.

"Talk to Mitch."

"Come on, Mercedes. He's being vindictive."

"Can you blame him?" Mercedes stood up. Only a skosh over five feet, she had the bearing of an NBA center. "You broke his heart, and with his best friend no less. And to add insult to injury, you stuck him with the wedding bills."

"Don't drag Jace into this. He had nothing to do with it. Now let me in my office before I call my lawyer." She was bluffing, because she didn't have a lawyer.

"I'm not getting involved. It's between the two of you."

Not getting involved, yeah, that was rich. "Come on, Mercedes, just let me in. It'll take less than thirty minutes."

"I won't go against Mitch's wishes. He's a good boy and you're a selfish girl. And Jace…I thought better of him."

"Jace and I are not an item. I don't care what Mitch told you, it's not true." Mercedes rolled her eyes and walked away.

"Dammit, Mercedes!" Aubrey called to her back.

"Don't make me call security, Aubrey."

"You're actually kicking me out of the building? The same building where I've worked for ten years?"

Mercedes turned around, looked down her stubby little nose at Aubrey, and lifted a perfectly penciled eyebrow. "You bet your ass I am."

Aubrey folded her arms over her chest. "You can forget me getting you that coffee table at cost." She rushed past Mercedes and let herself out the door before the witch sicced Leroy on her. The big lug was Mitch's cousin and was what passed for security around here.

She pretended to walk to her car, then cut around the side of the building. It was a two-story, circa 2010 stucco number with a flat roof. The window to her office was on the first floor, but still too high to reach from the ground. She looked around for something to climb on, remembered she had a folding lawn chair in the trunk, and headed back to her Volvo. A few minutes later, she pulled around the corner, parked her station wagon out of sight behind a dumpster, and unearthed the chair from under a stack of blueprints.

The nylon webbing was as old as Mercedes, and when Aubrey stood on it, her right boot went through the seat, nearly taking the rest of her with it. She caught her balance with her left foot and grabbed the window ledge to hold herself up. One-handed, she managed to pry out the screen and immediately went to work on the window. Thank goodness no one bothered with locks in Dry Creek. But when she tried to slide the window open, the damned thing wouldn't budge. Finally, after tugging with all her might, she got it to move a smidge. But not enough to wedge her arm, let alone her butt, through the crack.

"Dammit!" What she wouldn't do for a can of WD-40?

With her shoulder shoved into the sash pull, she pushed as hard as she could, feeling it give a little bit more. "Come on, you son of a gun."

The heat was stifling and Aubrey could feel a pool of perspiration collect in the bridge of her bra. At least her cowboy hat shielded the sun from her head and face.

"Come on, come on, come on." This time she jiggled the handle as she gave it another shove. Slowly, it began to move. First, just enough to slip her arm through, then wide enough to fit her head.

A truck whizzed by on Tank Farm Way and she held her breath, worried that someone had seen her trying to jimmy the window. Burglary was all she needed to add to her résumé after "cheating" and "breaking poor Mitchell Reynolds's heart." She laughed to herself, because Mitch didn't have a heart. What he had was an overactive penis.

She waited a beat, listening for sirens, hoping one of Jace's deputies didn't show up. But all she heard was a tractor in the distance and a few cars on Main Street. Relieved, she resumed her efforts. Whatever had jammed the bottom rails must've come loose because all of a sudden, the window slid open as slippery as the roads in winter.

Aubrey tossed her hat on the ground, grabbed hold of the sill, and hoisted the top half of her body through the window. Flopping around, trying to wiggle the rest of the way through, her skirt hiked up, giving anyone who drove by a nice view of her ass.

She reached back to quickly pull it down when a deep voice—one she recognized—said, "How's it going up there?"

Aubrey squeezed her eyes shut and counted to ten. "Uh...good."

"Seems like you're stuck."

"No." Her voice squeaked and she desperately searched for an excuse why she was dangling out of a window but came up empty. "Just hanging out."

"Hanging out, huh? Last I looked, breaking and entering was illegal." Spoken like a true FBI agent. Former FBI agent, Aubrey reminded herself. "You sure you haven't been drinking?"

He wasn't going to let that go.

"Quite sure," she said. "This used to be my office. I'm just getting a few sundries, that's all." She reached behind her to smooth down her skirt, hoping beyond hope that everything back there was covered.

"I guess this is easier than using the front door."

She couldn't see him but was pretty sure he was laughing at her. Funny, because she'd surmised that Cash Dalton didn't have much of a sense of humor. She supposed they were even now. Well, not quite even. His butt was a heck of a lot better than hers, and she'd seen much more than his ass.

"All right, if you must know, Mercedes wouldn't let me in." The news of her being booted from her old office would be broadcast all over town by tomorrow anyway.

"Ah," was all he said.

"Give me a hand, would you?" She wanted him to boost her the rest of the way in.

"And be an accessory to a crime? I don't think so." He was still laughing, she could hear it in his voice.

"Fine, then go about your merry way." She wondered what he was doing in town in the first place, hermit that he was.

But instead of taking off, he hoisted her up by her legs. "Be careful." "Just a few more inches." Okay, that sounded weird. *Oh for crying out loud, get your mind out of the gutter, Aubrey.*

He gave her another push, and as soon as her hands touched the carpet, she was able to flop her legs over the side. Thank goodness for men over six feet tall. She scrambled to her feet and went back to the window to find him still standing there. "Thanks," she called.

"How do you plan to get back down?"

She hadn't thought that far ahead. "I'll figure something out." She waited for him to walk away, but he remained as if he were contemplating what to do next.

"I'm only taking what's mine," she assured him.

He deliberated, then walked closer to the window. "Throw the stuff down to me."

She nodded, because she didn't know how she'd do it on her own.

"But hurry. I don't have all day."

She dashed to her credenza, grabbed an armful of catalogs, found a few empty storage boxes in the closet, and packed them with as many belongings as would fit, then tossed them down to Cash. For the next twenty minutes, she ran around the office like a chicken with its head chopped off, collecting her things. Paint chips, wallpaper books, wood samples, fabric swatches, tile boards, and anything else she could stuff in a file box or carton. The rest she'd have to come back for later, after she had her come-to-Jesus talk with Mitch. She loaded up her family pictures, wrapped them up in an old pashmina she'd found on the coatrack, took one last look around the room, and bid the place goodbye.

"This one is kind of fragile," she called to Cash, who stood below with a scowl on his face. She noted that despite his surliness, he'd organized all her worldly possessions in a neat pile on the ground.

"Just throw it down."

"Be careful, they're glass." She tossed the pouch over the ledge and he caught it with ease. The tricky part would be getting out the window without mooning him. This time, she planned to go headfirst.

She leaned out, hung her head and shoulders over the ledge, and lost her nerve. Time to go to plan B. Aubrey pulled back inside and straddled the ledge with one leg, silently berating herself for not wearing jeans.

Cash tilted his head up. "You planning to fly?"

"I'm just assessing the situation. Jeez."

"Swing your other leg over and jump. I'll catch you."

She wasn't a bundle of picture frames and outweighed the carton of tile boards she'd dropped down by at least a hundred pounds. "That's okay. I can do it."

"By using your skirt as a parachute? I don't think so. Just jump."

Jace's cousin was awfully bossy, but Aubrey was running out of options. So, she flipped her other leg over the windowsill and perched precariously on the ledge. "You sure?" It wasn't all that far down but enough to get injured if he didn't catch her.

He held his arms out and motioned impatiently with his hands for her to jump.

"Just give me a second." She held her breath and slowly lowered herself, using her forearms as leverage on the sill.

Impatient, Cash reached up, hooked his arms around her waist, and pulled her feet first to the ground. He let go too fast and she nearly lost her balance. After all that, wouldn't it be just like her to fall on her ass?

"You good now?" he asked, and she gazed around to see if anyone had witnessed her cat burglar routine.

"Uh-huh. Thanks for the help." She wiped down the back of her dress and felt around to make sure everything was covered. "What brings you to town?" Inane question, but he didn't seem to leave Dry Creek Ranch too often, and she felt like she ought to at least make conversation with him after he'd gone out of his way to help her.

He nudged his head at the storage company at the intersection of Main and Tank Farm. "I was headed to my unit to get a few things when I saw a suspicious woman climbing the building. Where's your car?"

"Behind the dumpster."

He hefted one of the boxes onto his shoulder and started for the Volvo. "This is really your stuff, right? You're not stealing from your ex?"

She shot him a look. "Of course they're mine; tools of the trade." Items she'd need when she found a new job, one hopefully as lucrative as working for Reynolds Construction had been.

Mitch's company developed ritzy planned communities across Northern California. Aubrey had been responsible for staging models and ultimately working with buyers on picking out everything from their flooring and wall colors to their countertops and bathroom fixtures. Besides being a nice living, Aubrey had enjoyed the work immensely.

She lifted the tailgate, and Cash made room in the trunk for the box. Aubrey considered asking about his daughter but wasn't sure whether Jace had breached a confidence by telling her or not. Besides, Cash didn't seem like a sharer. He'd said more to her today then he had in the entire two weeks they'd lived next door to each other. And, still, it wasn't much.

He made a couple of trips back and forth, loading the car with her stuff, occasionally grunting something unintelligible, which Aubrey suspected had to do with the lack of space in her Volvo. Before Mitch canned her, her car had been a mobile office and was still filled with samples and paperwork from various jobs. She hadn't bothered to clean out the detritus, focusing on her living situation instead. For a week after the breakup she'd couch surfed. When Jace offered her the cabin, her brother drove from Seattle and helped her move out of Mitch's to Dry Creek Ranch.

"What's this?" Cash held up a plaque that said, "The Sangiovese."

"It's the name of one of the models in a new development I was staging. Each floorplan is named after a wine varietal. 'The Albariño,' 'The Grenache,' 'The Colombard.'"

"Hmm." He lifted a brow. "Given my love for the bottle, maybe I should move there."

"You're never going to let me live that down, are you?" She took the plaque from him and tossed it back in her trunk. Technically, it was the property of Reynolds Construction. When Mitch got around to explaining himself, she'd return it.

Cash dropped the last batch of fabric swatches onto Aubrey's back seat. "That should do it."

She kind of wanted to hug him for getting her out of a jam but wasn't sure he'd appreciate the gesture after she'd practically called him a raging alcoholic. "Thank you," she said and wondered if she should shake his hand only to reject the idea. Too formal. "And I'm sorry for getting in your face this morning. I shouldn't have prejudged you."

He stuck his hands in his pockets and nodded. She got the sense he was searching for a pithy comeback but instead settled on, "See you around."

"Okay, then." She started to get in her station wagon.

"Wait a sec, you forgot something." He jogged back to the side of the building, swiped her hat off the ground, came back, and popped it on her head. "Jace is up for reelection next year."

Complete non sequitur, but Aubrey got his meaning loud and clear. "I know that."

Cash gazed at the open window in Aubrey's old office. "Good." And with that, he walked away.

She watched him cross the road to Dry Creek Storage. The truth was, she couldn't take her eyes off him and waited until he disappeared behind one of the storage units before getting in her car. Too moody, she told herself.

But at least they had one thing in common: They both cared about Jace. This rumor about her and him had to stop. But how did she nip it in the bud without doing any more damage?

It was a question she pondered as she pulled onto Tank Farm and headed to Sew What to pick up a pair of drapes she'd had custom made for one of her clients. Occasionally, she took on outside business, usually locals she grew up with or friends of friends. Now, the freelancing would come in handy until she found a steady gig. She was a little low on cash after pouring a good chunk of change into wedding deposits. Mercedes had been wrong about sticking Mitch with the bills. Aubrey had paid for half of everything, and there were no refunds this close to the reception date. She was now the proud owner of a truckload of linens, which, in her prewedding delirium, she'd decided was more cost-effective to buy than to rent.

Yet, despite all the fussing and planning—and years of envisioning herself as the future Mrs. Reynolds, as well as fulfilling everyone's expectations that she and her hometown sweetheart would find matrimonial bliss—Aubrey felt like she could breathe again. After Mitch had ruined everything, she'd come to the very swift conclusion that she didn't love him, at least not in the way you were supposed to love the man you were about to marry. She'd loved things about him—his warmth, his wry sense of humor, his natural charm, his capacity to take nothing and build it into an impressive enterprise—but there'd always been a part of him that he kept locked away from her. It was as if he only let her know the person he wanted to be instead of the person he was.

She swung her car into Sew What's tiny parking lot, got her purse, and stepped outside into the oppressive heat, hoping Wren's air-conditioning was working. The seamstress's shop was as ancient as Dry Creek itself, but her work was magical. Wren was a perfectionist, exceeding even Aubrey's exacting standards.

The bell on the door chimed as Aubrey stepped inside to a blast of cool air. It was working, thank the sweet baby Jesus.

"Yo, Wren," she called to an empty shop. "You back there?"

A few seconds later, Wren appeared, brushing past the bead curtains left over from her hippie days, holding a bowl of soup. "Well, if it isn't the talk of the town."

Aubrey huffed out a breath. "Don't believe everything you hear, Wren."

"Kind of hard not to when you moved in with Jace."

"I didn't move in with Jace." Aubrey planted her hands on her hips. "I moved to a cabin on his ranch. There's a difference."

Wren didn't say anything, just arched a brow dubiously.

"Oh for goodness' sake, don't tell me you're actually choosing sides?"

"The optics aren't good, Aubrey. You're living with Jace and Mitch has been a good friend. He fixed my leaky roof."

"Seriously, you're choosing friends based on who does you favors? If that's the case, Wren, I give you business." Wow, who knew she had to stoop that low? Aubrey thought she and Wren were friends. But throwing Wren sewing jobs—lots of them—should trump patching a leaky roof, in Aubrey's opinion.

"Look, Aubrey, I don't want to get involved. Dry Creek is gossipy enough." She put down her bowl, reached under the counter, and handed Aubrey a package. "I'm officially removing myself from the fray."

Aubrey stared down at the brown paper wrapping. It was the same package she'd brought to Sew What with her upholstery fabric. "This is the way you're staying out of the 'fray'?" She continued to stare at the package in disbelief. "You're not going to make my client's drapes?"

"It's a Stitch in Grass Valley can do it." Wren picked up her bowl and blew on her soup.

Aubrey knew first hand that It's a Stitch did alterations and didn't have the bandwidth to create pleated draperies. "You're really going to turn down my business over Mitch?"

"Please don't turn this into something it isn't." Wren took a sip of her soup.

"What is it exactly? Perhaps you should explain." Aubrey had promised her client to have the drapes hung by Friday, which was only four days away. This would put her in a real bind.

"It's not an indictment of you. I'm a feminist, Aubrey, I don't believe in slut shaming. But I don't want to take sides."

Aubrey had to keep from rolling her eyes. Not slut shaming her ass. "So the next time Mitch offers you free work, you'll turn him down, right?"

"Okay, you're being petty and making me extremely uncomfortable. I think you should leave."

"Wow, you're kicking me out of your store. I can't freaking believe this." Even Laney, who doted on Mitch, hadn't refused to serve her. But Aubrey's pride wouldn't let Wren say it twice. She clutched her package and walked straight out the door.

She opened the passenger side of her Volvo and shoved the drapery fabric next to the rest of her crap. A pickup almost as old as Aubrey's station wagon pulled up alongside her. Other than the wheelchair lift in the back, it looked like every other truck in Dry Creek. Dinged and scraped from carrying hay, barbed wire, and other farm supplies. Jill Tucker rolled down the window, and Aubrey braced her hand on the hood of her car.

"Not now, Jill."

Jill swung open her door and jumped down from the cab anyway. Aubrey couldn't help noticing how much she'd aged in the last few years. There were crow's feet around her eyes and brackets tugging at the corners of her lips. And although Jill had always been trim, her curves had given way to sharp planes. The truth was, she looked exhausted, as if stress and loss of sleep had hollowed out her cheeks and added a hardness to her face that had never been there before.

Yet Jill was still the most beautiful woman in Dry Creek. Long, silky blond hair, big brown bedroom eyes, and great shoulders. No one rocked a tank top like Jill Tucker.

"We need to talk," she said.

"No, we don't." Aubrey rounded the front of her car, trying to get away.

Jill followed and effectively blocked Aubrey from opening the door. With tears in her eyes, she pleaded, "If you tell, it'll kill him, Ree. It'll absolutely kill him."

Aubrey planted her legs wide. "How could you, Jill? Never mind the fact that we're friends—once best friends—but how could you do that to him?"

Jill sagged against Aubrey's station wagon. "It just happened. We didn't mean for it to happen and we certainly didn't set out to hurt anyone. But you don't know what it's like, Ree. The mood swings, the isolation, the— Sometimes it's like he's not even here on this planet. And we're broke. Who knows if we'll even be able to keep the house?"

"Stop." Aubrey held up her hand. "It's not an excuse, Jill."

"No, it's not." Jill wrapped her arms around herself as if to ward off the cold in the ninety-degree heat.

"I told Jace," Aubrey said and pinched the bridge of her nose. "Other than him, I'll never tell a soul." She muscled Jill out of the way and opened her car door. Then, fixing Jill with a look, she said, "I'm doing it for Brett, not for you. Not for Mitch. Because to do otherwise, Jill, would destroy your husband."

Chapter 3

Cash pulled into a 76 station somewhere east of Sacramento. The drive from the airport had been a blur, his head too filled with all the ways he could fuck up being a father. He knew he'd whisked Ellie away sooner than anyone had wanted, but it was only prolonging her pain and putting off a move that was inevitable.

Cash riffled through the console for his wallet, then checked his rearview mirror before getting out to fill his tank. Ellie lay in the back seat, sleeping. It was eighty degrees outside, but she'd insisted on wearing a tattered old sweater twice her size on the plane ride from Boston and hadn't taken it off since.

He just sat there for a few minutes, watching her sleep. She was smaller than he expected. From what Cash could remember, her mother had been tall, maybe five ten. Other than her blue eyes, he didn't see any resemblance between him and his daughter. But when he'd sent a picture of Ellie to his parents after the funeral, they'd texted back that she was the spitting image of him at that age. His mother had been dead set on meeting them at the Sacramento airport when they landed, but Cash wanted to give Ellie a chance to acclimate before throwing a lot of new people at her.

He closed the door softly so as not to wake her and pumped his gas. Through the window, he saw her bounce up and take in her surroundings.

He popped his head inside. "We're a little more than an hour from home. You want to grab dinner around here?" He'd stocked the fridge before he left. But it was getting late and would probably be easier to hit a restaurant.

"I'm not eating," she said.

"Right, hunger strike. Forgot." She'd been threatening to starve herself if he forced her to leave Boston. He was banking on the fact that she'd eat as soon as she got hungry but was starting to think that was a flawed plan. She was already so slight.

"I need to use the bathroom."

"All right. As soon as I finish here, I'll walk you in."

"I can go myself." She got out of the back seat and started for the ministore, the sweater hanging past her knees.

He topped off his tank and followed her inside. The store was empty, except for the attendant. Still, he stood sentry outside the ladies' room door. When she finally came out she seemed startled to find him there.

"You're gross." She shook her head, pulled her arms up until the empty sleeves of her sweater dangled loosely at her sides, and went back to Cash's SUV.

He unlocked the door with his fob and she climbed in the back again. "You sure you don't want to get something to eat? There's a Taco Bell across the street." He didn't even know if she liked Mexican, not that Taco Bell was remotely Mexican. Or food.

She responded by lying down, her face pressed into the seat. Ellie would eat when she was hungry, he continued to tell himself. He got back on the interstate while Ellie slept the rest of the ride. Or she played a damn good possum; Cash couldn't tell.

"Hey, Ellie, we're almost home." She didn't rouse, and he gave up trying after calling her name a few more times. It was too dark to see anything anyway.

When he was a kid, the drive from San Francisco to Dry Creek Ranch was the longest three hours of his life. He used to count the pine trees in anticipation of seeing his grandfather and cousins, memorizing landmarks to track the distance. And when they arrived, he shot out of the car like a bullet, ready to lose himself in Grandpa Dalton's world. Riding fences until they were bowlegged, moving cattle until they were rank and sweaty, and bathing naked in the creek until their lips turned blue.

He pulled through the ranch gate and took the fork in the road to the cabin. One of his cousins must've had the forethought to turn on the porch light to welcome them home. Even though the place was a dump, it looked homey in the amber glow. Cash opened the tailgate and grabbed his and Ellie's luggage. The rest of her stuff he'd packed and shipped from Boston and would arrive in a couple of weeks.

Ellie sat up and rubbed her eyes, then wordlessly peered out the window. It might not be much as far as houses went, but the scenery was breathtaking. In the morning, he'd show her the creek and take her over to Jace's place to meet the boys.

He carried their bags up the porch stairs and called, "You coming?"
She got one foot out, then froze, like she was paralyzed.

"Ellie?"

"I don't want to live here," she said softly. This time she sounded more scared than rebellious.

He dropped the suitcases, jogged down the stairs, and took her hand. "There's nothing to be afraid of, sweetheart. It's late. Tomorrow I'll show you around."

She reluctantly let him lead her inside. The door to the spare bedroom was slightly ajar, and Cash went to close it only to find that his stacks of file boxes had been cleared away. For the first time since moving in, he could actually see the floor. A box spring and mattress with fresh sheets and blankets had been set up against the wall. Next to it sat an old wooden nightstand and one of Grandpa Dalton's Remington lamps. Jace and Sawyer had been busy.

It wasn't anything like Ellie's bedroom in Boston—pink and frilly—but the room was a hell of a lot better than the way he'd left it and would do until he could come up with something better for her.

"This is where you'll bunk," he told her as she waited in the hallway, her arms pinned to her sides. The cabin seemed to terrify her.

"Hey, Ellie, honey, it'll be all right." He had no guarantee it would be for either of them, but a twelve-year-old who'd just lost her mother needed reassurance. He might be new to this whole fatherhood thing, but he at least knew that much.

He wheeled her suitcase into the room and tucked it inside the closet. Tomorrow, he'd hit Target for hangers and anything else she might need. "Let me show you where the bathroom is." In the condo where she and Marie had lived, Ellie had had her own bathroom. Here, they would have to share. The fixtures were old as dirt and he'd done little to make it appealing other than to scrub it clean.

He led her down the hall. "You ever take a bath in one of those?" Cash pointed to the clawfoot tub.

Ellie looked appalled and Cash couldn't tell whether it was the pronounced yellow ring around the tub or the fact that a stranger—a grown man no less—was asking her about her bathing habits.

"I know it's a little rough right now, but we'll go shopping and you can pick out a shower curtain and whatever else you think will gussy it up." She didn't respond, and he told himself to give her time.

Cash checked his watch. It was past ten. "What time do you usually go to bed?"

"Whenever I want," she said.

He highly doubted that, but that's what he got for asking. Eventually, he'd lay down the law about such things. For now, though, he'd let it slide. "There's food in the fridge and pantry; help yourself. If there's stuff you want and I don't have it, make a list and we'll pick it up at the grocery store.

"Tomorrow, I'll take you to see Jace's horses." He'd been surprised to see all the dressage ribbons in her bedroom. Apparently, she was quite an equestrian. According to Linda, Marie had been taking Ellie for lessons since she was eight. She didn't have her own horse but belonged to a stable that let her ride one of theirs in competitions.

For a second, she seemed to brighten; then, just like that, whatever trace of excitement he thought he saw was gone.

"We've got a big day coming, so we should probably hit the hay." He was dog-tired. Between Marie's funeral and dealing with a morose child, the last four days had tuckered him out emotionally. "You okay to get ready for bed by yourself?"

Again, she gave him a look of pure horror.

"Then I'll see you in the morning." He left her alone in the bathroom and made a beeline for his bedroom, where he found all his file boxes stacked against the wall.

To make room, he dragged a few of the cartons under the window and spotted the glow of Aubrey's light across the creek. Aubrey: he shook his head, remembering Monday and how he'd found her hanging from her old office window with her thong-clad ass on display. It had been quite a sight. The woman was different, that's for sure. Just thinking about her dangling ten feet in the air with her skirt rucked up over her hips put a smile on his face. And lord knew he could use a smile. The last few days had been tough, especially the funeral.

So he took that image of Aubrey with him to bed until he fell asleep, only to be awakened by a bad dream. It was the same one he always had. Casey Farmington's mutilated body tied to a tree, her eyes wide open, staring at him.

He got up to wash his face and was about to duck into the john when he heard a faint noise coming from Ellie's room. At first it was indistinguishable. But when it came again, he recognized it as a sob.

She was weeping, and the sound of her muffled cries made his chest hurt.

He started to go inside her room to offer comfort, but something told him that wouldn't go over well. It hadn't gone beyond his notice that he scared Ellie. He was an absolute stranger to her and not exactly Mr. Rogers. He was gruff, a little impatient, and had no experience with little girls whatsoever. She'd bristled whenever he tried, albeit awkwardly, to be demonstrative.

The fact was, he'd never been good at relationships, period, committing himself solely to his job.

If you'd given me a tenth of the attention you give your cases, I might've stayed.

Tamara, like the rest of his girlfriends, had walked out. No argument from him; he'd been a lousy boyfriend. But the stakes of being a parent were higher. Ellie needed someone dependable, someone who knew what the hell he was doing.

He continued to listen through the door, his heart folding in half at her hushed cries. At the funeral she'd been stoic, singing hymns and reciting psalms by heart, her face downcast as the priest led the Mass. He'd reached out and touched her shoulder and she'd leaned into him. And then, just like that, she'd pulled away, and the moment was gone.

He loitered in the hallway, waiting to see if she'd eventually fall asleep, feeling uneasy about leaving her alone. Yet he instinctively knew she wouldn't welcome his succor. The sad part of it was, he didn't know what to say or how to make things better—or at least not worse—anyway. He couldn't bring back Marie, and Ellie wanted her mother.

* * * *

When Cash went to wake Ellie the next morning, he found her room barricaded. She'd dragged the nightstand against the door. He was able to push it open without any trouble. The piece of furniture only weighed fifty pounds or so, but if God forbid he'd had to get to her in a hurry…

"Hey, Ellie, wake up."

She sat up and brushed the sleep from her eyes, trying to register where she was. Then withdrew the moment she took in the sparse bedroom.

"Honey, you can't do this." Cash waved at the nightstand and her door. "If there'd been a fire or an earthquake I'd need to get in here as quickly as possible."

She pushed off the blanket and threw one leg over the bed. Cash noted she'd slept in her oversized sweater.

"I hate it here." She was back to being defiant, which Cash felt more equipped to handle. Just ask the Bureau; defiance was his middle name.

"You've been here less than twenty-four hours," he said. "Let's have some breakfast and I'll give you the tour. Maybe seeing it in daylight will change your mind."

"I doubt it." She got up and searched for her suitcase for a robe. "And I'm not eating."

He clenched his jaw. Eventually, he'd have to put his foot down about the whole hunger strike thing. "Well, I'm having eggs and bacon. Feel free to join me or not join me, but be ready to go in forty minutes, okay?"

Cash left the room, giving her privacy to dress. About fifteen minutes later, he heard the water in the bathroom running, then a shrill scream.

Shit.

"Ellie?" He rushed across the hall.

"Don't come in here." Her voice was so filled with panic, he didn't know whether to obey or bust the door down.

"What's the problem?"

"There's a giant spider in the tub."

His own panic subsided. A spider. The girl better get used to them, living on a ranch. "Honey, how can I kill the spider if I can't come in?"

Silence. Then, "I'll be out in a second."

"Just tell me when you're ready."

There was rustling and then she finally opened the door, cinching the belt of her robe. He inspected the tub, found the spider, and flushed it down the toilet.

"Spider free," he said and smiled.

Her response was to shoo him out of the bathroom and slam the door in his face. A half hour later, she joined him in the kitchen, where he was frying bacon. When she didn't think he was looking, she snatched a piece off the plate he'd set aside. When he thought she wasn't looking, he scooted the plate closer to her. By the time the eggs were ready, a few more strips of bacon had disappeared. At least the hunger strike appeared to be over.

"So this is what I'm thinking: How 'bout I introduce you to your cousins and they show you the horses?" Cash thought maybe if she was around kids her age, it might help smooth the transition. "You good with that?"

She gave an evasive shrug.

"You'll like Travis and Grady," he said and casually put a dish of scrambled eggs and buttered toast in front of her. She toyed with the food with her fork, but he noticed she took a few bites. The kid was probably starving.

"You sleep okay?" He knew she hadn't, but at least it was a conversation starter.

She shrugged again. "How long do I have to stay here?"

Forever, kid.

COWBOY UP 35

She was stuck with him, but maybe not with Dry Creek Ranch. If he could persuade Jace and Sawyer to sell, they'd move somewhere where Cash could get a job. First, he had to figure out what his new career should be. He was a lawyer, though he'd never practiced a day in his life. But having a JD behind his name had helped him get hired at the Bureau.

"What do you say we take one day at a time?"

She didn't particularly like that answer but quietly nodded.

"When I was your age you couldn't get me to leave the ranch. My parents—your grandparents—had to force me into the car. Did you have a place like that in Boston?"

"No."

He had hoped she'd talk about the stable where she rode. That at least was common ground. "I think you'll like the barn with the horses. Have you ever ridden Western?"

"Only English," she said.

"It's not so very different." Cash used to have a girlfriend who rode hunters and jumpers. The tack, the clothes, the competitions had all seemed slightly prissy to him. He preferred jeans and a Stetson and the wide-open range. Not a lot of that in Boston, he presumed. "We'll clean up here and head over to the big ranch house where Jace and his boys live."

He did the dishes while she played with her phone. Cash wasn't so keen on giving kids that age expensive toys like smartphones, but Marie had been a single mom and a cop with unpredictable hours. A phone had probably been the best way to keep tabs on Ellie.

"You want to change before we take off?" She still wore the sweater, and the temperature was likely to hit ninety before noon.

"I'm good."

Hopefully, she had a T-shirt underneath, but Cash steered clear of pushing the issue. "Then let's roll."

She grudgingly followed him out to his SUV and, like for the ride from the airport, got in the back seat.

"Ellie, you know you can sit up front, right? You might be able to see more that way."

She switched seats with her head bent low. He waited for her to buckle in and took the fire trail that looped around the ranch. The road circled the outer perimeter of the property and only offered a periphery view. But at least the drive would give her a glimpse into the vastness and beauty of the ranch. Rolling hills of pastureland, dotted with oaks and pines and ponds.

"That's Dry Creek to the left. You probably heard the water from your bedroom last night."

She glanced out the window, doing her best to look bored, and didn't say anything. Undeterred, he continued to call out points of interest. "That spot of the creek right there is where I learned to swim. ...See that barn? That's where your cousin Jace and I found a musket ball left over from the Gold Rush. ...Sawyer and I built a fort in those trees when we were the same age as you. ...Over there is the chicken coop...that's where the eggs we ate this morning came from."

For Christ's sake, he sounded like a tour guide on steroids. *Stop trying so hard and let the poor girl take Dry Creek Ranch in for herself.* For the rest of the drive he shut up and thought she might've nodded off to sleep.

When they pulled up to the ranch house she stirred and pressed her face against the window as two of Jace's dogs ran around Cash's SUV in circles, barking. They jumped up on the door and she jerked back.

"They won't hurt you," he said, but she refused to budge from the truck.

Jace came out of the house and called the mutts away, then opened the passenger door and shook Ellie's hand in that low-key, warm way he had of putting people at ease. "Welcome to Dry Creek Ranch. Come inside; the boys can't wait to meet you."

Cash got out first, scratched one of the dogs that had come around to his side on the head, and helped Ellie out of the SUV. Grady opened the front door a crack and stuck one eye through. Cash winked at him.

"Can I come out, Dad?"

"Yep, but give Ellie room to breathe."

Grady burst through the door like a four-foot-two whirlwind. The eight-year-old was a handful but cute as hell.

He ran up to Ellie and wrapped her in a hug. "You want to meet my Uncle Sawyer? He lives down the hill." For some unfathomable reason, kids—and adults, for that matter—loved Sawyer.

"Hey, buddy, what did I tell you about giving Ellie some space?" Jace grabbed Grady's arm and tugged him away while Ellie stood ramrod straight with a dazed look in her eyes.

Travis came out and leaned against the porch railing. Jace's thirteen-year-old was more reserved than his younger brother. The kid reminded Cash of himself at that age. A little too serious. Since the boys' mama left, Travis had taken on the role of caretaker, and his shoulders practically sagged with the weight of it.

"Ellie, this is Travis." Cash waved the boy over. "I was hoping you guys would show her the horses later."

Travis nodded and stuck out his hand to Ellie, which made Cash smile. The boy was on his way to being a fine man. Ellie gave him a limp shake, then quickly hid her hands underneath the sleeves of that damned sweater.

"You eat breakfast yet, Ellie?" Jace put his arm around her shoulder and walked her inside the house. His cousin was a natural with kids, but then again, he'd had thirteen years of experience.

The place was its usual chaotic mess. A collection of boots, cowboy hats, and various clothing items filled the foyer. In the great room, the boys' video games were scattered across the coffee table, and the sofa pillows had somehow landed on the floor.

Jace led Ellie to the kitchen, where a pile of dishes sat in the farm sink and remnants of the morning's meal still lay on the counter. Yet even with the clutter, no place had ever been more majestic to Cash, or felt more like a home than the ranch house. It was a cowboy's castle, down to the rawhide furniture and the massive deer antler chandeliers.

The kitchen alone was twice the size of Cash's cabin. He could still remember his late grandmother cooking over the big six-burner stove and making homemade pizzas in the stone fireplace. At Christmastime, they'd sit in the massive front room, opening presents all morning long. Cash used to lay on the floor and stare up at the soaring, open-beam ceilings, wondering how his great-grandfather had gotten the heavy wooden trusses so high.

His great-great-grandfather began building the log house in the late 1800s, when he settled in Mill County to run cattle. Since then, his grandparents had added on and updated the ranch house to reflect the times.

Same with the cattle ranch.

When Grandpa Dalton had taken the reins, he turned it into one of the most prosperous spreads in the region. But a decade ago, when California experienced historic droughts, he was forced to cull the herd and was never able to recover from the financial loss. Jace had been supporting the place the best he could.

"What'll you have?" Jace asked Ellie as he pulled out a few boxes of the boys' cereal from the pantry. Sugary shit that made Cash wince. "Or should I make my famous pancakes?"

Ellie appeared to shrink further into her oversized sweater. Cash didn't know if she was shy or on a mission to reject anything that had to do with him.

"We had bacon and eggs," he said, and turned to Ellie. "But I can vouch for Jace's pancakes. You want a stack?" It wouldn't kill her to eat a little more. She looked as if she could blow away in a soft breeze.

Ellie shook her head. Cash pulled out two stools from the center island and motioned for her to sit and took the one next to her.

"Where's Sawyer?" he asked Jace. When Sawyer wasn't on assignment he'd sleep till noon.

"On his way over."

"He caught a fish in the creek yesterday. It was this big." Grady spread his arms two-feet wide.

"You eat it?" Cash grinned, because he knew the boys didn't like fish. To prove it, Grady made gagging noises.

"You missed out on some fine fish tacos," Jace said to Cash and winked at Ellie.

"We had the regular kind." Grady elbowed his way up to the breakfast bar. "Do you like tacos, Ellie?"

She shrugged, and Cash felt more of that gnawing regret. He didn't even know what foods his daughter liked to eat, the kind of books she enjoyed reading, her favorite color. Nothing. A week before she died, Marie had at least gotten him Ellie's medical records. By all accounts, his daughter was healthy.

The only other clues he'd gotten about Ellie's childhood had come from Linda and packing up Marie's condo. Judging by the photo galleries on the wall and Ellie's closet, Marie had doted on their daughter. There were pictures of her everywhere. Ellie as a toddler, Ellie at various holiday and birthday celebrations, Ellie on her first day of middle school, Ellie on a horse. The pictures were his sole glimpse into those milestones.

Between the photo albums, her clothes, and electronics, it had taken two solid days to box everything. Sorting through it, Cash hadn't found any evidence of a male figure in Ellie's life. According to Marie, she'd raised their daughter completely on her own. Cash hadn't felt right about pressing her on what, if anything, she'd told Ellie about him, not when she was in hospice care, dying of cancer.

"Why don't you guys show Ellie the horses?" Jace told Travis and Grady.

Travis pushed off the wall of the breakfast nook. "Come on, Ellie, let's go to the barn."

Ellie surprised Cash by following Travis without any resistance. He wouldn't go as far as to say she was enthusiastic about it, but maybe the boys could coax her out of her shell.

Jace waited for the kids to leave and said, "Looks like you could use a drink."

Cash let out an audible sigh. "She hates the cabin and wants to go home."

"It's a lot, Cash. Give her time."

"I know, but I had hoped we'd have a little more of a rapport. In the five days we've been together, she's barely talked, has refused to eat, and treats me like she's afraid I'm going to kill her in her sleep. Last night she shoved the nightstand against the door."

Jace burst out laughing, then held up a hand. "I know, not funny. But you are kind of scary." He leaned across the breakfast bar, glanced Cash over, and sniffed. "At least you shaved and showered. Kids are tougher than you think; she'll come around. How was the funeral?"

"You know the drill. Bagpipes, honor guard, lots of cops, lots of eulogies."

"And Ellie?"

"She held up, poor kid. Marie's partner and his family sat in the front row with us. Ellie seemed pretty tight with them, as well as Marie's best friend, Linda."

"It's good she had that support," Jace said, hesitated for a beat, then asked, "How come you think Marie never told you about Ellie?"

It was a hell of a good question. "I don't know. Maybe she wanted Ellie all to herself."

Cash had given it a lot of thought over the last two weeks and wondered if Marie had singled him out that night simply because she was looking for a sperm donor. All those years she could've gotten child support but never sought him out, not even to tell him she was pregnant.

They'd met at a law-enforcement conference in New Orleans, had gotten drunk at one of the bars in the French Quarter, and had wound up in bed together. That was the sum total of their relationship. The next day, they went their separate ways and never spoke again. It wasn't until Marie was on her deathbed that she'd contacted him about Ellie.

Since then, he'd gone back and forth between anger and, though it was shameful to admit, relief. When Marie got pregnant he was two years into his FBI career, had solved his first big case, and was enjoying a meteoric rise in the Bureau. Having a child would have thrown a monkey wrench into everything he'd worked for. Perhaps Marie knew that and was trying to do him a favor by not getting him involved.

"Other than she was a cop and lived in Boston, I knew nothing about her," Cash said. "So I couldn't begin to tell you what her reasons were."

"I don't want to speak ill of the dead, but it was pretty fucked up, if you ask me. Tell me again why it is that she didn't see fit to tell you about Ellie all this time but entrusted her care to you now? How'd she know you weren't a psycho? Weren't there other family members?"

Cash flicked a cereal crumb across the counter at his cousin. "Hey, brain dead, I was a respected FBI agent for more than a decade. As for family:

Her father died ten years ago, her mother is in a nursing home, and she and her brother don't speak. I'm it as far as relatives go." Still, there were friends like Linda who wanted Ellie. But Marie had said she ascribed to the old proverb, blood is thicker than water, which didn't make sense to Cash because she hadn't given a rat's ass about his familial status until she was dying.

"Hey, where is everyone?" Sawyer bellowed.

"We're in the kitchen," Jace called.

Sawyer joined them at the center island, sank into the stool Ellie had vacated, and took in the mess left over from breakfast. "Got anything to eat?"

"When are you going to start buying your own food?" Jace opened the refrigerator and pulled out a dozen eggs. "Make yourself an omelet, asshole."

Sawyer swiveled on the stool until he was facing Cash. "Just met Ellie. She and the boys were headed to the barn. Good-looking kid. Bright. You sure you're her father?"

Cash had the paternity test to prove it; Marie had insisted.

"Like all of us, the kid's got the Dalton blue eyes," Jace said, then proceeded to make Sawyer his omelet.

"Not too much cheese."

Jace tossed the eggshells in the garbage. "You ever think about getting a maid?"

Sawyer grinned. "Why, when I have you?" He got up, rummaged through the refrigerator, and popped two slices of bread in the toaster. While he waited for the timer to go off, he grabbed the butter.

"Jeez, you're eating me out of house and home."

"You two sound like an old married couple." Cash watched Jace plate the eggs, reached over with Sawyer's fork, and took a bite. With a mouthful, he said, "Thanks for cleaning up my spare room for Ellie, by the way. Let me know what I owe you for the bed."

"We took it from the guest room." Jace tipped his head toward the staircase. "It's old; you'll probably want to get something better at some point."

Cash nodded. Shipping Ellie's old bedroom set would've cost more than a new one. For now, the old mattress would do, but he'd have to get her something soon. "I think the cabin gives her the creeps. You two give any more thought to what we talked about?"

"Selling?" Jace flipped the omelet. "Never gonna happen." He nudged his head at Sawyer.

"Still no for me too. Fix the cabin up, Cash. This is a good place for Ellie. Grandpa Dalton would've wanted us to keep it, to raise our families here."

That was the thing: Cash didn't know what their grandfather would've wanted, because he'd failed to leave an instruction manual in his living trust. And he was tired of going around in circles with his two cousins about what they should do with the land. Sadly, they were operating under a democracy. Two against one, and even Sawyer, who had more money than both Cash and Jace put together, couldn't afford to buy him out. Cash figured if he kept chipping away at them, they'd eventually realize five hundred acres of prime California real estate was too valuable to sit on. And lord knew they didn't have the resources to return Dry Creek Ranch back to its former glory.

"Fine, we'll table it for now." Cash didn't have the wherewithal to get into it with them again. For now, he had to focus on Ellie and hoped the horses would be a nice bribe, because he had little else to offer. Tomorrow, after she'd had a chance to settle in, he'd take her riding. "I've got my hands full with Ellie."

"She really is a beautiful girl," Sawyer said. "A little skittish right now, but she'll get used to it here…to us."

Cash hoped he was right. "I'm planning to take her to Roseville today to buy supplies. If there's time, maybe we'll hit a few furniture stores and order a better mattress."

"You should talk to Aubrey." Jace dipped into Sawyer's omelet. "She gets all kinds of discounts."

Cash walked over to the coffee maker and poured himself a mug. "Did she tell you I helped her break into her office the other day?"

"No." Jace's brows winged up. "She said Mercedes refused to let her in on Mitch's orders. She broke in?"

"Through the window." Cash left out the part about her skirt riding up, offering him a delectable view of her ass.

"That sounds like Aubrey." Jace chuckled.

"People are talking, Jace." Sawyer spread so much butter on his toast that Cash's arteries hurt just watching him.

"In Dry Creek, they always do. It'll blow over. It's summer, folks are bored."

"According to Jimmy Ray, old Mitch isn't taking the breakup too well. He's been bad-mouthing you all over town. Not good when you're up for reelection next year."

"It's a county election," Jace said. "Dry Creek is Dry Creek."

The small ranching community had somehow managed to stay stuck in the twentieth century while the neighboring county had grown with the times. Retirees flocked to nearby Grass Valley after selling their million-dollar homes in the Bay Area and hippies and artists continued to flood Nevada City, just up the road. But even though it was a little more than an hour's drive to Sacramento, Dry Creek had stayed relatively untouched. The same families that had come during the Gold Rush were still here and still running cattle and raising horses.

"Don't think your opponent won't use it," Sawyer said.

"Nah." Jace waved Sawyer off, grinning. "No one gives a shit about sex scandals anymore. You, a big-wig reporter, should know that. But if it becomes a problem, I'll hire your parents to fix it," Jace joked. Aunt Wendy and Uncle Dan owned one of the largest PR firms in Los Angeles, handling damage control for stars and politicians caught in all kinds of kink.

"In a place like this, they might," Sawyer argued around a mouthful of omelet. He started to say more, but the sound of small feet racing down the hallway stopped him.

"You're back already?" Jace called.

Grady came into the kitchen out of breath. "Ellie tripped on a log."

"She's okay," Travis assured them as he trailed in. "We just came to get the first aid kit."

Cash got to his feet. "Where is she?"

"Bathroom," the two boys said at the same time.

Cash rushed through the hallway and banged on the powder-room door. "Ellie? You okay?"

"Don't come in," came a faint voice.

Here they went again.

"Then come out so I can see if you're hurt."

"I'm not hurt."

He put his hand on the knob. "Let me have a look."

When she didn't respond, he opened the door. She sat on the side of the tub with the leg of her jeans pulled up, exposing a bloody scrape on her knee.

"Not so bad," he said and crouched down for a closer inspection. "What'd you hit?"

"A rock." Her bottom lip quivered.

He was at a loss of how to comfort her. His mother would've kissed the "boo-boo," but at twelve she seemed too old for that sort of thing. There was also the fact that she recoiled every time he came near her.

Travis came in with the first aid kit and Cash immediately got to work on cleaning her cuts. At least he knew how to do that. Before long, Grady, Jace, and Sawyer were crowded into the doorway and Cash felt the bathroom shrink to half its size.

"A little space would be good."

Jace and Sawyer backed off, but Grady stayed put and gave Cash pointers on how to clean and dress the wound.

"He's got it, buddy." Jace pulled the boy by the back of his T-shirt and wrapped an arm around his shoulder.

Travis handed Cash a bandage from the kit.

"Did you get to see the horses?"

She nodded, and Grady took over, describing in vivid detail how they'd climbed over the corral fence to pet Amigo, Jace's prized gelding, when Ellie tripped over the log. "She came this close"—he showed them with his hands—"to smashing her head on the gate. Kapow!"

"Hey, Grady, enough," Jace said.

Cash applied the bandage and helped Ellie pull her pant leg down. "I guess we don't have to amputate after all." He winked, and she responded by staring at the tile floor.

Jace gave Cash a sympathetic glance.

"We best be on our way if we plan to drive to town." Cash stood up and offered Ellie a hand, which she instantly rejected, getting to her feet on her own.

As they walked out of the bathroom, Sawyer mussed Ellie's hair. "You did good, kid. Toughed it out like a real cowgirl."

Cash could've sworn he saw a ghost of a smile flicker across Ellie's face. That was Sawyer for you. He could charm a feral cat, proving there really was no accounting for taste.

"You want to go home first and change into something cooler than your sweater?" Cash asked as they walked to his SUV. The ranch house was only five minutes away from the cabin by car.

"No."

"All right. But if it's all the same to you, I'm going to change into a pair of shorts."

Cash took the fire trail back to the cabin and threw his SUV into Park. "You coming in?"

He expected Ellie to say she'd wait in the truck, but she surprised him by following. On the doorstep, someone had left a basket decoratively wrapped in cellophane, ribbon, and a bow. He carried the package into the house and set it on the table.

Ellie flopped onto the sofa while he went inside his bedroom to change. When he came out, she was standing over the basket, poking at the envelope that had been taped to the ribbon, and jumped away, afraid he'd think she'd been snooping.

"What does it say?" He hadn't noticed the enclosure card before and simply assumed the basket was from one of the ladies in town who'd heard about Marie's funeral and about Ellie coming to live with him and wanted to welcome her to Dry Creek. That's the way people did things around here. Grandpa Dalton used to send steaks. "Go ahead and read it."

"I just wanted to see if it came from Linda."

"It might've. Let's take a look," Cash said, though he didn't think companies like FTD delivered out here. He removed the envelope from the basket and noted that it was monogrammed. A. M. He sliced open the flap and pulled out a flowery piece of stationery.

"Thanks for helping me the other day. Enjoy the cookies." It was signed Aubrey.

He tore open the cellophane wrapper, plucked out what appeared to be a snickerdoodle, and took a bite. "Not bad. It's from the neighbor. Taste one, they're pretty good."

Cash pushed the basket toward Ellie, whose face fell. She'd probably been hoping for a one-way airplane ticket back to Boston.

"No, thanks." She wandered back to the couch.

"Should we make a list of supplies?" He thought if he included her, she might be less reticent, and got a notebook out of the kitchen junk drawer. "We'll add anything you think you'll need."

"Can't I just go home?"

This is home, kid. "Ellie, you're not even giving it a chance. I understand that this...me...is a big change from what you're used to. I really do. But I would appreciate it if you at least tried to get to know me a little."

"Why should I? You never got to know me."

Was that what Marie had told her? He wanted to ask, but less than a week after putting Marie in the ground seemed like the wrong time. "We can talk about that, Ellie, but not today. Okay?"

"Whatever." She shrugged, but he could tell she wasn't as apathetic as she let on. "I need a better pillow. The one you gave me is hard as a rock."

"I'll put it on the list."

Chapter 4

Aubrey peeked through the blinds for the seventh time, watching as Cash and his daughter lugged in at least a dozen packages. There were Target bags, grocery bags, and a giant sack from Bed Bath & Beyond.

Her curiosity got the best of her and she went outside to get a better look, pretending she just wanted to sit on her front porch in the hundred-degree heat. No sense in Cash thinking she was nosy, because no one wanted a snoopy neighbor.

His daughter was adorable but looked like she was sweltering in that heavy sweater. Aubrey wanted to introduce herself and ask if they liked the cookies she'd delivered that morning but didn't want to disturb him while he was busy unloading his SUV. Besides, she took him for the aloof type, even though he'd been kind enough to help her sneak in and out of her office the other day. Of course, there'd been the not-so-subtle hint about Jace and his bid for reelection. Looking back on it, that had probably been Cash's motivation for helping her in the first place.

Aubrey tried to look busy in her rocking chair, scrolling through her phone, all the while sneaking glimpses of the logos on the bags. It appeared Cash was planning some home-improvement projects, which was right up her alley. And less noisy than shooting Jim Beam bottles all day.

Cash shielded his eyes with his hand and gazed at her from across the creek. "Thanks for the cookies," he shouted over the rush of the water and went back to unloading.

She stood up and leaned across her porch railing. "I'm glad you liked them." Now that he'd opened the door, she felt emboldened to cross the small footbridge that separated their two cabins and say hello. "What have you got there?" She nudged her head at one of the Home Depot packages.

"We did a little shopping." He waved over his daughter, who'd for the most part been sitting on her hands while he did the bulk of the work. "Ellie, this is Aubrey, the cookie neighbor."

The cookie neighbor? She supposed she'd been called worse.

"Hi, Ellie, so nice to meet you." She couldn't help herself and gave the girl a hug. She looked like she needed one. "Welcome to Dry Creek Ranch."

"Hi." Ellie dropped her gaze to the ground shyly.

"Don't you just love it here?"

"I guess," Ellie said with about as much eagerness as a rock. "It's not as nice as Boston, though."

"It's different, I suppose. Have you gone swimming in the creek yet?"

"No, it looks cold." She toed a clod of dirt with her tennis shoe.

"It's not so bad," Aubrey said, even though she'd only dipped her feet in since moving to the ranch. Cash, on the other hand...She felt her skin flush at the memory of him swimming naked. He certainly hadn't shown any signs of shrinkage, so how cold could the water be?

Aubrey carried on a steady conversation with Ellie, enjoying her accent. It wasn't as thick as the Kennedys, but Aubrey noticed Ellie dropped her Rs from time to time. Out of the corner of her eye, she saw Cash leaning against the hood of his SUV, watching her.

When there was a lull in the conversation, he asked, "You break into any more offices lately?"

"Not lately." But if she didn't get a job in the next couple of months, she'd have to hold up a Bank of America.

"Planning a home improvement project?" Aubrey pointed at one of the shopping bags.

"We're fixing up Ellie's room. Jace said you might be able to help us with furniture."

"Absolutely." Ooh, Aubrey brightened. "What did you all have in mind?" A little project would distract her from the rumors swirling around town.

"Ellie needs furniture. A bed, dresser, desk, whatever else she wants."

"How exciting," Aubrey said, and noted the girl appeared anything but. "Do you have a style in mind, Ellie?"

Ellie hitched her shoulders and frowned. "I'm good with what's there because I'll be going home to Boston soon." She drilled Cash with a look.

Uh-oh; clearly Aubrey was missing something here. She didn't want to get in the middle of a family squabble but relished the chance to decorate a little girl's room. So much of her work was designed to sell homes, meaning the appointments had to be generic enough to appeal to a mass audience. She loved projects where she could let loose and build an entire space around one person's personality.

"Ellie, we talked about this," he told his daughter, sounding frustrated. Then he turned to Aubrey. "So you're willing to take this on?"

"Definitely. How about I bring over some catalogs and you and Ellie can show me the things you like?"

"Sounds good. When?"

She laughed. Cash Dalton got right down to business. That was okay, because Aubrey had nothing but time these days. Besides, she was intrigued by the father-daughter dynamic she witnessed, which, judging by their body language, appeared strained to say the least. "Why don't I let you put away all your purchases and I can come over in an hour or two. Does that work?"

"Ellie?" Cash looked at his daughter.

"Whatever." Ellie twirled her dark hair.

She was a beautiful little girl who looked strikingly like her father. Aubrey could tell she was also a handful like her dad. But she'd dealt with plenty of difficult clients. A twelve-year-old wouldn't be too tough to tame.

"See you in a few, then," Aubrey said.

She crossed back over the footbridge to her cabin, marveling at how beautiful the day had turned out. Even though it was hot, there was a nice breeze blowing through the trees.

She was loitering on the porch, taking in the view, when her phone started ringing. Aubrey rushed inside and grabbed it off the coffee table, hoping it was someone looking for an interior designer. She'd spruced up her Houzz profile and was in the process of updating her résumé.

"Aubrey McAllister here." She tried not to sound out of breath.

"Hi, Aubrey, it's Ruth Singleton." There was a long pause. "Um… bad news, sweetie. Cole and I have decided to put the pool house project on hold."

"Oh?" Aubrey dropped onto the couch, surprised. Just a week ago, Ruth had been gung ho about remodeling her thousand-square-foot pool house. They'd already special-ordered flooring and fixtures that were nonrefundable. "I'm sorry to hear that. Is everything okay?" It was probably unprofessional to ask, but she had a sneaking suspicion the sudden change of plan was tied to Aubrey's breakup with Mitch. Perhaps it was the saccharine quality of Ruth's voice, which sounded more affected than usual.

"Oh, you know… the money. It just got to the point where the project became cost prohibitive…and, uh, overwhelming."

"I understand, Ruth, and I'm sure Reynolds Construction does too."

Ruth responded with another awkward pause, telling Aubrey all she needed to know. Mitch still had the job, while Aubrey had been cut loose.

When the silence stretched to the point of being uncomfortable, Ruth finally found her voice. "Thank you for being so understanding," she said, sounding as phony and rehearsed as the rest of her spiel.

The Singletons had more money than they knew what to do with. For the last five years, Ruth and her husband had been using Reynolds Construction to add on to their already gargantuan home. A guest cottage, a game room, a garage for their Airstream trailer. The place was like the freaking Winchester Mystery House.

Cost prohibitive. Overwhelming. Bullshit.

"I know you have quite a few hours into the project," Ruth continued. "Please send me an invoice and I'll write you a check for what I owe."

Aubrey clicked off and slammed down the phone. She'd been hoping the commission from the pool house job would get her through the next few months. "Goddamn you, Mitch."

In anger, she scooped the phone back up and hit the Speed Dial button for her ex-fiancé. It rang and rang until she got voice mail. The son of a bitch was screening.

"Quit messing with my livelihood, Mitch," she yelled into the phone. "If you don't want the whole world to know what you did, stop interfering with my projects."

She knew Mitch wouldn't heed her threat. He'd done an excellent job of villainizing her to the point where no one would believe a word she said, even if it was the truth. More important, he knew she would never tell. So, basically, she was screwed fifty ways from Sunday.

On second thought…she scrolled through her contact list, found who she was looking for, and dialed. Within thirty minutes, she'd caught up with an old friend from design school who'd volunteered to talk to her boss, a developer in Las Vegas, about giving Aubrey a job. It was a shot in the dark but worth a try. Vegas was a fast-growing city, with planned communities cropping up as fast as crabgrass. She could do Sin City. In fact, her life could use a little glitter.

She celebrated her slim prospect of employment with a pint of Cherry Garcia and for the next two hours buried herself in sticking Post-its to pages in catalogs with furniture that might appeal to a twelve-year-old.

At six o'clock, Aubrey gathered up the catalogs, checked her hair and face in the mirror, and took the short walk to Cash's cabin. He was fixing dinner when she got there.

"Did I come at a bad time?" She didn't want to interrupt their meal.

"Nope. Ellie may or may not be on a hunger strike, depending on her mood. Either way, there's plenty for you if you're interested in overcooked pasta."

She went over to the stove and stuck her nose in one of the pots. "Sauce smells good."

He held up a jar of Newman's Own and grinned. "Tough to screw up."

"What the heck? I'll have some, if there's really enough."

Cash put another setting on the table and slid a loaf of garlic bread into the oven. Ellie sat in the corner, doing something on her phone. It was the first time Aubrey had ever been in the cabin, and she took the opportunity to look around.

The place really was awful, at least in its current condition. The cabin itself had good bones. A stone fireplace she thought was original. And the walls were made from white pine logs that had beautifully aged with time. Vaulted ceilings with exposed beams and an open floor plan in the common areas made the house feel airy.

With some rugs, better furniture, a kitchen update, and some colorful accessories, the place could be charming. Too compact to be a showstopper, but inviting and cozy. Currently, the oversize dun couch recliner wasn't doing the living room any favors. The coffee table looked like an upside-down chicken coop, which was a thing, but not the way Cash had done it. The walls were bare and the floors scarred. The house could benefit from a deep cleaning. It wasn't exactly dirty, but there was a patina of neglect that hung in the air like a dreary cloud.

With ten grand and some elbow grease, she could make the place shine.

"Spaghetti's on," Cash said.

Aubrey noted that Ellie hadn't moved from her spot. "Are you really on a hunger strike, Ellie?"

Ellie gave a little shake of her shoulders, clearly pulled between the sweet aromas coming from the kitchen and whatever it was she was protesting.

"Well, come sit with me at least." Aubrey beckoned the girl to the table.

Cash did a double take when Ellie actually joined them. When Ellie thought no one was looking, she sniffed the dinner Cash had laid out. Cash didn't say a word, but Aubrey noticed that he served Ellie a nice helping of spaghetti and salad.

He passed Aubrey the pasta. "Dig in."

They ate without talking, and Aubrey spied Ellie taking a few nibbles of the bread before breaking down and trying the spaghetti.

"It's delicious," Aubrey said.

"It's passable." Cash dusted the top of his with a thick coat of pepper. "What do you think, Ellie?"

"It's all right, not as good as my mother's. Hers was the best." The tremor in Ellie's voice was enough to break Aubrey's heart.

Cash fell silent, clearly stymied over how to respond.

"What else did she make?" Aubrey asked.

"Everything. Macaroni and cheese from scratch, Sloppy Joes, enchiladas. Just everything."

"Do you have her recipes? Because if you do, maybe you and your dad could try to recreate some of her dishes." Aubrey was probably butting in where she didn't belong, but she'd always been that way. Just ask anyone.

"We could do that," Cash said, jumping on the idea.

Ellie turned to Aubrey. "Maybe I could do it with you."

Well, hell. Aubrey hadn't seen that coming, not that she wouldn't want to cook with Ellie. But she'd been trying to throw a life preserver to Cash, who frankly appeared a little lost in how to deal with an inconsolable child. Not that Aubrey was any expert on it.

"Maybe we could all do it together," she said.

"Yep," Cash agreed, but this time less enthusiastically. "Gotta eat, and Aubrey lives next door. We could have Jace and the boys come too, make it a family affair."

Aubrey nodded. "Wouldn't that be fun?" Was it just her or were they trying too hard?

"That's okay." Ellie played with a piece of lettuce that had stuck to the side of her plate. "I'll probably be leaving soon anyway."

Cash started to say something, stopped, and shoveled another forkful of pasta in his mouth.

"In the meantime, I found some really cute ideas for your bedroom." If it was anything like the rest of the house, it would need all the help Aubrey could give it.

"It seems like a waste of money." Ellie glared at Cash.

"I won the lottery, so not a problem." Cash clasped his hands behind his head and leaned back in his chair.

They finished eating, and Cash did the dishes while Aubrey spread her catalogs and magazines across the old farm table—one of Cash's nicer furniture pieces, which wasn't saying much. Before they got down to business, she asked Ellie to show her the room.

"So this is it, huh?" Aubrey examined the space. It wasn't a bad size and there was a big window that looked out over Dry Creek. Other than that, there wasn't a whole lot to recommend it. The lighting was bad—just a lamp, which looked like a Remington if she wasn't mistaken, on a rickety nightstand—and the rug looked like something had died on the floor. The wall with the window was made from pine logs, like the front rooms. But the other three were drywall, painted in a drab color. Not quite beige and not quite white, just a dingy combination of both.

"What's your favorite color?" Aubrey asked Ellie.

"Pink, I guess."

"Pink, huh? I can work with that." It had been Aubrey's favorite color when she was Ellie's age. She continued to size up the room, looking for the best way to arrange the furniture. While the window let in what little light the room had and framed gorgeous views of the creek and mountains, its location made the room tricky for placing a bed. Aubrey preferred not to put a headboard against a window unless it was absolutely necessary.

Cash wandered in, curious to see what they were doing, and the room suddenly felt smaller. It wasn't just his sheer size; she was used to tall, broad men. Her brother, Mitch, Jace. No, Cash had a commanding presence, the bearing of a man who was used to being in charge. The power of it threw her off her game, and for a second, she had trouble remembering what she was in the middle of doing before he walked in. *Uh, furniture placement, stupid.*

"Do you have a tape measure?" she asked him.

He went off to find one and Aubrey ballparked it by walking off the wall opposite the window. That was where she planned to put the bed.

"I think you have enough room for a dresser, a nightstand, and a desk. It'll be tight, but I'll make it work."

Ellie continued to stand just inside the doorway, looking forlorn and bored.

"What would be your dream bedroom?" Aubrey hoped the question would coax some participation out of the girl. "Mine was a canopy bed with tons of ruffles." A canopy bed would certainly work in Ellie's room, given the height of the vaulted ceilings.

"I liked the bedroom I had in my Boston house."

"Shall we try to replicate it?" Aubrey asked, refusing to give in to Ellie's sulkiness. "Or should we go totally new and different?"

Ellie's response was to flop onto the bed and play with her phone. Undaunted, Aubrey decided to leave Ellie be. She'd come around eventually. What young girl could resist decorating a bedroom?

Cash returned. "What do you want me to measure?"

"I need the dimensions of the room and the width and height of the window." Aubrey looked for something to write on. "I'll be right back."

She got her sketch pad from the dining room and went back to draw a rough schematic of the room, using the measurements Cash called out.

"What do you think of stripes, Ellie?"

"Whatever." Ellie went back to burying her face in her phone.

Aubrey and Cash exchanged glances. She gave him a reassuring smile, as if to say *I've got this.*

"Let's go back in the dining room and go shopping."

When Ellie made no effort to move, Aubrey went over to the bed, tugged her up by the arm, and led her to the table.

"Start looking through this catalog and stick these to anything you like." Aubrey handed Ellie a pad of Post-its.

Cash joined them at the table and leafed through one of the bedroom magazines Aubrey had brought.

"This one is nice." He held up a picture of a panel bed with dark wood, heavy lines, and a decidedly nineties vibe. It was ugly as sin.

"I was thinking something a little less masculine." What she meant to say was something a little less hideous, but Aubrey was trying to put it as kindly as possible.

"Gotcha." Cash continued to flip through the pages. "What about this one?"

Aubrey thought the picture of the mahogany four-poster he waved in front of her face was better than his last choice but too old-fashioned for a twelve-year-old. And definitely too dark.

"Do you like this?" Aubrey slid a picture of a headboard and footboard made of white picket fencing under Ellie's nose. On each of the four posts sat a colorful birdhouse. Aubrey thought it was adorable.

Ellie managed to pull herself away from her phone long enough to give the catalog a passing glance. Then, boom, her face brightened and her blue eyes flashed with excitement. Ah, they were getting somewhere.

"We could do one wall in pink and white stripes with bedding to match," Aubrey suggested.

Cash made a face. Apparently, he wasn't feeling Aubrey's vision. But Ellie was, Aubrey could see it in her expression, no matter how hard she tried to hide it.

"We could do lots of pink and white fuzzy pillows and a fluffy rug in the center of the room." She handed Ellie the tape measure. Now that she had the girl's attention, she wanted her to feel like part of the process. "Tell me how much floor space we have for the rug."

Ellie plodded off to do Aubrey's bidding but did her best to act put out.

As soon as she was gone from the room, Cash said in a hushed voice, "You do know I was joking when I said I won the lottery?"

"Give me a budget and I'll stay in it."

Cash hesitated for a beat, then asked, "Will a couple thousand do it?"

Probably not, but Aubrey would make it work. "Yep, I'll keep it right at two thousand dollars as long as you're willing to pitch in with the painting. Are you handy?" Something about the question made her blush, and she turned away so he wouldn't see the red stain that had heated her cheeks.

"Handy enough," he said, the corners of his mouth ticked up in an arrogant smile.

Ellie returned. "I don't really know what you want me to do. I measured, but I don't think it's right."

"I'll remeasure, no worries." Aubrey took the measuring tape from her, planning to review the room one more time before she left. Turning her attention back to Cash, she asked, "Is it all right with you if I come by tomorrow to begin preparing the walls?"

"Sure." Cash draped his arm over Ellie's shoulders, the first sign of affection Aubrey had witnessed between the two. "I don't think we have anything going on tomorrow, so Ellie can help."

Ellie squirmed out from under Cash's arm.

"Then I think we're good here for now. I'll order the bed and start searching for the other pieces." She gathered up her sketch pad, catalogs, and magazines and stuffed them in her tote bag. "Is ten okay?"

"We'll be up."

"I'll just take that last measurement and be on my way."

She double-checked Ellie's room's dimensions and Cash walked her outside.

"Thanks for doing this," he said in that low, rumbling voice she'd first mistaken for surly and now thought was sexy.

"I'm guessing it hasn't gone beyond your notice that Ellie doesn't want to be here," he continued. "I'm not sure if a new bedroom will change that, but the room—the whole cabin, for that matter—isn't what you would call homey. Hopefully, this'll help."

"Absolutely it will. I'll make her bedroom so beautiful she won't want to leave." Aubrey didn't know what else to say, so she smiled, and Cash smiled back. But something in his blue eyes told her he wasn't altogether convinced. "I'll see you tomorrow."

Aubrey went home to her empty cabin. Ordinarily, she spent Sunday evenings getting ready for the long workweek ahead, organizing her calendar, packing her car with supplies, doing laundry. Because she had now joined the ranks of the unemployed, she had nothing to do but wander aimlessly around her tiny new home. Mitch had built them a four-thousand-square-foot two-story farmhouse with every modern amenity imaginable. The man knew his luxury homes; Aubrey would give him that much.

Instead of feeling sorry for herself, she filled the next hour by gathering what she would need to tape off Ellie's room for the pink and white stripes. A pretty room for a pretty girl. Aubrey thought Ellie looked just like her father: same blue eyes, same cleft chin. Neither of them smiled that often, which made her wonder about Cash's story and why he was no longer working for the FBI. Next time she saw Jace, she planned to wheedle it out of him.

Bored to tears, she got ready for bed and stayed awake, watching TV until half past ten. She turned on her side and glimpsed the shimmer of her wedding dress hanging in the open closet. Next Saturday would've been her and Mitch's wedding day. She stopped to think about that, to let it sink in. No regrets came, just a deep and abiding disappointment. In Mitch, for what he had done, and in herself, for nearly making the mistake of a lifetime.

She got up, shut the closet door, and went to sleep.

Chapter 5

Cash awoke in the middle of the night. At first, he thought he was having the dream again, but it only took him a few seconds to clear the sleep from his head and realize it was a noise coming from Ellie's room.

He got out of bed, went to her room, and listened. When he didn't hear anything, he cracked the door a few inches and peeked inside. Ellie's face was buried in her pillow and sobs wracked her small body.

Her pain tore his insides out and this time, whether she liked it or not, he wasn't walking away. He went to the side of her bed and put his hand on her shoulder. "Ellie?"

She shrank away from him, like he'd burned her with a match. "Get out of my room."

"Ellie, honey, tell me what's wrong." Cash scrubbed his hand through his hair, knowing it was an asinine question.

"I want to go home," she said through sobs. "Can't I just live with Linda?"

He sat on the edge of the bed, and she scooted closer to the wall. "Your mom wanted you to live with me. It was her dying wish, so it must've been important to her. Don't you think?"

"Why? Why was it important to her?" she asked, and he wished he had an answer that would make sense to her. "You weren't even in our lives and Linda was her best friend."

"It's not because I didn't want to be. You're my daughter, Ellie, my own flesh and blood."

"If you wanted to be a good father, you'd let me go live with Linda." She wiped her nose with the sleeve of that damned sweater.

A part of him wondered if she was right. He'd ripped her away from everything familiar, and Linda had made it clear that she and her family would be thrilled to take Ellie in. "I was hoping we could get to know each other."

"I don't want to know you, I just want to go home." She turned so that her back was facing him.

"We'll talk about it tomorrow." He didn't know what else to say… what else to do. He tucked her in, like his mother used to do to him, and remained at the edge of the sagging mattress. "What if I just sit here until you fall asleep?"

She responded with radio silence. So he watched over her until her breathing became even and her small back rose and fell with slumber. Watching her like that, so small and innocent, gripped him with emotion. And without thinking about it, he leaned over her and kissed the top of her head, whispering, "Night, Ellie."

Back in his room, he stared out the window into the darkness. Aubrey's front porch light was on, and he wondered if she was still awake. Nah, not likely at two in the morning. But it would've been nice to have someone to talk to about Ellie, and Aubrey seemed to click with his daughter. And he seemed to click with Aubrey in an entirely different way, which, given his newfound circumstances, wasn't good.

It took him an hour of tossing and turning to finally fall asleep, only to have dawn creep through his shades. He considered turning over and going back to bed when he remembered he had a kid to feed breakfast. It struck him that Ellie changed everything. He was no longer a bachelor, free to roam. He had someone who was completely reliant on him. The weight of that revelation pressed heavy against his chest. He pushed back and got up to take a quick shower.

In the kitchen, he found Sawyer pawing through his refrigerator.

"Did you eat through Jace's already?"

"Nope, just seeing what you've got. A lot of healthy shit."

Cash put on a pot of coffee and grabbed two mugs from the cupboard. "How's the book coming?"

Sawyer let out a loud yawn. "It's coming. I stayed up all night working on it." He'd always been a night owl and yet he was here at the ass-crack of dawn. "How's the kid doing?"

Cash groaned. "She's having trouble with the transition."

"Transition? It's only been two days."

"A decade in preteen years." Cash rubbed his hand down his unshaven face.

"I guess. You try buying her off? That's what my folks used to do with Angela."

Yeah, and look how well that turned out. "Anything new from that PI you hired?"

"Nada." Sawyer swiped a carton of milk from the fridge and poured himself a cup of coffee before the machine was finished brewing. "She's like a ghost."

Or worse, she was dead. In this day and age, even people who intentionally tried to disappear had a hard time doing it without leaving some kind of bread crumbs. But Cash didn't voice his thoughts. Sawyer knew his sister better than anyone, and it didn't take a hardened journalist to know that Angela lived a high-risk lifestyle.

"I miss her," Sawyer said, surprising Cash because his cousin rarely talked about Angela.

"We all do." Cash poured his own cup and they stood against the counter, sipping coffee.

Sawyer nudged his head in the direction of Ellie's room. "She's not up yet?"

"Rough night. She cried most of it."

"Ah, crap. Poor kid. You got plans for her today?"

"Aubrey's coming over at ten to help decorate her room. From what I can tell, it's going to involve a lot of pink and a lot of pillows."

Sawyer raised a brow. "Aubrey, huh?"

"It was Jace's idea. Ellie seems to like her." More than she did him anyway.

"Don't act like it's a hardship," Sawyer said and lifted that brow again, this time suggestively.

Cash shook his head. "Yeah, because I don't have enough to deal with."

"She's hot. Nothing wrong with looking."

"I'm not interested in looking at Aubrey McAllister." It wasn't altogether true, because he'd done plenty of looking, but that's as far as it could go. With a twelve-year-old living under his roof, he wasn't in the market for a woman. "A few weeks ago, she was engaged."

Sawyer shrugged. "So? She got herself unengaged, which means she's available." He grinned to drive home the point.

Aubrey was his neighbor and Ellie could benefit from having a woman next door, considering the rest of Dry Creek Ranch was filled with testosterone. Cash didn't want to screw that up by getting his dick involved. "Well, I'm not."

Sawyer held up his hands. "All right, no need to get defensive."

Cash heard running water in the bathroom. Ellie was up. "I'm making French toast for the kid. I'm assuming you want some."

"Your assumption is correct." Sawyer made himself at home at the table Cash had pulled out of storage. "You got real maple syrup or that sugary shit?"

Cash ignored him, got a loaf of bread out of the cupboard, and snatched the milk back from Sawyer. There were a dozen eggs from Jace's chicken coop in the fridge.

A few minutes later, Ellie wandered in, wearing the same sweater she'd slept in. The nasty thing needed a washing.

"Hey, Ellie." Sawyer pulled a chair out for her by the table. "Your old man's making French toast."

"How many slices do you want?" Cash asked.

"Two." She took the seat Sawyer offered.

Cash took some solace in the fact that she was eating regular meals and dipped the bread in batter, letting each slice soak long enough to get good and custardy. It was the way his mother made her French toast. "You want orange juice?"

"Yes, please." She wouldn't make eye contact, but at least she was talking.

"I hear you're getting a bedroom redo." Sawyer winked at her, then gazed around the kitchen. "The whole place could use a redo, if you ask me."

"No one did." Cash brought Ellie her glass of juice and swatted the top of Sawyer's head.

"Hey," he protested. "Where's my juice?"

"Get off your as—butt—and get it yourself."

Ellie giggled, seemed to remember she was supposed to be miserable, and abruptly stopped.

"Don't be afraid to laugh at Sawyer," Cash told her. "We all do."

"How are you related to me again?" she asked Sawyer.

"First cousin once removed. But you can just call me Uncle Sawyer." He put her in a headlock and she giggled again. The sound of it did something to Cash's insides.

He'd just put a few of his French toast slices on the griddle when a pounding came from his front door. Both Sawyer and Ellie jerked their heads at the banging.

"Police, open up!"

Ellie's eyes grew large as Cash went to the door and swung it open.

A laughing Grady fell across the threshold, holding his belly. "Tricked you."

Travis followed, rolling his eyes. "I told him not to do it. He's such a dork."

Cash grabbed Grady by his collar and threw him over his shoulder until the boy hung upside down. Grady howled with laughter.

"Can Ellie come fishing with us?"

"Where's your babysitter?" Cash asked and put Grady down.

"Dad has the day off," Travis said. "He's taking us to the lake and said Ellie could come too."

"Afterward we're getting ice cream in Nevada City." Grady wrapped himself around Sawyer like a monkey. "You want to come, Ellie?"

"I guess. I've never fished before." She turned to Travis. "Is it fun?"

"Yep. Do you know how to swim, because we're taking the boat out."

"I know how to swim." Ellie looked at Cash, who returned to the stove to flip the French toast.

She might've rejected him as her father, but she clearly knew he was in charge and wanted some kind of affirmation that it was okay for her to go. Cash knew Jace wouldn't let anything happen to her, yet he felt oddly conflicted. "What about Aubrey…your bedroom?"

"I'm not staying, so I'd rather fish."

Sawyer lips curved up. "Ah, let her go, Cash." A lot of help he was.

"All right," Cash told Ellie, though he felt hesitant about it. It was only her third day here. Then again, being with Travis and Grady, kids roughly her age, might make her feel more at home.

Grady pumped his fist in the air. "Let's roll."

"Ellie's got to eat first." He put plates in front of Ellie and Sawyer as well as a bottle of syrup. "You two hungry?"

"We already ate," Travis said, anxious to get started on their trip. Jace didn't get a lot of weekdays off. As sheriff, he was always on call, even on the weekends and holidays.

Ellie finished most of her French toast and ran off with the boys to the ranch house. As soon as they were halfway down the driveway, Cash called Jace. "You have an extra life jacket for Ellie?"

"Travis's old one. It should fit her."

"You'll keep an eye on her?"

"As if she were my own," Jace said. "The boys will watch out for her too. Relax; she'll be fine."

"Okay." Cash supposed he was being overly cautious. But his last case had done more than screw with his livelihood; it had screwed with his head. Not a day went by when he didn't see Casey Farmington's dead eyes staring back at him.

Sawyer cleared the table and was at the sink doing dishes when Cash got off the phone.

"Woah, you're actually doing dishes." Cash snapped Sawyer's leg with a dish towel. "I thought you had people for that."

"Yeah, you." Sawyer moved away and waved his hand. "Be my guest." Cash took over. "What are your plans today?"

"Sleep, maybe head into town later to do a little writing at the coffee shop."

"The place even have Wi-Fi?"

"I talked Jimmy Ray into getting it, told him it would increase business."

The old-timers and cowboys who ate at the coffee shop didn't strike Cash as being too concerned about Wi-Fi, but perhaps he was wrong. "Has it?"

"Yeah, it actually has. Ever since that Starbucks went in off the highway, Jimmy Ray has seen a slump. He's hoping the free internet will make a difference."

The coffee shop and Jimmy Ray had been in Dry Creek for as long as Cash could remember. Their grandfather used to take them there for chicken-fried steak and biscuits and gravy, delicacies to a city boy who'd been raised by health-nut parents.

"Progress in Dry Creek." Cash grinned. "Who would've thought?"

"It's a good place, Cash, especially to raise a family." Sawyer gave him a pointed look.

Cash got the impression his cousin wanted to use the spread as his personal retreat. He'd taken one of the barns on the ranch, hired a fancy architect to turn it into a Manhattan-style loft, and despite Cash's desire to sell, had begun construction. According to Jace, the project was costing Sawyer an arm and a leg.

Well, Cash didn't have that luxury.

"I'm not saying it's not. Like you and Jace, I love Dry Creek; always have. But it's impractical to sit on five hundred acres of real estate and continue to pay property taxes when we can't afford to do anything with the land."

"Jace wants to grow the cattle operation."

"Cattle operation?" Cash had to keep from laughing. "Jace runs sixty head. That's a petting zoo, not an operation."

Cash knew Jace sold his calves at market for a tidy profit, but at that scale it was just enough to keep his breeding herd fed and to afford a few splurges, like vacations and minibikes for his boys.

"We'll add to it," Sawyer said.

"Yeah, and who's going to oversee a working ranch? Jace has a full-time job as sheriff and is a single parent, and you travel more often than Southwest Airlines."

"Yep," Sawyer said and locked eyes on Cash. "I guess that leaves you."

"Uh-uh, not happening." Minus Cash's summers on Dry Creek Ranch, being an FBI agent was all he'd ever known.

Cash's own father had left the day after graduation and had gone straight into the San Francisco Police Academy. None of Grandpa's sons had been interested in ranching, except maybe Jace's dad. He, along with Jace's mom and baby brother, had been killed in an auto wreck more than thirty years ago. None of the Daltons had ever fully recovered from the tragedy. Even though Cash had been a little boy at the time, he'd never forgotten the pall that hung over his grandparents' house in those years following the accident.

"Why not? From where I'm sitting, you're in need of a job."

That was the truth. Instead of searching for one, Cash had whiled away the last four months drinking, dwelling on Casey Farmington and how he could've prevented her death, and mourning Grandpa Dalton. Then, two weeks ago, came the out-of-the-blue call about Ellie. Sometime soon, he'd have to knuckle down and get serious about finding himself a new career because his savings would only hold him so long. But ranching?

"First off, I don't know shit about the beef industry, and even if I did, we don't have the kind of capital to start a cow-calf operation that would support the three of us and this ranch, which, if you haven't noticed, needs a good deal of work. Expensive work."

"It's what Grandpa would've wanted."

It was the second time Sawyer had thrown around their grandfather's so-called wishes. "You think he wanted to saddle us with a bunch of debt, huh?" Cash regretted the words as soon as they left his mouth. They were harsh and uncalled for. The only thing Jasper Dalton had ever wanted for his grandkids was happiness. And to Jasper, Dry Creek Ranch was the essence of happiness.

"We can't do anything without Angie's permission," Sawyer said. "She's on the deed just like the rest of us."

Cash didn't respond. They both knew that if, God willing, Angela was still alive, she didn't want a run-down cattle ranch.

"And Jace and the boys," Sawyer continued. "This has always been their home, Cash."

Cash rubbed his hand down his face. "We've been over all this before. I feel like I'm talking to a brick wall. Let's change the damn subject." He didn't want to fight about this now, not with everything else he had to juggle. They had time before the taxes were due; they'd figure it out then. Who knows, maybe they'd win the lottery or strike gold in the meantime.

"Changing the subject works for me. What do you have planned today? Or should we stick to talking about the weather?"

Cash wasn't about to let Sawyer get a rise out of him. "As far as the weather, it's hot. Just like it was yesterday." He elbowed Sawyer in the ribs. "If it doesn't hit a hundred, I might waterproof the shed." Cash had tripped over one of the file boxes this morning.

"You better make it critter proof too." Sawyer glanced at his watch, then grabbed his sunglasses off the table. "I gotta roll; book deadline calls."

He watched through the window as his cousin hiked up the driveway. It was less than a mile walk to Sawyer's loft. Cash shook his head. Who the hell builds a big-city loft in a barn in the middle of nowhere?

He finished cleaning up the breakfast mess, which Sawyer had largely tended to, and went out onto the porch to assess the shed. The corrugated metal top was rusted and, in one corner, had folded up, leaving that side of the building completely unprotected. The damn thing needed a whole new roof.

"Morning," Aubrey called from across the footbridge while trying to balance a box filled with painting supplies, a big leather tote, and her handbag.

Cash hopped down from the porch and took the crate and tote from her. His hands brushed hers and her cheeks turned an appealing shade of pink that set off an equally appealing pair of green eyes. A man could drown in those eyes. He forced himself to look away and get back to the purpose of why she'd come.

"Do I need to go to town to buy paint?" He could get it at the hardware store while he was buying roofing materials.

"There's leftover primer and white paint at my cabin. I'd like to get a couple of coats on the walls and give it time to dry before I tape. Then we can focus on getting the right pink. The wrong shade will make the room look like a bottle of Pepto-Bismol."

"I guess that wouldn't be good."

"Nope." She shifted her purse to her other shoulder.

"I can get going on the primer, but I'll need a roller."

"I've got 'em over at my place, just couldn't carry it all."

"As soon as I unload this"—Cash shook the crate—"I'll go back and get it. Watch your step." The porch stairs were in as bad a shape as the shed roof. He shifted the crate and tote to one arm and gave her a hand.

"They're a little rickety, aren't they?"

"Another thing I've got to fix."

She tilted her head and gave him a long appraisal.

"What?"

"Nothing. It's just...never mind." She held the screen door open for him and they went inside.

Cash took the supplies to Ellie's room and left them on her unmade bed.

"You want coffee?" he asked Aubrey, who had followed him.

"If you've got some already made."

"Come in the kitchen." He checked to make sure the pot was still hot and poured her a cup. "Ellie went fishing with Jace and the boys."

"Oh." She looked at him, paused, and turned pink again. "That's nice...I mean for Jace, getting a day off. Good for him."

Cash enjoyed watching her try to gain her composure. Clearly, she was as affected by him as he was by her. Even if nothing could happen between them, that pull of attraction felt good.

He pulled the milk out of the fridge and set it out for her, not knowing how she liked her coffee. "I'll go get those rollers. Where are they?"

"I'll walk over with you." She followed him out, sipping her coffee as they trekked across the bridge.

She went up the porch stairs first and let him inside her cabin.

"Whoa." The house's layout was identical to his, but that was where the similarities ended. The place looked like a model home. "Did you do all this?" he asked, giving himself an uninvited tour.

The exposed ceiling beams were freshly stained in a clear varnish, the pine floors polished to a high sheen, the kitchen cabinets painted in a shade of green Cash had never seen before. A cowhide rug anchored the living room where two sofas faced each other and a large antler chandelier hung over the coffee table. There were drapes on the windows, paintings on the walls, and pictures on the fireplace mantel.

She laughed at his expression of awe. "This is what I do for a living."

"You're good. I don't know anything about interior design, but I know you're good."

She laughed again, a musical sound that was the nicest thing he'd heard in a long time. Except for Ellie's giggle that morning. The sound of it had hit him in the gut like a cannonball.

"Spread the word, because it appears I've been blacklisted by my old clients."

"Blacklisted?" He pushed aside a couple of the colorful pillows on Aubrey's couch and made himself at home. She had one of those window fans going, and the cool air was a welcome relief from the triple-digit temperature. He tilted his head and rested it on the back of the couch, taking a second to enjoy the breeze. The couch was comfortable and the cabin was a nice respite from his clutter. He just wanted to sit and take it all in. "Why's that?"

She huffed out a breath. "Mitch."

"Because he thinks you left him for Jace?"

She was quiet for a minute. "He knows I didn't leave him for Jace. He knows Jace and I aren't together. But he believes spreading rumors about us helps him save face."

"Save face because you dumped him?" It seemed extreme to Cash, not to mention a shitty thing to do to your best friend, but some guys didn't take rejection well, he supposed.

"It's a long story."

She clearly didn't want to talk about it and Cash was only too happy to avoid the topic. He tried to steer away from other people's love lives whenever possible, though he did admit being mildly curious. He wasn't sure if it was because he was a natural-born investigator or because Aubrey intrigued him.

In any event, it was easier not to get involved. He had enough swirling around in his own head. His grandfather's death, the Presidio murders, and losing his job. And Ellie. But it stuck in his craw that Jace was the innocent party here and the rumors could hurt his bid for reelection.

Cash would have to ask his cousin later why Mitch had dragged Jace into his and Aubrey's breakup. In the meantime, he continued to check out Aubrey's place, finding something new to look at with every glance. He'd never cared much about his living spaces, viewing them as just a place to lay his head. If they were clean, with fresh sheets on the bed, he was content. But he was impressed with the way Aubrey had transformed the cabin.

"You've only lived here a few weeks." Before she'd moved in, it had been in as bad a condition as his. Maybe worse.

She sat across from him, and he forced his eyes away from her legs. Long, lean, and tan. The denim shorts she wore weren't what he would call Daisy Dukes, but they had his attention just the same.

"I got sort of manic about it," she said, her eyes taking a turn around the front room. "And I've had a lot of free time on my hands."

Yeah, he could identify with that. Though he'd spent his drinking and plinking.

Despite resembling a spread in one of the home magazines his mother collected, the rooms were accessible. He could live here without being afraid to touch anything. It wasn't a museum. "It's remarkable."

"Thank you." She beamed, and the way her face lit up, the way her green eyes sparkled, had more of his attention.

Damn, she was beautiful.

And he needed to get out of here before he did something stupid. "Shall we get the rollers?"

He rose, waiting for her to point him in the right direction for the rest of the supplies. She clearly had no idea of the effect she was having on him. Cash told himself he'd gone too long without a woman, that was all. Still, for the first time since the Presidio case, he was thinking about sex, which should be the last thing on his mind in the middle of decorating his twelve-year-old's bedroom.

"They're in here." She led him to a storage closet in the hallway.

Once they returned to Ellie's room, she gave him instructions on how to prep the walls for priming. He found a ladder in the shed and hauled it into the house.

"You know, it wouldn't take all that much to fix up the rest of the cabin." Aubrey stood below the ladder as he filled holes with spackle.

"One room at a time." He had to conserve his money until he found work. Besides, as soon as he persuaded Jace and Sawyer to sell, he and Ellie would be moving on.

"Okay, but I've got ideas."

He leaned down from the ladder. "Like what?" He was interested to hear what she would do with the place. If he hadn't seen her cabin, he wouldn't believe there was any help for his.

"I'd paint your kitchen cabinets like I did mine."

"What's wrong with my cabinets?" He patched another hole, dabbing spackle in with his finger.

"They're great if you're nostalgic for the eighties."

"Hand me one of those rags." She bent down and her shorts rode up. And despite himself, he stared.

"I'd paint them blue." Aubrey handed him up one of the cloths she'd brought. "Not sky blue, something deeper but not quite navy. Then I'd replace the tile countertops with a solid surface."

It sounded expensive to Cash. "What about the floor?" he asked, merely to hear her talk. She had a nice voice, sort of husky.

"Refinish 'em."

"Is that what you did to yours?"

"I just gave mine a light sanding and a coat of polyurethane. That's what I'd do to yours."

He could do that himself. "Not a bad idea. Painting the cabinets...I'm not too sure about, though I liked yours."

"It changed the whole kitchen. Your living room just needs new furniture and maybe some window treatments. That's all."

"Maybe," he said and got down from the ladder so he could move it to the other wall.

"I think it would be good for Ellie if you made the place a bit homier, don't you think?"

He climbed up again. "I'm not sure we're staying." Cash didn't want to go into details. The last thing he needed was everyone in Dry Creek thinking they were selling the ranch, which they weren't. Yet.

"No? Why's that?"

She was a nosy little thing. "At some point I have to start working again. Dry Creek doesn't have a lot of options jobwise."

"Tell me about it. Sounds like we're in similar situations."

Except she had a vocation. He had to find one. Law enforcement was out of the question. "Why don't you go out on your own? What do you need Reynolds Construction for?"

"I don't. But Mitch has a lot of influence in this area. I've already had a couple of cancellations because of him."

"The rumors will die down, don't you think?" He finished the wall he was working on and moved to the next one.

"Hopefully, but maybe not soon enough for me to support myself."

"You got this job." Not that his measly two thousand bucks would go far. He grinned to let her know that he knew the bedroom assignment was peanuts in the scheme of things. Now, if he gave her the rest of the cabin to decorate, it might be helpful. The question was, to whom? He'd be lying if he said he didn't like looking at her. She was a nice distraction from everything else going on in his life. She was also a distraction he didn't need.

"One more wall and we've got the spackling covered."

She nodded. "We can have it primed today, and in this heat, it'll dry quickly and we can do at least one coat of white before I start taping off the stripes."

Cash stared at the wall where the stripes were going. "I'm not exactly seeing your vision for that, but you're the expert."

Her mouth curved up like he was being a typical guy. "When it's finished you'll love it, you'll see."

"I'll take your word for it." Pink and white stripes weren't his thing, but if they were Ellie's, he was happy. "What's important is that Ellie loves it."

"She will. I have yet to disappoint any of the children of my clients." She helped him move the ladder to the last wall. "She looks like you."

"You think?" People kept saying that, but he suspected she looked more like Marie, though she did have the Dalton blue eyes. "She seems small to me. You think she's small for her age?"

"I just think she's petite. Was her mother petite?"

Cash shook his head. "Tall, medium build. My mother's small, though."

"What about her family?"

"Don't know. Marie and I hardly knew each other. I never met any of her people."

"Did you keep in touch over the years?"

"No. I didn't even know I had a daughter until Marie called me a few weeks ago. She was dying and needed to resolve Ellie's future. That's when she told me." He didn't know why he was sharing such deeply personal information with her. He supposed it was because she'd been so free in discussing Mitch.

"That had to have been…complicated," she said.

"The situation or the conversation?"

"Both."

"Yep." He was still grappling with the fallout. Anger, denial, and fear continued to hit him in waves. "Under better circumstances, the conversation might've gone differently. But it seemed wrong to lay into a woman with stage four breast cancer. Marie had suffered enough."

Aubrey reached over and touched his arm. "I can understand why you would be angry. Anyone would be if they were kept from their child. I guess the fact that she was on her deathbed made her want to clear her conscience."

"Probably," he said. "Unfortunately, Ellie is the one to suffer. She's living with a stranger now, a stranger she's afraid of. My whole adult life I've lived to protect and serve, and my own daughter is afraid of me."

"Nah." Aubrey shook her head. "She's a kid in completely new surroundings. Her mother's gone and she feels alone. That's what it is. Try not to take it personally."

He gave a humorless laugh and climbed the ladder. "Working on it."

Around one, they stopped for a lunch break, and Cash went to the kitchen to fix them sandwiches. "Turkey or ham?"

"Uh, turkey, please."

"You want avocado?"

"Hell yeah, I want avocado." She came around the counter to help. "You have a well-stocked pantry." As soon as the words left her mouth, her face flushed.

He cocked his brows. "You think so?" She'd gotten a look at the full monty, after all, and he wanted to rub it in.

"Your kitchen." She elbowed him in the arm. "So you can get over yourself."

By three, they had the room primed, working well as a team. They stood back to appraise the job they'd done. Just that little bit of primer and already the room seemed cheerier, less dingy. Cash eyed Aubrey, wondering if she still wanted to paint and tape off the stripes. The afternoon sun beat down on the cabin, making it steamy as a sauna.

"Come here." Cash crooked his finger at her. "You've got paint on you." He took a lock of her hair and wiped away a smudge of white.

"Is it gone?"

Slowly, he let a few silky strands sift through his fingers. So soft. "Yeah, I think so," he said, and she looked up at him, her eyes widening a little. He bent lower, wanting so much to taste her lips.

A car door slammed, and he abruptly pulled away.

Chapter 6

Travis and Grady's dad told her she should call him Uncle Jace, but she didn't want to. He wasn't even really her uncle, just a distant cousin. What did Sawyer call it? First cousin once removed. Whatever that was. She didn't exactly know how she was related to Travis and Grady either. But they all kind of looked the same, except she was a girl and they had darker hair than hers. They were nice, though, even if Grady talked too much.

The whole time they were out on the boat, Grady made duck noises until Jace told him he was scaring away the fish. They all caught a fish, even her. But Jace said hers was too small to keep and threw it back in the water. She was sort of glad because a) it was gross, and b) the poor fish didn't deserve to die.

Jace caught two big ones and Travis a medium-sized one, and they were going to eat them for dinner, which sounded disgusting.

"Tell Cash we're eating at five," Jace called out his truck window.

"Okay." She started for the porch, then turned around and shouted, "Thank you for taking me fishing." It's what her mom would've wanted her to say, because it was bad manners not to. But she had had a good time on the lake.

It was something she could add to her bucket list before she went back to Boston. Fishing.

Tomorrow, if Travis and Grady's babysitter said it was okay, they were going to ride horses. That was pretty much her favorite thing to do in the world. Her mother had worked an extra job doing off-duty security for some rich lady so she could afford Ellie's stable and riding fees. Troubadour hadn't been hers, but she'd gotten to ride him whenever she wanted, including in equestrian events. Now, someone else would get him.

"Hey." Her father came out onto the front porch. "You have fun?"

"I guess. They want us to come over for dinner at five. Fish." She made a face.

"That sounds nice, I mean, besides the fish part." He grinned at her like he was the funniest guy in the world, which he wasn't. "You want to see what Aubrey and I have been doing?"

Not really, but she followed him inside anyway. Aubrey was in the hovel, otherwise known as Ellie's bedroom, painting the walls white.

Aubrey straightened up and stretched her back, and Ellie caught her father checking out Aubrey's boobs. Ew.

"What do you think so far?" Aubrey asked.

Ellie looked around the room and had to admit it looked brighter. It smelled better too, like paint instead of moldy yuckiness. "It's good."

"I'll just finish up and get out of your hair," she said, and Ellie wished she'd stay.

But Aubrey finished the last section of wall, packed up her stuff, said she'd do the taping on Tuesday, and left.

"You want to shower and change before we head over to Jace's?"

"I'm good." The tub in the cabin gave Ellie the willies. There were spiders everywhere and the toilet didn't flush right.

"Okay. I'll wash up and we can go. On the way over, you can tell me all about the fishing trip."

"There's nothing to tell," she said. If her mom was alive, she would've described to her the fish she caught and how Jace taught her how to bait a hook and cast a line. And how Travis had done a giant belly flop in the water.

"You catch anything?"

She hitched her shoulders. "We threw it back."

"You caught one your first time out? That's great, Ellie."

God, he was such a phony. What did he care whether she caught a fish or not? She waited for him to leave her room and threw herself on the bed. It was hot and she was pretty sure she smelled like trout and lake water. Her mother would've made her bathe.

She got up and found her suitcase in the closet. In the front compartment, she pulled out the pictures. The framed ones were coming with the boxes. But Linda had printed Ellie a few from her computer. She traced her mother's face in the first photo with her finger. "I miss you, Mom. I miss you so much."

As soon as she heard the water shut off in the bathroom, Ellie shoved the pictures under her pillow and sat on the edge of the bed, staring at the new white walls.

"You ready to go?"

She scrambled to her feet and waited by the front door.

"You sure you want to wear that sweater?"

Could he just leave her alone about the sweater? He was so annoying. She nodded and hopped into the passenger side of his SUV.

"Did you guys go for ice cream?"

"Yes." She'd gotten two scoops. Mint chip and strawberry.

"Did Jace feed you any real food?"

"We had sandwiches on the lake."

"That's good. Do you like fish?"

She scrunched up her nose. "Not really."

On Fridays at her school, they had a fish fry. She liked the breading, but everything else she left on her plate, even though Father John said it was wasteful.

"Neither do Travis and Grady. Jace'll make burgers on the grill. You like burgers?"

She nodded. She wasn't that picky, not like Mary Margaret O'Malley who had to become a vegan because she hated everything under the sun, even chocolate milk.

When they pulled up to Travis and Grady's house, the dogs started jumping on the truck, barking like crazy. She opened her door slowly, hoping they'd go away.

"They won't hurt you, Ellie. They're all bark and no bite." He came around to her side and lifted her out of the passenger seat.

"I'm not a little kid." She pulled away and went to the front door on her own.

Grady let them in. "Hey, Uncle Cash."

"Hey, pardner. How was the fishing?"

"Great. Ellie caught a baby fish and we had to throw it back."

"I heard. What about you?"

"I didn't get anything. Dad said it's because I talk too much. We're in the backyard."

They followed him through the house, to the kitchen, and out a side door to a big picnic table. There was a big rock fireplace and a built-in barbecue where Jace was cooking. Sawyer was there too. He waved and made room for them on the bench.

"How was the lake?"

"It was good," she said.

Her father went off to talk to Jace and she wished she could go inside and watch TV or something. It's not that she didn't like Sawyer. He seemed nice, even if he was old. But she kind of wanted to be alone. She thought that once they started eating she could sneak away. It wasn't like anyone would notice her absence anyway.

"Who wants burgers, who wants fish?" Jace was at the barbecue. He had on a funny apron that said, "Mr. Good Lookin' Is Cookin'."

"I'll have both," Sawyer said.

"Anything else I can get you, your royal highness?"

Travis and Grady laughed at their dad's joke and Ellie hid a giggle. Jace was kind of funny. The men were always poking at one another. She didn't think they were really trying to be mean, but her mom probably would've thought it was disrespectful.

"Ellie, what do you want?" Jace asked.

"I'll have a burger, please."

"Coming right up."

She wanted desperately to look at her phone to see if Mary Margaret had texted her, but her father didn't like it when she was on her cell. She could tell because whenever she got on it, his face scrunched up like he'd sucked on a lemon. Her mom used to take the phone away from her if she texted at the table.

He came back to where she and Sawyer were sitting. More than likely, he'd been checking up on her with Jace, making sure she hadn't been a brat on the fishing trip. He probably hated having to be her dad and wished she didn't exist. Ellie suspected that the only reason he wouldn't let her return to Boston was because he was a grown-up and had to be responsible.

Jace served her a burger. Somehow, he'd known how to make it the way she liked it. Not too pink. Pink meat made her want to gag.

"That's our beef. We raised it here on the ranch," Travis said. He seemed proud of it, but Ellie thought it was sad for the cows and was seriously thinking of becoming a vegan like Mary Margaret.

She took a bite of her burger and decided to become a vegan later. Her father put some salad on her plate, and when he wasn't looking, Sawyer passed her the bag of potato chips on the table. It was sort of nice eating outside. Even though it was hot, the trees were shady and she could see the horses in the distance. Grady sat by her but got up at least a million times to run around. He was sooooo hyperactive.

Ellie finished her burger, ate a few bites of the salad, and got up to head for the house.

"Where're you going?" her father asked.

She had to go to the bathroom and now he wanted her to announce it in front of the whole group. Great. "I need to go inside for a second." Hopefully, he'd get a clue and not embarrass her.

"Okay."

At least he wasn't a complete loser, she thought as she continued to the back door. Once inside the bathroom, she snuck a look at her phone. Mary Margaret hadn't texted her back. She put the seat down on the toilet, sat on it, and rushed off a quick text.

"Where are you? I hate it here."

She waited for a reply but was afraid if she waited too long, her father would come looking for her.

"Have to go," she wrote to Mary Margaret. "But I have two hundred and seventy-four dollars and forty-five cents in my suitcase. Do you think that's enough to buy a bus ticket home?"

She put her phone away, finished doing her business, and went back outside.

* * * *

Aubrey changed out of her painting clothes and headed for town. It was time to meet Mitch face-to-face to let him know his rumormongering was unacceptable. She couldn't afford to lose any more clients.

On the drive over, she tried to decide how to play this. If she told him she was going to rat him out—tell everyone in Dry Creek what he'd done— he'd call her bluff. She had to come up with something more creative. The problem was, she didn't have anything better than the truth, and the truth would devastate Brett.

Once she got there, she'd have to wing it.

Mitch was probably just getting home from work. She deliberated on whether to give him time to settle in. Her ex was more agreeable after a couple of beers. Then again, he deserved nothing more than to be ambushed.

At the only stoplight in town she pulled up to a red and caught Mitch's sister Joanne's Ford F-150 in her rearview. As soon as the light turned green, Joanne passed Aubrey on the right-hand shoulder, rolled down her window, and stuck her middle finger in the air.

"For crying out loud," Aubrey muttered. Even Joanne, who knew her brother could be a real douchebag, believed his lies.

She drove by Reynolds Construction on the way to Mitch's and considered breaking in again. Last time she'd forgotten a few things, including her favorite fringe jacket, which was still in the closet. She didn't need it right now, but come fall she'd miss it. More than likely, though, Mercedes was still there. On most evenings she put in a couple of extra hours to suck up to Mitch and avoid her husband, who, on a scale from one to ten, ranked a nine in the asshole department. It wasn't worth another run-in.

Aubrey didn't see Mitch's truck in the driveway when she pulled up. On rare occasions, though, he did park in the garage, probably to hide from an angry husband. Undeterred, she got out of the car and rang the bell.

Twice.

When Mitch didn't answer, she peeked through the front window, working her way around the house. It didn't appear that anyone was home. She continued to the back, peered inside the kitchen, and saw no sign of life there either.

Fine, she'd wait for him out by the pool. With all the lakes, creeks, and rivers in the area, she didn't know why they needed a pool. But Mitch had insisted on it, arguing that it would make the house more marketable if they ever decided to sell. Admittedly, the pool was gorgeous; the whole backyard was. Mitch had spared no expense. Imported tile, dramatic lighting, a waterfall feature, a hot tub, brick decking, and enough exotic plants to open their own nursery. He'd also insisted on an outdoor kitchen with a four-thousand-dollar grill when they didn't even use the range inside. With their busy lives, they'd either eaten at the coffee shop or takeout from nearby Grass Valley or Auburn.

She slipped off her sandals, walked to the pool's edge, and dipped her foot in. The water was warm. Knowing Mitch, he heated it, even in summer. She heard a car pull up and prepared herself for a showdown. Putting her shoes back on, she headed to the front of the house, ready to let Mitch know in no uncertain terms that he'd better stop screwing with her livelihood.

But it wasn't Mitch, it was Sally, his mother. She was rooting around in Mitch's mailbox and glowered when she discovered she had company. "What are you doing here?"

"Looking for Mitch. Do you know where he is?" Aubrey wouldn't be surprised to learn that Sally had a tracking device on her son. She wasn't a bad person, just overbearing and possessive.

"He's out of town, not that it's any of your business. You lost the privilege of knowing where my son is the second you broke his heart."

It would be fruitless to argue with her because unlike Joanne, who knew Mitch's foibles, Sally thought her son walked on water. "He and I have things to discuss." Aubrey wanted to add that it wasn't any of Sally's business, but why bother starting up with Mitch's mother? Aubrey and

Sally had never been what you would call close, but there was no reason to antagonize the woman.

"Things to discuss." Sally slanted an imperious brow. "Like how you stuck him with all the wedding bills?"

"Sally, you know we went halves. I lost just as much money as Mitch did."

"You're the one who called it off. As far as I'm concerned, you should have paid for the whole thing."

Aubrey prayed for patience. "There's more going on here than Mitch has led on."

"Like the fact that you ran off with Jace Dalton? Mitch didn't have to tell me, I heard it all over town. You always did have eyes for that boy. I warned Mitch about you, and now you've gone and humiliated him."

According to Sally, Aubrey had had eyes for every man in Dry Creek at one time or another. She probably thought Aubrey had the hots for Jimmy Ray too. "Stop being ridiculous; there's nothing between Jace and me. When is Mitch coming home?"

"I have no idea." Sally stuck her nose in the air.

Sally knew damned well when Mitch would be home. If Aubrey was laying odds in Reno, Mitch had gone on their Hawaii honeymoon trip early, the one Aubrey had paid for. And Sally knew his itinerary down to the second.

"Whatever, Sally. Just let him know I was here."

"You can be sure I will." Sally muttered something about Aubrey trespassing. "And tell your boyfriend Jace that if it was between him and the devil for sheriff, I'd vote for the devil."

"I'll be sure to let your son's best friend know that." Aubrey decided it was better to leave than argue any longer with Sally. She was going to believe the best of Mitch and the worst of Aubrey no matter what.

"Always a pleasure seeing you." Aubrey got in her car and drove away.

Instead of going to Dry Creek Ranch, she went to Auburn to hit a drive-through. She hadn't eaten since Cash had fixed them turkey sandwiches and was starved.

Cash. Now there was an enigma. He wasn't at all what she'd expected. Originally, Aubrey had concluded that he was a curmudgeon with a drinking problem. But alcohol didn't appear to be an issue. For good measure, she'd inhaled him while they'd worked on Ellie's walls. Just soap and the clean outdoors, which smelled distractingly good.

He did have complications, however, starting with his daughter. Besides that, Aubrey had a sneaking suspicion leaving the FBI hadn't been his idea. Even if he had quit, Aubrey sensed it wasn't an amicable parting. She'd wanted to ask him about it but had gotten the distinct impression the topic was off the table. She was actually surprised he had shared as much as he had about Ellie's mother. Cash didn't exactly seem like an open book. He did, however, have a fantastic cover; she'd give him that. He was even better-looking than Jace, who was hard to beat. Objectively speaking, Sawyer was probably the most handsome of the three cousins, but too pretty for her taste. Cash had that rough-around-the-edges appearance. Rugged, chiseled, and square-jawed.

Aubrey got her food, parked under a shady tree, and ate. Her mother texted and Aubrey ignored it, knowing it would be all about Mitch and what a good "provider" he was and how Aubrey should take him back. Aubrey had had her fill of Mothers for Mitch today.

She threw away her wrappers in the garbage and headed for home. Maybe she'd take a dip in the creek and catch up on invoicing. So far, nothing had come of her new Houzz profile and she could use a few checks to tide her over. Her savings wouldn't cover her forever. If she didn't hear anything in a few days, she'd check in with her friend about the Vegas developer.

No one appeared to be around at Cash's cabin, she noted as she drove up their shared driveway. Now, while she had relative privacy, would be a good time to take that swim. She rushed into the house, changed into a bathing suit, and waded waist deep into the water. Unlike Mitch's pool, it was cold, making her teeth chatter. She stood there, waiting to get used to the frigid temperature, before dunking her head in. The creek was full, and in spots she couldn't touch her toes to the bottom without the water going over her head.

When they were kids, they used to float in inner tubes they got from the Gas Stop in Dry Creek. The owner would sell the old tubes to them for a buck and they'd spend the bulk of the summer hanging out at the creek, tubing and swimming.

She was floating on her back, looking up at the sun, when she heard a truck engine. Cash's SUV. Two doors slammed, and she heard the squeak of the cabin's screen door swinging. She submerged her head again and when she came up with a splash, Cash was standing at the edge of the footbridge.

"How's the water?" he called to her.

"Cold but refreshing." She wondered if he wanted to join her, but before she could invite him in, he turned away and headed inside his cabin without saying a word.

Either he was back to being moody or not feeling particularly friendly this evening. Confounded, Aubrey went back to floating.

Chapter 7

Cash wished he could've joined Aubrey in the creek or at least seen more of her in the bikini she had on. But it was time for him to have a talk with Ellie. She'd been moping around ever since they got to Jace's and had avoided him throughout dinner. If they were going to coexist, they needed to come to an understanding.

First, though, he wanted to explain that he hadn't abandoned her twelve years ago, despite what she might think.

He went inside the cabin, the scent of fresh paint still thick in the air. It was better than the musty odor that had clung to the place like mildew.

"Hey, Ellie." He tapped on her bedroom door.

"I'm going to bed."

It was only a little past seven, but he supposed she was still operating on East Coast time. "I thought we could have a talk."

"I'm too tired," Ellie said, and he rolled his eyes because she was probably on that damned smartphone of hers.

The cell was one of many things they had to talk about. He didn't mind if she was communicating with her friends in Boston, but there had to be rules and boundaries. Cyberspace could be a dangerous place for a twelve-year-old.

"Why don't you take a nap and then we'll talk?" Cash decided it was a good compromise. The kid wanted him to cave, but he wasn't going to do it. He had twenty-four years on Ellie; he could out stubborn her.

She didn't respond, which didn't surprise him. In an hour they'd have their discussion. Cash decided to spend the next sixty minutes tidying up. Priming Ellie's walls—or perhaps seeing Aubrey's cabin—had motivated him to organize. Tomorrow, he planned to work on the shed and get his old case files out of the house. Then he'd go to work on the leaky toilet.

In the meantime, the bathroom could use a cleaning. On a hook behind the door, he found the sweater Ellie was so attached to. It was stretched and stained and smelled like a combination of fish and barbecue. He stuck it in the washer with a load of dirty laundry, even though he should've thrown the damned thing out and bought her a new one.

A car pulled up while he was in the kitchen, hunting up scouring powder. It was a little late for a visitor, at least by country standards. Cash went out to the front porch and found a familiar Ford sedan parked in his driveway.

Calvin Sullivan, known as Sully to everyone at the Bureau, alighted from the car and flipped up his aviators. "So this is Dry Creek Ranch?"

"This is it," Cash said, surprised his former colleague had made the trip.

"I expected something a little more, uh, ranchy." Sully looked up at the cabin, then turned slightly and stared off into the fields. "Where are the cows?"

"It's past their bedtime." Cash brushed away a few fallen leaves from a lawn chair and offered Sully a seat. "To what do I owe the pleasure?" His gut told him this wasn't a welfare check or even a social call. Sully was wearing a suit and his wing-tips were freshly shined. A G-man to the core. Even though they'd been good friends in the Bureau, there was no question in Cash's mind where Sully's loyalties lay.

"Can't I just say hi to an old friend?"

Cash cocked a brow. "You always were a bullshit artist, Sully. Hang on while I get us a couple of drinks." He fetched two beers from the fridge, popped the caps, considered glassware and just as quickly rejected the idea before returning to the porch. "How's Candy? Bet she misses me." He handed Sully one of the bottles.

"She's pissed at you." Sully took a long drag of his beer and wiped his mouth with his hand. "She liked it when you had my back."

Like you had mine? Ah, hell, it wasn't Sully's fault Cash got fired. It wasn't anyone's fault but his own. "Send her and the kids my love. We all caught up now?"

"Stop being an asshat, Dalton." Sully glanced out over Dry Creek Ranch and lingered on the creek. "You can fish from the porch."

"And I do. And on evenings like this, I watch the sunset," Cash said, taking a pull on his drink. It tasted good, like a hot summer night. "It's something out here."

Sully rose, walked to the edge of the porch, rested his elbows on the railing, and stared out over the western horizon. "I see what you mean."

The sky was streaked in bloodred, purple, and blue. In an hour, the sun would dip below the mountains, leaving shadows across the range, and then the stars would start to fill the sky. Hundreds of them. "You know you could come back if you truly wanted to."

That's right, all Cash had to do was adjust his attitude. Wasn't that what his boss had said in that thick Texas drawl of his right before he told Cash to pack his desk and use all his vacation time? With 365 days accrued on the books, Cash took the words for what they were: a verbal pink slip.

Sully sat down again. "We're not superheroes, Dalton. Sometimes the bad guys get one over on us. Live with it."

That was the problem: Cash couldn't. Not when innocent lives were taken because they'd made an epically bad call. He clasped his hands behind his head, leaned back in his lawn chair, and watched the colors of the sunset grow more vivid.

"Sully," he finally said, "I know you didn't drive all the way from San Francisco to tell me I could have my job back." Other than a sympathy card when Grandpa Dalton died, Cash hadn't heard from Sully since turning in his badge.

"I came for the fresh air." Sully took a deep breath and slowly let the air out of his lungs. "A guy could get used to this." He returned his gaze to the fields where Grandpa Dalton used to run his cattle. "How much does a place like this go for?"

Cash propped up his boots on the stair rail and felt it wobble. "More than you can afford."

"That's not saying much." Sully chuckled, then became contemplative. "Candy's always saying we should get a place in the country. Something small with a little land, where we can get away on weekends."

Cash had always had Dry Creek Ranch. Looking back on it, he wished he'd come more often, spent more time with Jasper. The old coot had been Cash's hero. "Yep, Candy's right, the country's good. Soothes the soul." Yet, as peaceful as it was here, he still had the dreams. Always Casey Farmington.

"What are you planning to do?" Sully asked.

"Haven't decided yet."

"I hear your cousin's the Mill County sheriff. Can he give you a job?"

"Not interested," Cash said. "It's time for me to do something else. Maybe put my law degree to work." Though the idea didn't much appeal to Cash. He'd come up with something sooner or later.

Sully tilted back his bottle and took another long pull of his beer. "They're serving you with a subpoena to testify at Whiting's trial."

So that's why he'd come.

"Who's they?" Sad to say, but Cash was probably more beneficial as a defense witness than he'd be for the prosecution.

"US Attorney, but for all I know, Whiting's federal defender is planning to call you too."

Cash pressed the cold bottle against his neck. "Great," he said. "Just what I need." The entire case had been a fiasco, but if his testimony helped put Whiting away, he'd be the first one at the courthouse. The problem was, he might do more harm than good. "Seems like a big risk to me."

"Why do you think they're subpoenaing you?" Sully said. "It's called damage control. As long as the prosecutor gets first crack at you, he can frame the narrative any way he wants. That way there are no surprises when the defense gets its cross-examination."

Yep, that was exactly the way Cash would've played it if he were prosecuting the case. "I won't lie on the stand, Sully. You can tell those sacks of shit that I'll tell the truth, the whole truth, and nothing but the truth. It's all I have left to give Casey Farmington's parents."

There was a long silence, then Sully said, "You always were a sanctimonious son of a bitch. No one expects you to lie, Cash. Jeez, you'd think we were the Antichrist."

No, just incompetent.

"Just as long as the brass knows what they're getting themselves into by calling me as a witness." They'd royally screwed up the case and he wouldn't hide all the things that had gone wrong. Not under any circumstances, let alone under oath.

The screen door squeaked and Ellie came out onto the porch. She looked half-asleep, and Cash wondered if their voices had awakened her.

"I didn't know you had company," Sully said, flummoxed by the appearance of a young girl. "And who is this?" He smiled at Ellie, who looked back at him with mild curiosity.

"This is my daughter, Ellie." Cash got to his feet. "Ellie, this is Calvin Sullivan. We used to work together."

Cash saw surprise streak across Sully's face and, like any good agent, he immediately masked his reaction. "Good to meet you, Ellie." He shot Cash a WTF look. They'd known each other more than a decade and Sully was obviously stymied by the revelation that Cash had a daughter.

You and me both, bud.

Nevertheless, Cash knew that before Sully got in his car and drove away he'd get an earful.

He nudged Ellie. "Hey, what do you say?"

"Good to meet you too." She stuck out her hand and Sully shook it.

"You ready?" Cash asked her. They still needed to have their talk, but he hoped Sully would construe the question to mean they had plans to go somewhere and take it as a not-so-subtle hint to leave.

Under different circumstances, he might've enjoyed visiting with his former colleague for a while. Tonight, he didn't want to have to explain Ellie's sudden appearance in his life or share FBI war stories over a couple of cold ones. He especially didn't want to talk anymore about Charles Whiting. The SOB had given Cash enough nightmares.

"I should get going." Sully stood and stretched his back. "Walk me to the car, would ya?" They strode down the driveway until they were out of earshot of the porch. "Since when do you have a daughter?"

"Since twelve years ago," Cash said and sighed. "It's a long, complicated story."

"I've got time." Sully rested his hip against the side of his car.

"I don't." Not too long ago, Cash had considered Sully a close friend. Not so much anymore. And while Ellie was by no means a secret, Cash didn't feel like sharing the details of Marie and her death with him. Not while Cash was still trying to sort it out for himself. "Ellie's waiting for me."

Sully gave him a long perusal and nodded. "Okay. It was good catching up, buddy. Things haven't been the same without you."

Cash went in for the one-second man hug, even though he knew Sully was full of shit. "Let's grab a beer sometime."

"Yep." Sully tilted his head toward the spot where Ellie was still standing. "You owe me that long, complicated story. Pretty girl."

"Yes, she is." An odd sense of pride welled up in his chest. Not because Ellie was pretty but because she was his. "See you around, Sully." Cash watched Sully do a three-point turn in the driveway, then headed to the cabin.

Ellie had gone inside and was fiddling with the television. "I can't get it to work."

Cash took the remote control from her hand. "Come sit at the table. I'd like us to have a real conversation."

She screwed up her face as if he'd asked her to eat all her liver and vegetables. Despite her aversion to him, she did as he asked, plopping down on one of the dining room chairs, then propping her elbows on the table, doing her best to appear put out. Which she no doubt was. He had that effect on her.

"Where's my sweater? It's not in the bathroom where I left it."

"I washed it," which reminded Cash that he still had to transfer the clean clothes to the dryer.

Ellie went white, then bolted for the washing machine.

"The sweater was filthy," Cash called after her, wondering what the problem was. It was a worn, old sweater that hung on her tiny frame like a gunnysack.

A door slammed, and Cash got up to find out what the hell he'd done wrong. He let himself into Ellie's room to find her sitting on the bed, the sweater cradled in her lap, crying.

"She's gone," she whispered.

Cash blinked, trying to make the connection.

"Who's gone?"

Ellie didn't answer.

He came a few steps closer, but she didn't look up.

"Who's gone, sweetheart?" he asked, softer.

"My mother." Ellie's voice was barely there.

Cash wrinkled his forehead. He still wasn't making the connection.

"Please," he said as gently as he could. "Explain what you mean."

Finally, Ellie looked up at him. "It doesn't smell like her anymore."

"Like who?" The mattress dipped from Cash's weight as he sat next to her on the bed.

"My mom." She hiccupped. "It was hers and now she's gone and now I can't even smell her anymore." Ellie began to sob uncontrollably.

"Ah, jeez." Cash scrubbed his hand over his face, at a total loss for what to do. "I screwed up, Ellie. Ah, honey...I had no idea."

"I want her back so bad," she said through tears. "Then I could leave this place and never come back again."

Seeing her this way made his heart fold in half. He reached for her, awkward at first. But when she showed no resistance, he pulled her closer. She buried her face in his chest and let the dam burst, soaking his shirt.

"I hate you," she said between sobs.

Cash rubbed her back like he'd seen Jace do when Grady was a newborn. Between Ellie and his old bosses at the Bureau, he wasn't too popular these days.

"Yeah?" he said. "Get in line, kiddo."

Chapter 8

Tuesday morning, Jace set out for the office early, hoping to enjoy his first coffee of the day in peace. Annabeth, his secretary, always made sure to set the timer on the grind and brew before she left in the evening so he was greeted with a fresh pot. But today he took a detour on his way to work and braved the long line of cars and pickups in the drive-through at Dutch Bros on Highway 49.

Ten minutes later, he sat in the Dry Creek City Hall complex parking lot, contemplating whether to crank up his AC and drink his travel mug from the comfort of his truck. But the stack of reports on his desk, which had probably grown in his one-day absence, beckoned, and he figured it was now or never. As he made his way to the sheriff's office, a 1920s' white-brick one-story, he checked his phone to see if the boys had run off yet another babysitter. Since December, he'd gone through four. Bellamy Woods had quit after Grady stuck a barn mouse down her shirt. The second, whose name now escaped Jace, left after three days, saying the boys were bad for her blood pressure. To be fair, Jace was responsible for chasing off the third sitter when he'd told her where she could stick her unsolicited parenting advice. Jana Horowitz had outlasted all three sitters put together but had resigned recently to move closer to her grandkids in Eugene, Oregon. At least that's what she'd told him.

"Morning, Sheriff."

Jace tipped his Stetson. "How you doing, Red?"

"I'm retiring in"—Red made a show of checking his watch—"ten days, two hours, and forty-two minutes and three seconds, so pretty damned good."

An investigator with the Bureau of Livestock Identification, Red Buckley had been stationed in Mill County for as long as Jace could remember. "Who's going to catch the cattle rustlers without you?"

With the price of beef being what it was, cattle theft was on the rise in California. Ranchers in the Golden State lost roughly a million dollars a year from rustling.

"Why don't you go for the job? It may not pay as well as sheriff, but the perks are good." Red nudged his head at the sheriff's building. "I don't remember the last time I spent a full day indoors."

No, Jace suspected Red spent most of his days in a four-wheel drive, riding across Northern California from ranch to ranch.

"I think I'll keep my current position until the good voters of Mill County kick me out." He slapped Red on the back. "See you around, buddy, and don't forget to invite me to the retirement party."

He avoided getting wet from the sprinklers on his way into the office and, as predicted, the stack of paperwork on his desk was a few inches taller than when he had left it. He finished his coffee while tackling reports. Annabeth trudged in a few minutes later and dropped a load of library books on her desk.

"Sure is hot out there," she said, then crossed the bull pen to the kitchenette to fix a cup of the herbal tea she drank instead of coffee and returned to his open doorway, clasping the mug her granddaughter had made her at one of those artsy ceramic shops in Nevada City. "You enjoy your day off?"

"Went fishing with the boys and Cash's daughter, Ellie. Had a barbecue in the afternoon."

Annabeth leaned against the doorjamb. "How's the little girl holding up?"

"As well as can be expected." It hadn't taken long for word to spread. By now, all of Dry Creek probably knew.

"I'm planning to hide in here for a while and get this paperwork done. If you don't hear any sounds coming from my desk, come inside and wake me up."

She tucked a wisp of white hair behind her ear. "Will do," she said and shut his door behind her.

Not twenty minutes later, there was a ruckus outside his office. Before Jace could get up and check out the commotion, Tiffany Sanders, his unofficial campaign manager, crashed through his door.

"I just got off the phone with Sally Reynolds. Do you know how much clout that woman has in this county?"

He leaned back in his chair and propped his Justin boots on the top of his desk. "Relax, Tiff. We've got sixteen months until the election."

"Did you forget the June primary? Count, Jace." Tiffany held up her hand and flicked off the months with her fingers. "Eleven months. Eleven freaking months. You and Aubrey need to hold a press conference. Now!"

"A press conference?" He screwed up his face. "You're kidding me, right?"

"Hell no, I'm not kidding you. How do you think a sex scandal will play here on *Little House on the Prairie*, huh?"

First, he took issue with her calling Mill County *Little House on the Prairie*. Last he heard, Chesterville was getting a Kohl's. Besides Dutch Bros, there was a Starbucks on the county line and an El Pollo Loco in Mill Town. And in Dry Creek…okay, here, time had stood still.

"It's not a sex scandal, Tiff."

She held up her hand. "Stop…don't say anymore. Whatever you two have going on has to end. She needs to move off the ranch…uh, like yesterday… and preferably out of the county. Then we need to find you a"—she shut the door on Annabeth, who had tried to block Tiffany's way in—"beard. Someone noncontroversial, preferably a Sunday school teacher who's never been married. Or a widow. A widow's good. Voters love widows."

"Not gonna happen, Tiff." He was sorely tempted to fire her on the spot even though she wasn't on his payroll. "Aubrey and I have been friends since kindergarten. That's it. And friends don't let friends marry assholes." Technically, he'd had nothing to do with Aubrey and Mitch's breakup, but knowing what he knew now, he would've advocated for it.

"Mitch is one of your best friends." Tiffany folded her arms over her chest.

"Was one of my best friends. 'Was' being the operative word. Now, I've got police work to do, so…" He swung his head toward the door.

"We need to talk about this, Jace, and get a strategy in place."

After running one successful campaign for an obscure candidate's bid for the state legislature, Tiffany now thought she was in the big leagues.

"My strategy is to be a good sheriff and let the people decide," Jace said, because in a perfect world that should've been good enough. Unfortunately, he knew all too well that there was no perfect world and voters could be fickle.

But instead of dwelling on something that was out of his control, he could finish his paperwork. So he herded Tiffany out of his office and shut the door.

* * * *

Aubrey arrived at Cash's a little past ten, giving both her clients time to sleep in. It was a good thing, because she found father and daughter in the kitchen fixing breakfast. And despite the eighty-degree weather, there was a distinct chill in the air. In fact, the hostility radiating off Ellie was palpable.

Aubrey exchanged glances with Cash, who silently relayed that he'd tell her whatever the problem was later.

"Ready to paint stripes?" she asked, her voice overly chipper.

Ellie's response was to shove a spoonful of cold cereal in her mouth while Cash answered, "Let's do it."

He followed her into Ellie's bedroom and leaned against the window frame. "I washed that sweater she wears every day, not knowing it had been her mother's. She'd been clinging to it because it still held Marie's scent. Now it smells like generic laundry detergent. Needless to say, she flipped out."

"Oh boy." Aubrey sat on Ellie's unmade bed. "Is there anything else of Marie's that can take the sweater's place?"

"Nothing I know of. We shipped a bunch of stuff from Boston that should arrive in a couple of weeks, though I'm not sure there's anything of Marie's in the boxes. Marie's best friend, Linda, was in charge of packing up her clothes, and because they're too large for Ellie, I assume she kept what she liked for herself."

Aubrey heard a television go on in the other room. Apparently, getting a new bedroom wasn't as fulfilling as *Full House.*

She glanced up at Cash, who looked like a hot mess. His dark hair was mussed, as if he'd run his hands through it a few too many times, and he hadn't shaved, though she liked the trail of scruff that covered his lower face. It enhanced that whole rugged thing he was working. He had on a Salinas Rodeo T-shirt and a pair of worn 501 button-fly Levi's. His feet were bare, and she noted that his toes were slightly furred. The entire package sent a tingle up her spine, an odd reaction when they were supposed to be talking about Ellie.

He sat next to her on the bed and she felt it again. Tingles. Which set off all kinds of warning alarms. *I'm not ready for these feelings of attraction, not after a breakup like the one with Mitch.*

"You got any other ideas?" he asked, absently touching his leg against hers. "I'm fresh out."

"Um…uh…I think we just need to find another talisman that will remind her of her mom, maybe a piece of costume jewelry that still has Marie's perfume on it. Could you call that Linda woman?"

"I'll do it this afternoon," he said, but didn't seem too thrilled about it.

"You don't like her?"

"It's not that. Linda's been very helpful; she loves Ellie. I just feel like I'm failing." He jutted his chin in the direction of the TV. "Last night, she said she hated me."

Something about seeing a two-hundred-pound male made of pure muscle appear so dejected by the offhanded scorn of a sullen twelve-year-old melted Aubrey's Mitch-hating heart.

"I'm no expert on kids, but I think it's fairly common for them to throw around the 'hate' word. There's a certain drama to it."

"I told her to get in line. Besides having a drinking problem—or maybe because of it—no one likes me." He smiled to show he was teasing, but it had a more sensual effect on Aubrey. The fact that they were sitting on a bed together only added to the sexual tension in the room.

"Right," she said, trying not to roll her eyes. "I'm guessing you have quite a fan club. Blondes, brunettes, redheads."

He chuckled but didn't deny it.

"What do you say we tape and paint the wall now?" Or else she might do something stupid and throw herself at him.

He winked and got to his feet to go in search of a ladder, leaving Aubrey to realize that Cash's surly shtick was quite possibly his version of dry humor with a bit of flirtation thrown into the mix.

Don't be getting any ideas. She forced herself back to business.

She took a few minutes to appraise their paint job. Not bad. Then she measured out the placement of her stripes, marking the walls with a pencil. When Cash didn't immediately return with the ladder, she headed to the living room, where Ellie had spread out on the couch. Aubrey brushed the girl's legs out of the way and plopped down next to her.

"I used to watch that show," she said as the Tanner family's living room filled the flat screen. "I bet your dad would take you to see the original *Full House* Victorian in San Francisco." Aubrey had read somewhere that it was in lower Pacific Heights and that the *Full House* creator had purchased it for over four mil.

"It's really there?" Ellie perked up. "I thought it was a set, like in Hollywood or something."

"They might've filmed some of the scenes in a studio, but part of it was the real house." Aubrey began stacking Ellie's breakfast dishes, which now cluttered Cash's poor excuse for a coffee table.

"How do you know about it?" Ellie asked, and actually got up to take her bowl and glass to the sink.

"I'm an interior designer," she called to the kitchen. "I take an interest in these things."

Ellie reclaimed her spot on the sofa. "My mom was a police detective." She puffed up with pride.

"That's what I heard. You know your dad used to be in the FBI?" It couldn't hurt to pump Cash up in his daughter's eyes. "I've heard he was a big-deal agent."

Ellie shrugged with indifference. "How come he doesn't work there anymore?"

Cash came in, carrying the ladder, and Aubrey said, "Why don't you ask him?"

But the opportunity was ruined when Travis and Grady followed Cash through the door like human tornadoes.

"Ellie, you want to go with us to the pool in Dry Creek?" Grady hopped up on the couch and bounced up and down as if the sofa were a trampoline. "Uncle Cash said you could."

"Hey, Grady, buddy, how 'bout you sit down and take a breather?" Cash propped the ladder against the wall. "You want to go, Ellie?"

In the summer, most of the kids swam in the creek, but in the last couple of years the high school had opened its pool to the public. Aubrey suspected it was a nice alternative because the pool had lifeguards, which probably put a lot of parents at ease.

Ellie appeared to be on the fence about it. Aubrey couldn't blame her; it had to be hard getting used to a new town with all its new faces.

"A lot of girls your age go," she said, knowing that Mercedes's grandkids were regulars, as well as Mitch's nieces. Apparently, all the middle-school girls had crushes on a few of the high-school lifeguards. "It would be a great way to make some new friends before school starts."

"I won't be here for school." Ellie lifted her chin in defiance.

Aubrey could tell Cash wanted to protest but thought better of it and instead said, "You may as well make the best of the place for summer. It's either the pool or painting, your choice."

"The pool!" Grady shouted.

"The pool," Travis seconded.

"All right, the pool," Ellie agreed. "I'll put on my suit."

"I've got to text Yoda and tell her we're waiting for Ellie. Otherwise, she'll call my dad and turn it into an international incident." Travis began tapping out a message on his phone.

"Don't call your sitter Yoda," Cash said and put Travis in a headlock. "Give me her number. I want to make sure it's okay if Ellie tags along."

"She said it was okay." Travis tapped a few more keys. "I sent it to your phone."

Yoda? Whoever Yoda was, she must be desperate for a job. Jace's kids were sweethearts in their own rambunctious way but rough as hell on nannies. They seemed to have made a game of running them off.

Ellie came out of her bedroom in a pair of shorts embroidered with tiny whales. The straps of her bathing suit peeked out from under a white polo shirt. It was more preppy than the kinds of clothes kids wore in Dry Creek. Most of the town's population lived on a ranch or worked at one. The uniform was basically cutoff jeans and tank tops. But Ellie looked adorable and not so different that she would stick out as an oddity.

It was sweet to see Cash fuss over her, making sure she had suntan lotion, a hat, and a towel before she left the house. The kids took off for Jace's to meet up with the aforementioned Yoda, leaving Aubrey and Cash alone.

"Who's Yoda?" she asked.

Cash's lips quirked. "The lady who used to work at the post office."

"Mrs. Jamison? She doesn't look anything like Yoda."

"Yeah. I don't know where they come up with half the stuff they do." Cash moved the ladder into Ellie's room and climbed up, motioning for Aubrey to hand him the roll of tape.

"Be careful," she warned.

He looked over his shoulder as if to say, *get real, woman.*

"Not the ladder," she clarified, though anyone could fall, even Mr. Bad-ass. "The walls are uneven, so you have to improvise to make the stripes trick the eye." She reached up and made some adjustments with the tape he'd begun to roll out until she was satisfied. "Do you have a level? If not, I could go home and get mine."

"I've got one." He came down the ladder and disappeared for a few minutes, only to return with a laser level.

"Nice!"

"You like my tool, do ya?" He said it to be funny, not pervy, and she laughed.

"No more construction jokes. Working for a development company, I've heard them all."

She and Cash hung the next strip of tape, working their way across the wall until they fell into a nice rhythm. He got the top of the wall and she got the bottom, tweaking as they went. A few times, their arms brushed and her heart raced.

And once, while fussing to get the tape perfectly straight, their faces nearly collided, and she rubbed against his stubble just a tiny little bit to see how it felt against her skin.

"Let me look." She stood back, trying to gain some distance, and double-checked their work before they started painting.

"Well? How's it coming?" He came down from the ladder and stood next to her.

"Good, I think. We'll know better after we start painting the stripes. Worse comes to worst, I can touch up with the white. You ready to stay inside the lines?"

"Inside the lines, huh?" He seemed to think about that for a while and finally said, "It'll be a new one for me, but I'll try my best."

She got the impression they were no longer talking about painting. "You must be a renegade, Cash Dalton."

He held her gaze, his eyes so blue they reminded her of Mill Lake in summertime. "Maybe, how 'bout you?" And then his eyes slid over her in a way that wasn't altogether respectable.

"Me? Uh...I'm pretty conventional."

"There's nothing about you a man would call conventional." He stepped in front of her and flicked a piece of tape off her shirt.

She lifted her face to his, hoping she wasn't misreading what was going on here. "Should I take that as a compliment?" *Are you making a move on me?*

"Damn straight it's a compliment." His lips twitched and he tilted his head down close enough that she felt his warm breath on her cheeks. "You know I nearly kissed you the other day? How weird would it be if I kissed you now?"

She chewed her bottom lip. "Probably pretty weird." But she didn't move away.

His lips hovered barely an inch from her mouth. "Should we try it? What's the worst that can happen?"

It was just a kiss, she argued with herself, trying to dismiss all the reasons it was insane, starting with the fact that she'd just broken her engagement to another man. Her head told her to back away, but her mouth said, *I don't see how it could hurt.*

COWBOY UP   91

And then, just like that, he covered her mouth with his, tasting her lips until the kiss grew deeper. She opened for him and his tongue slid inside her mouth and tangled with her tongue, hot and wicked. She reached up to hold on to his shoulders before her knees buckled. Lord almighty, the man could kiss. He hadn't even touched her with his hands, only his lips and tongue, and she felt it to the tips of her toes.

She pulled him tighter, and his arms went around her and his hands moved up and down her sides. Without realizing it, she whimpered, and he became more brazen, letting those clever hands of his travel under her T-shirt. He touched her back and belly, making her shudder. Then he kissed her again. This time softly, with a deliberateness that caused her whole body to react. Her breath quickened, her neck and chest flushed, and she was wet.

He too was aroused; she could feel the evidence of it pressed against her belly.

"Mm," she purred.

He backed her up to the bed and started to push her down, then muttered, "Shit."

"What's wrong?"

"This is Ellie's room…her bed."

Aubrey pulled away. May as well have poured a bucket of ice water over her head. They'd gotten caught up without thinking.

"You were right," she said. "Definitely weird."

Yet her body said something entirely different.

Chapter 9

Cash decided to drive to town and check up on the kids at the pool. He and Aubrey got the stripes painted, despite a bad case of blue balls. Although it had been a spectacular kiss, it had been a spectacularly bad idea. He needed to be focused on his daughter and his future, not on romancing his next-door neighbor.

Aubrey had been a good sport about their brief makeout session, laughing it off and blaming it on paint fumes. But they'd had a pretty intense few minutes, and in the interest of honesty, he'd wanted to take it further. Much further. She'd felt unbelievably good in his arms, curvy and soft.

It was a relief to want sex again. He suspected that had they been in his bedroom instead of Ellie's, they would've made a marathon session of it. And now he didn't know whether to thank fate or punch it in the mouth.

He passed the bus station, snagged parking in the high school lot, and cut across campus to the gymnasium. For a tiny town, the good folks of Dry Creek had raised enough cash with a bond measure for an outdoor, Olympic-size pool, open to the public in summer. Because there wasn't a lot to do in Dry Creek, it was considered quite a boon. Cash preferred the creek or Mill Lake, but he supposed the pool was more convenient for working parents who wanted a supervised environment for their kids.

He found Mrs. Jamison sitting with two other women under a big umbrella. The kids were in the pool. Cash hung back, taking a seat on top of a retaining wall at the far end of the deck. Travis was at the deep end of the pool with a few kids his own age. Grady was whooping it up on an inflatable bull float, pretending to be a rodeo star. The kid was the loudest one in the water, but Cash got a kick out of his exuberance.

Ellie was all alone, doing handstands in the shallow end. Cash scanned the area. There was no shortage of young girls, many of whom were laying on lounge chairs or towels, tanning themselves in the sun. There was a small clique that sat at the edge of the pool, dipping their feet in the water. Cash thought they looked about the same age as Ellie.

He watched for a while, hoping Ellie had had the opportunity to make a few new friends. But from what he'd observed so far, she was playing by herself. The kids in Dry Creek had grown up together and could be clannish. As a kid, Cash had benefited from Jace being a local and their grandfather being a big figure in the community. Still, he, Sawyer, and Angie had never been treated completely like insiders, and he was afraid Ellie would have trouble fitting in. Right now, she could probably use a few friends.

He continued to stay in the background because despite swimming by herself, Ellie seemed to be enjoying her time in the pool. Cash's presence would probably ruin that, given how she felt about him. At least Linda had called. Thanks to Aubrey's suggestion, Linda was sending one of Marie's old jackets to replace the sweater he'd ruined.

Jace came through the pool gate, spotted Cash, and waved, then stopped off to have a word with Mrs. Jamison. Several pairs of hungry eyes followed him.

After a short conversation, Jace made his way to where Cash was sitting. "When did you get here?"

"About ten minutes ago." Cash nudged his head at Ellie. "I was hoping she'd meet a few girls from the middle school."

"It's her first day in town, Cash. In the meantime, she's got the boys."

Grady shouted "Cowabunga" at the top of his lungs, and they quickly turned to see him cannonball into the deep end.

Jace tilted his head back to the sun as if he was praying for patience. "The kid never runs out of energy."

"You used to be like that before you got old," Cash ribbed him.

"I'm not old, asshole, just tired." He grabbed a spot on the retaining wall, and Cash noticed for the first time that his cousin had a few gray hairs. They were both the same age: thirty-seven. "My campaign manager thinks I have to do something about the Aubrey rumors. I know what Sawyer thinks, but what about you?"

"What does she want you to do?"

Jace snorted. "Hold a press conference. To announce that Aubrey and I are nothing but friends. People are just going to believe what they want to believe. It seems making a big deal out of it just adds fuel to the fire, you know?"

"How do you think the rumor started in the first place? Her moving to the ranch?"

Jace watched Grady perform another cannonball, then in a soft voice said, "Mitch started the rumor, even though he knows there's no Goddamn truth to it."

"Why?" Cash had learned a long time ago that nearly everyone had an ulterior motive for everything they did. Cynical? Maybe. But working many years in law enforcement had made him a cynical guy.

Jace shrugged, but Cash got the sense it was a studied nonchalance. There was more going on here than Jace was willing to let on.

"Would it be better if Aubrey moved off Dry Creek Ranch?" Cash asked. *Better for whom?* he thought to himself. The woman was certainly a temptation he didn't need.

"Nah." Jace shook his head. "I'm not kicking her out. She needs a place to live and we need the rent."

They'd lived without the rent all this time. Cash knew Jace was just being obstinate. It was in the Dalton DNA. Besides, he suspected there weren't a lot of rental options in Dry Creek. "Then what else can you do?"

"I could beat the shit out of Mitch," Jace said, but it was more to himself than to Cash.

"Yeah, probably not the soundest of plans. Abuse of power and all that."

Jace socked him in the arm. "Since when are you the voice of reason?" He got up and threw a beach ball lying on the ground to a group of kids in the pool. "On another note, an acquaintance of mine is retiring from the Bureau of Livestock Identification. You should go for the job."

Cash threw his head back and laughed. "A cow cop? That's pretty funny, Jace."

Jace turned to Cash and gave him a hard look. "You like being unemployed?" When Cash didn't respond, Jace said, "Yeah, I didn't think so. The pay is good, and you could continue to live on the ranch. And in my experience, cows are more amiable than people. The cattlemen around here need a good investigator and you're the best. Think about it, Cash. With a good word from me, you'd have an excellent shot at getting the job."

It was Cash's turn to pin Jace with a glare. "You sure about that?"

Jace flipped Cash his middle finger. "This shit with Aubrey will fizzle out." But just a few minutes earlier, Jace hadn't seemed so confident. "You interested in the job or not? A position like this won't last long."

"Nope, not interested." Cash was done with law enforcement of any shape or kind. Period. And it wasn't as if he knew a damned thing about cattle rustling.

"Suit yourself." Jace got to his feet, stuck his fingers in his mouth, and let out a whistle. It was something Grandpa Dalton used to do when he wanted to round up his grandsons.

Travis and Grady climbed out of the pool, and Jace huddled up with them for a few minutes, then strolled out of the pool area, presumably to return to his office. Ellie got out too, grabbed a towel, and found an empty chair as far away from Cash as possible.

The day had gone from hot to hotter, and a steady stream of kids and adults poured in. The place was starting to feel too crowded. Cash walked over to Ellie. He'd forgotten to give her money in case Mrs. Jamison took the kids over to the coffee shop or went to Grass Valley or Auburn for burgers at a drive-through.

"You having fun, kiddo?" He squeezed the back of her neck and she pulled away.

She lifted her shoulders, which Cash noted were getting sunburned. "The kids here are annoying."

"Annoying, huh?" He pulled up one of the last vacant chairs. "How's that?"

In her typical communicative way, she failed to respond. Like father, like daughter, he supposed. Cash had never been accused of being overly forthcoming.

"Perhaps you won't feel that way once you get to know them. They're just new to you, El."

"See that girl over there?" She pointed to a kid with red hair and freckles, who looked vaguely familiar. "She made fun of the way I talk."

He experienced a flash of visceral anger, which surprised him. Kids were notoriously insensitive, Ellie had to learn to stand up for herself. Yet, as overreactionary as it was, he wanted to call the redhead's parents and tell them to teach their little brat some manners.

"Kids around here probably never met anyone from Boston," he said. "I like the way you talk, Ellie."

She dropped her gaze to the ground. "Can we go home?"

"If that's what you want to do." He should've told her to tough it out and refuse to let some snot-nosed girl ruin her afternoon. But he'd gone soft. He supposed his dad genes were kicking in, which was an odd revelation. Until now, he hadn't thought he had any.

"I do." She wrapped her towel tighter around her and went over to Mrs. Jamison to collect her stuff.

Cash waved goodbye to Travis and Grady, motioning that Ellie was going with him. Grady hopped out of the pool and gave Ellie a great big hug. She pretended to be irritated when he got her wet, but she patted his back with affection.

"Want to grab a late lunch?" he asked as they made their way through the high school parking lot.

She surprised him by saying yes. "Mrs. Jamison was going to take us for ice cream later."

"Then we'll get some for dessert."

He drove the short distance to the coffee shop and asked Laney to seat them in one of the booths at the back of the diner. The restaurant held so many memories of Grandpa Dalton that sometimes Cash came in just to feel his spirit, though it was everywhere on the ranch, the place Jasper loved most.

On their way to the table, Jimmy Ray waved from the kitchen. "I'll be out in a few minutes to meet the little miss."

Cash got a kick out of the way Ellie studied the menu so intently. "What looks good?"

"I don't know. What do you like?"

"The steak sandwich." The beef was local and the sandwich was what his grandfather used to get. "You want to try it?"

"Sure."

It was only a steak sandwich, but he'd never seen her this agreeable. He decided to press his luck.

"What do you think of going riding tomorrow? I thought we could borrow two of Jace's horses and see the ranch from the back of a saddle." It would probably be hot as hell, but if they got an early enough start they could beat the heat. He'd missed riding, galloping across the open range at breakneck speed and watching the day come to life under a Dry Creek sky.

"Okay."

That was twice now. Still, Cash didn't get his hopes up that her sudden affability was a permanent thing.

Laney came to take their orders and Ellie shyly ordered her steak sandwich. A couple of the locals dropped by Cash's table to say hello and to say a few nice words about Grandpa Dalton.

"Who's Jasper?" Ellie asked.

"My grandfather, your great-grandfather. I'm sorry he died before the two of you got to meet. You would've loved the old goat." Everyone did.

Laney brought their drinks and rearranged the table settings.

"Did Travis and Grady know him?" Ellie asked, oblivious to Laney's eavesdropping.

"They lived with him right up until the day he died. He was a real-life cowboy who could rope and bulldog a steer and ride a horse like a champion."

"Woo-wee, that man was something," Laney said and put her hand on Cash's shoulder. "The whole town mourned when he died. And your daddy looks just like him. Spitting image. When your great-granddaddy was his age, your great-grandma had to hold the other ladies off with a stick. I swear it."

When Laney went off to the kitchen, Ellie asked, "Is that true?"

Cash's mouth quirked. "It was before my time, but that's the way I heard it. You can ask your grandpa about it when you meet him. He and your grandmother are planning to come soon."

Ellie's glance fell to the table and she grew quiet.

"You don't want to meet them, Ellie?"

She lowered her face until it was practically dragging on her napkin. Cash decided not to push. They'd circle back around to it eventually. Their food came, and Cash took the opportunity to change the subject.

"Did you and your mom eat in restaurants a lot?" he asked as she bit into her steak sandwich.

"Not that much. My mom had to save her money."

The words stabbed him in the gut. He could've helped with that. Raising a kid on a cop's salary in Boston couldn't have been easy, and yet Marie had made sure Ellie got horseback riding lessons, private schooling, and a nice condo in a decent part of town.

He nodded. "We have to talk about some stuff, Ellie, about why I wasn't around. I'd like to do that this evening when we're home." With no prying eyes and big ears.

"Whatever," she said and took another bite. The sandwich was so big, she needed both hands to hold it.

The door swung open and Aubrey walked in, out of breath. Her face was splotchy red, her shirt wet with sweat, and a few locks of hair had come loose from her ponytail and stuck to her face. She looked like she'd run a marathon in a hundred-degree weather. And damn if she didn't take Cash's breath away.

She leaned into the kitchen window. "I need to use your phone, Jimmy Ray."

"What's wrong with yours?" Jimmy Ray came out and untied his apron.

"It's out of juice." Aubrey held up her cell and pulled the ancient cordless out of its stand at the cash register. "What's the number for Mama's Towing?"

Jimmy Ray lifted one bushy brow. "What's wrong with your car?"

"Heck if I know. It got me here just fine. When I left the parking lot at the Dry Creek Market, I got a few blocks away and then it started puttering out on me."

Cash stood up. "Want me to take a look? I'm a decent mechanic." He used to help Grandpa Dalton repair the tractor on the ranch and one summer during college had worked in an auto shop.

She jerked back, surprised. "I didn't see you tucked in the corner like that." She craned her neck to get a better look at their booth. "Hi, Ellie."

"Hi." Ellie waved.

Aubrey turned her attention back to Cash. "That would be great, but I don't want to disturb your and Ellie's lunch."

"Come join us. As soon as we're done, I'll check it out." He was supposed to be distancing himself from her. Yet the minute she walked in the door, he felt his Goddamn blood rush south of his belt.

"Okay, but I've got perishables." Aubrey looked at Jimmy Ray.

"Oh no," Laney said. "Do not think you can come in here with your woe-is-me-my-car-broke-down story and think you can use our refrigerator. Why don't you go over to the sheriff's station and ask your boyfriend if you can use his?"

"Seriously, Laney, we're back to that?" Aubrey put her hands on her hips. "For the last time, Jace is not my boyfriend."

Laney stuck her hand in front of Aubrey's face. "Tell it to the judge, Aubrey McCallister."

Aubrey rolled her eyes. "Are you actually planning to let my groceries spoil to vindicate poor Mitch, who by the way, thinks your corn bread sucks. That's right, on more than one occasion, he complained that it was dry as dust. I quote: 'It's worse than the crap they serve at Reggie's Barbecue.'"

Laney growled—at least Cash thought it sounded like a growl—and pointed at the door. "Out! Get out, girl, before I forcibly push you out."

"Hold on." Cash rushed over and stepped between Aubrey and Laney. "Come on, Laney, be a good neighbor."

"Good neighbor, pfft. Over my dead body. She left a good man just to get between the sheets with your cousin." Laney walked to the door and opened it wide. "Out!"

Jimmy Ray came up behind his wife, lifted his hand, and pressed the door closed. "Now, sugar, be reasonable."

He turned to Cash and shook his head, as if to say he didn't know what had gotten in to either of them.

Laney poked Jimmy Ray in the arm. "Did you hear what she said about my corn bread?" She crossed her arms over her ample chest. "Everyone loves my corn bread, including Mitch." She jabbed her finger at Aubrey. "The girl's a liar."

Aubrey came out from behind Cash's back and got in Laney's face again. "Think what you want, but no one loves your corn bread. Not even Mercedes's husband, Joe, who'll eat anything on a plate. I once saw him dig an old Danish out of the garbage, that's how discriminating he is."

Laney made that low sound in her throat again, and this time Cash thought she might throw a punch. He tugged Aubrey's arm, a signal to shut up.

"Jimmy Ray, let Aubrey store her cold stuff in your cooler." It was more of a demand than a request. Cash didn't have a lot of tolerance for drama.

Jimmy Ray gave a slight nod and Cash nudged Aubrey to go get her groceries before Laney pitched another fit.

When Cash returned to his table, Ellie's eyes were big as saucers. "Finish your lunch," he told her.

"Why was that lady mean to Aubrey? Is Aubrey Uncle Jace's girlfriend?" Uncle? Ellie hadn't even called Cash Dad yet. And hell no, Aubrey McAllister wasn't Jace's girlfriend.

"It's just a misunderstanding." Cash scooted into the booth and pointed at Ellie's fries. "Come on, honey, eat up."

By the time Aubrey returned with two bags of groceries, Laney was bussing their table and looking like what Grandpa Dalton would've called "fit to be tied."

Aubrey swished by her and headed for the kitchen. While she was storing her perishables, he squared up with Laney at the cash register. Ellie stood by his side, and he got the impression she was intrigued by the circus. Probably not a whole lot of country crazy in Boston.

"Ready?" Aubrey came out of the kitchen, her white blouse plastered to her like a second skin.

"Let's go." He forced his eyes away from her chest and called back to the kitchen, "Thanks, Jimmy Ray."

They were barely out of the restaurant when Aubrey said, "God, she's such a bit—" and remembered they were in the company of a twelve-year-old. *Sorry*, she mouthed to Cash.

"Let's take my SUV." The market was just up the street, but Aubrey's car might need a jump and Cash figured she'd walked enough in the heat.

They piled into his Ford and pulled into the Dry Creek Market parking lot, where Aubrey's Volvo sat under a tree. Cash left the air-conditioner running for Ellie, popped the hood on Aubrey's car, and told her to start the engine. The ignition turned over, but just as quickly, the car stalled.

"Is this what happened before?" Cash asked.

She shook her head. "It started right up and I was able to drive it. I got as far as Tank Farm and all of a sudden the car wouldn't accelerate. No matter how hard I pressed the gas pedal, the car still didn't have any power. I was afraid it was breaking down, so I came back here."

"Try it again," he told Aubrey.

This time the Volvo wouldn't even start.

From what she'd described, Cash suspected the problem had something to do with fuel combustion. He twisted off the cap on her gas tank and tried to take a look inside.

"Well, do you see anything?"

"When was the last time you gassed up?" Perhaps it was bad fuel.

"A few days ago." Aubrey moved closer to Cash and tried to peer into the gas tank.

"Maybe someone put something down there," Ellie said.

Cash glanced over at his daughter, who'd gotten out of the truck. The girl had a suspicious nature. What did he expect when both her parents had been cops? "Let's not get ahead of ourselves."

"Like sugar?" Aubrey crouched down and tried to get a better look inside the tank, which was fruitless. "Who on earth would do something like that? Mitch is out of town."

"Look, we don't know for sure. It could be something with your gas line. Easiest way to find out is to syphon the tank and replace the gas."

"Should I have it towed and let a mechanic do it?"

Cash knew that between the tow and the hours it would take to diagnose the problem, Aubrey could wind up shelling out a few hundred bucks. "I'll do it." He gazed around the parking lot. "I can come back in the morning with tools and a can of gas. Will Stu and Marsh care if you leave the car overnight?" For as long as Cash could remember, the two brothers had owned the market.

"They won't mind and everyone knows this is my car."

There wasn't much crime in Dry Creek, so Cash wasn't worried someone would strip the ancient station wagon.

"You want to pick up your groceries and hop a ride home with us?"

"That would be great." She wiped her brow with the back of her hand. "I don't know how to thank you."

He could think of a couple of ways but kept them to himself.

Chapter 10

Her father wanted to have his stupid talk, but Ellie was tired. She didn't know why, because it was only eight. Her mom used to let her stay up until nine on weeknights and ten on weekends. So far, he hadn't given her a curfew. But one was coming; all signs pointed that way. Her father made believe he was laid-back, but Ellie could tell he was more of a hard ass than he led on. If she wanted to be fair, her mom had kind of been that way too. Maybe all parents were.

She took her time changing into a pair of sweatpants and to check out the new stripes on her wall. They were pretty but didn't go with the fishing comforter on her bed. Aubrey said she was searching for something pink to match the paint color.

Ellie used to think she wanted to be a detective like her mom, but being a decorator didn't seem like a bad job. She sort of liked the idea of picking out people's stuff and not having to pay for it. And Aubrey said she got to see a lot of big houses and snoop through people's bedrooms.

Of everyone, Ellie liked Aubrey the best. She was pretty but not stuck-up. And she'd told that lady off good at the coffee shop. Ellie still didn't understand why the woman had been so awful to Aubrey or what Grady and Travis's dad had to do with it. Ellie had kind of thought Aubrey was in to her father, which was…*uh, can't even.*

Tomorrow, when she saw Travis and Grady, she planned to ask them about it, mostly because she was curious. Grady was probably too young to know anything. But Travis was older than her by a year and was wicked cool. When that annoying red-haired girl had made fun of the way Ellie talked, Travis had told the ginger to shut the F up.

"Hey, Ellie, what's taking so long?"

"I'll be right out," she yelled back and threw herself down on the bed. Why couldn't he just chill? It wasn't like he even wanted a daughter, so why did he have to act all desperate?

"Everything okay in there?" He knocked on her bedroom.

She jumped off the bed and opened the door before he had an ulcer or a heart attack.

He pointed at the walls. "They look good, don't they?"

She nodded and followed him to the kitchen, where he'd set out two bowls and a container of ice cream. Vanilla, which was so boring. Even Mary Margaret, who hated everything, liked pistachio or mint chip when she wasn't being a vegan.

He served them both two scoops, put the ice cream in the freezer, and sat across the table from her. "Looks like you got a little sun. Should we put some lotion on your face and shoulders?"

"I can do it." He always treated her like a mutant.

"Okay, otherwise you'll peel."

She took a spoonful of ice cream, and the cold gave her brain freeze. "What did you want to talk about?"

He didn't say anything for a few minutes, and Ellie wondered if he was going to send her back to Boston. Linda would take her, even if she had two kids of her own. Or she could live with her Uncle Woody who wasn't really her uncle but had been her mother's partner at Boston PD. She really wanted to live with Mary Margaret and Miss O'Malley, but Ellie's mother would've had a heart attack if she were still alive. She thought Mary Margaret was a bad influence and Miss O'Malley was a pothead.

Her father leaned across the table. "What did your mom tell you about me?"

Ellie ate another spoonful of ice cream and lifted her shoulders. "That you had your own life and we had ours."

"Did she tell you who I was, my name, where I lived?"

"No, just that she met you at a police conference and that you were in the FBI."

He stuck his spoon in his ice cream bowl but didn't take a bite. "Did she say whether I knew about you?"

Ellie thought about it for a while. "I can't remember."

He nodded, then got up and put his bowl in the sink. When he returned to the table he said, "Until your mom called me a few weeks ago, I didn't know anything about you, Ellie."

Well, of course he didn't. He'd never met her before. "I guess you were too busy with your job or whatever." She looked down, picking at her nails.

He lifted her chin so they were eye to eye, and she tried very hard not to squirm, but he was being real serious and it made her nervous.

"No, not too busy," he said and was still looking at her. "I didn't know you existed, Ellie. I didn't know I had a little girl."

What? That had to be a lie. How could he not know? "I don't believe you."

"It's the truth, Ellie." She tried to look away, but he wouldn't let her. "I wanted you to know in case you thought I deserted you. I didn't; I just didn't know I had you."

It was a bunch of lies. Her mother would've told her.

She pushed the ice cream away and fisted her hands in her lap. "My mom must've known you wouldn't have wanted me." Her voice started to tremble and she swiped her eyes with her arm.

He handed her a napkin but didn't say anything. She was happy he didn't because she hated him. She hated everything about him.

"I didn't abandon you, Ellie."

"My mom must've thought you were really bad to keep me from you." She threw her ice cream bowl on the floor and ran to her room.

* * * *

The next morning, Cash asked Sawyer to sit with Ellie while he drove to Dry Creek to fix Aubrey's car. He'd promised to take Ellie riding, but after the way their discussion had turned out, he thought she might need a little time alone.

All night he'd gone over the conversation, wondering if he'd done the right thing by telling her. In essence, he'd thrown Marie under the bus. But what was he supposed to do, let his daughter forever think he'd ignored her for twelve years because she was too inconvenient?

He blew out a breath and played with the air-conditioner, trying to find the perfect temperature. Maybe he should have talked to a child counselor first, or called his mother. But the bottom line, whether it was selfish or not, was that Cash wanted to be straight with her. He didn't see how their relationship could move forward if he wasn't.

She'd always feel unwanted by him and he'd always feel like a martyr who had ruined his chance at having a meaningful bond with his daughter for a dead woman who hadn't given one thought to his feelings until she was dying.

But the implications of what he'd told Ellie were a lot for a kid to chew on. He knew that. And although he hadn't expected Ellie to immediately embrace him, he'd hoped the conversation would've gone better.

He pulled up to a stop sign on his way to town. Jace nosed in behind him and turned on his light bar.

"Ah, for Christ's sake," Cash muttered under his breath.

Jace stuck his arm out of the window and pointed to the shoulder. Cash shook his head but turned his SUV onto the narrow swath of gravel that joined an open field anyway. A few minutes later, Jace came up to the passenger side and motioned for Cash to roll down his window.

"License and registration, please."

"How about this instead?" Cash flipped Jace the bird.

"You see that over there?" Jace pointed to the stop sign and Cash snorted. "You know what you did when you saw it? The old California roll, which means you're in violation of CVC 22450."

Cash reached through the window and covered Jace's ticket book with the palm of his hand. "I don't have time for this, Jace."

"Where's the fire, Cash?"

"Aubrey's car broke down and I'm on my way to fix it." Cash pulled his hand back in and started to roll up the window.

"Where's her car? I'll come with you." Clearly, the sheriff was bored, not to mention that the idea of him tagging along was a terrible idea. Jace working on Aubrey's car in the very public parking lot of the only grocery store in town would only add to the gossip.

"Bad plan," Cash said.

Jace stuck his ticket book in his back pocket and furrowed his brow. "Where is it?"

That was Jace. Instead of letting the rumors die down, he had to be contrary just for the sake of it.

"You're an idiot. You know that, right?" Cash shook his head. "It's at the Dry Creek Market."

"See you there." Jace hopped inside his sheriff's SUV and tailed Cash to the grocery store.

Cash parked behind a delivery truck, got out, and walked up to Jace's vehicle while it idled.

"Where is it?" Jace asked.

Cash threw his arms in the air. "It was here yesterday afternoon." He fished his phone out of his pocket. "What's Aubrey's number? Maybe she called a tow truck after all." He didn't know why she would've after they'd agreed he'd fix it if he could.

Jace gave him the number and Cash plugged it into his phone, saving it to his contacts. Aubrey picked up on the third ring, sounding like she'd just woken up. Cash checked his watch. Seven.

"Your car's not here," he told her. "Did you have someone pick it up?"

"What? No. Hang on a sec."

Cash heard rustling in the background, probably Aubrey getting out of bed. A vision of her in her sleep shorts flashed in his head and he could feel the blood rush to his groin.

Aubrey came back on the line. "Are you sure it's gone?"

"I'm standing here in the middle of the lot. The only other vehicles here are mine, Jace's, and a few delivery vans."

"You think someone stole it?"

No, not too many folks in the market for a used Volvo that was probably older than he was. "I'll have Jace look into it, but I think it's more likely it was towed."

She was moving around, and Cash heard a whirring sound. Her coffee maker. For a second, he let his thoughts return to her sleepwear. If not the little shorts she'd been wearing the morning she'd complained about his target practice, a teeny nightie? A man could dream.

"Why would anyone tow me?" she asked, shaking him out of his daydream. "I'll call Marsh and phone you right back."

He leaned against Jace's SUV and waited. Jace got out, shaded his eyes, and scanned the lot. It wasn't large, maybe twenty parking spaces max.

"What spot was it in?"

"Over there." Cash pointed to the only tree in the lot.

Jace reached into his glove box and slipped on a pair of sunglasses, then made a call on his cell. "You wouldn't happen to know Aubrey's license plate number, would you?"

Cash made a get-real face. Jace moved to the other side of his vehicle to stand in the shade and described Aubrey's Volvo to whoever was on the other end of the call.

There was some back and forth on the phone before Jace finally called over the roof, "It's at the impound lot in Chesterville."

Great; either Stu or Marsh had had it towed. In San Francisco, between the tow truck and storage cost, it was something like three hundred bucks to free your car after the first day of having it impounded. Cash had no idea how much it would cost in Mill County, but it couldn't be cheap.

A few minutes later, Cash's phone rang. Aubrey. He answered, ready to deliver the bad news.

"Stu had my car towed," she blurted out, beating him to the punch. "I can't freaking believe it! My mother wheeled me around in a Dry Creek Market shopping cart before I was old enough to walk and that asshole had my car impounded. Now I have to figure out where the lot is before it costs me a fortune to bail out my car. I ought to sue Stu."

Cash didn't have the heart to tell her that it was private property and the owners could have anyone towed after two hours. There were signs in the parking lot that said exactly that, though he suspected Stu and Marsh had only done it a handful of times, if ever. The brothers appeared to be sticklers for the rules only when Aubrey was concerned.

"Did he tell you why?" Cash asked, but he already knew the answer.

Silence on the other end. Bingo. Mitch Reynolds certainly had a lot of pull in this town. Cash was beginning to think the guy needed a good whupping after all.

"I'll take you to get the car. It's in Chesterville," he said. Technically, he should be spending the day with Ellie. But it wouldn't take long to drive to Chesterville and back. It was only ten miles away and traffic free, if you didn't get stuck behind a livestock or farm truck.

"You're the best. I just have to jump in the shower. Give me fifteen minutes."

He signed off and found Jace staring at him. "What?"

"You and Aubrey have certainly gotten cozy."

"We're neighbors and she's decorating Ellie's room for practically nothing." But yeah, they'd gotten cozier than Cash was comfortable with, if you counted the kiss.

"Right," Jace said, a smart-ass grin on his face.

"Think what you want," Cash responded lamely, because Jace wasn't an idiot. "Or maybe you have a problem with Aubrey's and my friendship."

"Nope." Jace continued to smile like a loon. "She's my pal and you're my favorite cousin, except, of course, for Sawyer. Mazel tov!" He winked, and Cash returned a one-finger salute.

"As much as I like standing around supermarket parking lots with you, I've gotta go." Cash clicked the fob to unlock his Ford.

"You give anymore thought to that job I told you about?" Jace came around the side of his SUV and followed Cash to his vehicle.

"Cow cop?" Cash kicked a pebble with the toe of his boot. "Still not happening, Jace."

"What are you planning to do career-wise?"

"Don't know yet. Have you given anymore thought to selling? Maybe we could somehow split the property so you and the boys can keep the ranch house."

Jace looked Cash square in the eye. "It's not what Grandpa would've wanted."

"Not what Grandpa would've wanted or not what you would want?" Cash was getting tired of Jace and Sawyer throwing Jasper in his face. They all loved their grandfather the same; guilting Cash into keeping the ranch to uphold a romantic legacy wasn't going to work with him. He was too practical. "How are you planning for us to pay the property tax bill, not to mention the back taxes?"

"We've got a little time on that, I'm sure we'll come up with something."

Come up with something. He didn't have to tell Jace that the bills weren't going to pay themselves. "You let me know when you have an idea how."

"You'll be the first to know." Jace walked back to his SUV and tipped his Stetson.

Damned cowboy was a dreamer.

Cash shook his head and climbed in his driver's seat. He got home to find Sawyer and Ellie eating cereal in front of the TV. He checked to make sure Sawyer hadn't put on the porn channel and went inside his bedroom to change his shirt into something more acceptable than the holey one he'd put on to fix Aubrey's station wagon. When he came back out, Ellie was in the kitchen.

"Morning." He pulled her in for a little hug and felt her stiffen. They were back to being strangers again. Before their talk, he'd felt like they were getting somewhere. One step forward, two steps back.

"I talked to your grandparents and they're planning a trip here this weekend," he continued. Cash's mother was champing at the bit to meet her granddaughter. He couldn't hold her or his father off any longer. After twelve years, it wasn't right to keep his parents from their grandchild.

Ellie reacted with her usual indifference. "When are my boxes coming?"

"I'll check later. Are you okay here with Sawyer for a little longer? Aubrey's car got towed and I offered to take her to pick it up."

"How come it got towed?"

"Don't know," he said, because it was easier than explaining the situation. "Business owners usually don't like people to take up their parking spaces unless they're shopping in their store."

"Aubrey bought groceries there."

The kid might be lawyer material, he thought with pride. "Yep, but that was yesterday, and today is today."

Sawyer overheard the conversation and wandered in. "Stu and Marsh had Aubrey towed? Really?" He shook his head. "And so it begins."

Small town, big drama, Cash thought. "Mitch's got clout around here."

"Mitch is a douchebag," Sawyer said, covering Ellie's ears, which made her giggle.

"Who's Mitch?" she asked.

"Aubrey's ex-fiancé," Cash answered and got a bottle of water from the refrigerator.

"Aubrey was engaged?"

"What are you, a reporter?" Sawyer gave her a noogie and she giggled again.

Uncle Jace. Giggles for Sawyer. Nothing for Cash. He felt like a tool begrudging his cousins Ellie's affection, but it stung a little.

"You okay for another hour?" he asked Sawyer.

"Sure. Me and the little rug rat were thinking of walking over to the barn and petting the horses."

"Okay. But don't take her out on any of them." He wanted to be the one to show Ellie the ranch on horseback. As a city kid, it had been his wonderland. Acres and acres of open space and blue skies that went on forever. Cash used to explore the hills for hours and swim with his gelding in the creek. In the summers, they'd move the cattle down from the mountains into the valley. It was a four-day adventure, camping out on the range in bedrolls and eating over an open fire. Some of the hands had taught him how to pan for gold and he, Jace, and Sawyer would stand in the creek for hours, hoping to strike it rich.

"Nope," Sawyer said and squeezed the back of Cash's neck. "I'll save that for you."

"Thanks. I'll hurry so you can get back to writing." It was good of Sawyer to pull babysitting duties, and Cash wouldn't make a habit of asking.

"Take your time." Sawyer got that pained expression he always did whenever he had writer's block. "Nice of you to help Aubrey out."

You're not going to start in with that too?

"She's giving my kid a whole new bedroom," he said, trying not to act defensive.

"I saw the paint job. Cute for a young girl." Sawyer opened the fridge and stuck his head in. "Maybe I should have her take a look at my loft."

"She could use the work." But for some reason, he didn't like the idea of Aubrey working with Sawyer, which was crazy. He didn't want a girlfriend, not even a sex partner if it involved any kind of commitment whatsoever. His hands were already full.

"Make sure if you go out, Ellie wears sunscreen, okay?" She had fair skin, and Cash didn't want her to burn any more than she had at the pool.

"Where is it?"

Cash got the beach bag Ellie had used the other day and handed it to Sawyer. "Seriously, I won't be more than an hour.

"Bye, Ellie," he called to the living room, where she'd gone back to watching TV.

Not so much as a grunt. Cash sighed, Rome wasn't built in a day. It was a cliché, but it helped put things between him and Ellie in perspective. He was as much out of his depth as a father as she was being his daughter. *You're stuck with me, kiddo, so we better make the best of it.*

True to her word, Aubrey was ready when he got there. The second his SUV pulled up, she came out on the porch in a short skirt and a peasant blouse, her brown hair loose. He liked the outfit. Then again, he liked her in cutoff shorts and an old T-shirt, or a pair of jeans, or a thong. All of it worked for him.

He leaned over and pushed the passenger door open, and she got in.

"Thank you, thank you, thank you."

"You're welcome." His lips ticked up because he wasn't going to say it three times. "Maybe on the way to Chesterville we can talk about why your ex is making your and Jace's life uncomfortable."

She didn't say anything, just leaned forward and turned on the radio.

Under normal circumstances, it wouldn't have been any of his business, but she'd involved him in this strange pissing match. And Jace…whatever was going on here could hurt his cousin's reelection chances. "Aubrey?"

"Can't I plead the Fifth?"

"Why? Is there something that might incriminate you?" What exactly had she done to Mitch to make him so spiteful?

"No. I just don't want to talk about it." She fiddled with the dial until she found a station she liked. "I love this song, don't you?"

It was a country-western tune Cash didn't care for. He was a traditionalist: Hank Williams, Lefty Frizzell, Patsy Cline, Loretta Lynn, George Jones, the stuff his grandfather used to listen to. "I'm a professional interrogator, so if you think you can distract me with music, you'd be mistaken."

"Ugh." Aubrey leaned her head against Cash's leather seat. "It's not that I don't want to tell you, it's that I can't."

"Why? Something wrong with your tongue?" He knew firsthand her tongue worked just fine. Better than fine. The woman's kisses made him hotter than a four-alarm fire.

"I made a promise. And unlike Mitch, I keep mine."

He wondered if Jace had made a similar promise, because he'd been as reticent as Aubrey to open up about whatever was going on here. "To Jace?"

"No. Jace, unfortunately, got caught up in this by accident."

"Well, whatever it is, you and Jace need to fix it, because impound lots cost money and last I looked, you're unemployed. And Jace has two sons to support and he needs his sheriff's job." He absently put his hand on her knee. She didn't try to move it away, so he kept it there. Her skin was warm and soft, and if he moved his hand up her thigh, the skirt was short enough that he'd come in contact with her panties. "I don't know how big or small the infraction was, but Mitch seems loaded for bear, and he appears to have quite a bit of sway in Dry Creek."

Small towns could be like snake pits, Cash had learned over the years. Once, Grandpa Dalton had had a dispute with the owner of the local propane company over who had the winning bid for a kid's 4-H steer at the county fair. For three years, the company refused to deliver the ranch's propane. Jasper had to use another service in Auburn.

Jace had required them to invite the entire town to Jasper's funeral for fear that those left out would hold a grudge and, like the propane company, refuse service.

"Mitch does free small construction projects for everyone around here," Aubrey said. "Besides that, he's the closest thing Dry Creek has to royalty. You know he was a first-draft pick for the Colorado Rockies before he blew out his knee?"

Cash hadn't known Mitch had made the major leagues but remembered something about him being a ball player. "Still, I'm guessing you're pretty popular around here, too." How could she not be? "And Jace—everyone loves the guy, though there's no accounting for taste."

She gave him a quick jab in the arm with her elbow, and he pretended to struggle with the steering wheel. They'd already breezed through Dry Creek. The drive went fast with Aubrey in the passenger seat.

And his hand had made it to her thigh.

Chapter 11

It cost Aubrey $185 to get her Volvo back, not including the price of having the car towed to the ranch because it didn't run, and she was spitting mad. How could Stu have done this to her? It was a rhetorical question, of course. She knew exactly why. Stu Nally had been Mitch's dad's best friend since high school.

At least Aubrey's mom had dated the impound yard manager, who'd been kind enough to take twenty-five bucks off the bill. Good to have friends in low places.

The whole ride home, she'd planned her revenge on Mitch. Perhaps she'd sign him up for an escort service and have the company send him their sleazy brochures to Reynolds Construction. Or better yet, she'd report him to health services, tell them he had chlamydia and was infecting half the county.

"What are you doing over there?" Cash pulled her from her payback fantasies.

"Thinking of ways to get even with Mitch." She gave him a sideways glance. His blue eyes were hidden behind a pair of aviator sunglasses, but nothing covered that square jaw of his or the cleft in his chin. They really ought to take away licenses from men like him. Driving while sexy. It was too distracting to all the other motorists.

"Why don't you talk to him? If you want, I'll come with you."

She planned to have a talk with Mitch all right, but unless she was willing to out him, it wouldn't do much good.

"Why did you two break up anyway?" Cash was trolling for information. It didn't take an FBI agent to see that.

"He cheated on me." Aubrey decided it wouldn't hurt to give him half the story.

Cash turned in his seat to look at her, then shifted his eyes back to the road. "You know this how?"

Because she'd walked in on him when he and Jill were doing it on his desk. "Let's just say I have direct evidence as opposed to circumstantial."

"I don't get it." Cash drummed his fingers on the steering wheel as he waited at the stoplight. "If he cheated on you, what does he have to be so angry about? And why drag Jace into it?"

Because Jace knew his secret, and Mitch thought a good strategy was to discredit both of them in case they went public with his cruel affair.

"I can't tell you why. There are other people involved who would be hurt if this got out, so please keep what I just told you under your Resistol." She eyed his cowboy hat.

"Like who?"

She poked him in the shoulder. "Quit being an FBI agent and drive." She pointed at the light that had turned green some time ago.

"I stopped being an FBI agent more than four months ago. I'm just trying to put the pieces together, because frankly, none of this makes sense."

"How come you quit being an FBI agent?" She could just as easily turn the tables on him. Besides, she was insanely curious. "Was it the drinking?"

He shot her a glare. "Keep it up and I'll pull the truck over and spank you."

"You wouldn't dare." But she kind of wanted to see if he'd actually follow through. "Really, why did you quit? According to Jace, you were an amazing agent and solved all kinds of crimes."

"You're doing it again." He slid his hand down her back, pretending to go for her butt. "Changing the subject. We were talking about you and Mitch, remember?"

"I don't want to talk about me and Mitch. Me and Mitch are old news."

"Are you, though?" All playfulness had left his voice. "Because from my experience, two people don't go to war when they're old news."

He had a point, and under a normal scenario, she'd have to agree that a couple that was truly over moved on and didn't involve an entire town in their breakup. This, however, was not a normal breakup.

"We're definitely old news," she said. "Our conflict isn't about me wanting him back or him wanting me back. Or about me being jilted. It's way more complicated than that, and that's all I'm going to say about it."

"Okay. Fair enough. In the meantime, I'd find a new grocery store and dine at a different restaurant."

She blew out a breath. "At the rate I'm going, I won't be able to afford to shop or eat."

"Mama said she'd give you a good deal on getting your car to the ranch."

"Mama appears to be the only person in Dry Creek who's not taking sides." Though it had been Mama's Towing—the sole tow service in Dry Creek—that had done Stu's bidding, hauling Aubrey's Volvo from the Dry Creek Market to the impound lot. Aubrey didn't blame Mama. She was just doing her job.

Cash nodded. "As soon as she gets your car to the ranch, I'll fix whatever the problem is."

It was an old car with over 200,000 miles on it. More than likely her antique Volvo was just giving up the ghost. The prospect of having to buy new wheels was too depressing to contemplate.

"You're a prince among men, Cash Dalton." She leaned over, grabbed him around the neck, and planted a big kiss on his cheek.

Cash arched his brows. "You want me to pull over so you can thank me properly?"

"I thought we'd decided"—she wagged her hand between them—"this… us…was weird."

"It doesn't mean I don't want to finish what we started." His lips slid up in a grin that was all male. "But yeah, the timing's bad."

"Absolutely," she rushed to agree. "You've got Ellie, I'm going through an acrimonious breakup, we're both looking for jobs. Definitely bad timing." She stopped, having run out of reasons.

"Right," he said, and his mind seemed to wander off somewhere. Then, halfway home, he said, "I had a talk with Ellie last night about the fact that I didn't know of her existence until Marie was on her deathbed. I pretty much told her that her mother kept us a secret from each other. Needless to say, she didn't take it well."

"It's the truth, right? What are you supposed to do, let Ellie believe you never took an interest in her all those years?"

It seemed a shame that Cash had missed out on Ellie's formative years and that Ellie had missed out on having a dad. Aubrey's own parents had divorced when she was a little girl, and her father had died of a heart attack when she was only ten. Perhaps if she'd had a stronger male figure in her life, she wouldn't have settled for jerk-off Mitch.

"That was my thinking," Cash said. "But maybe I should've soft-pedaled it instead of making Marie look like the bad one."

"You didn't intentionally malign Marie, you were just trying to explain where you've been all this time. Ellie must understand that."

Cash looked dubious. "Ellie has me marked as public enemy number one. I don't think there's much I can do to change that, and yesterday's disclosure didn't help matters."

"You guys seemed good yesterday at Jimmy Ray's." The two of them had looked adorable, eating lunch together, like a daughter and daddy day out.

He hitched his shoulders. "I don't know about good, but at least we were communicating, as short-lived as it was." Cash slanted her a look. "She likes you, though."

"That's because I'm a girl." And not Ellie's parent, which made Aubrey the good cop.

He shot her another glance, this time more lascivious than the first. "Girls are good." He was back to being flirtatious. Just one sexy look from him and she was a goner. In a minute, she'd ask him to pull over. Bad timing be damned.

They drove through the ranch gate and found Ellie and Sawyer sitting on the front porch, killing any real chance of that happening.

"As soon as your car gets here, I'll take a look at it," Cash said and drove her up to her front door. "But first, I'm taking my daughter on a horseback ride around the ranch."

Aubrey unfastened her seat belt. "Nice." Before hopping out, she turned in her seat. "Again, I can't thank you enough for all your help."

"Don't mention it."

She slid over and gave him another peck on the cheek, because even though they'd decided romance was off the table, he'd become her friend.

"You trying to kill me?" he asked, holding her a little closer than the innocent kiss called for.

"No. I'm just an affectionate person by nature and you've been a lifesaver." It was the truth.

"I'm affectionate too." He squeezed her ass and winked. "Now, get out of my truck before our mutual affection gets out of hand."

Teasing aside, she got the sense he wasn't as under control as he led on. The evidence had pressed against her leg as he'd goosed her butt. And any semblance of willpower she possessed had deserted her halfway home. Cash Dalton was one of those once-in-a-lifetime men, the kind who could show you a night you'd never forget. His kiss alone still gave her shivers.

She hopped down from his SUV and, to remind herself they were keeping things platonic, she resorted to business. "I ordered Ellie's furniture. It should be here in less than two weeks," she said, then closed the door and climbed her stairs.

By the time she got inside and kicked off her shoes, Cash had backed down the driveway and parked next to Sawyer's Range Rover. She watched through the window as he went up onto the porch.

She didn't want or need a man anyway. Not until she got her life in order.

Today, her pocketbook had taken a major hit. Without work, she'd be scraping the bottom of her savings in no time, which reminded her to see if she was eligible for unemployment. Mitch had fired her for cause, some bullshit about her being insubordinate. The real reason, of course, was that she'd caught him boinking Jill on top of his desk. She didn't know where exactly that fell in the labor rules to collect.

She flipped open her laptop to check her Houzz profile and tweak her website a bit by adding some new before and after pictures.

Anything to drum up business.

There were a few new messages in her email, and she quickly scrolled through, deleting the penis enlargement ad and an alert that someone loved her Pinterest pins. And, much to her delight, an email from the Vegas developer. He wanted to set up a telephone interview in the next couple of days. She read the note three times, then dashed off a reply, trying not to sound too desperate.

Vegas.

Other than leaving for college, she'd never lived anywhere besides Dry Creek. Her mother had also been born and raised here and had recently moved to a retirement community near Sacramento, which wasn't that far away. Only her brother had ventured out of state.

Las Vegas, Nevada. A new place, a fresh start, where people didn't hate her because she'd dumped the town's golden boy. Yes, the change would be good, her head said. But her heart was already homesick.

Get over it, Aubrey. It's time to see something other than your own backyard.

Her cell rang and she rummaged through her bag, hoping the call was from Mama, letting Aubrey know her car was on its way to the ranch. But when she finally found her phone, the caller ID wasn't one she recognized.

"Hello," she answered, eager that it might be someone looking for a designer.

"Hey, Aubrey," the caller whispered.

"Who is this?" She got up and moved away from the fan so she could hear better. "Hello. Are you there?"

"I don't want Jill to hear me, she's in the other room." It was Brett.

Aubrey immediately went on alert. "Is everything okay?" No answer, just rustling in the background. "Brett?"

"Hang on a sec." More swishing noises that made Aubrey think Brett was outside. "Can you hear me now?"

"Much better. Where are you?"

"In the backyard." A year ago, Mitch had built two ramps at Brett's place so he could get his wheelchair in and out of the house. "Whaddya doin'?"

"Nothing much." Why tell him about the shenanigans with her car? It would only lead to questions she didn't want to answer. "What about you?" He sounded a little odd, or maybe because of his PTSD she was being overly sensitive.

"Making plans, but I need your help."

She flopped back onto the couch. "Sounds mysterious. What are you up to, Brett?"

"It's Jill's birthday next week and I want to throw her a surprise party."

"Oh," Aubrey said, trying not to choke on the single word, then immediately searched for a reason why she'd be out of town that day, even though she didn't know what day they were talking about.

"You're better at this stuff than me. I was hoping you could help with the details. Who to invite, decorations for the house, that kind of thing. I'm holding it a week from this Saturday. What do you say? You in?"

"Uh...I don't know, Brett." She stalled, trying to come up with a legitimate excuse to bow out. The hypocrisy of her planning Jill's birthday party was almost comical. Almost. If you had a sick sense of humor. "With the way things are with Mitch and...well, you know."

"Ah, come on, Ree. We're all adults, and Mitch doesn't have a problem with it."

"You talked to Mitch? When?" The son of a bitch was supposed to be out of town, presumably on their honeymoon. She popped her feet up on the coffee table and tried to keep from grinding her teeth.

"Earlier today. He was good with it, even volunteered to buy the keg." Sure he did, the complicit asshole. "You know who all of Jill's friends are. Can you make me a list?"

How the hell was she supposed to say no to that without looking like a total jerk? It would probably take her ten minutes to compile a list of names—if it took that long—and only slightly more time to create a group email or invitation.

"Sure, Brett. But I may be out of town next weekend for the party." She pinched the bridge of her nose. Damn, she was the world's worst liar. "I've got a job interview and they're flying me out."

"Oh yeah?" Brett sounded excited, which made her feel even more like a lowlife. "Where?"

"Las Vegas." It wasn't so much of a stretch. If she impressed the developer on the phone, he'd likely want to fly her out for an in-person interview. Then again, who scheduled job interviews on a Saturday? "They want me there for a few days to get the lay of the land."

Liar, liar, pants on fire.

"Holy shit, Ree, you're not planning to leave us, are you?"

Oh boy, she was digging herself in deeper. She reached under her shirt and unsnapped her bra. The underwire was cutting into her rib cage. She slipped her arms out of her sleeves and managed to take it off without removing her shirt.

"Ree?"

"Let's see if I get the job first." She tilted her head against the sofa backrest and banged it up and down. Since when did she make up stuff to her friends? Never, until now. But it was a white lie, she told herself.

A white lie that would save a good man and a war hero what little shred of joy he had left.

* * * *

Cash decided the horseflies were even worse than the heat. Still, it was a good day. He'd forgotten just how much he enjoyed being on the back of a horse, seeing his family's land—his land now—endlessly roll out in front of him.

Ellie came jogging up behind him. She had an excellent seat and, for a city girl, was fearless, choosing Sugar, one of Jace's more spirited mares for the ride. They'd brought her riding boots from Boston and Cash had borrowed one of the boys' helmets. But the girl needed a good sturdy pair of jeans instead of the stretchy riding pants she had on, which were better suited for riding in a ring than the rugged countryside.

He twisted around in his saddle. "How you holding up?" The heat wasn't ideal, but if she wanted to stick it out, he'd find a trail with some shade trees.

"Good." It was only one word, but it lacked her usual sullenness. Surprisingly, she looked happy, like she was enjoying the ride as much as he was.

"Should we head over to the east end? It won't be as sunny there."

"Sure. Can we canter?"

"You mean lope?" He winked. "No self-respecting cowgirl calls it canter." He tugged on her reins to pull her closer, reached in his saddlebag, pulled out a tube of sunscreen, and slathered a mess of it on her face. She tried to pull away, but he wouldn't let her. "You'll thank me later."

She attempted to wipe off some of the lotion, then cleaned her hands on her britches. He was quickly learning that a good part of raising a twelve-year-old was doing endless loads of laundry.

Sugar, anxious to get the show on the road, began to wander toward the fence. Ellie took control and deftly steered the mare alongside Cash's gelding. He couldn't help but reach over and tweak Ellie's button nose.

"How come you never called my mom after you met her?" she asked, her brows furrowed in challenge.

The question startled him because he thought they'd called a temporary truce, leaving the day to riding and exploring the ranch. But it was obvious she'd been giving their talk from the other night some serious thought and had some things she wanted to get off her chest.

The problem was, he didn't have a good answer, or at least an answer that was G-rated. Still, he wanted to explain the best he could. "I lived on the other side of the country and there was no expectation that we'd ever see each other again."

They let their horses wander idly across the field, leaving the lope—or canter—for later.

"You didn't like her?" Ellie asked, tugging Sugar's head up to keep her from munching the grass.

"I liked her a lot. She was smart, pretty, and from what I could tell, a terrific cop. But we were both young and not looking for permanent situations." Was there a way of candy-coating the fact that he and Ellie's mother had only been scratching an itch when he was talking to an innocent child?

"So you guys were just hooking up?"

Okay, not so innocent. Apparently, Ellie had learned more at her private Catholic school than Cash wanted her to know.

He blew out a breath. "We liked each other, Ellie."

"Just not that much?"

"I guess not." They were having a frank conversation and he wanted to be honest. He'd been twenty-four at the time, not ready for love or commitment.

"What if she had liked you?" She swatted a fly away from Sugar's neck.

"Then she would've called me, Ellie. She knew where I worked and where I lived, but she never did." Not even when she was pregnant with their daughter. "Look, there's no one to blame here. I told you because I didn't want you to think for all those years I didn't want you, that I didn't want to be your father."

Ellie measured everything he said. Cash could see her analyzing his words in her head the same way he did when he was trying to figure something out.

"I don't know why my mother would've kept you from me." She frowned. When he started to respond, she stopped him. "I don't want to talk about this anymore."

"Okay," he said, pulling his cowboy hat lower to shade his face from the sun. "Think about it for a while." It was a lot to digest. "I'm here for you any time you want to talk or have questions. For now, let's ride."

He took off, kicking his gelding into a gallop. Ellie caught up, and he tightened up on the reins because he didn't want her to go too fast until she learned the trail. Dry Creek Ranch wasn't an equestrian arena. The land was uneven, the trees had low-hanging branches, and there were plenty of distractions to spook a horse.

"I don't know about you, but after this I'm planning to jump in the creek," he said, wiping sweat from his forehead.

"Are there fish in there?"

"Yep, but they won't bother you, and you don't have to eat them."

"Ew." Her nose wrinkled up, making him laugh.

They rode for another hour, and Cash showed Ellie some of his old haunts, including a small pond where he, Jace, and Sawyer had built a raft out of dried logs and inner tubes to make it float. To test its buoyancy, they'd first sent it into the water with Grandpa Dalton's Australian shepherd, Ranger. The dog successfully made the voyage from shore to shore.

On their way home, they stopped by the big barn where Grandpa's ranch hands had once stabled their horses. Like his cabin, the old building was half rotted and looked like it would blow down in a strong wind.

"The place used to be something," he said reverently.

"What happened to it?" Ellie shielded her eyes from the sun and stared out over the brown fields, parched from lack of irrigation in the summer, a luxury they couldn't afford.

"Money. Your great-grandfather ran out of it."

He swung his leg over the side of his gelding and got down to check Ellie's cinch. Or rather girth, because it was an English saddle. Among the clutter in the tack room, he'd managed to find the old thing—probably a leftover from years ago, when Angie used to visit the ranch and ride the fancy show jumper her parents had bought her.

Cash planned to eventually teach Ellie how to ride using a Western saddle. It was how Cash's grandfather had taught them to ride from the time they were tykes, and no self-respecting cowgirl would use anything else. But if Ellie wanted to continue with dressage, he'd get her whatever she needed.

"Are you going to fix it up?" she asked curiously.

Her interest surprised Cash. Until this point, she'd seemed indifferent to the ranch, a place that never failed to make his chest fill with pride. There was something about the land, its sheer expanse of rugged beauty, that enthralled him and captured his soul. Grandpa Dalton used to say that Dry Creek Ranch ran through them like blood in the veins, yet none of his surviving children had seen it that way. That was why Jasper had left the ranch to his grandkids. Would he turn over in his grave knowing Cash wanted to sell?

"I'm not sure." He climbed back into his saddle. "Jace and Sawyer want to, but I don't know that we can actually afford it."

"What about you?" she asked. "Do you want to fix it up?"

Again, he was struck by her sudden inquisitiveness. "It's not a matter of whether I want to, it's a matter of coming up with the money." He eyed the barn some more, giving it a thorough examination. "It's a big place that requires a lot of upkeep and it's been badly neglected. You ready to head home?"

She nodded, and he lifted his reins and clicked his tongue. They continued on the trail leading back to the corral where Jace kept his horses. Both horses, sensing their day was coming to a close, picked up the pace. Cash tightened the reins. He was in no rush. It was a pretty afternoon and he and Ellie were making strides, even if they were small ones.

They didn't talk for a while, just letting the peacefulness of the countryside settle over them. Though Ellie was a skillful rider, she wasn't used to an open trail in the middle of nowhere and was taking it all in.

"You having fun?" He hoped their earlier discussion hadn't tainted the ride. But if things were going to work between them, if they had a shot at a real father-daughter relationship, she needed to know the truth.

"I guess," she said, and quickly turned from him as if not to give away any of her true feelings. "It's better than the pool. And it's better than TV, because you don't even have HBO or Showtime."

"HBO?" He lifted a brow. Surely her mother hadn't given her free rein to watch movie channels. "Basic cable must be pretty bad if you'd rather slum it with me." Cash gave her ponytail a tug.

When they arrived at Jace's barn, Ellie asked for her phone. Cash hadn't let her carry it, wanting her to focus on her horse and the ride. He retrieved it from his saddlebag and waited for her to dismount before handing it to her.

"I wanted to take a picture of me on Sugar and send it to Mary Margaret," she said.

"I'll take it." He tried to find the camera feature on her phone, but the screen was locked. "What's your password?"

She rattled off a number, which sounded like someone's birthdate to him, and he snapped the photo. It was at the top of his mind to tell her to change the code when three police vehicles sped up the road toward Jace's house.

He swung Ellie off her horse, impatient to check what was going on. Jace wasn't typically home this time of day, but the boys and their babysitter were, which worried him.

"You think they're here because of Aubrey's car?" Ellie stared across the field where the three SUVS had parked in Jace's driveway.

"I don't think so," he said, more to himself than to Ellie. "Can you finish up with the horses? Unsaddle and groom them?"

"Okay." But she seemed reluctant to stay alone.

"Only for a few minutes, sweetheart. Just long enough for me to make sure the boys are fine." He took off at a jog, calling behind him for her to go inside the barn.

By the time he reached the house, there was a small confab on the front porch. Jace was there, and Cash searched his face to get a read on the situation. Jace was in deep conversation with two deputies and a man in plainclothes, but Cash didn't see anything in his cousin's body language to suggest any harm had come to Travis or Grady.

Jace bobbed his head at Cash in acknowledgment, then motioned for him to come up on the porch.

"This is my cousin, the former federal agent," he told the others, who stuck out their hands to shake his.

"Everything okay?" Obviously it wasn't, judging by the grave expressions on the deputies' faces.

"Beals Ranch was hit early this morning," Jace said. "The fence was cut and two hundred head were loaded into a trailer with at least three ATVs. We found tire tracks."

That was a lot of cattle, worth a lot of money. Hopefully, the thieves hadn't snatched Bealses' breeding stock. A rancher spent years collecting extensive performance data on his cows and bulls, the animals responsible for building a herd. There was no way to quantify that kind of damage.

"Sorry to hear it," Cash said.

Beals Ranch was only a few miles away. Grandpa Dalton and Scott Beals had been longtime friends. Last Cash had heard, Scott's son, Randy, and

Randy's wife were running the ranch now. "I've gotta get back to Ellie, just wanted to make sure the boys were all right." He started down the stairs.

"You want to help us on this?" Jace scrubbed his hand under his hat, where a streak of sweat had stained the band. "Red's got his hands full planning his own retirement party." The two deputies and the man Cash assumed was Red—he had auburn hair—chuckled.

Cash wasn't a cop anymore. And Mill County wasn't such a backwater that Jace could just deputize anyone he wanted to, as if Dry Creek were the Wild West.

He shook his head, calling over his shoulder as he headed back to the barn, "I'd check with local slaughterhouses that have a penchant for shady business practices if I were you." One look at Beals Ranch's state-registered brand on each of the stolen animals and no legitimate auction house would take the livestock. And it wasn't as if you could sell two hundred head of hot cattle on eBay. Either the thieves had a buyer already lined up or they were selling the meat on the black market.

Red threw back his head and laughed. "The boy knows what he's doing."

Nah. Cash was just using common sense. "I'd also talk to places that rent stock trailers. Call it a hunch, but I'm betting your culprits don't own one." And for that many stolen cows, they'd need a hell of a lot more than one trailer.

"He's good," Red said. "Jace thinks you ought to apply for my job, and by golly, I think he's right."

"Nope." Cash rubbed the back of his hand across his forehead. "My days in law enforcement are over."

"Doesn't seem like it," Red called back.

Chapter 12

At five o'clock in the evening, four hours later than scheduled, Mama delivered Aubrey's Volvo. She unceremoniously dumped the station wagon on Aubrey's front lawn and stuck the bill in her face.

"You got cash?"

"No. I've got a credit card." Aubrey turned from the door to find her purse.

"Credit card companies charge a fee." Mama let herself in and looked around the cabin. "Nice place. A little fussy for my taste, but I could get used to it. Now that McMansion you shared with Mitch…well, that was just vulgar."

Coming from a woman who wore grease-stained overalls and a bandanna tied around her stringy hair, Aubrey considered the source and tried not to take offense. She'd decorated that McMansion from wall to wall. At least Mama didn't appear to be part of the Mitch cabal. No, she was rude to everyone. Aubrey's mother liked to call her earthy. Aubrey's take on Mama was that she was simply missing a filter. In any event, the tow-truck driver had been a staple of Dry Creek for as long as Aubrey could remember.

"Here you go." Aubrey handed Mama her Visa.

"I'm gonna have to charge you a few extra bucks for the credit card fee."

Aubrey wanted to argue that it was the price of doing business but decided it was more trouble than it was worth. The car had already put her in the hole. What was a few more dollars?

Mama returned to her tow truck to put the card through and Aubrey followed, hoping to hurry the transaction. She had a piece of leftover quiche in the oven.

"Stu must have it out for you real good." Mama fumbled with the swiping machine, and Aubrey was tempted to tell her she ought to look in to Square or any other credit-card processing system invented in the twenty-first century. "In all my years, I've never seen him have someone towed from that market."

"I guess I'm just special." Aubrey flashed a cheesy grin. "You could've refused, you know?"

Mama pulled the bandanna off her head and wiped her neck with it. "If it wasn't me, it would've been someone else."

She had a point. Still, Mama could've stood on principle. "You knew Stu was being vindictive…you know what this is really about."

Mama handed Aubrey her credit card and eyed her up and down. "You don't look any worse for wear. As far as I'm concerned, you got the long end of the stick. Despite what everyone thinks, Mitch Reynolds is no angel. But as far as you and Jace Dalton"—she cackled—"he ain't ever getting over that awful ex-wife of his."

For hell's sake, did Aubrey really have to say it again? "I didn't leave Mitch for Jace. Jace and I aren't together."

"It's no business of mine." Mama lifted her shoulders. "And if I were you, I'd tell this whole town to stick it where the sun don't shine." She climbed up into her tow truck, slammed the door shut, and took off down the driveway, raising enough dust to choke a person.

Aubrey went back inside the cabin and pulled her quiche out of the oven before it burned. Instead of sitting at the table, she ate in front of the TV. Nothing on but the news. She looked outside the window for Cash's SUV. Sometime around four, he and Ellie left, probably to get food. Aubrey would've fed them but didn't want to interfere with their father-daughter time.

He'd looked good in a black felt cowboy hat and a matching T-shirt. She'd enjoyed watching him wait for Ellie by the side of his truck, his muscular arm resting on the rooftop.

She remembered his hand on her thigh when they'd driven to the ranch after getting her station wagon out of car jail. It had been big, warm, and callused, and she'd nearly agreed to his suggestion that they pull over so she could thank him properly for his help.

That certainly would've gone over well with the prying eyes in this town. She could hear it now: *What's with Aubrey McAllister and those Dalton men?* There was no plural; there was only one Dalton who made her want to have car sex. And it wasn't Jace.

Hmm, that gave Aubrey an idea. Something that might put an end to the rumor about her and Jace once and for all. Like Jace had said, why not give the good folks of Dry Creek something to talk about?

* * * *

At nine the next morning, Aubrey found Cash syphoning gas out of her tank into an old bucket on the ground.

"Morning." He raised his head from what he was doing and flashed her a grin that was better than a first cup of coffee, which, to Aubrey, was pretty much the best thing in the world.

"Good morning." She sat down on the grass next to him, watching while he worked. "Where's Ellie?"

"The boys don't have a babysitter today, so Sawyer took them and Ellie to the waterslides in Roseville."

It seemed early to Aubrey, but in the summer the water park got so crowded they had to turn people away. "That was nice of him."

"More like brave." Cash removed the syphon tube from Aubrey's tank and nudged his head at a gas can a few feet away. "I want to let the tank dry completely before I add the new stuff."

"Okay." He seemed to know what he was doing and she didn't have a clue. "Can you tell if what you took out is contaminated?"

"It looks like water to me." He pointed at the bucket. "See the way the gasoline floats on top? That usually happens when there's water on the bottom."

She stuck her face over the bucket but pulled it away when the strong odor burned her nose. "It smells like gasoline to me."

He nodded and reminded her that water was odorless.

"How do you think the water got in there? A bad batch of gas?"

"Nope." He held her gaze and silently conveyed what she already knew. Someone had intentionally poured the water down her tank. Perhaps it had happened while she was shopping at the Dry Creek Market or on one of her other trips to town, but the bottom line was, someone had wanted to mess up her car.

"I can't freaking believe this." She pressed her forehead against the Volvo's door.

"You have any idea who could've done it?"

"Not a one." She didn't mention that Mitch had been back in town because she didn't think he would do something like this. It wasn't his style to lurk around, sabotaging people's cars. He was too busy spreading rumors. Even his henchwoman Mercedes wasn't devious enough. And Jill Tucker...what could trashing Aubrey's car possibly accomplish?

"We need to go to Jace and report it," Cash said.

"Uh-uh." She shook her head, adamant. "I don't want to get him involved. I've caused him enough problems."

"You at least need to put it on the record in case something like this happens again."

She couldn't afford any more acts of vandalism. If Cash hadn't volunteered to make the repairs, she would've had to dig even deeper into her savings.

"I'll just be more alert in the future," she said so as not to pull Jace into the drama. He had more at stake than she did. Not only did he need his job to support his family, he loved being sheriff. "I don't want people to think Jace is giving me special treatment."

Cash folded his arms over his chest, and she couldn't help noticing how his T-shirt stretched across his broad shoulders, and the way his biceps bulged.

"You're the victim of a crime and Jace is the sheriff," he said. "I don't see how reporting the incident gives you special treatment. It would be the same for anyone else in Dry Creek."

"Okay, I'll think about it." She pretended to acquiesce because she knew Cash wasn't going to quit until she agreed to go to the police. Aubrey turned her attention to the car. "How long do we wait for the tank to dry? I'd like to see if the car actually drives."

He rubbed the scruff on his chin. "An hour should do it. In the meantime, why don't you buy me a cup of coffee?" Cash hitched his head at her cabin.

"Welcome to Chez Aubrey." She swung her arm wide, gesturing for him to follow her up the porch stairs.

Aubrey headed straight for the kitchen and put on a fresh pot in her fancy grind-and-brew coffee maker, one of the things she'd managed to lift from Mitch's on her way out. And why not? She'd paid for the darn thing.

Cash came up next to her and washed his hands in the sink. She used to yell at Mitch that tending to basic hygiene should be done in a bathroom, not a kitchen. But as far as she was concerned, Cash Dalton could wash his hands anywhere he wanted to. He'd been her guardian angel these last two weeks while dealing with his own convoluted life.

"How's Ellie? Did she enjoy her ride?"

"Yeah." He dried his hands on a dish towel and cocked his hip against the counter. "We talked a little bit more about her mom and me. Not sure that went over too well. It's hard to tell what's going on in that small head of hers. One minute she seems receptive to making this work, the next, she's begging me to send her back to Boston."

"It's a lot of change at once. Give her time."

"That's what everyone says." He gazed out the window at the creek. "We'll see how it goes. My parents are coming this weekend. I'm hoping that'll help the situation. They're good people and are thrilled about having a granddaughter." He laughed. "I'm pretty sure they never thought it would happen."

"Are you an only child?"

"Yep." He turned and glanced at the coffee maker. "Is that done yet?"

The machine was still gurgling, but Aubrey pulled the pot away and stuck a mug in its place. She pulled out a carton of low-fat milk. "Sorry I don't have half-and-half."

"I take it black." He peered over her shoulder into her nearly empty refrigerator. "You got anything to eat in there?"

"Eggs, cottage cheese, and a couple of yogurts. I could make you a scramble and some toast."

"Sounds good."

He moved past her, unintentionally—at least she thought it was unintentional—brushing against her backside, and her body instantly reacted. Since finding Mitch with Jill, she'd expected to lose her sex drive. At least for a while. But with Cash, she seemed to be in a constant state of arousal.

To get her mind off the sensation of his groin pressing against her, she handed him the cup of coffee and started on the eggs. He made things easier by taking his mug to the table. That little bit of distance forced her to concentrate on cooking.

"Speaking of weekends, what are you doing next Saturday?"

"Nothing, as far as I know. Why?" His big hands clasped her good-sized mug, making it look like a demitasse cup.

"Brett Tucker is throwing a surprise birthday party for his wife, Jill, and I was hoping you and Ellie could be my plus two." She paused for a second. "I thought if we acted like we were sort of dating, I could lay these rumors about Jace and me to rest. I mean, only if you're comfortable with it. I wouldn't want to do anything that would be…you know, weird for you and Ellie."

He took a long sip of his coffee, watching her over the rim of the cup. "What exactly is 'sort of dating'?" He was being sarcastic.

"You know what I mean." She put her hands on her hips. "We don't have to be in everyone's face about it, which would probably look like we were putting on an act anyway. Just subtle stuff."

He arched a dark brow, his blue eyes dancing with laughter. "Subtle? What do you mean by 'subtle'?"

She could feel her face heat. "I don't know, maybe we kiss or something."

"Kiss, huh?" His lips quirked. He was enjoying this way too much.

But if she didn't think it could work, she wouldn't have asked him for the sacrifice. "You don't have to stick your tongue down my throat. Just a peck on the lips, and you could also put your hand at the small of my back…uh, to make it look authentic."

"Sounds like a lot to memorize."

She balled up a napkin and beaned him with it, then went back to finishing his scramble before he teased her anymore. "Well, are you in or not?"

"Sure…if you think it'll work." He said it as if he had his doubts. "What are you putting in those eggs."

"Cottage cheese. It'll make them fluffy." She turned around to find him standing there. The man moved like a ghost. "What?"

"Just wanted to see what you were doing." He held up his mug. "And get a refill." But he made no move to pour himself another cup. In fact, he put the mug down on the counter while he watched her pour the egg batter into a hot frying pan.

She reached over for a wooden spoon, and he caged her in with both hands. "Want to practice for the party?" Before she could answer, he crushed his mouth against hers.

"Like this?" he whispered against her lips, and wrapped his hands around the lower part of her back. "Or this?" He pressed against the vee in her legs and took the kiss deeper.

"Your eggs will burn," she said but didn't stop, twining her arms around his neck.

"I just want to make sure we get it right. One wrong move and the jig is up, right?"

"Exactly," she murmured, no longer able to hold a coherent thought. He was doing something with his hips that was driving her crazy. Aubrey reached behind her and turned off the stove.

He maneuvered her out of the kitchen, walking her backward.

"Where we going?"

"Bedroom."

She didn't know if she'd make the nine or ten feet down the hallway, but there were an awful lot of windows in the rest of the cabin.

"Ellie won't be home for a few hours," he said. "And you know what they say: Practice makes perfect."

"Mm-hmm." She slipped her hands under his shirt, dying to touch real skin. He shuddered in a breath, and she proceeded to explore, running her hands over his six-pack. Not once had she seen Cash in gym clothes. Either he had amazing genes or he worked out in the dark. Either way, the man's body was in tip-top shape.

When they got to the bedroom, he pushed her down on the bed and fell gently on top of her. His weight, pressing her into the mattress, made her moan. He kissed the side of her neck and throat, his hands roaming over the thin fabric of her camisole, touching her breasts. She wriggled out from under him, sat up, and pulled her top over her head, leaving her in nothing but a white bralette.

Cash hummed his appreciation, running his finger over the space where the lace met her breasts. "Is this for practice, or do you always wear stuff like this?" His eyes traveled over the lingerie, then stopped short where a good amount of her cleavage showed.

"Depends on the day," she said, rucking up his T-shirt for a sight of all those bunched muscles and tan skin. "Thursdays are white lacy bra day, Fridays are black, Saturdays are red." The truth: She was lucky to find something clean, let alone sexy.

"Black and red, huh? Let's practice tomorrow, and Saturday too."

"What do you have on?" She tugged at the waistband of his jeans and peeked down his pants.

He laughed. "Nothing that exciting."

"I'll be the judge of that." She fumbled with his buckle—damn Western belts—and when she couldn't get it undone, he performed the task for her.

Her fingers shook ever so slightly as he watched her unbutton his fly. When they were all undone, she spread the pants apart to find a significant bulge encased in black cotton. Boxer briefs. She liked. But she was pretty sure she was going to like what was inside of them even better.

He lifted his butt and pulled off his pants, belt and all, and dropped them on the floor. Aubrey dragged his shirt over his head, finding a furred chest with a happy trail that ended at the waistband of his shorts.

"What about you?" He stuck his thumbs in the belt loops of her cutoffs. "Does the bottom match the top?"

She assumed they were talking underwear and couldn't remember what she had on. If he was referencing something else...why yes, the bottom most certainly matched the top. "Only one way to find out."

This time he did the honors, tossing her shorts next to his pants on the floor. She looked down at her panties. White Jockey hipsters. Not her first choice, but from the silly smile on Cash's face, he was delighted.

"Nice." He rimmed the edge on the elastic of one leg with his finger.

"Utilitarian," she corrected and waggled her brows. "Sundays are thong days."

"Honey, I don't care if they're big, saggy bloomers." He cupped her crotch. "My only interest lies in what's under them."

She closed her eyes, luxuriating in the feel of his hand there. "Your turn, now."

With the modesty of a stripper, he stood up, hooked his fingers in the elastic waistband of his shorts, and jerked them down, showing off an impressive erection. Ah, who was she kidding? It was more than impressive.

He moved on top of her again, letting her feel the full extent of his arousal, and she purred like a cat in heat.

"Cash?"

He went up on both elbows, dangled his head over her breasts and kissed each one. "Hmm?"

"We're doing this, aren't we?"

"That was my plan, unless you say otherwise."

She raised her arms, wrapped them around his neck, and pulled him back down. "Help me get these off," she said, trying to shimmy out of her panties.

He slid his hand underneath his hips and dragged her underwear down her legs. "What about this?" Cash pulled down the straps of her bralette.

"Go for it."

He searched for a clasp and, when he realized there wasn't one, brusquely tugged it over her head, then pushed up to gaze down on her. "Damn, how did I get so lucky?"

Such a simple declaration. But the appreciation and desire she saw in Cash's blue eyes made her chest flutter and her body warm to a fever pitch.

He covered her breasts, weighing each one in the palm of his hands. She arched her back, desperate for more of him. His mouth moved over her, sucking and licking her nipples until she cried out. Then he began moving south, kissing his way down her belly to the throbbing need between her legs.

Oh boy. Aubrey nearly came off the bed. She fisted both hands in the sheets, thrashing her head from side to side.

As she intuitively knew he would, Cash Dalton could please a woman. "You okay up there?" he asked, a hint of amusement in his voice.

"Oh, oh, oh" was as articulate as she could get. "Cash...I need...I need..."

"What? What do you need, Aubrey?"

The man actually wanted her to spell it out.

"I'm going to...if you don't stop."

"I think that's the point, baby." He kissed her inner thigh while his fingers took over. "Let yourself go. I'll catch up...promise."

His mouth was on her again, laving and licking, driving her insane. Cash reached up and fondled her breasts, using his thumbs to circle her nipples. She shouted out his name as her body began to shake and tremble and strain toward him until she went limp on the bed, blinded by pleasure.

"How was that?" he asked in a throaty whisper.

She tilted her head back on the pillow. "Need you ask?"

"Ready for more?" He hung off the bed and grabbed his pants, and Aubrey heard the tearing of paper.

Then he kissed her, slow and deep, and with one long, hard thrust was inside her.

"That's so good," she said as he pulled out and thrust back in.

He put one hand under her bottom so he could go deeper, pushing in and out. To keep up, she threw her legs around his hips and met him thrust for thrust. Soon, he was pounding into her, harder and faster, making the pressure build.

Holy cow, she was about to have another orgasm. That never happened to her. In fact, she was lucky if she had one.

The hot pull of Cash's mouth on hers filled her with ecstasy. And when he slipped his other hand between her legs she reached for that final satisfaction.

"You almost there?"

"Yessssss," she said between breaths as her body began to spasm. "Oh Cash, oh Cash."

He took her higher and higher, grunting her name as he found his own release and collapsed on top of her. For a few seconds they stayed like that, tangled in each other's arms.

"Am I crushing you?" He rolled them both on their sides and shielded his eyes when the sun shone in his face. In their excited state, they'd forgotten to close the blinds.

"I'm good." And wasn't that the understatement of the world? "Good" didn't even begin to describe how she was feeling.

"I'll be right back." He climbed over her and headed for the bathroom, giving her a nice view of his ass, which she took plenty of time to admire.

She'd wanted to cuddle but now didn't know what she was supposed to do. Wait in bed for him or be supercasual about it? Nothing about them sleeping together had felt casual, but men were different about sex, at least judging by Mitch. Aubrey didn't want to make more of it than it was, so she gathered up her bra and camisole from the floor and slipped them on and found a fresh pair of panties in her drawer.

Cash returned as naked as when he'd left, saw her dressing, and put on his jeans.

"I guess we're done practicing," he said, a hint of disappointment in his voice—or maybe Aubrey had imagined it—and sat on the edge of the bed to pull on his boots. "Are you still offering to make me eggs?"

Was he kidding? She'd make him a twelve-course meal. "Of course. I might even be able to scare up some bacon."

"Yeah?" His lips curved up, and something in her chest fluttered. He tugged on his second boot, got up, walked over to her, and planted a sweet kiss on her lips. "Thank you."

"No, no," she said. "Thank *you*. I haven't had sex like that since...uh, never."

Chapter 13

Five minutes later, they were in the kitchen, practicing their domestic skills. The alternative to postcoital cuddling, Aubrey presumed. Oddly enough, it felt comfortable—and sexy—even though they were both fully dressed. Still, they wore the afterglow of being thoroughly sated. Aubrey in particular, though Cash appeared pretty damn happy.

"You want more coffee?" she asked, prepared to make a fresh pot.

"Nah." He opened the fridge, rested his arms on top, and leaned in. "Okay if I have some juice?"

"Knock yourself out." She tossed out the eggs she'd started earlier and scrambled three new ones in a bowl.

"Who else is going to this party?" He came up behind her and grabbed a glass from the cupboard, brushing her back with his chest in the process.

She tried to focus on the question. "Probably everyone in town, including Jace and the boys. You'll definitely know people."

"This Brett Tucker—he's Jace's high school friend, right? The one who used to play football."

"Right." Aubrey got quiet for a second, remembering the old Brett, the one who still had use of his legs. "He joined the army after graduation and was injured by an IED in Afghanistan that left him a paraplegic."

"The guy in the wheelchair who eats breakfast at the coffee shop?" Cash asked, and Aubrey could see him putting the pieces together. Dry Creek was small enough that a disabled man their age stood out.

"Uh-huh."

"Whoa, I didn't recognize him." Cash brought the glass to the table and poured himself some juice. "I don't think I ever met his wife. Jill, you said her name was."

"Uh-huh. She used to be Jill Beals before she married Brett. Pretty much the only reason Brett keeps it together is for her and his kids' sake. He's excited about throwing this party for her." It was the first time she'd seen an honest-to-goodness spark in him since he'd come back from the war. Most of the time, he only pretended to be his old self.

Cash took a swig of the juice and came over to help her with the bacon. "You sure other kids will be at this shindig?"

She stopped what she was doing and tilted her head to the side, as if to say *are you kidding me?* "This is Dry Creek; kids are always welcome. Ask Jace. Like I said, I'm sure Travis and Grady will be there."

"I guess it would be good for Ellie to meet some more young people her age. Her pool outing didn't go so well. Some girl made fun of her Boston accent."

Aubrey stifled a laugh. Kids were idiots. "She'll be fine. She may be a *ferner*"—she pronounced "foreigner" the good ol' Dry Creek way—"but at the end of the day, she's a Dalton. And around here, that means something."

"I don't know about that. Sawyer and I weren't around much before my grandfather died." He got down a pan from her pot rack and spread out the strips of bacon. "Will Mitch be at the party?"

"Probably," she said, as blasé as possible. But from the grim set of Cash's lips, he wasn't buying her attempt at nonchalance.

He turned to face her. "Are we pretending to be 'sort of dating' for Mitch, or to get negative attention off Jace?"

If Aubrey didn't know better, she'd think Cash viewed Mitch as a rival. "Mitch has nothing to do with this. He knows damned well Jace and I aren't an item."

"Which brings us back to why he started the rumor in the first place, now doesn't it?" His expression turned stern, and Aubrey got a glimpse of what he must've been like as an FBI agent. Formidable.

"I told you, it's complicated."

He made a point of staring out the window at her car. "It's not just complicated, it's criminal. What would've happened if you'd broken down on one of the isolated roads around here in the dark because some asshole decided to put water in your gas tank?"

She got the distinct impression he was thinking of one of his San Francisco cases and wanted to remind him that this was Dry Creek they were talking about. "It's a safe town, Cash; not a lot of crime here."

"Tell that to the Bealses. They just lost two hundred head of cattle in this safe town. What if your car had broken down and the thieves had come upon you? What if they'd been worried about having witnesses who'd seen their faces and could identify them? You ever think of that?"

"First of all, I wasn't aware that anyone had stolen the Bealses' cows, and second of all, this isn't the city."

"Crime happens everywhere, Aubrey, even in seemingly safe havens like national parks."

She had no idea why national parks had been thrown into the conversation. Last she looked, Dry Creek was a Gold Country ranching town. She assumed he was referencing the horrible serial killings in the Presidio that had been splashed all over the news last summer and made a mental note to research who the investigators were on that case.

"All I'm saying is, this stupid rumor about you and Jace has gotten way out of hand and it's time to put a stop to it. Jace obviously can't get involved outside the confines of the law because of his position. But I sure the hell can...and will. Before I do, it would certainly help to know the background."

Aubrey shook her head. "A little high-handed of you, don't you think? Is this because we slept together?"

"What?" he asked, confused. "What does one thing have to do with the other?"

"This is not your problem to solve and yet here you are, riding in on your white charger." She turned the bacon over and started the eggs to give him time to think about that. She'd asked him to fix her car, not her life.

"Jace is my cousin," he said weakly, because both of them knew Jace could take care of himself.

"What's going on with Mitch is tricky." She went up on tiptoes and kissed Cash on the lips. His desire to protect her was appreciated, but not necessary. She could do that herself. "I'm handling it the best way I know how. But thank you."

He rested his forehead against hers. "Just tell me what's going on. I was a federal agent. I know how to keep a secret."

She moved away before the eggs burned and served them on a plate. "Eat and I'll think about it." What would be the harm, other than breaking a promise to Jill? And given that Jill had cheated with Aubrey's fiancé, she wasn't exactly in a position to complain if Aubrey did anyway.

Aubrey brought the bacon to the table and sat while Cash ate. He'd worked up quite an appetite, because he was shoveling in the eggs like he hadn't had a meal in a week.

He stopped chewing when he caught her watching. "You want some?"

"Nope, they're all yours. Bon appétit." She pushed the bacon closer so he wouldn't eat the plate. "When were the Bealses' cattle stolen?" Aubrey was still digesting that. Cattle rustling had become a problem in California since the recession, but this was the first time she'd heard of someone in Dry Creek being victimized.

"The other night. Jace says they cut the fence and loaded the livestock into trailers with all-terrain vehicles."

"Wow, that sucks."

"Yep." He reached for a strip of bacon and looked at her before taking a bite. "Be careful when you're driving around these backroads alone."

She only drove the backroads when she had a client to visit, and because she was currently clientless, she had nowhere to go. "You too," she said.

He stopped eating long enough to raise his brows at her. Typical man. Nah, nothing about Cash was typical. Especially his bedroom performance.

Cash stared at her chest, as if he'd been reading her mind. "Your shirt is inside out."

She looked down, saw the seams of her camisole, and laughed. Then, for fun, whipped it off in front of him and turned it right side in.

"Feel free to leave it off." His eyes stayed pinned on her breasts. "It's hot out."

And it was getting hotter by the minute. She slipped the top back on and righted it to cover any spare parts.

He shrugged, then winked. "Suit yourself."

"Who knew you were such a flirt?"

"Who knew?" he said, then suddenly turned serious. "Uh, hey, for Ellie's sake, I'd like to keep this discreet. The party's fine as long as we're subtle about it. But after the conversation Ellie and I had about her mom, I wouldn't want her to get the wrong impression."

"What impression would that be?"

"You know...that I'm a player."

The comment rubbed Aubrey the wrong way. Why, she couldn't exactly pinpoint. It wasn't like their morning romp had filled her with expectations. She wasn't even interested in having a boyfriend; not so soon after her failed engagement. And obviously he wouldn't want his twelve-year-old to know he was having monkey sex with the woman next door.

But still, his words had kind of stung.

* * * *

Cash walked home after replacing Aubrey's gasoline and took a shower. After charging his phone, he started to call Sawyer to check on Ellie and stopped himself. The kid didn't need an overbearing old man. Knowing Sawyer, he was keeping Ellie, Travis, and Grady thoroughly entertained, and a call from Cash to make sure his daughter was staying hydrated and covered from the sun would put a damper on her day.

Hydrated. Covered from the sun. Damn.

He checked outside to see if Aubrey's Volvo was still there, but it was gone. He'd test-driven it around the ranch, and with the new high-octane gasoline it had run like a charm, confirming his theory that someone had sabotaged the car.

This bullshit had to stop.

The Aubrey-and-Jace rumor and the subsequent fallout had gone on long enough. Cash planned to coax the truth out of Aubrey, and soon. But after her white charger comment, he'd stopped pushing, especially in light of them sleeping together. Maybe jumping into the sack with her hadn't been such a prudent idea. Sure, his dick was still gung ho about it, but his brain was on the fence.

Or was it? That was the problem.

In any event, it had been some morning. One he wouldn't forget.

"Hey, anyone home?" Jace didn't wait for an answer, just let himself inside Cash's cabin.

Cash hadn't heard or seen his cousin's truck pull up. "You walk over?"

"Yep," he said and held up the beer in his hand. "Got off early because I put in an all-nighter after the shit show at Beals Ranch."

"You have any suspects?"

"Not yet." Jace sighed and nudged his head at the porch. "Let's sit outside. It's not too hot today."

It was at least eighty degrees in the shade. Cash was used to summer in San Francisco, where most days called for a fleece or hoodie.

"Let me grab a beer." Cash found a six-pack hiding in the back of the refrigerator and returned to the porch.

Jace pulled two lawn chairs under the eaves of the roof. He propped up his feet on the porch rail and they listened to the creek gurgle and flow.

"I was hoping you'd help me work through it." Jace took a swig of his beer and put it down on the floor.

"Work through what?"

"The Beals case. I'm starting to think it was an inside job."

Cash leaned against the wall in his chair. "How's that?"

"I hope I'm wrong." Jace shoved his hand under his hat and rubbed his head. "I've known that family my whole life. Grandpa was best friends with Scott. But things aren't adding up."

"What kind of things?" Cash asked before he remembered that he didn't want to get involved.

"Like how does nearly a dozen stock trailers get through Dry Creek unnoticed? Because not one person remembers seeing that kind of caravan go through town. Granted, people 'round here roll up and go to bed by nine. But come on! We're talking roughly a thousand pounds on the hoof for each animal; that's a hundred tons of live beef. How do you move that unnoticed? You might be able to in the middle of nowhere, where there isn't a person around for miles. But here? We're not that small, Cash. Denny's horse farm is right there on the road. They were up all night with a sick stallion. No one saw trailers come and go."

Cash had to agree. "What does the inspector from the Bureau of Livestock Identification have to say?"

"Red? He's got one foot out the door. Besides, he's friends with all these guys."

"So are you." It was the life of a country sheriff. Cash had seen the Bureau called in countless times to rural areas because the local lawmen were too cozy with the bad guys.

Jace picked up his beer. "You know me better than that. I don't roll that way."

Hell no, he didn't. He was raised by Jasper Dalton, who lived by the cowboy code. Honor, integrity, truthfulness, and defend the weak. Didn't Cash know the creed well. *Defend the weak.* It sure hadn't helped Casey Farmington.

"You think it's an insurance scam?" he asked Jace, because that was the only way the Bealses would benefit from stealing their own cattle. Slaughter the cows, sell the beef to a shadowy distributor, and report the livestock stolen.

"If they did it, yeah. What do you think?"

Cash hesitated a second. Accusing your neighbor of insurance fraud wasn't something he took lightly, even if it was just him and Jace throwing around possibilities. "It's a decent theory, but you need more than a hunch, Jace."

"I know that. And hell, Cash, I like the Bealses. It would kill me if they pulled something like that. But the cattle business is hard. The drought killed Grandpa. He had to cull half his herd."

Cash nodded. Saving a family business was a strong motivator, even to do something illegal. "Have you been in touch with the Bealses' insurance company? Do you even know if they were insured?" Agriculture insurance was expensive, and a lot of companies wouldn't even write the policies.

"Not yet. Red's looking in to it. The Bealses claim they weren't even home that week. They took their grandkids to Disneyland."

Cash took a sip of his beer. The cold brew tasted good in the heat. "That should be easy enough to corroborate. What're you thinking your next move is?"

"That's what I wanted to ask you." Jace scratched his chin. "How would you proceed?"

Cash got to his feet, walked to the end of the porch, and rested his arms on the railing. Jace was sucking him back in and he wasn't doing anything to stop it. It was just a puzzle, he told himself. He'd always liked puzzles. "When you were at Beals Ranch, were you able to take a good look around? If the Bealses are involved, it's a pretty good bet they slaughtered those animals right on the property."

"We were only in the pasture where the fence was cut and the ATV tracks were left."

"Did you collect the tire tracks? I'm guessing the Bealses have a couple of ATVs." Most ranchers did, for everything from rounding up cattle to getting to places where a truck wouldn't go. "It would be nice to make a comparison, but you'll want a warrant for that. And I'm not sure at this point you want to tip them off to the fact that they're suspects."

"Nope," Jace said. "But I'll go over today under the guise that I want to update them on the case, and have a look around."

Cash didn't need to tell Jace what to look for. Having grown up on a cattle ranch, Jace would know the signs of a makeshift slaughterhouse better than Cash would. While commercial livestock had to be slaughtered and processed at a USDA or California Department of Food and Agriculture-licensed facility, plenty of ranchers did it at home for personal use.

"They would've had to have cleaned the place with a toothbrush and a truckload of bleach to conceal the slaughter of that many animals," Cash said.

"If they did, they're looking at more than insurance fraud. They'll have the USDA and the CDFA up their asses."

And possibly other federal agencies if they were selling the meat on the black market.

Both Cash and Jace turned their attention to the driveway as Aubrey's Volvo nosed its way up the hill, a cloud of dust in its wake.

"I see her car is working." Jace stood up, shielding his eyes, and waved.

"The diagnosis: water in her gas tank." Aubrey would probably be pissed that Cash had told Jace, but he frankly didn't give a shit. It was vandalism, or worse, and the law needed to be aware of it.

Jace looked at Cash with the same intense blue eyes he saw in the mirror every day. "Water in the tank? As in someone intentionally put it there?"

"Yep."

"Goddammit." Jace took off his hat and scrubbed his hand through his hair. "Now this shit has gone too far. Does she have any idea who did it?"

"If she does, she's not saying." Cash gazed across the creek and watched her carry an armload of grocery bags into her cabin. "I don't think she knows, though."

"I'm gathering you're the one who fixed it." Jace followed Cash's line of vision.

Cash didn't respond, knowing where the conversation would go if he did. He and Aubrey were friends—friends with benefits, apparently. Other than that, there was nothing more to say on that topic.

That's why he quickly moved to a new one.

"I've got to ask you something." Cash grabbed his chair again. "The feds are planning to have me testify at Whiting's trial. It'll require a few days in San Francisco. I could leave Ellie with my folks, but I'd rather she stay here on the ranch." She'd meet his parents for the first time this weekend and would probably feel more comfortable staying with the boys until she knew her grandparents better.

"Sure, that's not a problem as long as you're okay with Mrs. Jamison."

"You mean Yoda?" Cash grinned.

Jace crushed his empty beer can and shook his head. "I don't know where Travis comes up with this crap. Trial, huh? I thought by now he'd plead out."

"His attorneys were trying for mental incompetence. The son of a bitch is as crazy as a fox."

Jace tossed his can into Cash's old wine barrel, went into the kitchen, and came back with another beer. "You okay with it? Testifying?"

Cash didn't say anything for a while. There were too many things filtering through his head, like how he'd have to tell a courtroom full of reporters and the victims' families how he...and the Bureau...had botched the case. "I want the piece of shit to fry."

"Yeah you do." Jace popped the cap on the bottle with his cowboy boot. "Whatever you need, Ellie's always welcome with us. With Sawyer too."

"Thanks."

Jace tipped back the bottle, took a long guzzle, and slapped Cash on the back, then handed him his unfinished beer. "I've got to get some laundry done before the kids get home."

He rose and halfway down the driveway called to Cash, "Be good to Aubrey or I'll kick your ass."

Chapter 14

Ellie posted a picture of Sawyer, Travis, and Grady to her Instagram account while they drove home from the water park and, like clockwork, Mary Margaret texted her.

"How's Daddy dearest?" Mary Margaret wrote back.

He was the bane of her existence. He tried to act like Ellie's mom had kept Ellie a secret from him, but she didn't believe him. It was obvious he just hadn't cared enough to go to Boston to visit her, or at least send a card on her birthday.

Even Mary Margaret's dad, who was supposedly "out of the picture," sent presents on Christmas and Valentine's Day. He also bought her a camera once, and a locket that Mary Margaret's mother said wasn't real gold.

Ellie's father hadn't given her the time of day until her mother died.

"How are you guys doing back there?" Sawyer asked while looking in his rearview mirror. "You're awfully quiet."

That was because Grady, who'd called shotgun, blabbed enough for all of them.

"We're good," Travis said and went back to his phone.

"Ellie?"

"I'm good too."

"Should we stop for food? That way I can save you from your dads' cooking."

Her father actually cooked okay; not as good as her mom, though. No one cooked as good as her mom. Every Sunday after church they used to make a bunch of meals and freeze them in case Ellie's mom had a big case to investigate and couldn't come home in time for dinner.

It was weird that her father didn't work. Every time Ellie turned around, he was there, telling her dumb things, like she needed to put suntan lotion on her face.

"Yes!" Grady did a fist pump in the air. "Tacos."

"What do you guys say? Tacos? Or we could get a pizza, or burgers."

"Pizza," Travis said.

Ellie wanted pizza too, but her mom had taught her that it was rude to ask for things. When she went out to dinner with other people, she was supposed to order the cheapest thing on the menu and not get a soda.

"How 'bout you, Ellie? You're the tiebreaker."

"Um...I don't care, whatever everyone else wants."

Sawyer adjusted his mirror and looked straight at her. "Hey, kiddo, Daltons aren't shy. Say what you want to eat and own it."

Everyone waited for her to say something. Grady twisted around in the front seat and Travis nudged her impatiently with his toe.

She was quiet for a long time. But because everyone was staring at her, she finally said, "Pizza."

Travis cheered, Grady did another fist pump, even though he wanted tacos, and Sawyer winked at her. Ellie wondered if they thought she was a Dalton now. Because she didn't feel like one. She still felt like Ellie Tosca from Boston, Massachusetts.

And she still wanted to go home.

"We'll stop at that pizza joint you guys like in Auburn," Sawyer said and grabbed Grady's foot. "Sit straight, buddy."

Travis went back to playing on his phone.

Ellie turned sideways in her seat and sent Mary Margaret one more text. "We're on our way to pizza, so I've gotta go. Hit me later. I've got a plan."

* * * *

On Friday morning, Aubrey stopped over at Cash's on her way to town. Brett wanted to meet with her to talk about Jill's party. As much as she dreaded being involved, she'd committed to it and had to follow through.

"Hey." Cash opened the door barefoot, with his hair wet.

Aubrey heard the TV in the background and assumed Ellie was catching up on another episode of *Full House*.

"Come in. You want coffee?"

"Just for a sec," Aubrey said and followed him, stopping in the living room on the way. "Hey, El, how were the water slides?"

"Good. We went for pizza afterward." Something happened on the show Ellie was watching and she became absorbed in whatever it was.

Cash lifted his arms and gave a half shrug. They went to the kitchen and Cash poured her a cup of coffee and pulled a carton of milk out of the fridge. "How come you're all dressed up?"

She glanced down at her dress, which was something she would've worn to work, as opposed to knocking around Dry Creek, and tried to act casual. "I'm meeting with Brett to go over the party." Aubrey hadn't worn the dress for Brett.

Cash didn't say anything but took his time looking at her.

"What?" She dropped her purse on the counter.

"You look nice, that's all."

"Thank you. I came over to let you know that Ellie's furniture has shipped. I was thinking she and I could go on a field trip to Roseville and pick out bedding."

"I'm not invited?"

"You're absolutely welcome to come. I just wasn't sure you'd be that into pink throw pillows."

"I like bedding as much as the next guy." He was joking, but there was a hint of flirtation in his voice.

She sipped her coffee, the second cup she'd had today, and held his gaze over the rim of her cup. "When are your folks getting here?"

"First thing tomorrow morning. You want to have dinner with Ellie and me tonight?"

"I thought we were keeping this—how did you say it?—discreet," she whispered, though she doubted Ellie could hear anything over the television.

He folded the dish towel he was holding and set it on the counter "Dinner is dinner, Aubrey."

Okay, he was being mature and she was being...bitchy. What did she want, day-after roses? They'd both gotten exactly what they'd wanted out of yesterday's hookup: good sex.

"Yes, I would love to have dinner with you and Ellie. What time?"

"Six? Or we could go to town earlier and do that bedding shopping. My parents are staying at Jace's while they're here because the ranch house is more comfortable. But I should still stop by a grocery store on the way home to pick up a few things."

"My meeting with Brett shouldn't take long. We could go as soon as I'm done." Traffic in Roseville on a Friday evening was no fun, everyone scrambling to get away for the weekend.

"Why don't you text me on your way home and I'll make sure the SUV is gassed up and ready to go?"

"Perfect." She put her cup in the sink and picked up her purse. "I'll see you later, then."

"The car running okay?" He followed her to the door.

"It's like there was never anything wrong with it."

"I'm glad." He touched her back. "I'll walk you out."

When they got to her Volvo, he opened the driver's door and waited for her to get in. She'd hoped for a kiss, but none was forthcoming. *Stop acting so needy, Aubrey.* She chalked it up to being on the rebound, even though it didn't feel that way. Nope, it felt like something altogether different, something she didn't want to look at too closely.

She backed out of the driveway and drove to town, hoping to keep party planning with Brett to a minimum. The e-vite was ready to go; all she had to do was hit the Send button. Brett just had to okay the guest list and add anyone Aubrey had forgotten. Jill, who'd married Brett right after graduation, still palled around with the same clique she did in high school.

Aubrey had been a year behind them and had idolized Jill back then. She'd been the girl everyone wanted to be.

A memory of Jill and Mitch playing around on the beach at Dry Creek flitted through Aubrey's head. It was before Mitch had been Aubrey's boyfriend—that hadn't happened until after Aubrey returned from USC—and they'd all met at the creek for a summer bonfire. Brett had gone into town because Jill wanted marshmallows for s'mores. While he was gone, Mitch and Jill started goofing around, chasing each other in a typical game of grab-ass. No one seemed to think anything of it, but Aubrey's sixth sense had kicked in, and she remembered thinking that their chemistry screamed of something more than friendship. The whole evening she'd felt slightly uncomfortable, like she'd witnessed a betrayal. But by the next day, she'd forgotten all about it.

Until today.

She slipped into a parking spot in front of the coffee shop and cut her engine. Brett was sitting inside by a window that faced the street. Aubrey gathered up her notebook with her list and went straight to his table, avoiding Laney.

She doubted the old crone had been the one to pour water down her gas tank but everyone was suspect.

"Hey, Brett, sorry I'm late." She scooted into the bench across from his wheelchair at the only ADA-compliant table in the place and neatly stacked her notes so she could go through the names with him and get the hell out of Dodge. Aubrey was looking forward to spending the day with Cash and Ellie.

Jimmy Ray came out from the kitchen and waved. It was more for Brett's benefit than Aubrey's, but at least it was cordial, which was more than Aubrey could say for Laney, whose resting bitch face was brittle enough to crack eggs.

Wren was on her way out and said hi to Brett without so much as looking at Aubrey. Another one to add to Aubrey's suspect list. She was feeling very Jessica Fletcher at the moment.

"You want coffee?" Brett started to call the waitress over, but Aubrey stopped him.

"I'm good." If she had any more coffee, she'd have to swim home. "I actually have an appointment and need to get through this as quickly as we can."

"Another job interview?" Brett appeared so hopeful, it filled Aubrey with guilt for lying.

"No, a client who needs bedding to match her new room." That part was completely true. The part about her sleeping with her young client's father she kept to herself. "And that other interview I told you about...uh, it got moved to another date."

Brett brightened, then must've remembered how badly Aubrey needed a job. "But they're still interested in hiring you, right, Ree?"

"We'll see." She had a phone interview with the developer on Monday. "If not, I'll find something else. Vegas isn't all that. Besides, I hate the Raiders." It was Mitch's favorite team.

He laughed and gave her a conspiratorial wink. "Me too. So what else do you have cooking?"

Nothing, that was the problem. "A few things here and there."

"Don't want to jinx it, huh? The good news is, you can come to the party now."

Yep, good news all right. "Uh-huh. And if it's okay with you, I'd like to bring a date and his twelve-year-old daughter."

"Yeah?" Brett pulled back in surprise. He must've believed the rumors about her and Jace like everyone else. "Who's the guy? Anyone I know?"

"He's Jace's cousin, Cash. We're neighbors, and his daughter recently came to live with him and could use some friends."

"Oh, yeah, sure. That's nice of you to include 'em, Ree. And of course they're welcome. Anyone related to Jace is a friend of mine." He flipped through her notebook. "Is this the list?"

"It is. All I need is your approval and I'll get the invites out tonight." Even in Dry Creek, where no one stood on ceremony, a week was awfully short notice for a party.

He perused the list. "I don't see Letty Hall here. She and Jill have gotten real close."

"I'll add her," Aubrey said, distracted. Mitch had come in through the other door and had grabbed a seat in the back. She didn't think he would dare confront her with Brett there, but he was unpredictable these days. "Anyone else?" Aubrey wanted to get the show on the road, especially now that her ex was in the restaurant. There'd been enough drama the last couple of days. She wasn't in the mood for a showdown.

"No, it looks real good, Ree." Brett turned his head. "Who's got your attention back there?"

"Mitch came in. He's sitting in the back." Brett started to turn his wheelchair around and then thought better of it. "You want to go someplace else?"

As if there were any other restaurants to go to in Dry Creek. She supposed they could go to the VFW Hall, but they were here now, and she wouldn't let Mitch Reynolds run her off. "I'm fine."

He leaned forward in his chair. "I don't know what's going on between you two and what Jace has to do with it. But I know that besides Jill and the kids, you're my three favorite people in the world. I wish you could all get along."

"Perhaps someday." It was the best she could offer under the circumstances. And sometime soon, she planned to have words with Mitch. But not now. Not when she was in a rush to meet up with Cash and Ellie. "You want to give the list a second look?"

"Anxious to get to that appointment, huh?" He turned slightly, trying to catch a glimpse of Mitch without being too obvious about it.

"I have to maintain what business I have left."

"It's been that bad, huh?"

She contemplated whether to tell him about the water in her gas tank and how Stu had had her car towed from the market and decided against it. The less he knew the better. "I'm just not used to being unemployed." Aubrey patted his hand. "But something will come up."

Two men joined Mitch at his table. They were probably prospective clients, though Mitch usually met development partners at the job site. She tried to focus on her conversation with Brett, but one of the men was laughing at something Mitch had said and he looked vaguely familiar, though Aubrey couldn't place him. On closer inspection, the third guy

she recognized as Jill's brother, Pete Beals. Last she'd heard, he'd moved
to San Jose and was involved with a startup there.

"I didn't know Pete was in town."

This time, he turned his chair to have a look. "Yeah. The ranch was
robbed the other day by rustlers. Jill's folks lost two hundred cattle. Pete
came home to help them sort out the financials. The other guy, the dude
with the red hair, is a cattle inspector with the state."

"I heard about it from Cash." She took Brett's hand. "I know it must
be a big setback for Jill's parents. I'm so sorry, Brett." Aubrey glanced at
the back of the dining room again. "What does Mitch have to do with it?"

"Nothing." Brett wheeled his chair closer to the table. "He's probably
just saying hi to Pete."

Sure enough, Pete and the red-haired man stood up and got their own
table. Mitch buried his head in his cell phone while sipping his coffee. If
Mitch had seen Aubrey watching him, he was putting on a convincing act
that he didn't know she was in the restaurant. Not once had he so much
as glanced her way.

"Can I keep the list?" Brett asked, bringing her back to their meeting.
"I'd like to have it in case there's anyone else we forgot."

"Absolutely." She tore the pages from the notebook and handed them to
him. "Everything is set up online, so just email me anyone else you want
to include and I'll shoot them over an invite."

"Thanks, Ree. I couldn't have pulled this off without you."

She'd made a lousy list, which had taken less than an hour. In the old
days, before Jill had cheated, Aubrey would've helped Brett with everything
from the food to the decorations. Under the circumstances, though, she
didn't have it in her to be that big of a phony.

Aubrey got up, walked around the table, and gave Brett a kiss on the
cheek. "*De nada*, my friend. I'll see you at the party next weekend."

"Get there a little early. I really want it to be a surprise."

"You got it."

Aubrey waved goodbye to Jimmy Ray and snuck another peek at Mitch.
He wasn't as unaware of her as he pretended to be. And if he was the one
who'd vandalized her car, so help her...she'd wring his thick neck.

A blast of hot air hit her as soon as she stepped outside. On her way to
the car, Mitch's sister, Joanne, zoomed down Mother Lode Road in her
F-150, leaned on her horn when she saw Aubrey, and flipped her the bird.

"Nice, Joanne. Stay classy," Aubrey yelled, then quickly darted a glance
around to make sure no one had witnessed her outburst. Let Joanne make
a spectacle of herself. Aubrey wanted to keep her dignity.

She stood on the sidewalk, searching her purse for her car keys. That's when she saw the bright red word scrawled across the side of her baby blue Volvo: "Hore."

Oh, for God's sake, at least spell it right.

Stunned, she continued to stand there, staring at the writing, willing it to go away. It was broad daylight. Whoever had painted her car had done it in broad freaking daylight on the most traveled street in Dry Creek. She stepped off the curb and touched the door, smearing red paint all over her hand.

Aubrey ran back inside the coffee shop to get a wad of napkins, hoping she could wipe off the paint before the sun baked it on and ruined the finish of her car. As she brushed past the hostess stand, she smacked straight into Mitch's arm.

"Hey, slow down!" He moved in front of her and blocked her from getting by.

"Get out of my way, Mitch. So help me God, if you don't, I'll…"

"You'll what?" He moved into her personal space, towering over her in a way that could only be described as menacing. "What, Aubrey, what will you do about it?"

Out of the side of her eye, a flash of Brett's wheelchair glinted off the chrome on Laney's cash register.

He rolled to where they were standing and craned his neck up at Mitch. "Knock it off, Reynolds."

Mitch threw his hands in the air. "You're right, Brett. I don't know why I let her antagonize me with threats. If you have something you want from me, Aubrey, just say it. Right here. Right in the open," he challenged, a smirk spreading across his face.

She shook with rage. The bastard was actually egging her on, daring her to spill the beans. He'd pushed her too far this time. He had an alibi. But whoever had graffitied her car had done it because of him and his lies.

Hore. She wasn't a hore. She wasn't even a whore.

Enough already. Aubrey was ending this once and for all. She began to speak, took one look at Brett in his wheelchair with the guest list for Jill's birthday party scattered across his lap, and shut her mouth. That was when everything started moving in slow motion.

There was a hazy recollection of a carafe filled with scalding coffee. Mitch's arrogant face. Broken dishes. Shouting. And finally, Jace standing over her with a pair of handcuffs.

After that, everything became appallingly clear. For the first time in Aubrey's life, she was going to jail.

Chapter 15

"Did you really smack a guy with a coffeepot?" Ellie asked.

Cash draped his arm over Ellie's shoulder. "Not now, kiddo." They'd have plenty of time for Aubrey's version of the story when they got home. The duty judge had released her on her own recognizance.

"I...uh...need to get my car. It's parked in front of the coffee shop."

"Jace took care of it." Cash opened the passenger-side door so Aubrey could get in, then made sure Ellie was buckled up in the back seat.

Ellie continued to pepper Aubrey with questions the entire ride home. Cash had never seen his daughter this involved in a conversation.

Frankly, he had quite a few questions himself but was waiting until he and Aubrey were alone. He'd heard about the car. Jace was convinced Mitch had had nothing to do with the graffiti.

"You okay?" He reached over and put his hand on her knee. Her arms were wrapped around herself as if she was cold, so he turned down the air-conditioning.

"Ashamed, mostly. I made an ass of myself."

Ellie stuck her head between the two bucket seats. "Did he hit you first?"

Aubrey shook her head. "He was trying to get a rise out of me, trying to show that he had me over a barrel, and I let him do it. I let him push me until I almost tol—"

"You almost what?" Cash asked.

"Nothing. Never mind. I've already spent too much energy on Mitch Reynolds today." She rested her hand on top of his. "Thank you for bailing me out." She let out a rusty laugh. "That's a sentence I never thought I'd say."

"No bail. I just picked you up."

Aubrey turned to the back seat. "I guess it's too late to go bedding shopping. Sorry, Ellie. We'll go after your grandparents leave."

"That's okay," Ellie said and resettled herself in her chair, resting her cheek against the window.

"Anyone hungry?" he asked, then addressed Aubrey. "Or did you eat in holding?"

She swatted his arm. "No prison jokes. At least I had the cell to myself. And, yes, I'm starved."

"You want to stop somewhere, or I could fix us something at home?"

"Home," she said.

He looked in his rearview at Ellie, who was staring out the window. "Is home okay, Ellie?"

"Uh-huh."

They pulled into Dry Creek Ranch and he took the fork in the road to his cabin. The sun was setting, and the sky was white, filled with streaks of color. When they pulled up in the driveway, Ellie hopped out and ran for the door. Cash suspected she'd left her phone at home when he'd gotten the call about Aubrey and had rushed her into the SUV to go.

He and Aubrey sat in the vehicle for a few seconds, letting the silence stretch between them. Then he leaned over the console and kissed her. She clutched his shoulders with both hands and held on so tight, Cash let the kiss go on longer than he should have. He just sank into her, stroking her hair and back, reveling in the way she fit so perfectly into his arms.

When they finally pulled apart, he said, "Are you over this Mitch guy or not?"

The question seemed to shake her. "Over him? Is that what you think today was about, me not being over him?"

Cash didn't answer, but throwing a hot coffeepot at her ex-fiancé didn't exactly sound like an act of indifference.

She leaned her head against Cash's leather backrest and pinched the bridge of her nose. "You do, don't you?"

Again, he treated her to silence. He didn't want to identify the reasons why it mattered to him, but it did. It mattered a lot, even though he wasn't in a place to offer her anything more than friendship. And sex.

He had a grieving daughter to take care of and a case that still gave him nightmares. He hadn't been able to protect Casey Farmington; how was he supposed to...he just wasn't in a position to offer any more than he could.

She blew out a breath and hit her head against the seat. "Remember I told you that Mitch cheated on me? Ugh...I can't believe I'm about to tell you this. You have to promise you won't tell a soul."

"What happened?"

"He had an affair with Brett Tucker's wife, Jill. Brett came back from Afghanistan broken, Cash. I don't mean the lower half of his body. I mean…everything. He's a shell of the happy-go-lucky man he used to be. The football star, the hometown hero, the man voted most likely to take the world by storm. Gone. All those men are gone.

"You know how many times Jace has had to rush to the Tuckers' house because Brett was threatening to…The only thing that keeps him going, the only thing, is his children and Jill. He's loved Jill since they were fourteen years old."

She took a deep breath. "And Mitch, Brett's alleged best friend, took her from him too."

"Shit." Cash rubbed his hand down his face. "So Jace also knows about this?"

She nodded. "I told him when I didn't know what else to do."

"And it's his opinion that you should both take this to the grave with you?"

She reared back. "You sound like there's another option."

"Yeah. It's called the truth. You just got done telling me how this guy has lost everything. You want him to lose his dignity as well? Jeez, his wife is running around on him with his best friend. If you and Jace know about it, there's bound to be others who do too. You think he won't eventually learn of their duplicity? His wife's infidelity? Of course he will. Then he's going to blame you two for trying to keep him in the dark about it."

He stopped, trying to contain his irritation. Lies ruined lives. If Marie had told him the truth about Ellie, he would've known his daughter. If his bosses had told the public the truth about the Presidio murders, they might've caught a killer before he struck again. Lies didn't just ruin lives, he corrected himself, they caused people to die.

"No, Aubrey, you're not doing the man any favors. You're just killing him softly, that's all. And for what? So you can be the town pariah and have your car vandalized and towed. Lose work accounts. So Jace can hand his opponent the perfect ammunition against him and get himself creamed in the election?"

Aubrey did a double take. "My God, I can't believe you're that heartless. Brett can't take another hit, especially not something like this. Brett is disabled, Cash. Do you know how much it would kill him to know that his best friend is doing what he can't do with Jill?" It wasn't a question, it was a rebuke.

"Are you privy to what Brett can or cannot do?" He nudged his chin at her in challenge. He doubted Brett had shared his sexual capabilities with

Aubrey. Just because he was paraplegic didn't mean he couldn't perform in the bedroom. "You do know that women have affairs on nondisabled men every day of the year?" The point was that only Brett and Jill knew what was going on in their marriage, and it might not have anything to do with Brett's injuries.

She unbuckled her seat belt. "So basically, you're telling me I should blow the whistle?"

He didn't know if he would call it blowing the whistle. But, yeah, she should stand up for herself. "What I think is that lies have a way of biting people on the ass and hurting the ones you're trying to protect. That's what I'm saying."

"I'm not lying," she said, and reached for the door. "I'm just not telling. There's a difference."

Not as far as Cash was concerned. Omitting the truth was the same as a lie, plain and simple.

She got out of the SUV and started walking toward the footbridge.

"Hey, where are you going? I thought I was making us dinner."

"I've lost my appetite." She kept walking.

He followed and caught her arm. "Don't do this. We were having a frank discussion and I gave you my opinion. I think your heart is in the right place, Aubrey. But I think your logic is skewed."

She spun around. "I can't ask you to understand. Brett isn't your friend and you have no idea what he's going through."

"Nope, I don't." But he had an inkling of what she was going through. She'd just spent the last five fucking hours in a jail cell because that asshole Mitch had pushed her to the brink.

She took his hand and laced her fingers in his. "I'll take a rain check on that dinner. I'm tired, grouchy, and want desperately to shower."

He got it. He was disappointed, but he got it. "If you change your mind, you're always welcome." If it wasn't for Ellie, he'd offer his shower, a glass of wine, and his bed as long as she was interested.

Cash returned to his cabin to find Ellie pawing through the pantry. She was standing on a footstool, trying to pull something down from the top shelf. His stomach pitched at the sight.

"Hey, kiddo, let me get it. I don't want you to fall." He took down the box she was reaching for. "Cereal? Don't you want a real dinner?"

"Cereal is a real dinner." She hopped off the stool as spry as a goat and got a bowl and spoon out of the cupboard.

"You've been hanging around Uncle Sawyer too much." He opened the fridge and searched the contents. The day had gotten away from him with Aubrey's arrest and he'd failed to shop. "How about pasta?" It was his go-to dinner these days.

She reached around him and got the milk. "Cereal's good."

He swiped the box off the counter and read the ingredients. "You know how much sugar this stuff has in it?" Why the hell had he let her put it in his basket the last time they'd grocery shopped? "We're going to have to hide this from your grandmother."

She grabbed the box, piled it on top of her bowl along with the milk, and took it to the table.

"Why do I have to meet them?"

He held on to his patience. "Because they're your grandparents, your flesh and blood, and they're dying to meet you."

"Why? Why all of sudden do they want to meet me?"

"All of a sudden?" He joined her at the table. "We talked about this, Ellie. They learned about you when I did." Not much more than a month ago. "Had they known about you sooner, nothing could've dragged them away."

Her small, heart-shaped face scrunched up. "Right."

They were back to this again. "El, how about you give them a chance? I don't think you'll be disappointed."

"I don't want to," she said and stared into her cereal bowl. "I don't want to meet any new people. It's hard enough keeping everyone that's supposedly related to me straight."

His first inclination was to tell her she was being a spoiled brat. That his parents weren't getting any younger and they deserved to know their grandchild. But when her bottom lip began to quiver, he saw something other than obstinance; he saw fear, and his heart melted.

"They're going to think you're great, Ellie." He picked up the box of cereal and poured himself a handful.

"I don't care," she said with a steely stare, trying her damnedest to sound indifferent. Tough. But Cash saw the vulnerability in her blue eyes.

"Okay." He stuffed the cereal in his mouth. "Then it shouldn't be a problem, right?"

He could feel the anger vibrating through her clear across the table. She'd wanted him to fold and let her have her way. *Not happening, kid.* She'd thank him for it later.

Ellie got up from the table, washed her bowl out in the sink, and stormed off to her bedroom. By ten, her bedroom had gone dark, and Cash assumed Ellie was fast asleep. Tomorrow would be a big day for both of them.

Twice, he considered calling Aubrey to see how she was doing and convinced himself she was probably asleep. Besides, he wasn't her boyfriend. Yet he went out on the porch to see if her cabin lights were still on or a reflection from her TV. Nothing.

He stood at the railing, smelling the sweet scent of pine trees in the breeze. In the distance, the hoot of a lonely owl echoed off the creek, breaking the stillness of the night. The sounds and smells brought him back to his childhood, to summertime at Dry Creek Ranch when life was uncomplicated. Taking a deep breath, Cash stared up at the star-filled sky.

At midnight, he turned in, sleeping soundly only to be awoken a few hours later. At first, he thought it must've been the nightmare that still plagued him. But as his eyes began to adjust in the darkness, he saw a shadowy figure standing next to his bed. Cash moved so fast, he nearly knocked the lamp off his nightstand.

The figure jumped back and let out a bloodcurdling scream.

Ah, Jesus. Ellie.

Cash flicked on the light and reached for her. "What's the matter, sweetheart?"

"You scared me."

That made two of them, because she'd nearly given him a heart attack. He pulled her onto his lap and cradled her head against his chest. "Sorry. I was asleep."

It took a while for it to register, but she was letting him hold her. Not just letting him, she was clinging to him like a barnacle.

"I had a bad dream," she said, her voice shaking.

He knew something about bad dreams. "What was it about?" he whispered.

"My mom. She didn't have a face anymore. Worms had eaten it off. And she was trying to talk to me, but she didn't have a mouth." Ellie snuggled closer.

"I've got you, sweetheart."

"It was so horrible." She shuddered, and he tightened his arms around her, brushing the back of her hair with his hand.

"I have them too, sometimes. They're awful."

"What are yours about?" She seemed to relax somewhat, pressing her cheek against his shoulder.

"A case I had. I dream about it a lot." They often kept him awake into the morning. The circumstances of the nightmare varied, but it was always Casey Farmington's dead eyes staring back at him.

"Did someone die?"

"Yes." Maybe he shouldn't have told her that, but her mother had been a homicide investigator. "The bad guy is in jail now. So when I have the dream, I just think about that and it goes away."

"What can I think about to make mine go away?"

He pondered it for a while. "You could remember her face, the way it really was. How does that sound?"

She sniffled, and he found a handkerchief in his bedside table and wiped her nose.

"Sometimes I'm worried that I'm starting to forget what she looked like."

"Nah," he said. "You'll never forget her. When your stuff comes, we'll frame a big picture of her and hang it on the wall, and we can get a small one made and put it in your wallet. But, Ellie, you won't forget your mom. She'll always be with you." He touched her heart and then her temple. "Here and here."

"I don't want to forget her." She swiped Cash's handkerchief across her eyes. "I miss her so much."

"I know you do, sweetheart." He took the handkerchief from her and wiped her tears with his two thumbs, wishing he could take the pain away. "You want to stay in here tonight?"

"Maybe just for a little while." She yawned, and her eyes drooped to half-mast.

He pulled the blanket down and settled her under it on the other side of the bed. She looked so tiny laying there that it brought out all kinds of paternal instincts he didn't think he had. Suddenly, he wanted to hunt the monsters under her bed and wipe out the bad dreams in her head.

He leaned over and smoothed her brown hair away from her forehead and kissed the top of her head.

"Sleep tight, little one. I'll be right here if you need me."

In a groggy voice, she said, "Okay, Dad."

He froze. She'd never called him that before. The sound of it—Dad—made something move in his chest.

Chapter 16

The Bealses had indeed been to Disneyland with their grandkids the week their cattle had gone missing. Jace had a plane manifest and a slew of time-stamped pictures at the Magic Kingdom to prove it. They most definitely had an alibi.

What they didn't have was a motive.

As it turned out, the Bealses didn't have livestock insurance; it was too expensive and "not worth the paper it was written on," according to Randy Beals. So the working theory that they'd stolen their own cattle and made it look like someone else had was a nonstarter, leaving Jace at square one.

"How the hell does two hundred head of cattle disappear into thin air, that's what I want to know?"

"Were you able to get a look around their ranch?" Cash sat in the chair on the other side of Jace's desk.

"Just from the driveway to the house. What's the point, if they're no longer the suspects?"

"You said it before." Cash flicked a speck off his boot. "Two hundred cattle didn't beam themselves up, Scotty. Someone either snuck them off the property very quietly or they were slaughtered there."

Jace tilted his chair against the wall until it rested on two legs. His head hurt from trying to crack the case.

He turned his attention to Cash and examined his cousin. Since the weekend he'd been a little off. "What's going on with you and Aubrey? Why didn't she come to the barbecue Sunday afternoon before your folks left?"

Cash let his eyes wander around Jace's office, pretending he was too caught up in his own thoughts to thoroughly answer the question. It was a mechanism for avoiding something he didn't want to talk about. Jace knew, because he did it himself, and he suspected Sawyer did it too. Daltons were cowboys at heart, and cowboys weren't sharers when it came to personal stuff, at least in Jace's experience.

"Cash!" Jace stuck his finger in front of Cash's face and guided him back so they were locking eyes. "Aubrey. We were talking about Aubrey."

"You were talking about Aubrey. I was talking about the case." He sighed, resigned. "She's pissed at me and I'm a little pissed at her...and at you."

"Me? What did I do?"

Cash got up, shut the door, and leaned against Jace's file cabinet. "I know about Mitch and what he did and how he's holding it over both your heads because of some heroic notion that you and Aubrey have."

Jace should have seen this coming. Pillow talk. Jace was far from an expert when it came to relationships—just look how his own screwed-up marriage had gone—but he was pretty sure Cash and Aubrey were tangling up the sheets together.

"It was Aubrey's call to keep it secret," he said. "But I can't say I disagreed with it. I don't want to be the guy who tells one of his best friends that his wife is stepping out on him, especially a friend who's been to hell and back."

Cash walked to the window and gazed outside, resting his hands on the sill with his back to Jace. "It's not my business," he said. "And I'm certainly not going to tell anyone. But lying...it has a way of catching up with you, Jace."

It was something Jace had had to wrestle with. If his friends had only come to him with how unhappy Mary Ann had been, maybe they could've fixed their marriage. By some divine intervention, Jace had been able to hold it together when she'd walked out on him and the boys.

He wasn't so sure Brett could. Not too long ago, Brett was in such a funk that Jace feared he'd do something stupid. Jace didn't want to send him back to that place. And finding out about his wife and Mitch would surely make Brett spiral. "Brett isn't wired to handle the truth right now."

But Cash was avoiding the real question, and Jace wasn't about to let him get away with it. "So this is why Aubrey didn't come to the barbecue?"

"You'd have to ask her," Cash said.

He was doing that Dalton thing—deflecting—which told Jace there was more going on between Cash and Aubrey than recreational sex. For now, Jace decided to leave it alone. His cousin's personal life was Cash's to screw up any way he wanted. And Aubrey was no fragile daisy. But the town had picked sides in the Aubrey-Mitch marriage debacle, and she could use some backup. In other words, now wasn't a good time for Cash to be throwing a bunch of morality at her. She wanted to protect Brett at all costs and that was her prerogative as far as Jace was concerned. After all, she was the one taking the bulk of the shitstorm for it.

"Fine," Jace said. "Change of subject. How do you think it went with Ellie and your parents?"

"As good as can be expected. They, of course, were crazy about Ellie. Ellie...well, she's still testing the waters."

His mom had brought a dozen presents. Ellie had certainly liked that, though she'd pretended to be indifferent. Even his dad, who was quiet and often remote, had been so attentive that Cash had asked his mother, "What have you done with my real father?"

"Oh hush." She'd swatted him. "This is a dream come true for both of us. The only thing that could possibly make it better is you finding a nice woman to settle down with."

He'd laughed because it was her constant refrain.

By the end of the visit, Ellie had warmed up somewhat, taking her grandparents to the barn to show them some of her dressage moves on Sugar. No easy feat, because the horse had been trained to cut cattle, not perform in an arena.

His folks reacted with so much pride, Cash thought they'd burst from it. And though Ellie had remained aloof, he was pretty sure she'd been tickled by the attention.

Cash's only regret was that Ellie hadn't been more affectionate. Her grandmother had wanted to snuggle with her and Ellie had drawn an invisible line in the dirt.

"It's normal," his mother had assured him. "In fact, I'd be worried about her if she was too open, too accepting. She's a smart, cautious girl, just like her father." She'd poked him to get her point across.

All in all, it had been a positive visit. He just wanted Ellie to find her footing with him.

"Let me ask you something." Cash turned his focus back to Jace. "When Mary Ann left, did the boys have nightmares?"

Jace tried to remember. It had been more than two years since she'd walked out. "Nah, but they were clingy. Grady used to hold on to my leg to keep me from going to work in the morning. I think they thought I'd walk out and never come back." Like Mary Ann had. "Why, is Ellie having nightmares?"

"Yeah. You think I should get her grief counseling?"

"I suppose it couldn't hurt." Jace hadn't done it when his ex deserted them; perhaps he should've. But other than chasing off babysitters, which the boys did for sport, they seemed fairly well adjusted. At least, he thought they were. "But kids are pretty resilient, Cash. Ellie's in mourning and she's in a new place. There's bound to be a bad dream or two. I wouldn't worry too much about it."

Cash sank into the chair again. "That's the thing; since she came into my life, I worry about everything. Is she eating right? Is she getting too much sun? Is she on her phone too often?" He rubbed his chin. "I'm crazy, right?"

Jace chuckled. "Nope. Welcome to parenthood. Word on the street is that the worrying never ends, so get used to it. In the meantime, I wouldn't get too worked up about the bad dreams. All kids have them."

"I'll see how she does." He stared at the wall for a few moments, lost in his own thoughts, then, just as quickly, snapped back. "You need to get on to the Beals property again to take a good look around."

Cash had returned to his default: the case. He could tell himself he was through with law enforcement all he wanted to, but Jace knew it for the bullshit it was.

"My gut tells me those cattle never left the ranch," Cash continued.

"You still think it was some sort of a mobile slaughterhouse setup?" Jace asked.

That would've been mighty brazen, unless, of course, the thieves knew the Bealses would be away for the week. Jace didn't know how many employees they had or whether their hands even lived on the ranch. It was something else to look in to.

"That would be my hunch."

Cash's hunches were usually spot on. He was one of the best investigators Jace knew.

"What's Red say about all this?" Cash asked.

"Not a lot; he's too busy planning his retirement party. He did contact about a dozen auction houses, though, to see if any cattle with the Beals brand had shown up. *Nada.*" He leaned across his desk and jabbed Cash in the shoulder. "You should take the job."

Cash got to his feet. "Nope, I'm done."

Funny, for a done guy, he'd just spent forty minutes going over the case with Jace as if he was the lead investigator.

"Gotcha." Jace flipped a pencil at him. "Sawyer and I think we should build up the ranch again, start a cow-calf operation like Grandpa had. Why don't you run that?"

"With what money?" Cash asked. "We can't even afford the property taxes. How do you plan to pay for a breeding herd, a new barn, feed when we experience the next drought? Hell, we don't even have enough to fix the fencing."

"That's what banks are for, Cash. The land, the houses, it's all paid off. A lender would give us a loan in a second. Half the developers in Northern California, including Mitch, would sell their firstborn for Dry Creek Ranch. But we're not selling, I can tell you that right now."

"You have to make payments on loans. Do you and Sawyer have a plan of how to even pay the taxes? Because I sure the hell don't."

He grabbed his hat off Jace's rack and put it on his head. "The Bealses. Get a warrant if you have to, but make sure an evidence crew combs that ranch with a fine-tooth comb ASAP. Mark my words, your answers are there."

When Cash left, Jace got on the phone. It was time to do a little judge shopping.

* * * *

Cash found two things on his porch steps when he got home: a subpoena to testify at Whiting's trial and Aubrey.

"When I accepted it from the guy, I thought it was mail, like a certified letter," Aubrey said as she read the subpoena over Cash's shoulder. "Are you in trouble or getting sued? Did I screw up?"

"Nah. I'm a witness in a murder trial." It was a simplification. He'd been the lead investigator on the Whiting case until he'd gotten taken off it. "I don't know why they just didn't email me." Being served on his family's ranch seemed like overkill. It wasn't as if Cash would skip the date. He wanted justice for Casey Farmington and the three other women Whiting killed.

"The Presidio murders?" Aubrey sat on the top step and hugged her knees, drawing Cash's attention to her long bare legs. They were tan and perfect, and he remembered every inch of them wrapped around his waist.

"Yeah," he said, not surprised she knew about the case. It had been splashed across the news for twelve straight months. The entire year, reporters had dogged him. The Bureau had a strict policy against talking to the press. Everything had to go through the public information officer. Cash had made the critical mistake of following the rules. Maybe if he hadn't, Casey would still be alive today.

He sank down next to her, put his face in his hands, and massaged his eyes.

"You don't want to do it? You don't want to testify?"

Not particularly. Besides not wanting to relive Whiting's vile confession, which surely would be the bulk of Cash's testimony because he'd been the one to get it, he didn't want to have to discredit the agency he'd given his life to. "It's complicated."

"Does it have to do with the reason you quit being an FBI agent?" she asked.

"I was fired." He took off his hat and put it down on its crown.

"Why?"

It was a fair question, but Cash had avoided talking about it in any great depth because despite everything, he still felt loyal to his former employer. "My bosses and I had a difference of opinion."

Aubrey gave him a long assessment. "What does that mean?"

"It means I didn't agree with the way we were handling the case."

"Weren't you entitled to your opinion?"

He laughed, but there was no humor in it. "Let's just say there was a lot of politics behind the scenes, supervisors who were hoping to make their bones on the case. I got in the way of that, and because I was lower on the pecking order...well, you know what they say: Shit rolls downhill."

"I don't understand. What does politics have to do with a murder investigation?"

Beautiful, smart, and perceptive. Where had she been all his life?

"You would think," he said and brushed a strand of hair that had come loose from her ponytail out of her face. "You still mad at me?"

"I was never mad. And you're changing the subject."

"Yes, I am." He leaned over and kissed her. She tasted good, like maple syrup and coffee. "Did you have pancakes for breakfast?"

"Uh-huh." She fisted her hands in his shirt and pulled him in for another kiss. Whether she'd been angry with him before was up for debate. But clearly, she was over it now judging by her kisses. "How about you? What did you have for breakfast?"

His hands wandered, roaming freely over her blouse. It was loose and easy to get under, and he took full advantage, fondling her breasts. "I went to the coffee shop after I dropped Ellie and the boys off at rock camp."

"Rock as in music?" She moved onto his lap.

They were still kissing, and he wanted to focus on that instead of talking. Actually, he wanted to focus on a whole lot more than just kissing.

"No, as in rocks. Gemstones and that kind of thing. Wanna go inside?"

"Okay," she said, a little breathless.

He didn't bother to wait for her to follow him across the porch. Impatient, he scooped her up and carried her inside. She giggled, and for some crazy reason it made him even harder than he already was.

"Don't drop me."

He gave her a look like she'd insulted his masculinity, then proceeded to pretend to drop her. More giggles, and his fly strained to the point of bursting.

"We might have to skip foreplay," he whispered in her ear.

"I like foreplay." She played with his belt buckle as he made his way to the master bedroom. If she didn't stop, he was going to take her up against the wall in the hallway.

"Then we'll have foreplay," he said and brushed her hand away. "But don't blame me if I don't make it to the end of the rodeo."

"I have the utmost faith that your ride will be a heck of lot longer than eight seconds." She dragged his shirt over his head and ran her nails down his chest, making him suck in a breath.

He pulled down her shorts—thank God for elastic waistbands, because he was too hurried to mess with buttons and zippers. This time, she had on a thong similar to the one she'd worn on the day he found her climbing through her old office window. Just a mere scrap of lace that was hotter than hell.

She started to take it off and he immediately pressed her hand down. "Leave it," he said in a growl.

The blouse and bra, though, had to go. He wanted his hands and his mouth on her breasts. With some dexterity, he managed to get both off in about a second flat. The bed was a few feet away and he didn't know if he'd make it without being inside her first. Cash had never felt this kind of urgency before. He'd always had a hearty appetite for sex, but this was different, like a craving that couldn't be quenched.

She began working on his jeans. He could do it more deftly, so again, he pushed her hands away and somehow managed to get the legs off over his boots.

"That's a good look." She laughed as he stood there in nothing but black cowboy boots.

"Hush." He pressed his mouth against hers and kissed her long and hard, shoving her against the wall. "Not gonna make it to the bed."

Cash pushed the thong to one side and felt her. "You're so wet for me." Knowing that he could arouse her that way, that fast, whipped him higher.

He rubbed his erection against her, and she moaned with pleasure and threw her head back against the wall. Cash lifted one of her legs and hooked it around his hip and entered her with one hard thrust. Aubrey whimpered, and for a second he thought it may have been too much. But when she grabbed his ass and pushed against him, he wrapped her other leg around him and carried her to the bed, walking and moving within her at the same time.

By the time they got to the bed, he remembered that in his desperation for her, he'd forgotten a condom. "Shit."

"What?"

"No protection," he grunted, knowing he should stop but finding it next to impossible.

"I'm on the pill." She pulled him to the edge of the mattress and thrust up, pleading for him to go faster. Harder.

He slid his hands under her and pushed her further back on the bed so he could mount her. Then he reached in his nightstand and pulled out a strip of condoms. Marie had said she was on the pill too. He didn't for one minute think Aubrey was lying, but it wasn't in his DNA to take risks. His job was to protect her.

"Hang on." He pulled out, feeling immediately bereft of her warm tightness.

"No, come back," she protested, trying to pull him back down on top of her.

"One second, I promise." He suited up, cupped her ass, lifted her up, and slammed back in. She whimpered, then clawed his back to urge him on. Cash pumped into her a like a crazed man. "This okay?"

"This…this is amazing," she said in a breathy voice.

He kissed her breasts and worked his way up to her neck and throat, ending at her lips. Who knew that maple syrup was an aphrodisiac? His hands fondled and rubbed her full breasts. Whoever said more than a handful was a waste was full of shit. He'd never been particular about size, but Aubrey's breasts did it for him. They were round and firm and high, with pretty pink nipples. Her legs—damn, he loved Aubrey's legs—gripped him hard.

"You ride horses?" he said against her mouth.

"Occasionally, why?"

"Strong thighs." He lifted her bottom so he could go deeper.

"Oh, oh, Cash." She clung to his shoulders as she tried to meet him thrust for thrust. "This is soooo good."

"Let's slow down." He wanted it to last, to make it as good for her as humanly possible, even though he was holding on by a thread.

She twined her arms around his neck and scraped his earlobe with her teeth. It was erotic as hell. He let her roll him over so she could get on top and she rode him that way, giving him a spectacular show. God, she was gorgeous.

Cash gripped her hips, guiding her faster, and when he could tell she was close, he touched her with his finger, drawing circles around her center. She cried out, and he could feel her convulse around him, her whole body shaking. He thrust up, over and over again, trying to draw out the orgasm for as long as it would last.

Then he rolled her under him to take his turn. He tried it slow at first, staring into her green eyes, feeling his throat clog with every stroke. It was the eyes, he told himself. Bottomless pools of emerald. They were bewitching him.

He increased the pace, losing his ability to hang on any longer. She moved with him, keeping the tempo he'd set. And before long, he felt himself standing at the top of cliff. With one fluid stroke, he tumbled down, calling her name.

Afterward, they lay there for a while in each other's arms, silent except for the whir of the ceiling fan and their breathing. He was slick with sweat, and Aubrey's skin was rosy. She curled up next to him and rested her head on his chest.

"That was intense."

A little too intense, Cash thought but didn't say anything. She'd crept in too deep, and he didn't know what to do with that. Not now, when everything else was so complicated.

He played with her hair, which had completely fallen out of its rubber band and was now spread across his chest. It was soft and smelled like fruit and he liked twirling it around his finger.

"Why didn't you come to Jace's barbecue?" He hadn't planned to ask her that, or to let on that he'd been disappointed when she hadn't shown. But this was what happened after mind-blowing sex. You opened yourself up to feelings you didn't want to face.

"I thought it should just be family. For Ellie. And for your parents, who are just getting to know her."

"Not because I disagree with your handling of Mitch?"

She snuggled closer. "No. You're entitled to disagree and I'm entitled to handle the situation any way I see fit."

She was indeed. But Cash fervently thought she was making a mistake. Lies begot more lies until the lies blew up in a person's face.

"When do you have to testify?" she asked, segueing back to their unfinished conversation about the case.

"Next Monday. Jace said he'd take Ellie for the night while I'm in San Francisco."

"I'd offer to come with you for moral support, but I have a job interview."

"You do?" He rolled over to face her. The news had surprised him, though he didn't know why. Obviously she needed employment, and from what he could tell, she was a top-notch designer, someone who would be sought after.

"Mm-hmm. I had a phone interview this morning. It went pretty well, I guess, because he's flying me out to Las Vegas Monday morning."

"Vegas?" He didn't want to call it panic, but the idea of her moving away...well, she'd just sprung it on him and he hadn't been prepared. "Is that where the assignment is, or would this be permanent?"

"Permanent. They're huge developers, much larger than Reynolds, and they have residential projects across Nevada. Unlike Mitch's company, they have an entire staff of interior designers. If I get it, I would have minions."

He should've been more enthusiastic for her. Aubrey certainly was and why shouldn't she be? It sounded like a great career move. Big company, a growing city, minions. "They pay well and offer benefits? I hear Nevada employers don't have the same labor requirements as California." The truth was, he didn't know dick about Nevada's labor laws.

"I'll find out if they offer me the job," she said, running her fingers through his chest hairs.

"But you'll probably get it, right? I mean, they wouldn't fly you out unless they were serious."

"I hope so."

She sounded so damn happy about it that he felt like a forlorn idiot and tried to remind himself that they were neighbors with benefits. Friends. Nothing more. He'd wanted it that way. In fact, he'd been the one to insist they keep anything remotely romantic on the down low.

"You okay?" she asked, cocking her head to one side.

"Sure. Why wouldn't I be?" He kissed her, trying to make it light, not desperate. But he couldn't control the urgency in which he took her lips and her mouth, because by this time next week, she might not be around to kiss anymore.

She wrapped her arms around his neck, fully giving herself over to him. "You do realize your boots are still on?" she whispered.

He stared down at his feet and saw the black Justins. "Ah hell, I didn't kick you, did I?"

"Not at all, or maybe you did, but I was too busy feeling amazing." Her face lit up. Cash had a sudden compulsion to tell her not to go on the interview, but what good would that do? He stopped himself.

What was the point?

"I guess we got a little carried away." He kicked off the boots and heard them hit the ground, then rolled her under him.

All thoughts of Vegas could wait.

Chapter 17

Aubrey's bedroom was starting to resemble a dressing room at Nordstrom. There were so many clothes strewn on the bed, she could no longer see the comforter. Jill's surprise birthday party shouldn't have been a big deal dress wise. A pair of jeans, boots, and a T-shirt was pretty much the dress code for any Dry Creek affair, including weddings. Sometimes, the ladies changed it up with denim skirts and lace tops, but that was as formal as it got.

This time, though, she wanted to make a bold statement. Something that said don't mess with me.

"I liked the black one." Ellie lay in the middle of Aubrey's clutter, watching the fashion show.

"The dress or the pantsuit?"

"The dress, the one that's cut out in the back."

Aubrey liked it too, but it was a wee bit over-the-top for a backyard barbecue with vinyl tablecloths and buckets of Budweiser. "You don't think it's too dressy?" Why was she asking a twelve-year-old when she knew damned well it was too much?

Ellie shrugged. "It's my favorite."

It was Mitch's too, another good reason not to wear it.

"What about this one?" Aubrey twirled in the floral halter dress she had on. "Too Laura Ashley threw up?"

"Who's Laura Ashley?"

Kids these days. "A famous fashion designer."

"Never heard of her."

"That's probably because they don't sell her clothes at Hollister." Aubrey checked her ass in the mirror on the back of the door. "Well, what do you think?"

Ellie propped herself up on a couple of throw pillows and appraised the dress. "I still like the black one better."

"The black one's out, so stick to the program. We're focusing on this one now."

"It's okay. I like the top part."

That wasn't very helpful. She wondered if Cash would like it. "Does my butt look big?" How could it not with giant posies plastered on her derriere?

Ellie studied her behind. "No. It's good in that."

At least that was something. Aubrey could tone it down with flat sandals, instead of the three-inch heels she usually wore with the dress when she met with her city clients. She took another look in the mirror. "Then this is it."

"What should I wear?" Ellie asked.

It was on the tip of Aubrey's tongue to say anything Ellie wanted, but what would be the fun in that? "Should we check out your closet?"

Ellie shrugged. "Okay."

Cash had gone with Jace on something that had to do with the Bealses' stolen cattle. He'd been tight-lipped about it and had asked her to watch Ellie for an hour or so, which wasn't a hardship. When Ellie wasn't being sullen, she was delightful.

Ten minutes later, they played *Project Runway* in Ellie's room. This time, Aubrey sat on the bed while Ellie tried on clothes. For a girl who'd worn uniforms to school, she had quite a few outfits. Jeans, shorts, skirts, and dresses.

"I like those," Aubrey said of a pair of white jeans with little daisies embroidered down the sides.

"I don't think kids around here wear stuff like this." Ellie went to the bathroom to check herself out in the mirror. Another thing for Aubrey to add to the list. They could get a full-length mirror to hang behind the door at a Walmart or Target as soon as they went on that shopping expedition.

"Sure they do," Aubrey called to her. "What we need to get you are some cowboy boots." She'd put that on the list too. That was something Cash and Ellie could do together. The man knew a thing or two about boots. She laughed to herself, remembering him in bed with them on.

Aubrey laughed a lot these days, despite losing her job, her home, and a fiancé she never really loved. Her whole world had been turned upside down, yet she'd never been happier.

With Mitch, everything had been a test.

Although they'd grown up together, they'd only started dating when she'd come home from college and Mitch had hired her to work for Reynolds Construction. He'd been a great boss, rewarding her with bonuses and commendations when they made their sales goals. And in the beginning, the romance had been sweet. Not the kind of stuff musicians wrote songs about but steady and solid. He'd bring flowers every Friday night and make her breakfast in bed on Sundays. And for the first couple of years, that had been enough.

But after a while it became apparent that her place in the relationship was to be the woman behind the man. When she made him look good, he reciprocated by giving her a trinket or whisking her away for the weekend to stay at a fancy resort. The rest of the time, their relationship stayed flat. Basically, roommates with benefits whose sole conversations revolved around work.

She'd chalked it up to the highs and lows of any long-term partnership. But as the years went by, the romance continued to stagnate. Her mother and her friends convinced her that marriage would infuse new life into the relationship.

It wasn't as if Mitch hadn't pressed the issue. Every year at tax time, he proposed, usually with a quip about how much they could save if they filed jointly.

Each time, she threw out a lame excuse for why they should wait. Until one day she decided she wasn't getting any younger, wanted to have kids, and had already invested ten years in the relationship.

What a mistake that had been. Not once had Mitch made her feel the way Cash did. Like every day held more promise than the last.

In just a few weeks, Mr. Cash Dalton had left his mark. But could a woman fall that quickly for a guy, or was she simply on the rebound? The question would be moot if she got the Vegas job. It was an eight-hour drive from Dry Creek Ranch, too far to maintain a relationship. Maintain? What she and Cash had could hardly be called a relationship, she reminded herself.

"Aubrey, there's a spider in here," Ellie yelled from the bathroom. "Could you kill it?"

Aubrey found Ellie standing on the toilet seat, a daddy longlegs creeping along the old linoleum floor. She ripped off a piece of toilet paper, snatched the spider up, and took it outside to let it go.

Ellie followed her to the porch. "Why didn't you kill it?"

"Because it wasn't hurting anyone and spiders eat flies."

"I'd rather have flies in the house than spiders," Ellie said. "I hate them."

"Tell your dad; he'll kill them for you." Aubrey suspected Cash would do anything for his little girl. Case in point: Ellie's pink bedroom redo.

"He has before," Ellie said in such a matter-of-fact way that it made Aubrey grin.

As they stood on the porch, talking about spiders, a delivery truck came up the long driveway. Aubrey shielded her eyes to see if she could read the logo on the side of the truck.

"I think that may be your furniture," she told Ellie.

Ellie climbed up on the porch railing to have a better look and nearly gave Aubrey a heart attack. The rotted wood wasn't strong enough to hold even a petite child.

Aubrey circled Ellie's waist and lifted her off the top rail. "It's not safe, El."

Together, they went down the stairs to wait. Furniture deliveries to Aubrey were something akin to Christmas morning. She loved watching her clients' reaction and joined in their excitement. From Ellie, though, she wasn't feeling it.

"Well, are you anxious to see how everything looks?" She draped her arm over Ellie's shoulder.

"I guess," Ellie said, with the same reaction Aubrey showed when her mother made split pea soup. "Was it superexpensive?"

"Not too bad." Aubrey pulled Ellie in for a hug. It was sweet of her to be conscientious about money, especially because Cash was out of a job. "Your dad just wants you to enjoy it, so no worries."

Ellie didn't say anything, but Aubrey sensed she was conflicted. Perhaps money had been really tight for her and her mother.

The truck got up to the house, then hung a U-turn so the tailgate faced the porch. Two strapping guys hopped out, one holding a clipboard.

For the next thirty minutes, they unloaded while Aubrey told them where to place the pieces she'd picked out. When the deliverymen left, Aubrey played with the positions of the furniture until she got everything just right. The room was coming together.

"Put that over there." She handed Ellie a lamp and pointed to the nightstand. "When we go to town we'll get a better lampshade." The one it came with was plain white, not very imaginative.

They heard tires crunching gravel and dirt. Cash was home. Ellie ran to the living room to look outside the window.

"It's not my dad," she called to Aubrey, who was trying not to look overanxious.

"No? Who is it?" Sawyer probably. Aubrey knew he came over a lot to raid Cash's refrigerator.

"I don't know, but whoever it is has a truck like Uncle Jace's."

Well, that described 99 percent of the vehicles in Dry Creek. Aubrey strolled into the living room to see who it was only for the truck to continue up the road and stop directly in front of her cabin.

She squinted at the familiar-looking Ford and watched Mitch get down from the driver's seat. What the hell was he doing here?

"Do you know him?" Ellie asked.

"Yep. Satan has come calling. Let's see what he wants."

The two of them headed outside and crossed the footbridge to Aubrey's house, Ellie trying to keep up with Aubrey's long strides. Mitch, who'd been standing in front of Aubrey's door, must've heard them over the roar of the creek and turned around.

"What do you want, Mitch?"

Mitch crossed his arms and started to say something profane, then stopped himself as soon as he saw Ellie. At least he had the decency to realize his language wasn't fit for a child.

"You and I need to talk." He looked at her, and then at Ellie, as if to say *get rid of the kid*.

Aubrey wasn't afraid of Mitch Reynolds. But the idea of keeping Ellie around just to irk him was appealing, even though she had no intention of putting Cash's sweet little girl in the middle of this.

"Hey, Ellie, there's ice cream in my kitchen. Why don't you go fix yourself a bowl. I'll be right in."

"No, thank you." Ellie wouldn't leave her side, bless her heart.

With arms akimbo, Ellie tried to mimic Mitch's stance. Aubrey noted that she still had on the white jeans with the daisy embroidery. There was a smudge on the knee, probably from moving the new furniture around.

"El"—Aubrey bent down and kissed the top of her head—"Mitch and I have to have a grown-up discussion. Go inside and eat some ice cream, please." As Ellie started for the stairs, Aubrey whispered in her ear, "I'll tell you everything, promise."

As soon as Ellie disappeared behind the door, Mitch said, "What kind of crap are you up to, Aubrey?"

"I have no idea what you're talking about."

He was psycho. She couldn't remember what she'd seen in him in the first place. Compared to Cash, Mitch looked like an overgrown frat boy. Everything about him reminded Aubrey of a self-indulgent child.

Cash, on the other hand, was all man. All cowboy.

"You know exactly what I'm talking about."

"No, I don't. What I do know is, the rumor you've spread about Jace and me has caused me no end of problems, including my livelihood, and if you keep it up, my lawyer says we're going to sue." Okay, she'd pulled that one out of her ass. She didn't have a regular manicurist, let alone an attorney. But Mitch, being in construction, knew all about lawsuits and how they could grind his business to a halt. Why not put the fear of God in him?

"Who's your lawyer?" He bobbed his head at her. "Who?"

She reached for a name, any name, and came up with "Jean Luc Mennard, that's who. Go ahead and look him up. He'll chew you up and spit you out like that disgusting tobacco you put in your mouth."

Mitch leaned against his truck, like he wasn't the least bit worried. "You're still a total whack job, I see." He tilted his head at Aubrey's living room window, where Ellie's face was smashed against the glass, spying on them. "Who's the kid?"

"Cash Dalton's daughter, not that it's any of your business."

"You throw Jace over for his cousin?" Mitch laughed, and she wanted to shove her fist in his face.

"Did you throw Jill over for another one of your best friend's wives?" She squinted up at him defiantly, letting him know she had the goods to crush him in this town. "Don't mess with me, Mitch."

He let out a bark of laughter. "The best thing that ever happened to me was the day you walked out. To think, I could've been stuck with you for the rest of my life."

To think she could've been stuck with a man who had so little honor that he'd boff his best friend's wife. "Mitch, what do you want?"

"I want you to stay away from Jill's party on Saturday. Knowing you, you'll make a scene and blow everything out of proportion, like you did at the coffee shop. Save us all the drama, Ree, and make yourself scarce. I'll even get your car detailed for you."

So, Mitch was running scared. Interesting that he'd brought up her car. "Brett wants me there, Mitch, and I wouldn't miss it for the world." She flashed a big saccharine smile. "Jace will be there too, and he knows what you did this summer."

"God, you're crazy. Why don't you move to Sacramento or San Francisco, where you can get the help you need?"

"Did you pay someone to graffiti my car and put water in my gas tank, Mitch?" He probably put Leroy up to it. Leroy was the only person she could think of in town who couldn't spell "whore."

Mitch made the cuckoo-cuckoo sign with his finger. "I'm serious: get some help. And if you and Jace care about Brett, you'll keep your mouths shut. It's not like anyone would believe you anyway."

Probably not after Mitch had started his ugly rumor campaign.

"Brett would," she said. "But the difference between you and me is that I could never hurt Brett. Never."

"Whatever, Aubrey." He opened his truck door and started to get in. "Just try to contain the crazy for an afternoon. No one needs another replay of your coffee shop melt down. You're lucky I dropped the charges."

After she'd spent five hours in a cell that reeked of stale urine.

"You're lucky I didn't aim higher with that carafe."

He rolled his eyes, got in his truck, and slammed the door closed.

Aubrey had no intention of letting him drive off without giving him a piece of her mind. And a warning. "Don't you dare screw up Jace's chance at reelection. Do you hear me, Mitch?" She jerked the door open before he could drive off. "I'm talking to you."

"Let go of the door, Aubrey."

He tried to wrestle it closed and knocked over a Dutch Bros coffee cup in the struggle. The lid popped off and coffee spilled all over the passenger seat. "Goddamn it. Now look what you've done." He hurriedly cleared a stack of papers before they got soaked.

A parcel map caught her eye and she leaned in to get a closer look. "What's that?"

He jerked it away, but she'd worked at Reynolds Construction long enough to be able to read a plat upside down.

"That's Beals Ranch." She knew from the road designations that flanked the property lines.

"What it is is none of your business." He hastily tried to cover the map, but it was too late. She'd seen the red markings that carefully blocked sections of land.

Someone was planning a housing division.

Mitch shoved the map along with a pile of other papers behind his seat, then searched through the glove box for napkins. She stood there, trying to process what she'd seen, while he cleaned up the mess. As far as she knew, Beals Ranch wasn't for sale. The property had been in Jill's family for generations and was still a working cattle ranch. If it had been on the market, everyone in Dry Creek would've known about it. The Bealses, like the Daltons, were an institution in the area.

Maybe someone had made them an offer too good to refuse. Surely not Mitch. Reynolds Construction did well, but not well enough to afford a thousand California acres of flat, usable land. And if someone else had purchased the property and hired Mitch's company to develop it, word would've spread through the valley like wildfire. Mitch also wouldn't have acted so squirrelly when Aubrey saw the plat. The blowhard would've bragged about bagging the biggest project in the valley and how rich he was going to get.

No, something was up. Before she could probe for more details, Mitch slammed the door, spun his truck around, and sped away. Ellie raced out the door and down the porch steps.

"What did he want?"

Aubrey caught Ellie in a hug. "Nothing important."

"He looked mad, like he was going to do something to you."

"Nah, that's his everyday look." Jackass, moron, cheater, take your pick.

"Does my dad know him?" Ellie stared past the trees, where they could still see the back of Mitch's truck jackknifing at the end of the road.

"I don't think so, but your Uncle Jace does. They used to be best friends."

"They're not anymore?"

"Nope." Aubrey ruffled Ellie's hair. She was an inquisitive kid, that's for sure. "They had a falling out. Let's go finish your bedroom."

* * * *

Cash couldn't believe he was getting sucked into this. Jace had rolled up to the cabin at nine in the morning, said he didn't need a warrant because the Bealses had given him permission to search their property, and he wanted Cash to come along. For some deranged reason Cash didn't fully understand, he had agreed. Almost gleefully.

So here they were, trying to find where thieves might've set up a mobile slaughterhouse without drawing attention from any of the neighboring ranches. It was a big spread, and there were lots of pockets where there wasn't another house for miles. The closest neighbors were Denny's horse farm and Dry Creek Ranch. They all shared the same artery—Dry Creek Road—to Highway 49, which turned into Main Street and went straight through town. There was no other way in and no other way out unless you went by helicopter. But with acres and acres of land between ranches, a person could set up any number of illicit enterprises and no one would be the wiser.

That was why Cash was working under the theory that the thieves had literally set up a chop shop on the ranch rather than drawing attention to themselves by trucking all those cattle through town. Black market meat was a good business. Shady restaurateurs, grocers, butchers, and even some distributors could snatch up prime cuts of beef for a fraction of the price of USDA-approved meat. It happened all the time in San Francisco.

"I'm not seeing anything that raises suspicion," Red said. The inspector had met them at Beals Ranch and had walked the barns with them.

If the animals had been slaughtered on-site, chances were good they'd find traces of blood, bones, hide, or even some whole carcasses. There was a lot of ground to cover. Cash had suggested searching the barns first because they were controlled locations that would serve an illegal slaughterhouse setup well. But that didn't mean the thieves hadn't used one of the Beals pastures.

"Let's go back to where you found the ATV tracks," Cash said, even though Jace had said they'd thoroughly combed the area. Still, it made sense that the thieves would stay as close to the cattle as possible, instead of moving them to another location. It would've taken too long, for one thing, and herding two hundred head on the backs of three-wheelers was a noisy enterprise.

"I think that's a waste of time." Red checked his phone; perhaps he had another appointment. "Truthfully, I think this whole expedition is futile. By now, any evidence left behind is either in the ground or has been eaten by birds and animals."

He was probably right, but if they found something, even something small, it could turn into a good lead. Right now, they had nothing.

"If you've got somewhere to be, Cash and I can finish up here." Jace sounded cordial enough, but Cash knew his cousin well enough to recognize annoyance. He thought Red was phoning it in.

"Nah," Red said. "Let's go check it out; it certainly can't hurt."

That was Cash's way of thinking. They piled into Jace's truck and Red followed them in his own vehicle. It took about twenty minutes to get to the pasture where the cattle had been grazing, the scene of the crime. Some of the drive was on a well-maintained dirt road, but a good chunk of the trip required all-wheel drive across rutted and bumpy fields. Because of the heat, the fire danger was high, so Jace took it slow. All it took was one spark in the grass from a hot exhaust pipe or muffler.

Unlike Dry Creek Ranch, the Beals had managed to weather the drought. Their fences were sturdy, their outbuildings well kept, and the land hadn't been overtaken by weeds.

"Nice place," Cash acknowledged out loud.

"Yep. This is what Dry Creek Ranch could look like."

"If we won a Powerball jackpot." When was Jace going to get it through that thick head of his that reviving the property was a pipe dream? "I think Beals Ranch is twice the size. It must be worth a pretty penny."

Jace slid him a sideways glance. "Is that all you can think about? There's history here, Cash. This is the Bealses'…our …heritage, for God's sake. But all you seem to see are dollar signs."

Cash resented the remark. It made him sound like a money-grubbing piece of shit. "Unlike you, I'm practical. You know what you could do for the boys with the proceeds from Dry Creek Ranch? For one, you could send them to college."

Jace visibly bristled. "We do fine."

"Oh yeah. Then I gather you're socking away money for Travis and Grady's education."

Silence. Yeah, that's what Cash thought. A sheriff in a small rural county didn't make a big salary, and unfortunately, that's what it took to raise a family in California.

"The way things are going, you don't even know if you'll get reelected," Cash said.

"Then I'll become a full-time cattle rancher."

Cash laughed, because no one in this state ranched full time anymore. The land was too valuable to run cattle. Most ranchers had day jobs to make ends meet. They raised livestock because they wanted to preserve a culture and lifestyle that had been handed down to them through the ages. But if they wanted to pay their mortgage and put shoes on their children's feet, they needed an outside income.

"Get real, Jace."

Jace steered around a grove of trees where a small herd of Angus had assembled to take advantage of the shade. "We'll come up with something, Cash. But we're not selling."

They'd had this conversation so many times, Cash didn't bother to argue. For now, Dry Creek was a good place for Ellie. Safe, with plenty of room for a kid to stretch her legs. He wanted her to have it long enough to make the same kinds of memories he'd made here as a boy. What happened after that…well, they'd have to wait and see.

Jace cut the engine where the fence had been repaired, the point of entry where the thieves had unloaded their ATVs. Cash got out and walked off the area.

"How big was the cut in the fence?"

Jace came over and pointed to two yellow markers that were spaced at least fourteen feet apart. Definitely enough room for a large rig to get inside. Cash crouched down, dug under the grass, and let a scoop of dirt sift through his hands.

"Over there is where we found the tire tracks."

"Do the Bealses have ATVs?" Without the insurance component, it pretty much ruled them out as suspects. Still, the suspects could've used the Bealses' ATVs in the theft and—in a perfect world—left evidence that would help identify them. Sure, like a business card. Wouldn't that be nice?

"Yep. We already checked that out. They don't match the tracks."

Red pulled up behind Jace's truck and took his time joining them. It looked to Cash like he was on the phone. The Bureau of Livestock Identification, an arm of the California Department of Food and Agriculture, was probably like any other state agency. Strapped for resources. Cash assumed Red's territory was a large swath of the state. And with the rise in livestock thefts, he had his hands full.

Jace wasn't as sympathetic. He gazed over at Red's truck and rolled his eyes.

"When is he retiring?" Cash asked.

"Officially, a couple of weeks. Unofficially, it looks like today."

Cash had to admit that Red didn't seem too invested in the investigation. This wasn't your average cattle-rustling case; two hundred head was a big deal. He would've thought Red would be more involved, retirement or not.

Cash stood by the fence, gazing over the land, trying to identify where he would've set up shop. The field was fairly remote, though sound carried in the still of the night. And in darkness, the thieves would've needed light.

"Any electricity out here?"

"Nope. They probably brought a generator."

Cash nodded. "What's over there?" He directed Jace's attention fifty or so feet away and started hiking toward the spot.

"Where?" Jace came up behind him.

"Over there." Cash pointed. It could've just been a trick of the eye, but the grass looked flatter there than it did in the rest of the field.

As they got closer, he could see tire tracks and didn't think they belonged to an ATV. But there hadn't been a trail from the fire road where the fence had been cut. Whoever drove here came from another direction.

Red's truck door slammed. He cupped his hands over his mouth and shouted, "Did you find something?"

Jace waved him over.

"I think this is where they set up some kind of staging area," Cash told Jace and walked around the disturbed ground, trying to find the continuation of the tracks.

"There." Jace pointed. "They came from there."

Red joined them. He was out of breath and sweat had soaked through his Western shirt. "What did you find?"

Cash kicked the tracks with his foot. "See the way the grass is flat and the ground indented? I think they parked a trailer here."

Red squatted and took a closer look. "How do we know this wasn't one of the Bealses' rigs, delivering water or feed? It wasn't here before."

"Or we didn't see it before." Jace made eye contact with Cash.

"It was pretty easy to miss. If that herd over there"—Cash pointed at the trees, where more than twenty cows stood in the shade—"had been here, I probably wouldn't have noticed anything."

Jace followed the tracks for a distance. "Check it out. If I'm reading it right, we're talking multiple tires."

That was Cash's initial impression when he'd first seen the tread marks. "A semitrailer. But where did it come from?"

"Beats the hell out of me." Red snapped a few pictures with his camera.

"I'm thinking they barreled right through the fence." Jace continued to scan the area and kicked the dirt. "The ground is so dry, it didn't leave impressions until they parked, and with the weight of the cattle inside…"

It was as good a theory as any, Cash supposed.

"I don't know; we saw the ATV tracks clear as day," Red said.

That could've been intentional, Cash thought. "I'm operating under the theory they did everything right here."

"Slaughtering two hundred head? That would've taken hours and hours," Red said, unconvinced.

"Convenient that no one was home." Jace exchanged another glance with Cash.

Red looked at both of them. "Inside job?"

It was a good guess. The question was, if not the Beals, then who on the inside was behind it?

Chapter 18

"Well, did you solve the case?" Aubrey greeted Cash at his own cabin door.

He took quick stock of the empty front room and crushed Aubrey's mouth with his. "Where's Ellie?" he whispered.

"In her new room. Furniture came. Want to see?"

"I want to kiss you a little more first while we still have some privacy."

"Kiss away." She wrapped her arms around his hips and pulled him firmly against her because she was a troublemaker that way.

A door squeaked, and they both pulled apart, knocking off Cash's cowboy hat in their rushed attempt not to get caught.

"Hey, Ellie." Cash bent down and collected his Resistol from the floor.

Ellie turned to Aubrey. "Did you tell him?"

"Tell me what?"

Aubrey waved him off. "It's nothing. Come see Ellie's room." She grabbed his arm and pulled him down the hallway. They could talk about Mitch later, or never. As far as she was concerned, the topic of her ex-fiancé was boring with a capital B.

"Can I at least wash my hands first?"

"Yes, but hurry. We worked really hard—didn't we, Ellie?—and want to show off the fruits of our labor."

Cash ducked inside the hallway to use the bathroom.

"You didn't mess up the bed, did you?" she asked Ellie. Even though they had to make do with the old bedding, which was beyond ugly, Aubrey had fluffed the comforter the best she could and made a nice arrangement with the pillows.

"No, it still looks good."

Despite Mitch's unannounced visit, she and Ellie had had a terrific time today, decorating and talking and eating peanut butter and jelly sandwiches together. And although Ellie wasn't as excited about the new furniture as Aubrey would've expected, she seemed to be coming around.

New dad, new place; all these things took some getting used to for a little girl.

"All right." Cash came into the living room. "Let's see this masterpiece of a bedroom."

Aubrey jumped up from the couch, but Ellie seemed reluctant. "Don't you want to be the first to show your dad, Ellie?"

Ellie rose slowly, walked to her bedroom, swung open the door, and waved her hand over the threshold, inviting Cash to step in.

"Wow, this is some bedroom," he gushed. "It's like something out of a magazine." He examined the birdhouses on each bed post, crouching down to assess the workmanship, which, for the price, was pretty good. Sturdy and made from real wood.

Aubrey had never dealt with the vendor before and was pleased that the real thing had been a close replica of the catalog picture. Often, that wasn't the case. Aubrey had had to return more products than she could count because they were anemic versions of what was advertised.

Cash sat at Ellie's desk, and Aubrey laughed when he tried to stuff his knees underneath.

"You like it, Ellie?" He got up and gave Ellie's shoulder a squeeze.

His expression was so hopeful, Aubrey's throat clogged. There was something about a big, strong cowboy working so hard to please a child that made her heart race.

Ellie's eyes filled with tears and she rushed out of the room. A few seconds later, the screen door slammed.

Cash threw his arms up in the air. "What did I do wrong?"

"You didn't do anything but be sweet." She took his hand and laced her fingers with his. "If you want my armchair analysis, Ellie wants to love it, but she feels like she's betraying her mom."

Cash appeared baffled. "But Marie would want her to have a nice bedroom...hell, the one she had in Boston was decked out."

"Exactly. Don't you see, if she loves this one, it's like giving up the one that her mother made her. She isn't ready to let go of that yet."

"Why does it have to be either/or?" He sat on the edge of Ellie's bed, looking completely puzzled.

"Because she's twelve, Cash. At that age, things are black or white. There are no shades of gray."

He scrubbed his hand down his face. "Should I go after her?"

"Give her a few minutes." Aubrey sat next to him. "She and I had such a lovely day together. The kid gets me right here." She tapped her chest with her fist.

Cash took a visual turn around the room. "You worked some magic here, Aubrey. Thank you. I'm sorry Ellie didn't appreciate it more, but I do."

Ah, he was worried her feelings were hurt. She stood up, put her hands on his shoulders, and bent down to kiss him softly. "Don't worry about me." She turned to linger on the pink stripes they'd painted together. "This was a joy to decorate, and Ellie will come to cherish the room, not because of my prowess as a designer but because her daddy did this for her, mark my words." She chucked him on the chin. "I'm taking off now so you two can have some time together."

Cash got to his feet. "Thank you for watching her today."

"It was my pleasure. And later, I want to hear about the investigation; that is, if you're allowed to tell me."

"Aubrey, I'm not a cop. I was just along for the ride." He walked her to the door. "I'll call you later."

They didn't kiss, but Cash stood on the porch and watched her walk home. She waved across the creek once she got inside the door. And then, for no reason at all, she sat at her kitchen table and cried. She supposed it was for Ellie and all the pain she must be going through, and for Cash, who was trying so hard but couldn't seem to catch a break where his daughter was concerned. And she supposed some of her tears were for herself, for Cash, and their colossally bad timing.

* * * *

Cash grabbed two apples from the fridge and went in search of Ellie. The girl couldn't have gone far, and he had a sneaking suspicion of exactly where she might be. Ten minutes later, he found her sitting under a blue oak tree, next to the horse barn. Her knees were pulled up to her chin and her face was streaked with tears.

"You got room under there for one more?" He ducked under a low-hanging branch and took the spot next to her, leaning his back against the fat trunk of the tree. "I come bearing gifts." He tossed her one of the apples.

She polished the fruit with her shirt and took a bite. The juice dribbled down her chin, and Cash wiped it away with his thumb. For a while, they just sat there, taking advantage of the slight breeze and watching the horses graze on patches of dandelions.

"I used to sit here sometimes when I was a boy and talk to the horses. See that tree over there?" He pointed out a valley oak that had to be at least a hundred years old. "Grandpa Dalton hung a rope swing for us there. Jace, Sawyer, Angie, and I used to take turns swinging on that thing."

"How come it's not there anymore?" Ellie wiped her mouth with her shirtsleeve.

"Good question." He'd have to ask Jace. It seemed to him that Travis and Grady would've made fine use of that swing. "That was some twenty years ago."

"We couldn't have a swing set at the condo, but my mom used to take me to the park."

"That's nice too." He tilted his head so they could be at eye level. "Don't you like your new room, Ellie?"

"I like it," she said, and stared down at the dirt where she tried to get a ladybug to crawl on her finger. Cash thought it was odd given her aversion to spiders.

"But?" he asked.

"But what if I don't stay?"

His MO would've been to give her the cold hard facts. *This is it, kid; you're stuck with me until you're eighteen.* But something told him that wasn't a good way to handle the situation. A twelve-year-old thrust into a completely new—and probably scary—situation wanted to feel like she had some modicum of control. Some power.

"I was really hoping you'd want to stay," he said, careful about the wording. While he didn't want to come off as a dictator, he also didn't want to give her the false impression that the choice was completely up to her.

She didn't say anything and he didn't push. He was betting on Aubrey's read of Ellie's mind-set. She was experiencing a mixture of grief and guilt.

"I do think your lack of enthusiasm may have hurt Aubrey's feelings. She worked hard to make the room special for you."

Her head jerked up. "I didn't mean to. Aubrey's super nice."

"She feels the same way about you. So maybe when we get home, you could go over to her cabin and tell her how much you appreciate everything she did." He lifted her chin when she lowered her eyes. "Ellie, what's bothering you, honey?" He hoped she might open up and they could have an actual conversation.

"Nothing."

"You know you can tell me anything, right?"

She nodded, but it was a tentative sort of nod. A nod that said, *Not really.*

They needed more time, he told himself. More time, and then she would open up.

"So what did you and Aubrey do all morning besides decorate your room?" He was going for a neutral topic.

"Did she tell you about the man who came over, and how he was yelling at her?"

"No." Aubrey hadn't told him any such thing and he wasn't too happy about it. "What happened?"

Ellie dried her eyes with the palm of her hand. "I couldn't hear a lot of it because Aubrey made me go in the house. But I peeked through the window and he was all like up in her face. I almost called 9-1-1. Do you think I should've?"

It was a tricky question because hell yeah. He wished she would've called him or, at the very least, Jace. But he also didn't want to put that kind of responsibility on the shoulders of a child. "It sounds to me like you read the situation and didn't feel like it warranted the police. You went with your gut, right?"

"I wanted to go outside and tell him to leave, but I was afraid Aubrey would be angry."

"Nope. You did the right thing. But next time, El, call me. Okay?"

She nodded. "Who do you think he was?"

"The man talking to Aubrey?" He didn't know for sure, but he was betting Mitch. He planned to broach the subject with Aubrey later but assumed it had something to do with her breakup, the secret she was keeping, and the absurd notion that she was protecting Brett. "I don't know, honey, but I'll ask her about it."

"You should tell him off. He was a big guy with a bad attitude, but he'll be afraid of you," Ellie said.

A smile spread through his chest. His daughter thought he was formidable. On second thought, maybe she just thought he was terrifying, which wasn't exactly a compliment.

He draped his arm over her shoulders and pulled her in for a squeeze. She was letting him do that more and more, which he considered progress. "What do say we go home, huh, kiddo?"

"Okay." She got up, took one look at her white pants, and grimaced. "I guess I can't wear these to the party tomorrow."

"I'll wash 'em for you." Laundry had become his new life's work.

They walked back to the cabin, her short legs trying to keep up with his. They were halfway home when Jace drew up next to them.

"Want a lift?"

"It's a five-minute walk." And it would mean Jace would have to double back. "You done for the day?"

"Yep. I did a little more digging on our cattle case." *Our?* It was Jace's case, not Cash's. He was only helping his cousin. "I want to run a few things by you, but the boys will be home any second."

"Call me later, then," Cash said, and told himself he was only doing it to help Jace. Jace, who needed job security.

"Ellie, you want to hop in the truck and have dinner with us? It's chicken strips and tater tots tonight."

Cash cringed. He doubted there was even any actual chicken in those processed strips Jace liked to buy. And tater tots had absolutely no food value. But Ellie stared up at him imploringly.

"Can I go?" She was either jonesing for kids her own age or junk food.

"Sure, but eat something green." He poked his head in Jace's window. "Make sure she eats vegetables."

He gave Ellie a conspiratorial wink and told Cash, "Roger that."

Ellie hopped in the truck, and Cash walked the rest of the way home lost in his own thoughts. Despite Ellie's words to the contrary, she appeared to like the ranch, especially the horses. He'd known all along that the barn was where she'd go. Somehow, he'd also known that she'd pick the blue oak tree. It had been his spot of choice as a child and the kid had his DNA. Their similarities didn't stop there. Her consternation over whether she should've called for backup when Aubrey's visitor had worn out his welcome...well, she was a chip off the old block.

Aubrey should've told him about the confrontation if, indeed, it was a confrontation. Ellie might've read it wrong, though he didn't think so. Not if Aubrey had sent Ellie inside the house. Perhaps it had been Brett and the cat was out of the bag. But Brett was in a wheelchair, and that was something Ellie would've been likely to notice and mention.

At his cabin, he took a detour across the footbridge and knocked on Aubrey's door. She answered in a pair of cutoffs and a white tank top. No bra, which threw him off his real purpose for coming.

He went inside, pressed her against the wall, and kissed her neck. "I came to talk, but I don't see that happening now."

"Is Ellie okay?" She stroked his arm.

"Ellie's fine. She went over to Jace's for dinner."

"Ah," she said and went up on tiptoes to kiss him on the lips, then fisted his shirt in her hand and dragged him into the bedroom. "Want to make out for a while?"

"I do. But first I want to know who came over this morning. Ellie said he gave you a hard time."

She let go of his shirt and plopped down on the side of her bed. "Way to be a buzzkill. It was Mitch. He doesn't want me to go to Jill's birthday party, the one I was roped into helping plan."

"That's what happens when you keep secrets." He pulled her up and led her to the living room. It was too hard to concentrate with Aubrey on a bed, and he wanted to have a discussion. "What do you mean, Mitch doesn't want you to go? Did he threaten you? Ellie said it got heated."

"It was nothing I couldn't handle. Remember, I have the upper hand in this situation." She smirked.

"You only have the upper hand if you're willing to rat Mitch out. Somehow, I think he knows you won't or else you would've done it by now." She should've done it the first time her car was vandalized.

"I don't know what he knows and frankly, he's not worth thinking about. I'm going to the party...with my date and his little girl. I'm going to stick a fork in these rumors once and for all."

"Tell me exactly what he said to you." Cash knew she was downplaying whatever had happened between them this morning. It wasn't as innocent as Aubrey was making it out to be or else Ellie wouldn't have been so rattled.

"I don't even remember, it was so insignificant. Something like, 'Aubrey, you better not go to that party.' And, 'Aubrey, you and Jace better keep your mouths shut,'" she said, mimicking Mitch. "I don't know what he was hoping to accomplish other than to be ridiculous."

For a ridiculous person, Mitch had caused Aubrey and Jace no end of problems.

"I hope it didn't scare Ellie, but it was really nothing."

"I just wished you would've told me about it," he said, trying not to sound like one of those guys who thought he had to go around protecting the fairer sex, even though he probably was one of those guys.

"What for?" She shrugged. "Between Ellie and the trial, you've got enough on your plate, Cash. I don't need you or Jace fighting my battles."

Jace? Wow, she was lumping him in with Jace? That kind of put him in his place.

What do you expect, asshole; you're not her man. She's moving to Vegas.

"Oh, but while he was here, I found out something interesting. He's planning to develop Beals Ranch. I didn't know they were selling, did you?"

"What?" Cash wasn't sure he'd heard right. "Beals Ranch? Are you sure?" The Bealses hadn't told Jace anything about a development. It seemed to Cash that something like that would've come up either during the course of the cattle-rustling investigation or in general. Dry Creek Ranch was their neighbor after all, and the real estate implications of a development would be significant.

"I saw a plat map in the front of his truck. When I asked about it, he got pissy and told me to mind my own business. I never thought they'd sell. The land has been in Jill's family for ages. In fact, Pete was just up from San Jose to help his parents sort out the financial mess of losing all that cattle."

Cash vaguely remembered Pete from when they were kids. He was a year or two younger than him and Jace. About the same age as Sawyer.

"Are you sure the map was for a development? Is there a chance you misunderstood?"

She shot him a look. "Cash, I worked for Reynolds Construction long enough to learn to read a plat. There's no question in my mind that Mitch is planning a development. He didn't give me a chance to study it, so I can't tell you what kind of development, but I know what I saw."

"And he got flustered when you saw the map?" Cash was trying to parse the information.

The idea of a planned development next to Dry Creek Ranch, his family's legacy, made him queasy. Then again, he wanted to sell the ranch, and who the hell did he think would buy the land? A Buddhist monastery? Get real. The Bealses were doing exactly what he'd been advocating: taking the money and running.

Besides the personal consequences, as an investigator—or rather a former investigator—he had to believe this new revelation somehow fit into the cattle-rustling case. Because in his experience there were no coincidences.

"I wouldn't say flustered exactly. But there was no question he didn't want me to know about it."

Cash didn't want to read too much into that. There could be a lot of reasons for secrecy, including the fact that he and Aubrey had become opponents of sorts. More realistically, Mitch was a good businessman and wanted to keep plans for a major development—because a thousand acres was definitely major—proprietary until the city signed off on it. Cash more than likely would've done the same. But the Bealses, on the other hand, should've shared the information with their closest neighbors.

It was a chickenshit move to keep it a secret, and Cash planned to raise hell over it as soon as he got Aubrey naked.

Chapter 19

"Ooh," Aubrey cooed. That thing he was doing with his fingers was…
"Cash, no more. I can't take…I want…please."

He managed to shed his boots this time, and lose his pants in a quarter of
a second flat. And when she thought she couldn't wait any longer without
jumping out of her skin, he was deep inside her, thrusting in and out until
she thought she'd lose her mind.

How had she let this become more than it could be? She was falling for
a single father who was currently unemployed. And just a few weeks ago,
she was engaged to be married. This wasn't supposed to be happening, but
as much as Aubrey wanted to deny it, she was crazy about Cash. Crazy
about his daughter. And pretty soon she'd have to leave them both, as well
as the ranch, which she'd also grown crazy about, for a job. Because she
certainly couldn't work here.

She rolled on top of him, gripping his shoulders to stay up as she rocked
back and forth. The way he filled her was so overwhelming, she thought
she'd die from the sheer exquisiteness of it. He stared up at her, his blue
eyes clouded with desire. Seeing him that way, knowing how much he
wanted her, only heightened the experience. She didn't think anyone had
ever looked at her that way, like they wanted to protect and devour her
both at the same time.

He reached up and brushed her hair away from her face, then fondled her
breasts, holding each one in his large hands. She closed her eyes, letting the
sensation of his touch wash over her. Leaning up, he kissed her over and
over again, the warm pull of his mouth first on her lips, then her nipples.
Cash sucked and laved until she couldn't take it anymore. She let go in an
earth-shattering crescendo and collapsed on his chest.

He rolled her over, spread her legs wide and thrust into her with such utter desperation that it made her realize how much control he must've exercised to maximize her pleasure.

She wanted to give him everything he'd given her and more. Hooking her ankles around his hips, she ran her hands up and down his back, pressing his butt, urging him to go deeper. He pumped into her three times before throwing his head back, the muscles in his neck taut, and shouting out her name.

For a minute, they lay there, absolutely still, except for the beat of their hearts. In that moment, she wondered if he had fallen for her as hard as she had for him.

"I should check on Ellie, see if she needs me to pick her up."

"Okay." But she wanted him to stay in bed with her.

He hovered over her mouth, swooped down and kissed her, long and passionately. Then he rolled off her and searched the floor for his jeans. In a soft voice, he said, "We didn't use anything," and slipped on his boxer shorts.

She shrugged. "I told you, I'm on the pill."

He didn't say anything, but she could tell he was silently chastising himself.

When Cash was completely dressed, he leaned over the bed and planted another kiss on her forehead. "I'll pick you up for the party tomorrow."

She took a handful of his shirt, pulled his face back down, and sat up to give him a real kiss. "See you tomorrow."

When she heard the door click behind him, she got up and got dressed. It was only five and she thought about how she could spend the rest of the evening. Friday night and nowhere to go. Or, if she wanted to see her cup as half full, she could remind herself that it wasn't even dark outside and she'd already gotten laid.

"That's right, missy, and it was a US prime lay. Not your garden variety lay," she said aloud and went into the kitchen to fix dinner, trying not to think about her upcoming interview 526 miles away.

* * * *

Cash walked to Jace's.

Temperatures had cooled to a balmy eighty-five degrees. And the short hike would give him time to think.

He and Aubrey were getting involved deeper than he wanted to, and yet he couldn't seem to stop it. He was forever looking for excuses to spend time with her when he should be dedicating all his energy to Ellie and to finding a job, like Aubrey had done.

Cash crossed through the trees, shunning the well-traveled trail that cut across the field from the cabin to Jace's place. Even in July, the pine trees reminded him of Christmas. And the towering oaks, heavy with leaves, formed a thick canopy that kept the late afternoon sun from beating down on the brim of his hat. He interrupted two deer foraging for acorns. As soon as they felt his presence, they pounded past him, vaulting over a broken split-rail fence.

On the other side of the trees, he heard the rush of Dry Creek. The smell of wet soil, fish, and vegetation swamped him with so many boyhood memories that for a minute he was lost in time. The screech of a nighthawk pulled him back, and he quickened his pace.

He got to Jace's just in time to help clean up the dessert dishes. Sawyer being Sawyer had brought artisan ice cream from a sweetshop in Nevada City.

"What's the difference between artisan ice cream and the stuff they sell at Safeway? It all tastes the same to me." Jace put the carton in the freezer.

"That's because you're a cretin and think Arby's is haute cuisine."

Sawyer was a snob, yet here he was, living in a barn on an old cattle ranch in Timbuktu.

"Don't you have a book to write?" Jace shoulder-checked him.

"I'm taking a break and giving the creative juices time to catch up."

"Is that a fancy way of saying you have writer's block?" Cash tossed a dish towel at him so he could help dry the stuff that wasn't dishwasher safe. Sawyer had a funny way of making himself scarce during KP duty. Cash chalked it up to the fact that he'd grown up with maids and cooks and chauffeurs and enough hired help to fill AT&T Park. But on the ranch they all pitched in. It was Grandpa Dalton's rule.

"Let's just say the words aren't coming to me as fast and furious as I'd hoped." Sawyer let out a hard breath. "At this rate, I'm pretty sure I won't make the deadline."

"Can you do that, miss the deadline?" Jace asked.

Sawyer lifted his shoulders in a half-hearted shrug. "There's some time built in, but it's better if I don't. More than likely I'll wait until the eleventh hour, tank up on a week's worth of coffee, and write like a fiend."

Cash lifted a brow, because it sounded insane to him, not to mention irresponsible. But that was Sawyer for you.

He stepped into the hallway to make sure he could hear the kids. They were in the family room, watching a movie. Ellie was laughing at something Grady said, and he smiled. He was still wearing the smile when he returned to the kitchen.

"They remind me of us when we were kids," Jace said.

Yep, except there were four of them with Angie.

Cash pulled out a kitchen chair and straddled it. "Mitch came to see Aubrey today. During the course of their meeting, Aubrey saw a map in his truck. She says it was plans for a development on Beals Ranch."

Two blank expressions stared back at him, then Jace's became mottled with anger.

"What do you mean, a development?" he asked in a raised voice.

"A housing development, like a planned community."

"That's impossible." Jace stood up and started pacing the floor. "No way the city signs off on that without getting input from the neighbors. Hell, I'm not even sure the land is zoned for a housing division."

"Could Aubrey be wrong about what she thought she saw?" Sawyer was the voice of reason in the family. Cash suspected it was because he was a journalist and was very analytical and methodical in his thinking. "Was this something that looked official or was it drawn on the back of a napkin?"

"Nope, she's pretty emphatic that what she saw was a plat, like a blueprint. It could just be that Mitch is delusional. Maybe he thinks that after the Bealses' recent bad luck, they'll sell." Cash looked at Jace, who knew their neighbors better than he and Sawyer did.

Jace shook his head. "The Bealses said nothing to me about selling, and Mitch is an asshole, but he's anything but delusional. If he went to the trouble and expense of having formal plans drawn up, there's something going on. And if Aubrey says she saw plans, she saw plans. She lived and worked with the guy. She knows Mitch's business and how he operates."

The reminder that Aubrey had come close to walking down the aisle with him made Cash's stomach pitch. He didn't want to think about her being with another guy, let alone being engaged to him. And what did that say about him? It said he was screwed, that's what it said.

Jace went to the mudroom and grabbed his hat. "You guys stay with the kids while I go over to the Bealses'. If they're selling, we have a right to know, goddamn it."

Both Cash and Sawyer jumped up at the same time.

"Slow down, cowboy." Sawyer moved in front of Jace to block him from leaving. "Not a good idea. It would be better if Cash or I did it, not the sheriff. Get my drift?"

"No, I don't." He pushed Sawyer out of the way.

But this time Cash blocked him. "Sawyer's right. Now's not a good time, not when you're up to your eyeballs investigating something that happened on their property."

"I'm going over there as a neighbor, not as the sheriff."

"Don't you see, Jace, you can't separate the two. If they are selling and they know you're angry about it, they'll accuse you of shortchanging the investigation out of spite. It's a classic conflict of interest." Cash stood his ground, even though he could see Jace was fuming. They all loved Dry Creek Ranch, but for Jace, the place had been his home all his life, and a haven after his parents and little brother died. He took anything that threatened the ranch and their grandfather's legacy as a personal affront. "Let Sawyer go. He's the most diplomatic of the three of us, and he has no conflicts of interest."

Sawyer would handle the situation without letting emotions enter into the equation. He'd been raised by parents who dealt with controversy for a living.

"I don't want to be diplomatic. A housing development…do you know what that'll be like? It'll be like living in the goddamn city. Next thing you know, the new neighbors will be complaining about the horse and cow shit and the tractor noise, and fighting over water rights. I don't want to be diplomatic, Cash. I don't want them ruining our way of life. The life Grandpa gave us."

"I don't see how you can stop them from selling if that's what they want to do." Cash had proposed the same thing. "But you…we…could fight the development." He didn't know what good it would do. He suspected Mitch knew city and county zoning better than they did. But the Dalton name did hold weight in this county, or at least it used to.

"Let me go, Jace. Let me see what I can do," Sawyer said. "There's a chance this is all a big mistake."

Cash had a more cynical take on it, but he'd save that information until he had more facts in evidence. Again, he didn't believe in coincidences. And the timing of the Bealses losing hundreds of thousands of dollars' worth of cattle and Mitch's plans for a planned community raised a million warning bells in Cash's head.

Jace threw up his arms in defeat. "Fine, you go. But I want a word-for-word account of what Beals says."

"It's suppertime," Sawyer said. "Why don't I go tomorrow?"

Jace shook his head. "They'll be at Jill's birthday party tomorrow. Go now, or else I will. I don't need a goddamn sleepless night. I get plenty of those being sheriff."

Sawyer tacitly agreed and Cash followed him to the front door.

"Don't bring up the cattle-theft investigation," he told Sawyer. "If they bring it up, act like you only know what you've heard through the grapevine."

"I won't have to act," Sawyer said and grabbed his hat off the hall tree. "All I know is what Jimmy Ray and Laney told me. Pretty wild, huh? Cattle rustling." His lips curved up in amusement. "Thought that only happened in old Westerns."

"It happens more than you think. Sheep and goats too. Anything worth money."

"Yeah, I guess so." Sawyer nudged his head toward the kitchen. "Between the Aubrey rumor and him going ballistic over Beals Ranch, he's going to screw himself in the upcoming election."

"Let's take it one step at a time."

"Okay, but you know I'm right."

"What I know is that people have short memories. Let's hope for Jace's sake that by the time the primary rolls around, all this will be old news."

But if the Bealses were truly selling and a housing division was in the works, Cash knew Jace would go to war. And Cash and Sawyer would be loyalty bound to go with him.

Life was already too complicated. Next week, he had to sell the agency he'd given his life to down the river. He had a daughter who didn't want anything to do with him. He had no job and no prospects for one. He had a ranch he loved but no way to pay the taxes or the upkeep on it. He had a next-door neighbor he couldn't get out of his mind when all he should be doing was focusing on fixing his broken life.

And tomorrow, he had to pretend to be her boyfriend.

Chapter 20

Cash waited by the door while Ellie took twenty minutes longer in the bathroom than usual. He didn't want to embarrass her, but they were going to be late to pick up Aubrey for the party.

"Ellie, are you okay in there?" He could hear her moving around, so at least she hadn't cracked her head on the tub. The water went on, but she still didn't answer. "El, honey, what's going on?"

Silence, then what sounded like a whimper. He deliberated on whether to force open the door.

Finally, in a small voice, she said, "I need Aubrey."

"Is it something I can help with?" He was her father after all, not Aubrey.

"No," came a quick response. "Don't come in here."

He leaned sideways against the door, resting his arm on the frame header. "Sweetheart, I won't come in. But I need to know if you're okay."

"I'm okay." But she didn't sound okay; she sounded distressed.

Whether that was because she was having a bona fide emergency or something as frivolous as a wardrobe malfunction he didn't know, because Cash's experience with twelve-year-old girls could fit in a thimble. But if it was indeed a problem with a zipper or a button, he was handy with a needle and thread.

"Please get Aubrey."

He didn't want to get Aubrey. If his daughter had a problem, he wanted to be the one to fix it. He wanted to be the one she turned to.

"Just tell me what's going on. Is it another spider?"

The toilet flushed and the water in the sink went on again.

"Ellie?"

"No, it's not a spider. Just get Aubrey."

He went to jiggle the doorknob. If his daughter was sick, he didn't want a locked door between them.

"Don't," she shouted, and there was rustling, like she was hurrying to cover herself.

He deliberated on what to do, reluctant to relinquish his parental duties to someone else. But whatever drama was playing out in there, Ellie didn't want Cash's help. She'd made that abundantly clear. She wanted Aubrey. Or maybe she just wanted a woman. It was that last revelation that made him give in and finally call Aubrey and explain the situation.

Not five minutes later, she appeared at his front door in a backless, armless dress that took his breath away.

"Wow! You look fantastic." He wanted to linger on the dress, on Aubrey's rocking body in the dress, but his kid was waiting.

"Thanks." Aubrey gave him a peck on the lips and brushed by him, going straight to the bathroom. "Hey, Ellie, can I come in?"

The door opened a crack. Ellie stood behind it with only her head poking out. She ushered Aubrey in and closed the door behind them. Cash paced the hallway, wondering what the hell the crisis was and why he wasn't the one tending to it. There was a lot of whispering going on inside, none of which Cash could actually make out.

A few minutes later, Aubrey emerged.

"Well?" He scrubbed his hand over his face.

"I'll be right back," she informed him but gave nothing away, which was starting to piss Cash off.

Aubrey wasn't gone long, and when she returned she had a tote bag with her. It better not be filled with makeup was his thought as Aubrey slipped back inside the bathroom. Cash didn't want his little girl wearing any of that stuff until she was eighteen. Or twenty.

Another fifteen minutes passed. At this rate they'd be late to the surprise party, not that Cash even knew these people. But he liked to be prompt. Tired of wearing out the wooden floor, he moved to the living room and waited on the couch.

"We'll be ready in a sec." Aubrey popped her head in and just as quickly disappeared.

Cash could hear activity in Ellie's bedroom. A short time later, they came out as if nothing had happened. Ellie was dressed in a pair of jeans, not the white ones he'd laundered. Something in Aubrey's body language told him to leave it alone and not make inquiries. He followed her lead, though a small part of him was perturbed that he was being left out of the loop.

"Shall we go?" Aubrey smoothed her dress and grabbed the pie she'd brought over and had left on the table by the front door.

Cash fetched his hat and trailed the ladies to his SUV. "Where's the house?"

Aubrey gave him directions and they headed out to Highway 49 into town.

Cash checked the clock on the dash. "We're cutting it close."

"We'll be fine." She smiled at him, and Cash could've sworn his heart stopped.

Something about the way Aubrey sat across from him, a commanding yet calming presence, felt so right. With Ellie in the back seat, the ride reminded Cash of his childhood when his own parents used to load him into the car to make the two-hour trek from San Francisco to Dry Creek Ranch.

"Turn right here," Aubrey said as they entered a residential section less than a mile off Main Street.

The homes were modest but well-kept, with grassy front lawns and attached garages that backed up to open fields where cattle grazed. A few kids ran in and out of the spray of a garden sprinkler.

"The Tuckers are up there on the corner." Aubrey pointed to a one-story ranch house where the paint job had faded to a dull yellow and the flower beds had turned weedy. There was a pickup with a wheelchair lift parked in the driveway, next to a pole flying the American flag. In the front yard, someone had posted a sign that read, "A combat veteran lives here. Please be courteous with fireworks."

Cash parked in the cul-de-sac. Together, the three of them walked to the house. Brett greeted them at the door in his wheelchair.

Aubrey leaned down and gave him a hug and introduced him to Cash and Ellie. "We're here; put us to work."

"Mercedes and Laney are in the backyard, setting the tables. The kids are putting together some kind of horseshoe arcade kind of thing on the side of the house. Travis and Grady are out there if you want to join them." He smiled at Ellie, who ran off to find her cousins. "If you two wouldn't mind carrying the drinks out to the ice chests, that would be a great help."

Cash followed Aubrey into the kitchen. She seemed to know the layout of the house fairly well. Then again, it was your basic California rambler, one long rectangle. There were cases of soda, beer, and bottled water stacked near the pantry.

"Hey"—Cash reached for Aubrey's arm as she put the pie down on the counter and started to lift a case of cola—"what was that about with Ellie?" He took the case from her and rested it on the counter.

"She started her period. First time."

"Oh" was all he managed to say, because that possibility hadn't even occurred to him. But yeah, it made sense now why Ellie had insisted on Aubrey coming to her aid instead of Cash. Shit, would he have even known what to do? "Uh, did she have what she needed?" Another thing he was ill-equipped for. He hadn't thought to buy those kinds of supplies.

"No, but I took care of it. We should probably stop off at the store later to stock her up. Try not to make a big deal out of it, though. She's shy about it and just a wee bit hormonal."

"Okay, but should I at least mention something about it?" Not that he had the foggiest notion what was appropriate to say when a young woman got her period. He inwardly groaned, because he didn't want to think of Ellie as a young woman. It was bad enough that he'd missed her first step, her first word, her first lost tooth. He still wanted to get to know his daughter as a little girl.

Stop complaining, he told himself as a wave of guilt hit him. At least he was a part of this milestone for Ellie, unlike Marie. Marie would never get to see her daughter go to the prom, graduate from college, walk down the aisle, and all the other momentous things mothers longed to witness their children do.

"It's probably best if you don't say anything. Maybe buy her a pint of Ben and Jerry's and call it a day."

He nodded, deferring to her recommendation, secretly feeling relieved. He gathered up a second case of soda and carried them both to the ice chest outside. There was a small crowd of helpers in the yard, tending to various party tasks. Cash couldn't help but notice that as soon as they spotted Aubrey, they started whispering behind her back. Angry, he slipped his arm over her shoulder. The move was intentional, a signal to the others to back off.

Without any conscious thought about it, he kissed her. The move was also intentional, a signal that he couldn't keep his hands off her. She kissed him back, of course, but he wasn't sure if she was merely playing to the crowd.

Brett called out that it was ten minutes until show time, and everyone went back to their respective party preparations. A couple of kids streaked by, and Cash grabbed Grady's collar.

"Hi, Uncle Cash. I can't talk to you now, I'm in the middle of something."

"I wouldn't dream of interrupting you. Where's Ellie?"

"She's working with us on it."

"What's *it*?" he asked, just in case they were playing with matches or cooking meth in one of the bedrooms.

"We're building a game out of horseshoes and bowling pins. It's so awesome."

"All right, just checking. Look out for her, okay? She doesn't know the other kids like you and Travis do."

"We will." He took off. The kid had so much energy, it was a wonder he didn't ignite into a burst of flames.

He helped Aubrey spread out the drinks, cognizant of the fact that the other partygoers were staring. Cash recognized some of them, including Laney, Jimmy Ray, and Mrs. Jamison, aka Yoda.

Jace was at the barbecues—there were at least three of them at last count—preparing the coals and woodchips.

People continued to trickle into the yard with salads, casserole dishes, bowls of guacamole and bean dip, and desserts of all varieties. Someone came with a crate of stone fruit from his orchard. Another guest brought six bottles of Bordeaux from his winery. Jace had evidently supplied the burgers and tri-tip from the ranch. It was how Cash remembered life in the country, where everyone shared Northern California's food bounty.

Jace waved Cash over, and he left Aubrey alone to chat with Mama.

"You talk to Sawyer?" Cash asked Jace out of earshot of the others.

"Yep. The Bealses said they don't know anything about a development, that their ranch isn't on the market."

"Do you believe them?" Because Cash had faith that Aubrey knew what she saw.

"I do." Jace stoked the coals, letting them turn an even white. "But this is where it gets interesting. Randy told Sawyer that they're upside down on the ranch. Everyone but Grandpa took out big loans during the drought so they wouldn't have to cull their breeding herds. The Bealses were hoping to pay down a huge chunk of that debt when they sold their yearlings in the fall. Then they get ripped off and guess what?"

"They can't pay back their loan."

"Bingo."

Cash rubbed his jaw. "So they're forced into a short sale, a perfect opportunity for the local developer."

"Yep," Jace said and pulled Cash into a quiet corner, away from a few guys who'd started to assemble in front of the grills. "I've known Mitch my whole life, Cash. I can't believe he'd do something like this."

This was the same guy who was cheating and lying and screwing with people's livelihoods. And Jace didn't think he was capable of swindling his neighbors? Call Cash a cynic, but as the old saying went, if it walked like a duck…"Aubrey saw what she saw, Jace. Pretty strong circumstantial evidence if you ask me."

Brett interrupted their conversation with another announcement. Jill was only a block away. Aubrey left her conversation with Mama to join Cash and Jace's huddle.

"You two look like you're conspiring over here. What's going on?"

Cash wrapped his arm around her waist. "Just talking. Want to get a beer?"

Even though they were supposed to be putting on a charade to quiet the rumors, it didn't feel that way. In the short time they'd been…doing whatever the hell they were doing…things were starting to get real. Cash still hadn't decided how to feel about that. Aubrey was on the rebound and Cash didn't want to drag women in and out of Ellie's life. It was no longer just him anymore; everything he did had to include how it would affect Ellie.

And Aubrey was moving to Vegas.

There was a slight commotion near the gate by the side of the house. The designated lookout signaled that Jill was here, and Brett motioned for everyone to hush up and take their places. Cash had never known a surprise party that had actually been a surprise, but he hoped for Brett's sake that it went off without a hitch.

He and Aubrey stood by the fence, waiting for the guest of honor to make her grand entrance.

When Jill came in with Mitch, Aubrey pinched him. "Can you freaking believe it?" she asked under her breath. "Poor, trusting Brett must've had Mitch keep Jill occupied until the party started. Little does he know how Mitch was occupying her."

"That's why you and Jace keeping it a secret is facilitating the situation," Cash whispered. Poor trusting Brett was not only being duped by his wife but by his two best friends.

"You've made your opinion known on this," she hissed. "I'm not telling."

"Surprise!" everyone yelled at once.

Either Jill was a good actress or she really was surprised; Cash didn't know her well enough to judge. Mitch scanned the crowd, zoomed in on Aubrey, and scowled. Cash disliked him on sight. Then again, it was hard to be objective given all he knew about the guy. He moved a few inches closer to Aubrey and tightened his arm around her.

Message delivered.

Mitch quickly looked away. Cash watched him take another visual lap around the yard. This time, Mitch focused on Jace.

Feeling cornered?

Jill had thrown herself into Brett's lap and they were kissing. A cheer went up, and Aubrey whispered, "This is more than I can take."

Cash started to tell her that she was part of the lie but held himself in check. Her mind was made up; nothing he could say would change it.

Mitch joined the happy couple and did a fist bump with Brett. Cash observed the three of them talking, and that old spidey-sense that had once made him a great agent crawled up his spine.

Cash made eye contact with Jace and held it for a few seconds. *Are you thinking what I'm thinking?*

* * * *

Ellie slipped away from the party just long enough to send a text to Mary Margaret.

"I finally got my period and it was horrible," she wrote.

Mary Margaret had been the first of all their friends to get hers and had acted like it was life-changing. Like all of a sudden she was superior to everyone in seventh grade. All Ellie felt was nauseated and embarrassed, especially that her dad knew. Aubrey said she had to tell him because it was like a medical issue or something. At least she'd been the one to bring Ellie a tampon. If her dad had done it, Ellie would've died.

Mary Margaret pinged her back. "You're a woman now."

That made Ellie want to barf. She didn't feel like a woman, unless feeling like a woman meant being this close to crying all the time. If her mother were still alive, she would at least have someone to talk to about it, although Aubrey said she and Ellie could have a sleepover and some "serious female bonding."

But first, they had to come to this stupid party where Aubrey and her dad could feel each other up in public. When they didn't know Ellie was looking, she'd seen them kiss. They'd probably get married someday and have their own kids. Where would that leave Ellie? She'd be odd girl out, like an orphan, which she pretty much already felt like anyway.

Next week, her dad was going to San Francisco for his old job and said she had to stay at the ranch with Uncle Jace and her cousins. More proof that he really didn't want her around. At least her mother used to sometimes let her come to the station and go out to lunch with her and Uncle Woody. And afterward someone would drive her home or take her to a horseback riding lesson in a patrol car.

If her father had really wanted her around, he would've come for her a long time ago. She was better off in Boston, where she knew people and had friends.

Ellie was just about to send another text when Grady found her standing under the flagpole in the front of the house and wrapped his skinny arms around her legs.

"Ellie, we're waiting for you. What are you doing?"

"I'll be right there." Gosh, he was such a pest, but she couldn't help herself and gave him a hug.

"They're about to cut the cake and there's ice cream too."

"All right, all right. I'm coming. Meet you there."

Before he hounded her to death, she dashed off one last message to Mary Margaret. "See you soon," it said.

Chapter 21

After the party, Aubrey sat with Cash on his front porch. Ellie was in her room, supposedly taking a nap. But Aubrey bet she was on her phone with her friends in Boston, gabbing about her day.

At least one Dalton was feeling chatty.

It wasn't that Cash was morose, but to Aubrey, he seemed quieter than usual. He'd been attentive and friendly to everyone at Brett and Jill's but had barely said anything on the ride home. Either something—or someone— at the party had upset him, or the anticipation of having to testify in the Whiting case on Monday was weighing heavy on him. She was guessing it was the case, because every time she'd broached the subject with him, he instantly became withdrawn. How could she blame him? It had been an unimaginable series of crimes. Who wouldn't be reticent to talk about it?

In total, four women had been murdered while jogging in the Presidio, a national park near the Golden Gate Bridge. Charles Whiting had sexually assaulted the victims, mutilated them, and tied their dead bodies to a tree.

Cash had been the one to get Whiting's confession. She'd read snippets of the killer's statement in the newspaper, but according to Cash, it was four hours long and most of it too gruesome for print. The prosecution was planning to play it for the jury while Cash was on the stand.

"Are you nervous about next week?" She took his hand and gave it a squeeze.

Cash huffed out a breath. "Not nervous…just not looking forward to it."

"Is that why you're being so quiet?"

"I didn't realize I was being quiet," he said, stretching out his long denim-encased legs and clasping his hands behind his head. "What do

you want to talk about?" He turned his lawn chair so it faced her. "Want
to talk about your interview? You can practice on me if you want."

He'd just deftly changed the subject. If she hadn't seen him do it in the
past, she would've missed it. But she was on to his tricks now.

"I've got it covered," she said. "You want to practice your testimony?"

"Vegas, huh?" He leaned his chair back. "It's even hotter there than
here in summer."

She poked him in the arm. "We both know what you're doing."

"Yeah, what am I doing?"

"You're trying to distract me from talking about the trial. And it's not
working. What is it that happened in the case that got you fired?"

He righted his chair and stared off into the creek. The water level had
dropped, as it usually did in August, but the creek was still running hard.
With the rain and snow in winter, the level would rise again.

As the time stretched on, she assumed that once again he was evading
the question.

"How closely did you follow the case?" he finally asked.

"A little bit. It was hard to ignore." The murders had been on every
newscast and on the front page of every newspaper. "I know that four
women were murdered while jogging in the park and that the FBI arrested
someone early on, but he turned out to be the wrong person."

"I told them he was the wrong person," Cash said, his voice laced with
anger. "But at the time, my supervisors didn't see it that way."

"And that's why you got fired?" It seemed rather extreme to Aubrey,
especially because Cash had ultimately been right.

"It wasn't as cut-and-dried as that, but it was at the root of the reason.
First, they took me off the case. Ultimately, what did me in was that I told
the special agent in charge that he had blood on his hands." Cash's mouth
ticked up in a wry smile. "I also threw a chair at the wall. Not my finest
moment."

"Because they wouldn't listen to you when you said they had the wrong
person?"

"Partly." He shook his head. "But it all came to a head when they held a
press conference announcing they had the killer in custody." Cash let out
a rusty laugh. "The dirtbag they had in jail didn't have enough brain cells
to tie his own shoes, let alone carry out three murders without leaving a
trace of evidence. There were so many indicators that he wasn't our guy,
so many telltale signs. But the killings were getting a lot of international
attention because one of the victims was an exchange student from Brazil,
and the brass desperately wanted to close the case and look like heroes. So

instead of handling it the responsible way by sticking to protocol, the boss stood on the steps of the federal building and told the world we had the culprit behind bars. Our unsub hadn't even been indicted yet, but suddenly it was safe to go jogging again in the Presidio." Cash clenched his fists.

"Casey Farmington," she said softly, almost afraid to voice where she thought Cash's story was leading.

"She might still be alive today." He rubbed his hand down his face. "And what did I do? Not a goddamn thing."

"What do you mean?" Aubrey was confused. "You told them they had the wrong man and you were taken off the case. What more could you have done?"

Cash moved in his chair and it squeaked. "This porch could sure use some real deck furniture instead of these crap folding beach chairs," he said and let out a tight, unconvincing laugh, clearly trying to recover some composure before giving up and blurting out, "I should've gone to the press and told them the truth, that we probably had the wrong guy. And that women should stay the hell away from the Presidio until we had the right guy. Instead, I followed the damn rules."

Aubrey reached for him, but he got to his feet and wandered over to the porch rail.

"Cash, you can't be serious. How could you have stopped a mad man from killing someone if you didn't even know who he was?"

"I knew who he wasn't! And yet I let the special agent in charge tell everyone that we'd nabbed him." He rested his elbows on the railing and took a couple of deep breaths, as if he was trying to hold on to his rage. "Casey Farmington saw that press conference on the news and felt safe to go running again. Safe to use the trails in the park."

"How can you possibly know that?"

"Because her father told us," Cash said, pulling the lawn chair away from the cabin wall and sinking back into it. "He'd warned her about being careful and she'd responded by saying, 'Daddy, they have the killer behind bars.' Those are the words that haunt me every night before I fall asleep."

It was a lot of responsibility to heap on himself, and now Aubrey understood why he'd been so miserable in the days before Ellie came to live with him. But Cash wasn't being fair to himself. The turn of tragic events had been out of his control. The idea that he could have gone to the press and prevented Casey's murder was beyond ridiculous. If that was the case, lone wolves would have changed the course of history. Not to mention that Cash would've come off as a rogue agent, a crackpot, and the press more than likely would've taken his boss's word over his.

People believed what they wanted to believe, especially if the truth was ugly. And having a serial killer still on the loose was about as ugly as it got.

"Cash, you can't take responsibility. You didn't kill Casey Farmington, Charles Whiting did. There's nothing that would've changed that. And if you had gone to the press, they likely wouldn't have taken you seriously. You'd been taken off the case, to some extent discredited, right? Why would anyone believe you over the top person at the agency?"

She wanted to wrap her arms around him and make the unwarranted guilt he felt go away. Cash Dalton was a good man. There was no doubt in her mind that he'd done everything he could.

"How come it was you who did the interrogation if you were taken off the case?" Aubrey didn't know anything about the workings of the FBI or criminal investigations except what she saw on TV. Yet it seemed odd that he would've been involved at that level if he'd been marginalized.

He let out another cynical laugh. "That happened by accident. Someone called the tip line and said Whiting had bragged at a bar that he knew who the killer was. We get about a hundred of those a day, mostly nutjobs or well-meaning people who lead us on dead ends. One of the supervisory agents thought it would be hilarious to get me out of bed at the break of dawn on a Sunday to hunt down Whiting. Payback for my so-called 'independent streak.' Turned out the joke was on them because when I found Whiting, something about his demeanor told me it was a good lead. The more I talked to him, the more he divulged. First, it was 'I know a guy who fits the description of the person witnesses describe as being in the park at the time of the murders.' Then it was 'The guy's a good friend of mine,' which eventually became 'he told me he did it.' Serial killers love to taunt law enforcement, and that's exactly what Whiting was doing. He thought he was smarter than everyone else and could toy with us.

"I offered to give him a ride to the other side of town, and by the time we got there, my gut told me he was our guy. After feeding his ego, I got him to come in for a formal interview to talk about his 'friend.' Twenty-four hours later, I had the full confession. It was strictly luck, being at the right place at the right time."

Aubrey slipped her hand into his. "Luck had nothing to do with it. You knew when the FBI had it wrong and you knew instinctively that Whiting was somehow involved. Ultimately, you convinced him to spill his guts. You're the unsung hero in this whole thing, Cash. To hold yourself personally accountable for the FBI's screw-up is nuts."

"Tell that to Casey Farmington and her family," he said, unwilling to forgive himself. Carrying around the blame was too much, even for someone with his resilience. "Can we talk about something else now?"

"Like what?" There wasn't a lot more to say. Soon, their summer fling would be over and she'd be moving away. If it wasn't Vegas, it would be somewhere else. Somewhere where she could make a living.

And while it made sense in her head, the rest of her hadn't caught up yet. This thing with Cash…was good. The kind of good that, if nurtured, could've turned into forever. But Cash hadn't said anything that made her think they had a future. In fact, to borrow a cliché, the silence on his end had been deafening.

He glanced at the door, probably wondering what Ellie was up to.

"Do you need to check on her?" Aubrey asked.

"Yeah, I really should. Never a good idea to leave a twelve-year-old to her own devices too long."

"Gotcha. I should get home and start packing." Being the organizational freak she was, she'd already packed. But she hoped the reminder that she was leaving on Monday for a job interview might spark a meaningful conversation about the two of them.

"Vegas, huh?" He'd already said that. *Vegas, huh?*

"Yep." She waited, and when he didn't say anything else, turned to go, telling herself that it was for the best. He had too many demons to fight, and she was done battling her own.

* * * *

Two days later, Cash sat on a bench outside a federal courtroom, compulsively checking his phone for a text or an email. By now, Aubrey was in Las Vegas, probably just about to start her interview. He should've been consumed with the case, about testifying, but all morning he'd been distracted by the prospect of Aubrey moving away and starting a new life.

Sully came out of the courtroom and sat next to him in the hallway. Cash wasn't allowed to sit in on the trial until after he testified. Those were the rules unless he was the lead investigator on the case, which he no longer was.

"The lawyers are in chambers," Sully told Cash. "I think they're working out a deal."

It wasn't unusual to pick a jury and then have a defendant realize he liked his chances better with a plea bargain. The prosecution was seeking the death penalty but might settle for life in prison without the possibility

of parole to save the victims' loved ones from having to go through a
lengthy trial.

"How do the families feel about it? Are they okay with a deal?" Cash
asked.

"Diego Vasquez is a strict Catholic; he'd be good with a life sentence.
The Farmingtons are flat-out anti-capital-punishment. The other two
families"—Sully shrugged—"I don't know."

"It would save all of them from having to listen to the confession tape."

"Yup. It would be good for everyone all the way around." Sully nudged
his head at Cash, his meaning clear. Cash wouldn't have to testify and
detail just how badly the case got screwed up.

Cash checked his watch. "They'll be breaking for lunch soon. You think
the judge will let the jury go for the day?"

"It'll depend on if and how fast they can hammer out an agreement.
Why have the jury come back tomorrow only to excuse them from the
case?" Sully said, and Cash nodded.

"I'll be back before lunch with a status report." Sully rose and returned
to the courtroom, careful to quietly close the door behind him.

Cash bobbed his head at two deputy US marshals he recognized as
they passed in the hallway. The Phillip Burton Federal Building was huge,
taking up an entire city block. The FBI's San Francisco field office was
on the thirteenth floor, and for many years, he'd roamed the building as if
it were home. Even now, the smell, a combination of old wood, cleaning
solution, and human sweat, was as familiar as his own aftershave.

He mulled the possible plea bargain and measured his reaction. If anyone
deserved to be executed for his crimes, it was Charles Whiting. But Cash
wasn't averse to taking death off the table. The important thing was that
Whiting would be locked away forever and could never hurt anyone again.
And if it would give the victims' families closure without them having to
sit through the torturous details…well, he was all for that.

The part he was conflicted over was not having to testify. On one hand,
he had no appetite for finger-pointing. On the other, divulging the agency's
missteps might be cathartic. Although the press had already told part of
the story, few outside the Bureau knew the full extent of just how far south
the investigation had gone. As far as Cash knew, reporters weren't wise to
the fact that he'd been thrown off the case for sparring with his superiors
over the direction they'd taken.

Cash wished he could talk to Aubrey about the plea bargain, get her
thoughts.

And then was surprised by the path his mind had veered on to. When the hell had that happened? He'd always been a lone wolf, and suddenly he was bending the ear of his beautiful neighbor. Spilling his guts about the case that kept him awake at night. Asking for advice on his daughter. Telling her about Marie and voicing his regrets about not knowing Ellie.

He checked his phone again. Early this morning, he and Aubrey had exchanged texts, wishing each other luck. He'd driven to the city the night before and stayed at his parents' house. Aubrey had been running errands most of Sunday, so they'd never gotten to talk before he'd left for San Francisco. Now, the texts felt pro forma and impersonal.

Cash started to send her a message, but Sully exited the courtroom and came toward him, and he put his phone away.

"They've got a deal. LWOP, not death," he said. "The judge is excusing the jury now. The Farmingtons asked if they could talk to you."

Cash tensed but nodded. He'd dreaded this moment, but it was time to cowboy up and tell them how damned sorry he was. How he wished he could turn back time and do right by their daughter.

"As soon as the jury's gone, the judge said you could use his chambers. I'll come get you when it's time."

"All right," Cash said, girding himself for the Farmingtons' anger and pain. He'd only had Ellie a month and he already felt her blood flowing through his veins. If anyone ever physically harmed her or stood by while someone else did, there was no telling what he'd do.

Sully slipped back into the courtroom, leaving Cash alone with his thoughts. Again, he was tempted to call Aubrey but didn't know how much time he had to talk or whether he'd be interrupting her. Instead, he paced the hallway, waiting for Sully to wave him into the courtroom. About ten minutes later, one of the deputy marshals escorted him into the judge's chambers.

A couple younger than Cash's parents sat on a love seat with their hands folded in their laps. Though he'd never met the Farmingtons in person, only on the phone, he recognized them instantly from the pictures he'd seen in the newspaper. They got to their feet the moment he entered the room. Cash went to shake their hands, but Mrs. Farmington enfolded him in her arms.

"I hope it's okay for me to hug you," she said, her voice trembling.

Cash was caught off guard and for a beat didn't say anything, letting his arms dangle at his sides as he stood stiffly at attention.

"Betsy, let the man breathe," Mr. Farmington said and rubbed his eyes.

Cash rebounded and politely hugged Mrs. Farmington back. "It's all right," he told Mr. Farmington but felt like the worst kind of phony. If he'd only spoken up, Casey might be alive today.

"Thank you," Mr. Farmington said. "Thank you for everything you did."

"You mind if we sit down?" Cash planned to tell them the truth and needed out of this clinch to do it.

Mrs. Farmington was reluctant to let go, clinging to him for a few seconds longer, before breaking the embrace. Mr. Farmington took her arm and they returned to their places on the sofa. Cash sat in the chair facing them.

The judge's chambers were large and reminded Cash of a drawing room you'd find in an old home in Pacific Heights. Masculine, with dark wainscoting, rows of bookcases, an antique mahogany desk, and a seating area that felt more like a living room than an office.

"We didn't want to put you on the spot, Special Agent Dalton. We just wanted to extend our appreciation for all you've done...the confession... putting Charles Whiting away for life."

The title didn't escape Cash. Special Agent Dalton had been his identity for more than a decade. "I'm no longer with the Bureau. Please, just call me Cash." He cleared his throat, struggling with how to explain. "The fact is, I wish I'd done more. A lot more. I might've been able to save Casey's life." He paused, hoping to let the gravity of that statement sink in.

Mr. Farmington held up his hand. "We're aware of the facts, Special... Cash. Casey was everything to us, and I made it my life's mission to ferret out the truth. We know you disagreed with your superiors on the original suspect. We know the mishandling of the case may have contributed to Casey's death and spent much of the grieving process fuming at law enforcement. But with time comes clarity. Casey loved running those trails and was a fearless young woman. Obstinate too. We raised her that way and were proud of the person she had become." Mr. Farmington faltered with emotion, then pulled himself together.

"What I'm trying to say is that we'll never know for sure whether Casey would've heeded the warning to stay out of the park. The only thing we know for sure is that Charles Whiting was a monster who took the lives of four innocent women, including our precious daughter. If it wasn't for you, the mystery of who killed her might not have been resolved. If it wasn't for you, that son of a bitch might still be walking the streets, free to kill again."

Mr. Farmington broke down, sobbing into his hands. His wife pulled him close, and they cried in each other's arms. Their love for their daughter and for each other was so palpable, it was powerful. It should've been heartachingly sad, but it coursed through Cash like a river of hope. All he could think about was Ellie and the love a father had for his daughter. And Aubrey, a light so bright it illuminated a path through the dark these last few weeks.

"You're our hero," Mrs. Farmington said through tears. "Thank you for giving us closure. For giving Casey justice."

* * * *

Cash canceled dinner plans with his folks, hoping if he left the courthouse now he could avoid most of the traffic on I-80 and be at Dry Creek Ranch before nightfall. He drove with the music on, feeling lighter than he had in months. Not completely absolved, but the heavy weight that had been pressing on his chest for months had been lifted. He could breathe. And maybe, just maybe, the nightmares would go away.

At a stop sign, he checked his phone. Nothing from Aubrey, but what did he expect? She thought he was in court and was probably consumed with the possibility of a new job, not with him. He made his way across the city onto the Bay Bridge and rolled down his window, enjoying the cool coastal breeze. When he got to Fairfield, he considered stopping for lunch. All he'd had for breakfast were two slices of toast and a cup of coffee and he was starved. But he decided to push on to beat rush hour in Sacramento.

He was thirty minutes away from the capitol when his phone rang. Disappointment stabbed him when his caller ID showed it was Jace, not Aubrey.

"What up?"

"Where are you?" Jace asked, sounding anxious.

"I'm on my way back, Whiting took a deal and the judge sent the jury home. You catch a break in the Beals case?"

There was silence, and for a minute, Cash thought he'd lost the call. "Jace?"

"Ellie's gone."

Chapter 22

The man sitting next to Ellie smelled like a combination of pot and BO and he kept staring at her. She wanted to move to another seat, but the bus was crowded and she was afraid he'd get angry if she got up. The minute he'd stepped onto the bus, Ellie had gotten a sick feeling in the pit of her stomach. Her mom called it an "instinct." Maybe it was, but the man just looked like bad news to Ellie.

He had a tattoo on his face and these really scary rings in his nose, and his clothes were dirty and sort of tattered. And he seemed mean, like he never smiled or anything. And he kept looking at her in a way that gave Ellie the creeps.

She desperately wanted to call her dad to tell him she'd made a big mistake, but she'd lost her phone. Maybe it was still at the pool, or she might've dropped it on her way to the bus station. She'd been in such a rush to get away before Travis or Grady noticed she was gone that she'd been disorganized. The worst part was, she'd had to travel in a bathing suit, cover-up, and a pair of shorts. Anything else would've made Mrs. Jamison suspicious. She was smarter than she looked, which meant Ellie hadn't been able to bring a suitcase with any of her clothes with her.

So here she was next to a perv, who was probably wanted for assault and battery. He kept checking out her legs, making her want to puke.

In two hours, they were supposed to reach Reno, where she had to transfer buses. Hopefully, at that point she'd lose him.

Without her phone, she couldn't even call Mary Margaret to let her know when she was getting in. Three days, according to the schedule. Seventy-seven hours and fifty minutes to be exact. Then she'd be back in Boston and she could visit her mom's grave and figure out where to live. Either with Linda, Uncle Woody, or with Mary Margaret, if Miss O'Malley said it was okay.

For some reason, none of those options sounded that good anymore. Linda and Uncle Woody had their own families, and she might feel like a mooch living with them. And Mary Margaret could be superphony sometimes, like when she would tell Father John he was the best and make fun of him behind his back. Mary Margaret was also kind of competitive. One time, she made Ellie cry for being too skinny.

Right now, Ellie was sort of missing her dad, even though he would probably be happy she was gone and out of his life forever. At least if he was here, though, he wouldn't let the creep next to her keep checking her out.

Thank God, he'd fallen asleep. Ellie scooted to the edge of her seat to avoid having his greasy head on her shoulder, wishing she could steal his phone and call her dad. Even though her dad wouldn't miss her, he'd be worried because he used to be an FBI agent. She could at least tell him she was okay.

Sort of.

A tear leaked from her eye and she swiped at it with her hand before anyone saw. As it was, the driver had thrown her some serious side-eye when he scanned her ticket. The grouchy lady at the Greyhound station hadn't questioned her too closely. Ellie had had to show ID, and the only one she owned was a student body card from St. Agnes, which said Tosca, not Dalton. Otherwise, the lady might've called her dad or Uncle Jace.

It was weird, because it had only been a couple of hours and she already felt homesick for the ranch, which wasn't even her home. Her home was in Boston. But Dry Creek Ranch was kind of cool, especially the horses. And she liked having cousins; she didn't have any with her mom. And Travis and Grady were fun, even if they were spazzes. Uncle Jace and Uncle Sawyer were cool too. And she'd really miss Aubrey, who was moving away to Las Vegas anyway. So what was the point of Ellie staying?

Her dad would probably follow Aubrey there, and they'd get married and have a bunch of kids. And he would love Ellie even less than he loved her now, which was more a responsibility type of love than the real kind.

Still, she was having second thoughts and wished she'd stayed at the pool with Travis and Grady and Mrs. Jamison.

"You got a cig?" The creepy guy was awake and breathing his bad breath on her.

"No." It wasn't like he could smoke it on the bus anyway. What he really should be asking for was deodorant, he stunk so bad.

Ellie tried to ignore him, but he was back to staring at her. "Please don't do that." She turned in her seat so he couldn't look at her anymore.

"How old are you?" He slid closer to Ellie, and she almost threw up.

"Sixteen," she lied, hoping it might scare him. If he knew she was only twelve, he would think he could get away with stuff.

"Sweet Sixteen, huh?" He raised his pierced brow and eyed her boobs. Ellie didn't really have any, not like Mary Margaret, who already wore a bra. "Where you going, Sweet Sixteen?"

She stammered, afraid to tell him the truth. What if he followed her to Boston? "Texas," Ellie said, because Dennis Thomas had moved there in the fourth grade and Sister Diana had made them all look at Texas on a map.

"Me too." He grinned, and his teeth were really yellow, like he hadn't been to a dentist in two or three years. "We could hang out." He brushed up against her and she wanted to cry, wishing someone on the bus would notice and let her sit by them.

"My dad's in the FBI," she blurted out. It made her sound like she was a six-year-old, but she didn't care. Ellie just wanted him to leave her alone and thought if she told him her father was a cop it might scare him.

"Is that why you're running away?" He laughed like it was a big joke, his garbage breath stinking up the entire bus.

"No, I'm going to visit my friend in Boston." Oops, she'd already told him Texas. Ellie hoped he hadn't noticed the slipup. As her mom would've said, he didn't seem like the sharpest tool in the shed. He might've even been on something. PCP or crack.

"Boston? What happened to Texas?"

Ellie wanted to bite her tongue off. How could she be so stupid?

He slung his arm over her shoulder and she wanted to die. "Let's stick it to Daddy when we get to Reno."

She didn't know what that meant but was smart enough to know whatever it was, it wasn't good. Ellie wanted to fold herself into a tiny ball so he couldn't put his grubby hands on her. And she wanted her father. Even though he didn't love her, he wouldn't let anyone hurt her. She at least knew that much. He'd let her stay in his room that night she'd had the bad dream and was always globbing suntan lotion on her face and killing all her spiders.

If the bad man knew what was good for him, he'd keep away from her. Because if she ever got her hands on a phone, her dad would make him sorry.

* * * *

Cash's heart stopped.

Later, he'd remember how he'd managed to pull off the exit and find his way to a Denny's parking lot without losing his mind. His immediate reaction was to lash out at Jace—then Mrs. Jamison. But it wasn't either of their fault, and playing the blame game wasn't going to get Ellie back.

"What are the boys saying?" he asked Jace, trying to stay calm as he clutched the phone to his ear. It was another hour to Dry Creek and he'd have to rely on his cousins to search until he got there. Right now, he wanted to flag down a fucking airplane.

"That she left the pool to go to the bathroom. About twenty minutes went by before Mrs. Jamison became alarmed. When she went to check the ladies' room, Ellie was gone."

"Did anyone see her in the bathroom?" Cash started his engine. He was holding on to his sanity by a thin thread, but he needed to keep moving.

"Nope. One of the girls at the pool went to the locker rooms about the same time as Ellie and swears she didn't see her in the restroom."

"Ah, Jesus." Cash's mind was swirling a thousand miles a minute with every possibility. All of them horrible.

"Let's not overreact. She probably got upset about something, maybe felt like a fish out of water with some of the other kids, and took off for the ranch."

Dry Creek Ranch was more than six miles from the high school, much of the route along the highway.

"I'm getting back on the road," he told Jace. "Do you have a deputy going over there? How about 49? Is someone searching for her along the highway?"

"Of course, Cash. I've got at least five deputies fanned out across town. She couldn't have gone far."

By his calculation, more than ninety minutes had elapsed since she left the pool. She could be in Nevada by now. He prayed she hadn't hitched a ride with a stranger or anything else equally stupid.

"Are you sure Travis or Grady don't know where she is? Maybe she confided something in them, something that could help us find her."

"I tried that already. Nothing. I know my boys, Cash; if they were keeping something from me, I'd see it in their eyes."

Cash peeled out of the parking lot and hopped back onto I-80, cursing himself for pulling over in the first place. Too much lost time. But when Jace had first told him, he hadn't been able to focus on the road, just on Ellie. Then he'd tried a dozen times to call her.

"What about her phone?" Lord knew she didn't go anywhere without it. "Are you tracking that?"

"Yep. I've got one of our techs on it. You wouldn't happen to have one of those apps on your phone that shows where she is at all times, would you?"

Cash pressed a hand to his temple and rubbed. He should've done that. A good father would've thought of it. "No."

"That's okay. We'll find her, Cash. You take it easy; don't drive recklessly. All we need is for you to wind up in the hospital."

Cash signed off with Jace and broke every speed limit there was. He was approaching Roseville when Jace called again.

"We found her phone. It was at the Greyhound station. The woman at the counter isn't from around here, says she's filling in for Phyllis while she visits her kid in Portland. She doesn't remember a twelve-year-old coming through here, but I think she's lying."

Cash loosened the tie around his neck, finding it difficult to breathe. "Why the hell would she lie?"

"Because minors traveling alone need a guardian to fill out a permission form at the counter. My guess is, the clerk was too busy watching her soap to give a shit and doesn't want to get fired. Do you have a recent picture of Ellie you can send me?"

"Hang on a sec." He fumbled with his phone, trying to access his photo gallery while he drove with one hand. "Better yet, I snapped one of her on Sugar with her phone. Show that to the clerk."

"I would if I could get in. Her phone is password-protected."

That's right. Cash had been meaning to tell her to change the code. It had been something obvious, like a person's birthdate. He searched his memory, saw the numbers clearly in his head, and called them out to Jace. "Try that. Maybe there's a clue in there of where she went."

Cash's biggest fear was that she'd struck up a relationship with a predator on the Internet. *Please, please, please, don't let that be the case.* "She's been begging me to let her go back to Boston," he said...to thin air.

Jace was no longer on the phone. Cash could hear him in the background talking to the clerk and assumed he'd gotten into Ellie's phone. He came up behind a Prius doing fifty-five in a sixty-five-mph zone and laid on his horn before passing him in the right lane.

Greyhound.

How the hell had she even afforded a ticket? He didn't want to contemplate the alternatives, like a pedophile buying the fare for her. Over the years, Cash had seen a lot of bad things, and every one of them was playing out in his head right now.

Jace came on the phone again, sounding out of breath. "She suddenly remembers her. She says she originally said no because she thought Ellie was eighteen."

Ellie didn't even look twelve. The clerk was covering her ass. He'd deal with that later. His immediate concern was finding his daughter.

"Did she take a bus to Boston?"

"The 8302, which is bound for Reno, where she has a two-hour layover before she catches the next bus to Salt Lake City. The bus is running on time, which means it'll hit the Reno Amtrak station in approximately twenty minutes."

Shit, it was more than an hour to Reno from where he was, and he was closer than Jace. "Can we have someone from Reno PD pick her up?"

"On it, but we're cutting it close. Just in case, I'll call Greyhound to see if someone will hold on to her until an officer arrives."

Cash let out a breath. If all went to plan, Ellie would be safe until he got there. But when the hell had everything gone to plan? Not in Cash's lifetime, that was for sure.

"Did she get on the bus alone?" he asked.

"As far as the clerk could tell. She hasn't been the most reliable witness, though. But Cash, it'll be fine. Ellie will be home, tucked safe in her bed, by tonight."

Except Ellie would rather travel across the country, alone, on a Greyhound bus, than be with him. That was how bad he'd screwed this up.

"Call me if there are any updates," he told Jace and flew past the exit to Dry Creek, his boot heavy on the gas pedal.

Weaving in and out of lanes, he told Siri to call Aubrey and was surprised when she picked up.

"Hey. I didn't expect to hear from you today. Have you testified yet?"

"Whiting asked for a deal and they dismissed the jury. I'm on my way to Reno. Ellie ran away. She's on a Greyhound bus, presumably to Boston via Reno."

"What? Hang on a second. I'm in the airport and it's noisy." There was rustling, and a few minutes later, she came back on the line. "Sorry. Ellie ran away? When? Why?"

"This morning, Mrs. Jamison took them to the pool. Ellie said she was going to the bathroom and never came back. She lost her phone and Jace traced it to the Greyhound station in Dry Creek, next to the high school. Jace is getting a Reno cop to babysit her until I can get there."

"I can't believe it," Aubrey said. "You must be freaking out."

"Freaking out" didn't begin to describe it. But hearing Aubrey's voice had taken the edge off.

"What're you doing in the airport? You're done with your interview?"

"Yep," she said. "We'll talk about it later. Should I catch a plane to Reno and meet you there? I'm right here. I might even be able to beat you there."

He hesitated, because he wanted her to come, to drop everything, including the job in Vegas, and be with him. It was selfish, because she had her own life to deal with. And he needed to do this on his own.

Stop being a fucking island. Sawyer's words rang in his ears, but he pushed them away.

"Nah, you should go home. It's been a long day for you, right? Have a glass of wine...celebrate."

There was a long silence, then, "You'll call me to let me know Ellie's okay, won't you?"

"You bet. Hey, Aubrey, let me ask you something: Am I a lousy father?"

"What? No, of course not. You're not blaming yourself, are you? Cash, she's been talking about going back to Boston from the moment I met her. She's a kid who lost her mother and is acting out. That's all. You'll work through it."

"I hope so," he said. "I love her." The words startled him, but they were the truth. Despite twelve years of lost time, she was a part of him, and he felt it down to his marrow.

"Of course you do. You're sure you don't want me to come? Or should you do this yourself?"

Ellie probably would've preferred to see Aubrey, but he should do this by himself. He was Ellie's father...and Aubrey was leaving. "Yeah, I've got it," he said with more confidence than he felt.

"Cash..." she faltered, then quickly amended, "Good luck with Ellie. I'll talk to you soon."

The second Aubrey hung up, he experienced a depressing sense of loneliness that seeped into his bones like the chill of a foggy Sierra morning. He tried to shake it off, telling himself it was ridiculous, because he liked being alone. He thrived on it. He was a cowboy at heart, only comfortable in his own company. But with Aubrey it was different. She finished his rough edges and made him feel like he was part of a whole, instead of solitary but incomplete.

He squinted into the glare of the sun on his windshield and forced himself to focus on Ellie. *Ellie*, he sighed. Would she run away again as soon as he got her home? Would he have to handcuff her to the cabin?

Cash took off his tie, threw it in the back seat, and checked the time. He'd hit Reno right around rush hour. A text from Jace came in. The police were sending an officer to the bus/Amtrak station. Cash felt a modicum of relief but wouldn't be completely reassured until he had Ellie safely where she belonged.

His cell rang. It was Thing Two.

"Hey, Sawyer," he answered, hands-free.

"You almost in Reno?"

"About thirty minutes if I don't hit bad traffic. Reno PD is sending someone."

"Good. Ellie will be fine. It's a three-hour bus ride where she can't get herself into trouble. What can I do? You want me to meet you in Reno?"

By the time Sawyer got there, Cash hoped to be halfway home. "Nah. I've got it covered. Thanks, though."

"Just say the word and I'll hit the road. Jace said Whiting took a plea. Are you cool with that?"

"The son of a bitch will never see the outside of prison walls, so yeah, I'm okay with it."

"Uh…how did it go otherwise?"

They both knew what Sawyer was dancing around.

"Better than I thought," Cash said and changed lanes. "The Farmingtons met with me. They've made peace with the Bureau…with me."

"That's good. Healthier. Did you hear about Crandall?"

Crandall was Cash's former boss, the special agent in charge of the FBI's Northern California division. "No. What about him?"

"According to the *LA Times*, he announced his early retirement today. He's leaving to 'pursue other interests.'" Sawyer let out a loud belly laugh. "Pursue other interests. Yeah right. The asshole was canned."

"Sounds like it," Cash said, surprised that Sully hadn't mentioned it at court that morning. He tried to summon his inner schadenfreude but came up dry. Crandall's resignation/firing wasn't going to bring back Casey Farmington. And the time had come for Cash to let it go. He also had what suddenly felt like much bigger problems to solve.

"I bet you can get your job back."

"That ship has sailed, Sawyer. I don't want my old job back. It's time to do something different." Cash was still working on what that something different was. But this morning he'd been able to lay the case that had haunted him for more than a year to rest. Tomorrow was time enough to start thinking about his future.

Sawyer didn't say anything at first and was probably cooking up a new way to entice Cash into running their nonexistent cattle operation. "Gotcha. Let's do something when you get Ellie home. We could do a night ride and a bonfire, like we used to do with Grandpa, and make her an official Dalton."

"I'm down with that, depending on how it goes with her. I'm wagering a guess she'll be pissed off at the world and not feeling family friendly. But we'll see."

"Call me when you get her."

"Will do," Cash said and clicked off.

For the next thirty minutes, he watched the clock as he maneuvered through traffic, breaking a number of traffic laws on the way. There was a parking space on Center Street. He wedged his SUV between a Ram pickup and a Chevy Volt and ran in search of the bus stop.

Amtrak and the Greyhound depot were housed in the old Southern Pacific Railroad station, a historic landmark that had been completely renovated to include a new building. And though it was nicer than most transit terminals, an air of desperation hung over the waiting room like a gray cloud. Perhaps it was the aura of gamblers down on their luck. Or maybe it was his own desperation to find his daughter.

He cut in line at the counter and explained to the clerk about Ellie. The clerk had a guard escort him through a wing of offices in the new building to a small conference room. When he opened the door, Ellie came rushing at him and threw her arms around his waist.

"Daddy, you came."

Cash held her so tight, he was afraid he'd crush her and loosened his arms, backing away just enough to have a look at her. Ellie's face was streaked with tears and grime. Her bathing suit cover-up was torn and one leg of her shorts was smudged with dirt.

His chest constricted, making it difficult to breathe. "Ah, sweetheart, I was so worried about you."

"I'm sorry, Dad." She hiccupped on a sob and pressed herself against him, hanging on to his shirt like it was a lifeline.

Cash's hand brushed the back of her hair, trying to soothe her. "What happened to your shirt, honey?"

"I tore it when I got off the bus, trying to get away from this disgusting guy who sat next to me."

"But you're okay?"

"I am now. I wanted to call you from the bus to come get me, but I lost my phone." She started crying again and between sobs said, "I changed my mind. I just wanted to go home to Dry Creek Ranch."

A female police officer came forward. Until now, Cash hadn't noticed her. She stuck out her hand and introduced herself. Cash managed to shake it without letting go of Ellie.

"I just got a call," the officer said, indicating that she had to leave. "Just need to see some identification."

He flipped open his wallet and showed her his driver's license. She nodded and headed for the door.

"Thank you," he told the officer, then kneeled and wiped Ellie's face with his handkerchief. "Who was the disgusting guy?"

Ellie shrugged. "Just a creep. Officer Hu was waiting for me in the station. As soon as he saw her, he took off."

"Let's sit down for a second." He led Ellie to a chair and joined her at a round conference table. The room was likely used for staff meetings. Other than the black-and-white pictures of old trains from the 1920s, the space was mostly utilitarian, with no windows.

"I know we don't know each other well," he started. "And I know you don't want to like me. But I love you, Ellie."

"Only because you have to, because I'm your kid," she interrupted.

"Nope. I'm supposed to love you because you're my kid; I don't have to. But the thing is, I do. From the moment I saw you, I knew. It was like something deep inside me busted wide open. And right then and there I knew you were a part of me. And that I wanted to watch you grow up and take care of you. Do you hear what I'm saying, Ellie?" He tilted his head so they were eye level. "I want us to make up for all the time we lost together. Nothing makes me happier than to be your dad, and I don't ever want you to run away again. Can you promise me that?"

She nodded, swiping at her eyes.

"Say the words, okay?"

"I promise." She sniffled.

"I love you, Ellie. I may not be good at saying it, but I do. And I always will. Always. Even when we don't agree, even when I do something to make you angry and vice versa…even when I want to beat up your boyfriends."

"I don't have any boyfriends."

Not yet, thank God. "You will, and I probably won't like them." He winked, and Ellie broke into a smile that spread through him like warm liquid.

"Well, you might like them," she said. "I like Aubrey."

He pulled her onto his lap. She was still young enough not to resist her old man. "Life's not fair and Aubrey's not my girlfriend." But he'd fallen for her, hard, no doubt about that. "You hungry, kid?"

"No, I just want to go home."

"Then let's giddyap."

Chapter 23

The flight from Vegas to Reno was only one hour and nine minutes. Aubrey didn't have the first clue where the Greyhound station was, but if she didn't find it soon, there was a good chance she'd miss Cash and Ellie.

Of all her crackbrained schemes, this one could seriously backfire. It was pretty damn presumptuous. She and Cash weren't a couple and she wasn't family to Ellie.

But the kid and the kid's father had wedged their way so deep inside her heart, even a crowbar couldn't get them out. So here she was, sticking her nose where it didn't belong, prepared to be rejected.

"Do you know where the Greyhound bus station is?" she asked the Lyft driver as she scooted into the back seat of the woman's compact car.

"There are more than one. There's one on Stevenson and there's one at the Amtrak Station on Center Street, which is just a bus stop. Which one do you want?"

Aubrey didn't have the foggiest notion. Despite wanting it to be a surprise, she dashed off a text to Cash. After a few minutes had passed and the driver grew impatient, she asked, "Which one is closer?"

"They're about the same distance, fifteen minutes. They're only five minutes apart. You want me to go to the one at Amtrak first?"

"Sure," she said, hoping Cash would see the text as they crossed town.

She stared out the window, watching buildings and an occasional casino go by. It wasn't like Vegas, with its glittery strip of luxury hotels. It was more like rows of strip malls and big-box stores.

Her phone hadn't chimed with a return text from Cash and she was beginning to fear that her coming here like this was a giant mistake. For all intents and purposes, Cash had told her to stay away.

You should go home. It's been a long day for you, right? Have a glass of wine. Celebrate.

Yet she continued to insinuate herself where she didn't belong, knowing full well that Cash was a heartbreak waiting to happen. Her throat closed up just thinking about leaving. How had she let this happen? Not only had she fallen for her unavailable neighbor, she'd fallen for his sweet little girl.

"This is it," the Lyft driver said as she pulled up next to the Amtrak Station. "You want me to wait?"

Aubrey had no idea where to go or where Cash and Ellie would be. No sense asking the woman to hang around while she searched through the building. "You said the other station is only five minutes away, right?"

"By car," the Lyft driver responded.

Aubrey sucked in a breath. "I'll take my chances. Thanks for the ride."

She checked her phone again just in case she missed a text from Cash, but there was nothing. For a second, she considered hightailing it back to the airport to catch a flight to Sacramento, where her car was parked.

You're here, she told herself, *at least try to find them.*

She asked the first person she saw for directions to where the Greyhounds came in. He stared at her with a vacant expression in his eyes and she moved on. There was a woman by the vending machine who was kind enough to point Aubrey to the location. But when she got to the bus stop, there were only a few people milling around the platform. Ellie's bus would've come in more than an hour ago.

Stupid idea, Aubrey.

She wandered the halls of the station, hoping to spot a tall cowboy with a petite twelve-year-old. There were lots of cowboys, but none of them were Cash.

She was just about to give up when a high-pitched voice shouted her name. "Aubrey! Aubrey!"

Next thing Aubrey knew, Ellie was wrapping her arms around her. Cash, who she'd never seen in a suit before, stood there with an oversize grin on his face, looking better than any man had a right to.

"I can't believe you're here." He blinked at her a few times, like he wasn't quite certain she was real, then took her in—all of her—until she felt butterflies in her stomach.

"I'm here," she said in a rush. "Group hug." She pulled him against her, sandwiching Ellie in the middle, and they just held on to each other for what felt like forever.

Ellie eventually squeezed out of the circle. "Do you guys want to like kiss or something?"

In a deep baritone voice that gave Aubrey goose bumps, Cash whispered against her ear, "Later. Thank you for coming. It means a lot to Ellie and me."

"You're welcome," she whispered back.

Sensing that they were probably making a spectacle of themselves, they pulled apart, and Aubrey instantly missed having Cash's strong arms around her. A second passed, the two looked into each other's eyes, and then the moment was gone.

"What do you say we go home?"

Aubrey nodded and Ellie took each one of their hands. The three of them headed for the sidewalk, swinging their arms. They did that all the way to Cash's SUV. Aubrey suspected that to anyone walking by they looked like a family.

"Ellie's decided to put her move to Boston on hold," Cash announced as they piled into the vehicle.

"I'm glad to hear that," Aubrey said.

"What about you?" Cash waited for everyone to buckle in, then turned to her. "Vegas bound?"

"Uh, we'll see if they make me an offer."

"They will," he said with total confidence.

It wasn't the words Aubrey wanted to hear. In fact, she kind of wanted to slug him and say, "Wake up, you idiot. I don't want to move to Vegas."

She didn't of course. Instead, she pasted a smile on her face. "They seem really enthusiastic about me, so, yeah, I think so."

Cash didn't say anything, just started his engine and nosed out onto the street with one hand on the wheel. "Where's your car?"

"Sacramento International Airport. Kind of out of the way." It would take an extra two hours. The logistics had escaped her when she'd dropped everything to go to Reno.

He caught the freeway and glanced in his rearview mirror at Ellie. "How would you feel about me taking you tomorrow to get it? I'd like to get Ellie home."

"That works." She twisted around to smile at Ellie, who appeared to have nodded off, and turned back to Cash. "Running away must have been exhausting. Ellie's out. Finish telling me what happened in court today?" With all the chaos, she hadn't gotten any of the details about Whiting.

All the way home, he told her about the plea bargain, how the Farmingtons had asked to meet with him in private, and how they'd thanked him for bringing Whiting to justice for Casey. He said it all very matter-of-factly, but he seemed more at peace with the case than he had before he'd left for San Francisco. The edge was gone, replaced by a sense of calm.

A drowsy Ellie pressed her face between their seats. "What are you guys talking about?"

"How your dad solved a big case for the FBI and how he's a superhero." Aubrey poked Cash in the arm. "Isn't that right, Superman?"

Cash shook his head, ignoring Aubrey's teasing. "Sawyer wants to go on a night ride, a Dalton family tradition. You two up for it?"

"Tonight?" Aubrey didn't know if she had the stamina and was surprised Cash did after the day he'd had.

"I'm in!" Ellie said, showing a new, enthusiastic side of herself that Aubrey had always known was lurking in the girl.

"Really?" Aubrey groaned. "You don't want to stay in? We could paint our toenails and make s'mores."

"S'mores sound good," Cash said. "Painting my toenails? Yeah, not really feeling it. I could probably talk Sawyer into postponing until tomorrow, though."

Cash's cell rang and Jace's number lit up on the dashboard display before Aubrey could interject that she was willing to go tonight if everyone else was.

Cash answered on Bluetooth and told Ellie to say hi.

"Hi, Uncle Jace."

Cash slid her a sideways glance. "Tell him you're sorry you ran away and you'll never do it again."

"I'm sorry I ran away and I'll never do it again, Uncle Jace." She sounded truly contrite.

"We love you, kid. Travis and Grady want you home; they missed you today."

"Sorry," Ellie said, her voice full of shame.

"We're on our way home," Cash said, saving Ellie from having to grovel for forgiveness on speakerphone.

"Good. Because we got a break in the case."

"The cattle-rustling case?" Cash came to attention, practically vibrating with interest.

Aubrey noted that he appeared pretty invested for a man who'd given up law enforcement. Then again, the Bealses were neighbors, and the theft probably felt like an invasion to everyone in the area.

"What's going on?" Cash asked.

"Thanks to you, I made four arrests about an hour ago."

"Me? I didn't have anything to do with it. Inside job?"

"Oh yeah," Jace said. "Jill and her brother Pete."

Cash didn't appear the least bit surprised, but Aubrey felt like she'd had the wind knocked out of her.

Jill Tucker?

"What about Mitch Reynolds?" Cash glanced over at Aubrey, whose mouth fell open.

"Up to his eyeballs in it," Jace said, and Aubrey's mouth fell wider.

She remembered the plat map and how secretive Mitch had gotten when she'd seen it. Still, she didn't understand how stealing cattle had anything to do with developing the Beals Ranch. "How was Mitch involved?"

"Aubrey?" Jace's voice filled the Ford's cab. "I thought you were in Vegas, doing an interview."

"Took a detour on my way back to the ranch. How is Mitch wrapped up in this, and why would Jill and Pete steal from their own family?" It didn't make sense, none at all.

"It's a long story," Jace said. "You can read all about it in the papers."

Typical tight-lipped Jace.

"Hey, I'm a material witness," she said, trying to pry the information out of him.

"Tell Cash to explain it to you. Hey, Cash, come over as soon as you get home. We've got stuff to discuss."

"Let Sawyer know I got Ellie, okay?" Cash hung up, and Aubrey regarded him suspiciously.

"How is it again that you're part of this investigation?"

"I'm not."

"What's a cattle rustle?" Ellie asked.

Cash reached between the seats and tweaked Ellie's nose. "It's when someone steals someone else's cows. Or, in this case, their own."

It sounded as if Mitch had really landed himself in some serious trouble. Jill and Pete too. The cattle weren't theirs; the herd belonged to their parents, and last Aubrey looked, it was still a crime to steal from your parents.

"Are you going to tell me what this is all about?" she asked Cash. "Does it have something to do with that plat I told you about?"

"I'm pretty certain it does. But I won't know for sure until I talk to Jace."

It seemed to Aubrey that Cash was being intentionally obtuse. By now, all of Dry Creek probably knew. It wasn't every day the town's golden boy was implicated in grand larceny.

* * * *

Jace held a big noisy dinner at the ranch house for Ellie when they got home. Grady hugged her so many times, she was probably bruised by now. Even Travis, who was less demonstrative, had showered her with attention.

A smile bloomed in Cash's chest. Just like him and his cousins, the next generation of Daltons would grow up together, thick as thieves.

After dinner, the kids went off to play a game of horseshoes while the adults settled in at the dining room table so Jace could give them a detailed account of the arrests.

Cash was anxious to hear the particulars. Between Ellie's misadventure, Cash's recounting of Whiting's plea bargain, and Aubrey's summary of her interview, they hadn't had time to discuss the Bealses' cattle.

"Spill," Aubrey ordered. "Tell us everything."

"It's all going to be in the paper tomorrow, so I don't feel like I'm divulging anything that should be kept under wraps," Jace said.

Sawyer grabbed a bottle of wine from the counter and refilled everyone's glass. "Let me guess: Jill and Pete were a little low on cash, so they waited until Mom and Pop went to Disneyland and slaughtered themselves two hundred cattle to sell on the black market. What I don't get is how Mitch the Bitch fits in."

"That's because the only thing you got right was the low-on-cash part." Jace flicked the wine cork at Sawyer. "Jill and Pete were looking for a much bigger payoff than two hundred head of cattle."

"Like the profits from a high-end real estate development," Cash interjected.

"Bingo." Jace pushed away his plate.

Aubrey began clearing away the dishes, and for a second, Cash got lost in watching her. She'd come all the way to Reno and ditched her car in Sacramento just to be with him and Ellie. A pang of longing hit him so hard, he was momentarily paralyzed by it.

"Is that how Mitch fits in?" she asked. "And how exactly does Jill and her brother benefit from a high-end real estate deal when it's their parents who own the property, not them?"

It was a good question, one Cash was about to ask himself. Though he was pretty sure he'd already figured out the answer.

"Mitch conspired with Jill and Pete," Jace said. "Basically, they were trying to put Randy and his wife into a situation where they were forced to sell."

"I get how Mitch the bottom feeder profits from this. but what's the benefit to Jill and Pete? Their parents are the ones who would get the proceeds from a sale, not them."

Cash couldn't help it: he rested his forehead against Aubrey's. "You should've been a cop because you're asking all the right questions. We call it motive. What was Jill and Pete's motive?"

"Well," she crossed her arms over her chest, "what was it?"

"Mitch planned to give them a piece of the action," Jace said. "A big piece, because without their role, the Bealses never would've been desperate enough to turn half their property into a golf-course community."

Aubrey let out a gasp. "A golf course? That's what that plat map was?"

Cash was a little stunned himself. But it was kind of genius. Retirees were already flocking to nearby Grass Valley. Dry Creek was a world of untapped potential.

"Shit," Sawyer said. "We could've been living next to Leisure World."

"You've got that right," Jace said. "A three-hundred-home planned community for seniors."

Cash let out a low whistle. Three hundred homes. "Are the Bealses still planning to sell?" Arrests were good, but the Bealses weren't getting their cattle back. "How else will they pay their note?"

Jace shrugged. "Dunno. But get this: they're not pressing charges."

"What?" Sawyer jerked back in surprise. "Their kids cost them their livelihood, possibly their family ranch, and they're just going to let it slide?"

"Apparently, Pete's startup is about to file for Chapter 11 and Jill and Brett are having financial problems. Randy's willing to forgive," Jace said. "I don't agree, but it's not my call."

Would Grandpa Dalton have been as forgiving as Randy Beals? Cash didn't know. Which brought him back to the question that continually haunted him: Would his grandfather turn over in his grave if they sold Dry Creek Ranch? They weren't selling—at least not yet—so Cash didn't have to face that conundrum. Not now anyway.

"What about Mitch?" Sawyer took a sip of his wine. "Are you pressing charges against him?"

Jace began loading their dinner plates into the dishwasher. "Without Jill and Pete, I don't have a case against Mitch. He wasn't directly involved with stealing the Bealses' cattle, though there's no doubt in my mind he knew about it. His defense will simply be that he entered into an agreement with Jill and Pete to build a development on their family's property with their parents' consent."

"Consent?" Sawyer scoffed. "More like coercion."

Aubrey rested her face in her hands. "I can't believe this." She turned to Jace. "But you arrested them anyway?"

"They were arrested and released. I don't have a case to submit to the district attorney without the Bealses' cooperation. What galls me is the fourth person in this enterprise getting away with it."

Six pairs of eyes stared Jace down. Cash had almost forgotten that Jace had mentioned a fourth person. "Who is it?"

"Red. The son of a bitch arranged for the mobile slaughter operation and for the sale of the meat in exchange for a cut of the proceeds. The whole time we were out there, combing the fields for clues, he knew. The SOB knew. It makes me sick. He's supposed to be one of the good guys." Jace pinned Cash with a look.

Yeah, yeah, Cash read him loud and clear. Jace wanted Cash to be a cow cop.

"You've got to go to the California Department of Food and Agriculture," he told Jace. "The taxpayers shouldn't have to pay his pension."

"I'll do what I can," Jace said but didn't sound confident. "It'll be tough without a conviction. The good news is that by tomorrow, the whole county will know what the four of them did. I made sure a few good reporters got the police reports."

"How'd you put the pieces together?" Cash wanted to know. For him, it had started coming together at Jill's surprise party, but at that point it was only a hunch.

"Brett," Jace said, and again six pairs of eyes snapped to attention.

Aubrey reared back. "Brett!"

"Apparently, Jill was so racked with guilt, she told Brett everything." Jace put his hand on Aubrey's shoulder. "Everything."

"Oh boy." She grimaced.

"He came to me, and I suspect he'll be calling you tomorrow," Jace continued.

Aubrey glanced at Cash, let out a long breath, and asked Jace, "Is he mad that we didn't tell him?"

"Nope." Jace rubbed his eyes. "Right now, he's got enough to deal with."

"Poor Brett."

Cash reached for Aubrey's hand under the table. "Does Brett know who sabotaged Aubrey's car and painted the graffiti?"

Jace slowly nodded his head. "Joanne, according to what Jill told Brett."

"Joanne!" Aubrey nearly came off her seat.

"Who's Joanne?" Cash had never heard her mentioned.

"Mitch's sister," Aubrey answered. "Seriously, the woman can't spell whore?"

Sawyer threw his head back and laughed. Jace didn't appear to think it was funny, though. Truth was, he looked weary as hell. There probably hadn't been this much drama in Dry Creek since 1976, when Jimmy Carter visited on a campaign stop. Grandpa Dalton had gotten to escort his detail around town and used to talk about it every chance he got.

"Do you want to press charges?" Jace asked Aubrey.

"Damn straight she wants to press charges," Cash answered for her. "The damage cost Aubrey a pretty penny, not to mention the aggravation."

"I don't," Aubrey contradicted Cash. "I'd have to testify, right? I won't be here. I'll probably be living in Vegas by then."

The room got instantly quiet, and both Jace and Sawyer stared daggers at Cash.

What did they want him to do, tie her to a hitching post on the ranch?

Chapter 24

Aubrey put off getting her car the next day. Brett wanted her to meet him at the coffee shop, and she suspected whatever he had to say would take some time. She hitched a ride into town with Jace and a commitment from Cash that he'd pick her up later.

Commitment? A funny word to use in the context of Cash—at least where she was concerned. It was for the best, she told herself. The timing was all wrong, and if she got the job in Las Vegas, she'd be starting a whole new life. A life in a big glitzy city. Wouldn't that be exciting? She suppressed an eye roll.

She passed Wren on her way inside the coffee shop.

"Morning, Ree."

Aubrey stopped in her tracks. They hadn't said two words to each other since their scene at Sew What. "Good morning, Wren." She waited for a snarky reply or a cutting remark, but Wren simply waved like they were the best of friends and went on her way.

Okay.

Jimmy Ray, Laney, and few of the restaurant staff were gathered around the cash register, hunkered over the *Mill County Times*. They couldn't tear themselves away from whatever they were reading long enough to seat her. Brett hadn't shown yet, and Aubrey wanted the one table in the restaurant that was wheelchair accessible.

She cleared her throat and waved at Laney, who grabbed a menu and started to show her to her and Mitch's old table. That was a switch. Last time Aubrey had been in the coffee shop, Laney had called the cops.

"Brett's meeting me." Aubrey nudged her head at Brett's usual booth, and Laney sat her at that one instead.

"You read the news?"

Aubrey didn't have to ask what news Laney was referring to and refrained from saying, "Look at your prodigal son now." She merely nodded. "I heard about it."

"I'm not surprised about Pete. He always was too hoity-toity for this little town, always looking to make a quick buck so he could live like a king. But Jill"—Laney shook her head—"that one surprised me. Poor Randy and Marge. Heard they're not pressing charges, even though this'll put 'em in a big black hole."

Nothing about Mitch, Aubrey noticed. But the fact that Laney—and Wren—was even talking to her showed that perhaps people in town were rethinking their opinion of Prince Charming.

"It's very sad," she told Laney, unwilling to dish, lest it get back to Brett. He had to be going through hell.

"And that cattle inspector…Red something or other…just despicable." Laney shook her head.

Aubrey realized now that Red was the man she'd recognized with Pete that day in the coffee shop. The bell above the door rang, and Brett wheeled his chair in.

Laney immediately hushed up and grabbed another menu and waved him over to the table. "How are you, sweetie?"

"Fair to middling," he said, trying for a smile. "Just coffee for me, Laney, and whatever Aubrey wants."

Laney wandered away to get them both coffee, but Aubrey could tell she was trying to eavesdrop. The big snoop. Brett pecked Aubrey on the cheek and maneuvered his chair to the other side of the table.

"How are you really?" she asked and reached across to take his hand.

"Pretty shitty. Jill and I are taking a break."

"I'm sorry, Brett." She didn't know what else to say.

"She told me everything." He locked eyes with her. "I'm sorry she and Mitch betrayed both of us, Ree. And I'm sorry you got treated the way you did for covering it up to protect me."

Aubrey swiped at a tear with her hand. "I'd do it again."

"Ah, Ree, you're an amazing friend. But I could've taken it, you know? I survived two tours of duty. I'll survive this."

The way he said it, strong and resolute, made her believe him and feel slightly silly for treating him like a piece of china. Perhaps Cash had been right. Brett was stronger than she thought.

"What'll you do?" she asked.

"I'm moving to Sacramento for a while. There's a vocational program there that trains disabled veterans. I'm taking up carpentry and hoping to join my uncle's cabinetry business."

"That sounds great, Brett." Despite everything, he seemed focused.

Laney came with their coffees. Aubrey ordered the breakfast special and waited for Laney to leave.

"Do you think you and Jill can work things out?" He loved her so much and Jill must've felt something for Brett. He was such a wonderful man; how could she not?

"We're gonna try. We've got an appointment with a marriage counselor." He choked up a little. "I've put her through hell, Ree. What she did to her parents...well, there's no excuse. But she did it to save our family. That's got to count for something."

It seemed pretty misguided to Aubrey, but she was trying not to judge.

"We're planning to sell the house, and anything we make on it, we'll pay back to Jill's parents. She and the kids will move in with them so Jill can help around the ranch. Mitch has promised to write them a check for the cattle as restitution." He paused, staring down at the table. "I don't know how Mitch feels about Jill, but she says she doesn't love him, that their affair was just an escape from what was going on in our home. Honestly, I'm still trying to deconstruct that. I haven't reached forgiveness yet, but I'm working on it."

"That's good," Aubrey said. "No matter what happens between you two, forgiveness is healthier."

Laney brought Aubrey's breakfast and showed great restraint by not loitering. Anyone could tell that Brett was emptying his soul to Aubrey and needed privacy. Kudos to Nosey Parker Laney.

"What about you?" Brett asked. "Can you forgive Mitch?"

She took a bite of her eggs, stalling to form her thoughts and to give the most honest answer she could. "I don't know if I can ever forgive him for what he did to you, and later to Jace. But the truth is I never felt the anger I should've that he cheated on me, that days before we were to be married he slept with another woman. All I felt was relief, because he'd given me an excuse to break off the engagement and move on." It wasn't a flattering assessment. If anything, it was weak. She'd been willing to marry a man she didn't love for the simple reason that it was easy. "Does that sound weird?"

"That you wanted an out and he provided one by sleeping with Jill?" Brett hesitated, then said, "I once told Jill that I didn't think you loved Mitch. At the time, I was sort of pissed off about it. He was my best friend and I thought he deserved a woman who was crazy about him. Jill said I was being ridiculous, and I figured she knew more about women than I did." He stopped and held eye contact. "But it sounds like I wasn't far off the mark. So to answer your question, no, I don't think it's weird. Do you love Jace's cousin?"

"Cash?" Her eyes went wide. "Wha…what…makes you think that?"

He picked a potato off her plate with his fork and took a bite. "You two were standing by the barbecue at Jill's party, talking. Your face lit up at something he said, and I watched those green eyes of yours dance with pure joy, and I remember thinking I wished Jill still looked at me that way. That's when I knew. I knew you loved him."

Her throat clogged, and it took everything she had to hold back tears. "Bad timing."

"Huh?"

"His daughter's mother just died and he's just getting to know Ellie. And I just broke up with Mitch. Plus, I might get this really amazing job and…Well, you know how it is."

Brett tilted his head to the side and looked at her. Really looked. "No, what I know is love is a gift that doesn't come around every day, and when it does, you freaking hold on to it with both hands. You fight for it, even when it's the hardest thing you've ever done. Even when you're lying bloody and battered by the roadside not knowing if you'll ever walk again and it might just be better to die. But you fight…you fight for love."

He turned his head away, because he didn't want her to see him crying. But if he'd looked, he would've seen that she was crying too.

* * * *

First thing the next morning, Cash picked up Aubrey to take her to get her car. He got out of the cab to open the passenger door for her and couldn't keep himself from pulling her into his arms and kissing her hard on the mouth.

"You smell good and taste even better."

"Mm." She leaned into him, her full breasts pressed against his chest.

In another second, he was going to carry her back into the cabin, leaving her car for yet another day in the pay lot. But Aubrey abruptly pulled away and quickly straightened her blouse.

"We should get going. I've got a full day," she said and immediately put space between them.

234   Stacy Finz

He wondered at her sudden coolness. It was as if she was angry with him and had momentarily forgotten her ire during their kiss. Or maybe she just had a lot on her mind.

"Everything okay?"

"Of course," she said. "Why wouldn't it be?"

"I don't know, you tell me."

"I suppose I'm just anxious." She slipped into his SUV and buckled up.

"About the job in Vegas?" All night, he'd mulled the prospect of her leaving and had finally come to the conclusion that they were at stages in their lives that didn't intersect. He had a daughter who needed his full attention and she had a shining career ahead of her that would flounder here in Dry Creek. It was what it was, he tried to tell himself, and accelerated out of the driveway. "You haven't heard anything yet?"

"It's only been a few days," she said defensively.

He held up his hands in surrender. "I wasn't passing judgment, Aubrey. It was simply a question."

"Steer." She put his hand on the wheel. "I'm just a little on edge and it makes me grumpy."

Cash supposed he was too. "Don't worry about it." He reached over and tried to take her hand, but she tugged it away on the pretense of finding something in her purse.

"If I get this job, you're not even going to ask me to stay, are you?"

Cash was a little taken aback by the accusation in her voice. He was working under the assumption she'd wanted the job and was as committed as he was to keeping their summer romance casual. "It would be selfish of me, don't you think?"

She didn't respond, just continued to search through her purse as if it contained the goddamn holy grail. He drove through Dry Creek and headed to the interstate, getting more aggravated with each passing mile.

"Aubrey, don't throw out a question like that if you plan to be passive-aggressive about it."

"I was curious is all."

He shot her a look, calling bullshit on her feigned indifference. If she had something to say, she should spit it out. "Are we about to have our first fight?"

"It's not our first. We had one over me not telling Brett about Jill and Mitch."

He hadn't considered that a fight, just a difference of opinions, but okay. "How about you tell me what we're fighting about, because apparently I'm dense."

"That's an understatement," she muttered under her breath.

What the hell had he done? Five minutes ago, he'd had his tongue down her throat and she was grinding on him like she thought he was a pretty good guy. Now, he was suddenly Satan personified. This was exactly why he'd never had much luck in the relationship department. Women were just so damned mercurial.

"Aubrey—"

Her phone rang, and he stopped talking as soon as she picked up. She was being pleasant enough with whoever was on the line, which confirmed that her hostility—because it was definitely hostility—was directed solely at him.

The call went on for ten more minutes, and by the time she hung up, he'd gleaned it was the Vegas development company making her an offer. His stomach churned and he told himself it was something he ate for breakfast.

"Sounds like congratulations are in order." He tried to act pumped, but it felt like a vice was squeezing his chest.

"Yep, they made me an offer," she said, more angry than happy. "I'm supposed to take a couple of days to think about it."

"Is it a good offer, salary-and benefit-wise?"

"Uh-huh, very generous."

"That's great," he said a little too brightly.

"Just fantastic," she returned, doing little to hide her annoyance with him.

She spent the rest of the ride dicking around with her phone. And he did what he always did when it came to relationships. Nothing. Not a goddamn thing. It was easier that way.

When they got to long-term parking, she showed him where her Volvo was. He pulled into an empty space next to it, cut the engine, and got out to open her door. But she didn't wait, jumping down before he could get there. She shoved her key in the lock of her station wagon and jerked open the door.

He gave her heap a fifty-fifty chance of making it home. Maybe with all that money she'd be making in Vegas, she could afford to buy herself a new car. "I'll follow you."

"Not necessary." She started to get in, then stopped. "FYI: I'm in love with you, idiot. If you asked me to stay, I would."

He stood there, feeling the full weight of what she'd just said. *I'm in love with you.*

I'm in love with you.

I'm in love with you.

Minutes ticked by, and he didn't say anything back. He just continued to stare at her with his hands shoved in his pockets, unable to utter so much as a word. He really was an idiot.

A shuttle pulled up to a plexiglass bus stop in the corner of the lot and a family of five got on with their luggage. The noise from cars whizzing by grew louder. And the hot rays of the sun beat down on the asphalt, making him see wavy lines in the blacktop.

"It can't work," he finally said. "I've got a twelve-year-old who needs my full attention, a ranch that's falling down with no way to fix it, a thirteen-year career that's over and nothing to show for it. You deserve a man who can focus on you…give you everything you need and then some. I'm afraid that man isn't me."

He started to walk away when she called, "You give me everything I need and then some." She held his gaze, willing him to respond, willing him to love her.

But he couldn't. He couldn't give her what she wanted, so he got in his truck, wishing he could drive her out of his mind…out of his heart. Forever. Just get on the interstate and go north, past the Oregon border, across Washington State, all the way to Vancouver if he had to. Anywhere but here, where the hope in Aubrey's eyes was like a dagger in his heart.

Then he thought about Ellie waiting for him at home, about how Dry Creek Ranch wasn't going to take care of itself, and he did what he always did and put responsibility first. But the whole ride home was filled with Aubrey. Her face, her voice, her laugh, the kindness she showed to his daughter, the way she made him feel. Like a good man, like the best man he could be.

You give me everything I need and then some.

But it wasn't true. All he could give her were the leftovers, and that wasn't enough. Not for him and not for her. In Vegas, she'd have opportunity and a chance for career advancement. Here, she'd have none of that.

Cash rested his head against the steering wheel as he sat in front of his cabin. He snuck a look at Aubrey's driveway, but she hadn't arrived home yet. Maybe she wasn't coming home. The realization that she'd be leaving for good left a stabbing pain in his chest. He didn't expect the ache to go away any time soon. But he told himself he'd done the right thing, even if it hurt worse than anything he could remember.

Ellie came out onto the porch, and when she saw his SUV parked in the driveway, came running down the stairs. He forced himself to get out of the truck.

"Hey, kiddo. Where's Uncle Sawyer?"

"In the house, writing. I guess he finally figured out what to put in his book."

"That's good." Cash tried to smile and ruffled her hair. Her short-lived attempt at running away had brought them closer together. The previous night, she'd snuggled up to him on the couch and they'd watched TV until her bedtime. When he'd kissed her good night a wave of protectiveness washed over him like a tsunami.

Why was it that Ellie had filled him so completely, but he couldn't make room for Aubrey?

"Dad, can I ride Sugar today?"

"Kind of hot for riding. But if you're okay with the heat, we'll go."

Soon, fall would be upon them and the days would turn crisp and cool. Ellie would start school and Cash would have to find a job.

"First, I want to send a few pictures of my new bedroom to Mary Margaret. Can I have my phone back?"

He'd kept the phone in his possession after Ellie's bus ride to Reno. From now on, he planned to keep better tabs on his daughter's texts and install a find-your-kid app. Damn right it was an invasion of privacy, but Cash's only concern was keeping Ellie safe.

"Sure, you can have it back, but with some rules," he told her. "Tonight, we'll talk about them."

"Okay."

Sawyer popped open the screen door and stuck his head out. "Where's Aubrey?"

"She had some errands to do," Cash said, but it was clear from Sawyer's expression that he saw right through the lie.

Cash went inside the cabin, got Ellie's phone from his bedroom, and gave it to her. She ran off to take her pictures. He went into the kitchen to find Sawyer cleaning up.

"Ellie said you've conquered your writer's block."

"Let's just say I had a good day. Got two thousand words down. What's going on with you and Aubrey?"

"Nothing. That Vegas company she interviewed with offered her the job."

Sawyer gathered up his laptop and notes and stuffed them in his briefcase. "And you're planning to let her go?"

"Last I looked, women weren't chattel." Cash made himself busy washing out the coffeepot Sawyer had left in the sink.

"Ah, bullshit, Cash. You're doing what you always do. You get fired from your job when you should've been given a commendation and what do you do? Nothing. Absolutely nothing. You decide you deserve to be fired because you couldn't save the whole fucking world. Grandpa leaves us this ranch and all you want to do is sell it. Why? Because you won't be able to bring it back to its former glory." Sawyer lowered his voice. "A woman keeps your child from you for twelve years and you tell yourself it's your fault because you wouldn't have been a good father. For God's sake, Cash, you're fallible like the rest of us. Stop putting so much damn pressure on yourself. You'll never be perfect, so stop trying and then beating yourself up when you don't get there.

"I watched Aubrey the other night. The woman is so damned in love with you that it filled Jace's entire kitchen. And I know you, Cash. I know you like you were my own brother. You're every bit as in love with her as she is with you."

Sawyer slung his briefcase strap over his shoulder and headed for the door. "If you let her go, you'll be sorry. For once in your life, let your heart lead you instead of your insatiable need to save the planet. Take a chance on love and cowboy the fuck up."

Cash watched Sawyer hike across the field. His cousin ought to stick to writing and not tell people how to live their lives, especially because Sawyer wasn't exactly a poster child for perfection. As far as Cash could tell, his cousin had no love life.

"Okay, I'm ready." Ellie came into the kitchen in a pair of riding pants and her equestrian boots. Cash reminded himself to take her to Tractor Supply for cowboy boots and a few pairs of Levi's the next time they were in town.

"Then let's go."

They walked to the barn, and Cash saddled up Sugar and Amigo. He helped Ellie onto Sugar's back even though she was perfectly capable of doing it herself and mounted his own horse. They walked through the meadow at a leisurely pace.

"What's wrong, Dad? You seem sad."

"I do?" He forced a smile. *See, nothing but happiness.*

"Are you and Aubrey in a fight?" She clicked her tongue to bring Sugar up alongside Cash.

"Not a fight. She's got a job offer in Las Vegas. I guess I'm a little sad that she'll be leaving." Yet she'd stay if he asked her too.

"Are you going to move to Las Vegas to be with her?"

"First of all, it's *we*. Wherever I go, you go. At least until you're thirty-five. Then you can live wherever you want. But no, we're not moving to Las Vegas."

"Why not? Don't you want to be with her?"

Cash exhaled and glanced over at Ellie. "It's complicated." Because how did you explain to a twelve-year-old the complexities of an adult relationship?

"What's so complicated about it?" She leaned over Sugar's head and swatted away a horsefly. "Either you want to be with her or you don't."

Cash laughed to himself, because the simplicity of her analysis made him think that perhaps she was the adult here. "How about you? Do you want to be with Aubrey?"

"Me?" Ellie asked, confused. "What do I have to do with it?"

He chucked her on the chin. "Everything. We're a team now, which doesn't necessarily mean I'll choose my girlfriend based on your opinion, but I sure couldn't be with someone who didn't meet your approval. Your view matters. A lot."

"It does?"

He nodded. "I hope that when it comes time for you to pick a boyfriend, my opinion will matter a lot too."

"I thought you were going to beat up my boyfriends."

Cash tugged her ponytail, which she'd pushed through the back strap of her riding helmet. "Yep, to bloody pulps."

She giggled, and the sound of it was like sunshine. Pure sunshine.

"I like Aubrey," she said. "I think you two should stay together. But I'd rather we lived at Dry Creek Ranch instead of Las Vegas, even though I've never been there before. And if you guys ever have kids, that you won't forget me."

Cash pulled back on his reins. "Forget you? Ellie, I could never forget you. Ever. You don't really think that's possible, do you?" Ellie looked away, and Cash knew instantly that his daughter had thought about it. Worried.

He slipped his finger under her chin and turned her so she was facing him. "Ellie, listen to me. No one, ever, will come between us. No one can take your place. And if I ever have another child—which, by the way, we're getting way ahead of ourselves here—we'll be a family. All of us. And I'll love you the same as I always would. It's you and me, kid, until the end of time."

Ellie's eyes watered and she swallowed hard. "Promise?"

"With everything I've got."

"Then in that case, I think you and Aubrey should for sure be together." She sniffed, and he leaned over and kissed her forehead. "Are you going to tell her not to take the job or are we moving to Las Vegas?"

"Don't know yet, kiddo." But the fact was, he suddenly knew with every fiber of his being.

* * * *

Cash was waiting on Aubrey's porch when she got home. It was almost dark, and under the porch light, he looked tired and a little ratty, if truth be told.

"Have you been drinking again?" she asked and climbed the stairs.

"No, but a shot of Jim sounds good right now. How 'bout you? You climb into any windows today?"

"Nope. I'm retired from that sort of thing." She passed by him and started to unlock the door of her cabin, hoping he'd get the point and go away.

"We've got to talk."

This was the part of the program where he apologized for not being in to her as much she was in to him. She knew the spiel, had heard it a dozen times before. "Whatever you have to say, I'm not in the mood to hear it. Let's just promise to be friends forever and call it a day."

"I don't want to be friends," he said, which was pretty shitty. Then again, neither did she. It would hurt too much.

"Okay, then let's send each other cards at Christmastime. That's nice and impersonal." For some reason, her damn key wouldn't work, or maybe it was because her hands were shaking.

He got up, crossed over to the door, and touched her arm ever so slightly. "Please. Just hear me out."

The crickets played a sad country song, because Aubrey knew this wasn't going to end well. Still, she would listen to what he had to say, even though she should slam the door in his face. For hours, she'd been aimlessly driving around, trying to imagine life without Cash. Without Ellie. And all it brought was sorrow. A sorrow that burrowed deep inside her gut and cut like a knife to her soul.

"Did you accept the offer?" he asked.

Not yet, but she planned to first thing tomorrow. "We're negotiating." The fact was, she would take the offer just the way it was, because any salary was better than staying in Dry Creek and having to see Cash every day, living his life without her. That would be a special kind of hell.

"Don't take the job," he said.

At first, she didn't think she'd heard right. "Excuse me?"

"Don't take it, or take it, but take us with you." He maneuvered her into one of the rocking chairs, crouched down, and took her hand in his. "I love you, Aubrey."

"A few hours ago, you said it wouldn't work." The man was mystifying.

He took off his cowboy hat and ran his hand through his hair. "I don't give a damn what I said before. I was wrong. As long as you're willing to take us on, we'll make it work. I love you, Aubrey. I love you so much, it's making me crazy."

She longed to kiss him, to touch him to make sure he wasn't a mirage, something she'd conjured up because she wanted him so much, she'd become deeply delusional. To test it, she put her finger on his lips. They were soft and moist and oh so real. "Why did you say no before?"

What's the matter with you? she chided herself. *Just take what he's offering, you fool.*

But she'd done that with Mitch. She'd settled. And if Cash wasn't sure, or didn't really love her, he'd just be settling. And while losing Mitch had been the best thing that had ever happened to her, finding out later that Cash wasn't in it for the long haul would destroy her. It would leave her crushed beyond repair.

So she repeated the question: "Why, Cash? Why the sudden turnaround?"

He stood up and pulled her out of her chair and into his arms. "Because the prospect of loving and losing you scares the shit out of me. I've got complications, Aubrey. A daughter, a ranch that's a few months away from foreclosure, and a career that's over because of a case that made me question everything about myself, including my ability to protect the people I love. I have no job and a future that's hazy at best. The only thing I can see clearly is you.

"You're my future, Aubrey. You and Ellie. You're my heart, my life, my everything. Please say I'm yours."

"You are." The lump in her throat was so large, she could barely get the words out. "I love you, Cash. I love you so much, and Ellie too. You and she are my future."

Aubrey wrapped her arms around his neck, because all she wanted to do was to feel him. Feel the shelter of his arms and the warmth of his chest and the beating of his heart. He tightened the embrace, and she hung on with all her might.

"What do we do now?" she whispered.

His lips curved up into a smile. A beautiful smile that she traced with the tip of her finger as her heart hammered in her chest.

"We do this." He kissed her, the hot pull of his mouth making her delirious with love.

Epilogue

"Oh boy." Aubrey looked around Cash's new office and grimaced. "I've got my work cut out for me."

"Don't go overboard." He kissed her. Her kisses had become an addiction with him. Scratch that; she'd become his addiction. "I'm an inspector for the Bureau of Livestock Identification, not a corporate executive."

"No worries. I'll decorate it superalpha. Lots of wanted posters of cattle rustlers." She rolled her eyes, and he chuckled.

He placed a box on his desk and figured he'd get around to unpacking eventually. He'd been on the job three weeks and had been called out so many times, he hadn't had a chance to move into his new office.

"Come here." He crooked his finger, and Aubrey slid into his arms. "Don't worry about the office; focus on your business—and on us."

Back in the town's good graces, she'd started her own design company, teaming up with an architecture firm in Nevada City. She had projects in three counties. In Aubrey's spare time, she put the finishing touches on her cabin to make it more comfortable for the three of them. Cash and Ellie had moved in and were planning to someday build their dream home.

"I can multitask, you know?" She wrapped her arms around his neck and reached up to kiss him. "You deserve a nice office, a manly office."

"What I don't deserve is you." She was the best thing that had ever happened to him besides Ellie. Sometimes, he'd wake up in the morning and hold her close just to make sure she was real. And the nights...she fulfilled every one of his fantasies. Needless to say, the nightmares of Casey Farmington were gone.

Ellie's too.

During the holidays, he planned to take his daughter to Boston to visit her mother's grave. But for now, she was settling in nicely at school. She, Travis, and Grady took the bus together every morning and either he, Aubrey, Jace, or Sawyer picked them up in the afternoon. She'd made a few nice friends, and Mary Margaret was planning to come for a week in the summer.

Cash checked his watch. "We've got to get going if we want to be on time for Sawyer's big surprise." He suppressed an eye roll. His cousin, up to something, had been sneaking around the ranch for weeks.

"I'm ready when you are. Should we pick up the kids?"

"Jace got them and is meeting us at home."

They crossed the City Hall complex to the parking lot and drove to Dry Creek Ranch. Cash still marveled that the countryside was not only his backyard but the place where he went to work every day. Being a cow cop had its perks. Though he hated to admit it, Jace had been right. He loved the job and was currently investigating a large-scale interstate cattle-theft operation that was drawing on his experience as a special agent. And to think he'd thought his new position would be dull.

"What are you daydreaming about over there?" He tapped Aubrey's leg. She rested her head on his shoulder. "That we have a very nice life."

And he was going to make damned sure it stayed that way. By Christmastime, he planned to put a ring on Aubrey's finger, and by summer to make her Mrs. Dalton. Ellie was in on the plan and was constantly showing Cash pictures of engagement rings on the Internet.

As they passed through the ranch gates, a rush of nostalgia for Cash's grandfather came over him. He didn't know how long it would last, but for now, he, Jace, and Sawyer were living the life Grandpa Dalton would've wanted for them, and that made Cash proud.

"Sawyer just texted." Aubrey studied her phone. "He wants us to meet him in the south pasture."

"Why there?" Cash had no idea what this surprise of Sawyer's was.

"I don't know. But we'll find out soon enough."

Cash bypassed the cabin, taking a dirt road to an old structure that used to be the main barn for the ranch. He stared into the sun at the building.

"Well I'll be damned." Someone had rehabbed the decrepit old barn. It now had new siding, a new roof, and a new paint job.

He pulled in next to Jace's truck, and he and Aubrey got out to find Ellie, Travis, and Grady sitting on the top rail of the fence, staring out into the distance.

"You fixed up the barn," Cash called to Sawyer, and Jace pointed to the field that had the kids' attention.

There were at least three dozen head of cattle that hadn't been there before. Cash and Aubrey joined everyone at the fence. "These yours, Sawyer?"

Sawyer poked Cash in the shoulder. "They're ours, the beginning of a solid breeding herd for a cow-calf operation."

Cash shook his head but couldn't help grinning. "You don't give up, do you? Where'd you get 'em?"

"Auction," Sawyer said. "I did my research. The rancher who sold them was leaving the business, but he kept good records." He watched a few stragglers that had found a patch of green grass to munch on. "They're excellent producers. I figure we can keep some of their calves in the beginning to build the herd."

They still had no way of paying the property taxes, so investing in cattle seemed crazy to Cash. At the very least, it was premature until they sorted out the future of Dry Creek Ranch. He glanced at Jace, wondering if he was thinking the same thing. But his cousin had a smile on his face as big as California.

Damned cowboy.

Cash had to admit that their excitement was infectious, though. Even he felt a pang of anticipation at the prospect of preserving the life their grandfather had worked so hard for.

Still, he couldn't help being a naysayer. "How do we plan to pay for it?" he asked, feeling like a broken record.

Sawyer hitched his shoulders. "We've still got a few months to figure it out. We'll come up with something."

They stood at the fence a long time, gazing out over Dry Creek Ranch, remembering how it used to be.

How it could be.

Sawyer and Jace were right: it was a good place to raise a family.

Cash looked at Ellie, perched on the wooden railing with her cousins, then at Aubrey, who grew more beautiful every day.

"Yep," he said. "We've got a few months. We'll figure it out together," because right now, his heart was so full of love that anything was possible.

CPSIA information can be obtained
at www.ICGtesting.com
Printed in the USA
LVHW010515120321
681318LV00029B/216